Midnight Convoy & Other Stories

S. Yizhar

MIDNIGHT CONVOY
& OTHER STORIES

WITH AN INTRODUCTION BY

Dan Miron

The Toby Press

Midnight Convoy & Other Stories,
Second Revised Edition, 2007
The Toby Press LLC

POB 8531, New Milford, CT 06776-8531, USA
& POB 2455, London WIA 5WY, England
www.tobypress.com

Introduction copyright © 2007 by Dan Miron

Grateful acknowledgement to the Institute for the
Translation of Hebrew Literature (ITHL) for their support
and help in the preparation of this anthology.

Original Hebrew text copyright © The Estate of S. Yizhar
and Zmora Bitan Publishing House.

"Ephraim Goes Back to Alfalfa," trans. Misha Louvish.
"Habakuk," trans. Miriam Arad.
Midnight Convoy, trans. Reuven Ben-Yosef.
First published in *Midnight Convoy and Other Stories.* ed. Murray Roston,
Tel Aviv *&* Jerusalem: The Institute for the Translation of Hebrew
Literature & Israel Universities Press, 1969. Copyright © ITHL.

"The Prisoner," trans. V.C. Rycus. First published in *Israeli Stories,* ed. Joel
Blocker, New York: Schocken Books, 1962. Copyright © V.C. Rycus.

"The Runaway," trans. Yosef Schachter. First published in
Hebrew *Short Stories: An Anthology,* selected by S.Y. Penueli *&* A.
Ukhmani, Tel Aviv: The Institute for the Translation of Hebrew
Literature & Megiddo Publishing, 1965. Copyright © ITHL.

"Harlamov," trans. Hillel Halkin. First published in *Modern
Hebrew Literature* 18, 1997. Copyright © ITHL.

ISBN 978 159264 183 3, *paperback*

A CIP catalogue record for this title is available from the British Library.

Printed and bound in the United States by Thomson-Shore Inc., Michigan.

Contents

Introduction

I

Amos Oz dubbed him "The most important writer in Israeli literature," and A.B. Yehoshua concurred, referring to his crowning achievement, the mammoth-size novel, *Days of Ziklag* as "The most important book written since the foundation of the State of Israel." Thus crowned by two of Israel's most popular novelists as well as by every Israeli literary critic of note, S (milanlsky) Yizhar (1916-2006) enjoyed an unchallenged high status in Israeli writing throughout his almost seventy-year long literary career. He was and still is commonly regarded as both the founding father of Israeli literature and its chief master of prose fiction. However, this superlative assessment demands further exploration. For even the lesser of these two accolades—the author's position as the first master builder who laid the foundations of Israeli literature as a whole—has never been clearly explained or convincingly demonstrated.

There are two mutually complementary supposed facts that are habitually cited to prove Yizhar's historical role as a literary founding father. The first is that he was the first modern Hebrew writer to be born and raised in Israel, in contrast to all his predecessors who had been born in the Diaspora, did not speak Hebrew as a mother tongue, and received at least a part of their formative education in non-Israeli educational institutions, whether traditional or modern. The implication is that Yizhar's unique position as a "native" allowed him to develop his extraordinary sensitivity to the Israeli landscape, and played an integral role in his approach to Hebrew as a literary language based on the *spoken* rather than traditional, written, idiom. It is also assumed that Yizhar's "native" childhood and adolescent experiences played a part in his choice to focus, perhaps more than any other writer, on the birth pangs of Israel both throughout the last decade of the pre-state period (his first extended short-story, "Ephraim Goes Back to Alfalfa" was published as early as 1938) and particularly during the War of Independence, which supplied background for the largest chunk of his fictional works

The second supposed fact pertains to Yizhar's alleged role in the emergence of the so-called "literary generation" of the 1948 War, also known as "The Palmach Generation" in reference to the special commando unit which played a crucial military role during the first months of the 1948 War. The importance of the Palmach led to its name being adopted as an appellation for the entire 1948 generation as well as for the group of writers who became active and gained some public presence right before or during the Israeli War of Independence. S. Yizhar was located within this generational framework and associated with the above mentioned literary group, in spite of the fact that he is at least a half a decade older than the oldest among those regarded as representative members of the Palmach Generation, and had emerged as a distinct literary presence close to a full decade before the most precocious and prominent among them had gained recognition. The chronological gap seemed to strengthen his right to primogeniture, which was acknowledged by the members of the group who hailed him as their precursor and trailblazer.

However, on close examination both these proofs of historical primacy are revealed to be closer to myth than fact. S. Yizhar was indeed born in an agricultural settlement on the southern Israeli coastal plain to a family of pioneers, farmers and writers who had arrived in the country some twenty-five years before. His father, Ze'ev Smilansky (1873-1944), arrived in Palestine when only eighteen years old, and throughout a multi-dimensional career served as an agricultural worker, a teacher, and a writer. A self-taught scholar, he was the first professional statistician of the Zionist project in Palestine, as well as one of the founders of the Socialist but non-Marxist party *Hapo'el Hatza'ir* (which would eventually form part of Ben Gurion's centrist Labor Zionist party MAPAI). He was also a regular contributor to its important weekly. Yizhar's uncle, David Smilansky (1875-1953), one of the founders of Tel Aviv, was a businessman and an occasional writer as well. His great-uncle, Moshe Smilansky (1874-1953), was a farmer and public figure representing the liberal, right-wing organization of the farmers of the established "old" settlements; a popular historian of the early days of the Zionist endeavor in Palestine, he was also a courageous propagandist advocating Jewish-Arab peaceful coexistence, and a widely read author of popular novels and short-stories set in Palestine, in which the romanticized figures of the Palestinian Arab and Bedouin were first introduced to modern Hebrew literature. Thus Yizhar, in spite of the fact that his family never achieved financial security and could not afford to give him anything beyond the bare essentials in his childhood, certainly belonged within the small, elect, "Mayflower" group of the Zionist founding fathers, and can indeed be regarded as the first Israeli-born writer to emerge from this specific group. Nonetheless, this hardly means that he is the first Palestinian "native" Hebrew writer. He had been preceded by about a dozen other "natives" who were sensitive to and knowledgeable about various aspects of life in Palestine with which he would never gain sufficient acquaintance to incorporate into his fictional portrayal of the land. Thus, for instance, the important novelists of Palestinian-Sephardic extraction, Yehuda Burla (born in Jerusalem, 1886) and Itskhak Shami (born in Hebron, 1888), brought to Hebrew

None of these characteristics fit either the biography or literary work of S. Yizhar. Even if we discount the aforementioned chronological gap that separates him from almost all members of the Palmach Generation, we still have to take into account several distinct differences. First, ideologically and politically he was brought up in the heart of the anti-Marxist, utopian socialism of *Hapo'el Hatza'ir*, and never had any emotional or intellectual affinity with communism in general and with that of Stalinist Russia in particular. Philosophically he was never influenced by the prophets of dialectical materialism, and was, more than anything else, a romantic informed by the Nietzschean vitalism he had absorbed through the teachings of the "Cosmic Zionism" propagated by A. D. Gordon, the guru of the Second Aliya, who believed that the Jewish historical identity had to be supplemented, if not altogether superseded, by the identity "normal" nations acquired through their contact with the "cosmos", i.e., with the elements. Throughout his life Yizhar remained close to centrist Labor Zionist trends, and served for seventeen years (1949–1966) as a representative of Ben Gurion's MAPAI in the Israeli Knesset; this during the period in which the relationship between this party and those of the radical left, with which most of the members of the Palmach Generation were affiliated, was strained.

Second, his formative experiences only partly overlapped with those of the younger writers. Central to his consciousness were the pre-1936 Arab-Jewish clashes. He vividly remembered the Arab riots of May 1921, in which the writer Y.H. Brenner, sequestered in a house near Jaffa, was murdered. The 1929 riots, and particularly the fall of Hulda, the first Zionist agricultural settlement to be abandoned under the pressure of Arab attacks, were so central to his world view that he dedicated his first full-length novel, *The Grove on the Hill*, to the Hulda battle. The clash of Fascism and Communism in Europe as well as World War II were never as important to him as they were to the aforementioned younger writers. His visionary world was thoroughly Palestinian and intentionally of a limited scope. He was interested in botany, geology and music rather than in class struggle and world history. Although in his early youth he served as a teacher in some kibbutzim, and even described them in his very first novellas, he never entertained a particularly high opinion of the communal-egalitarian lifestyle. As a sworn individualist, he found it repugnant, something to flee from, if possible. He never frequented the tents of the Palmach, was not on the same spiritual wavelength as the mentors of the Palmach group, and had little if any appreciation for the Palmach celebrated lifestyle and slang (if he would intertwine some of these in the fabric of a few of his stories, it was usually in an ironic context). What is more, he did not take part in nor was he committed to paramilitary underground activities. Throughout the 1940s, he was rather a teacher and professional writer. He never published a word in any of the periodicals frequented by the members of the Palmach Generation, and never acknowledged the authority of A. Shlonsky. On the contrary, in search for a publication outlet for his first novellas, he turned to the semi-conservative monthly *Gilyionot*, whose editor, the erstwhile expressionist poet Y. Lamdan, was a bitter enemy of Shlonsky and his neo-symbolist group. Artistically, he had no use for the blatant realism of the representative members of the Palmach Generation, nor did he ever think highly of them as writers. His models were not the latter day developers of essentially nineteenth-century narrative modalities, whether American or Russian, but rather the early twentieth-century pioneers of Hebrew modernism, with U.N. Gnessin, the great initiator of both stream of consciousness and symbolist-"symphonic" narrative modalities in Hebrew literature, as his immediate inspiration. He was also greatly influenced by the chief practitioners of British and American stream of consciousness fiction, such as William Faulkner and Virginia Woolf.

In short, there is no reason to regard Yizhar as even belonging to the literary generation he supposedly founded. The fact that the War of Independence occupies so central place in his writings—from 1948 until the publication of *Days of Ziklag* in 1958, nearly a full decade, his work for adult readers dealt exclusively with that war in its various phases—does not in itself render him the contemporary of the young soldiers he portrays. A helpful comparison in this context is the poet Nathan Alterman, who dedicated the better part of his work

throughout the 1950s to the war and its historical significance: this
does not bridge the generational gap separating him from the youngsters who had shouldered the burden of fighting, the lad and the lass
he eulogizes in his famous ballad "The Silver Tray". Essentially, Yizhar
was annexed to the Palmach Generation by literary-political strategists
of this movement, who, under heavy critical attack for real and imaginary shortcomings, regarded his formidable prestige as an important
asset. He himself consistently objected to this annexation—so much
so that he rather unnecessarily developed less-than-convincing theo-
retical pseudo-formalist arguments refuting the very applicability of
the concept of "generation" to art in general and to literature in particular. He maintained that only the individual artist and the specific
art object represent an authentic artistic phenomenon, while historical generalizations do not correspond to any verifiable artistic reality.
This rather crude rejection of any supra-individual aspects of artistic or
literary development is completely alien to the views of sophisticated
formalists such as V. Shklovsky, Y. Tinyanov or B. Eichenbaum, and
should be regarded as little more than Yizhar's rather hopeless attempt
to throw off his literary back the company of Shamir, Meged, *et al.* The
fact that his theory is not sustainable, however, does not imply that
Yizhar, *malgre lui*, should in fact be affiliated with this company.

2

Yizhar's role as founding father is something far more subtle then
than his "nativity", or his ties with a specific literary group. Rather it
lies in the conjunction of certain narrative and ideational elements in
his work that together form a fictional world which was felt to have
encapsulated the basic rudiments of an Israeli condition or mindset.
We shall attempt to isolate these elements, and analyze their essential
"Israeli" qualities. However, before doing so it is important to note
that Yizhar's fictional world, at least the one he constructed through-

out the first two decades of his career (1938–1958), when he made his seminal contribution to Israeli literature and culture, is a very narrow one, incomparably smaller than that of the older pre-Israel masters (such as S.Y. Agnon or Haim Hazaz) or even that of some later Israeli novelists (such as Moshe Shamir or Amos Oz). It is contained within a rather limited geographical, chronological, psychological and situational territory.

Geographically, it rarely extends beyond the boundaries of the southern Israeli coastal plain as it gradually changes from the reddish Hamra fertile soil, dotted with the lush greenery of the densely settled and well irrigated Jewish settlements and Arab villages, to the yellowish, arid hills of the northern Negev, sparsely populated by flock-tending Bedouins and a few frontier kibbutzim resolved to eke agricultural product from the soil of the desert. Chronologically, it is bracketed by the three major military confrontations between Jews and Arabs in the pre-Israel, British mandatory era, the riots of 1929, the 1936–1939 Arab Revolt, and the 1948 War of Independence. Situationally, it concerns states of strife—either with an unforgiving natural world which one must struggle to domesticate, or, more often, with an unrelenting human enemy in the framework of war.

In terms of character, Yizhar's early stories are mostly peopled by Israeli-born young men in their twenties, interspersed with an occasional, more mature, father-figure, and blurry, semi-idealized yearned-for girls, who either appear in a manner marginal and unspecific enough to feed the daydreams of the immature male protagonists without ever directly engaging them either physically or socially, or are not present at all except as fantasized introjects. The young men themselves, no matter how many of them are present in any specific story (*Days of Ziklag*, for instance, is populated by many dozens of them), can also be classified to four main archetypes: the sensitive and diffident youngster, usually described as physically unprepossessing and not altogether socially-adapted, emotional, yearning for beauty and a freedom that is rarely defined; his opposite, the robust, virile and self-confident young man, who often is also a braggart and teller of tall-tales of exceptional prowess and courage; the learned young man with vast, if spotty, erudition in matters pertaining to fauna, flora, geology, astronomy, music and archaeology; the *fallah*, a youngster who having grown up on a farm is constantly preoccupied by notions of farming, and possesses "good hands", a knack for dealing with dysfunctional machines, and an inbred understanding of tools and their uses.

It is only in his very late works, written and published in the 1990s after three decades of eschewing prose fiction, as well as his stories written for youngsters, such as those collected in *Six Summer Tales* (1950) and *Barefoot* (1959), that Yizhar transcends, to a certain extent, these narrow boundaries. However, it was this very aspect in his major works (all of which had been written before he was well into his forties), this unrelenting focus on a limited inventory of themes, characters and fictional situations, that rendered Yizhar the trailblazer and the cultural and literary pioneer that he was. For as monotonous as his narrative could be, the paucity of thematic and characterological innovation was not only compensated for by the overwhelming richness of descriptive detail, the symphonic stylistic orchestration of the author's distinctive Hebrew, and the intense emotional impact of the dangerous situations he portrayed, but also, and more importantly, that very paucity was felt to be the essence of a highly significant cultural and literary innovation. It was as if Yizhar had managed to identify the core of a new condition and obsessively attach himself to it. The few narrative components he worked with represented the rudiments of a new mindset that was seen as quintessentially "Israeli". Yizhar's stories, with their meager thematic contents and oversized descriptive and linguistic apparatus seemed like the necessary and logical results of the author's uncompromising delving into the infrastructure of "Israeliness". This targeted, pinpointed delving necessitated a certain shrinkage, as depth replaced width. The multifariousness of a literature that had encompassed the entire Jewish world, spread over four continents and a millennial history, had to be replaced, at least for a certain period, by a fervent homogeneity. To adjust the ear to catch the new musical register, a certain monotony had to be embraced.

3

First and foremost it was the all-encompassing monotony of open spaces. The emphasis was almost from the very beginning on wild, uninhabited or semi-inhabited spaces: a landscape of fields, wild patches, sands and desert reaches, is the usual arena in which the stories are set. This arena affords almost no room for the complex living entities of space as adapted to the vital and constant requirements of normal human existence. A few fragmentary descriptions of kibbutzim and collective villages appear in the early stories, but these serve only as a foil to the great openness of a wild world bereft of shelter and human order. The sheer linguistic and descriptive triumphantly successful grappling with the description of this wild world is a great, indeed, unique, artistic achievement not only of Yizhar but of modern Hebrew culture as a whole. For about a century and a half the so-called "New" Hebrew literature, triggered by the modernist revolution of the Enlightenment, had set as one of its chief cultural and artistic goals the reawakening of a sense of "place", of being in a concrete world, of directly negotiating existence with the elements and with nature (all of these had been very much alive in biblical times). It not only ascribed tremendous value to every form of information which would enhance the sense of space, encouraging the publication of popular books on geography, ecology, astronomy and biology, but also desired to develop the experiential reality of space through emotive and mimetic rendering. Every advance in this direction was celebrated as a victory. Thus Bialik dubbed S.Y. Abramovitsh the founding father of Hebrew prose fiction in honor of his contribution toward placing Hebrew literature within a "concrete world". According to Bialik, Abramovitsh lifted the curtain of biblical quotations, replacing the blurry silhouettes with a clear, fully focused and living narrative space.[1] With the early twentieth-century

---

[1]   See Bialik's essay "Mendele usheloshet hakerakhim" (1912), in H.N. Bialik, *Divrey*

of space serve as correlatives to romantic cravings for total freedom, total liberation from routine and conventionality—an ideal for which all of the author's protagonists yearn, and strive in vain to realize in their lives.

Thus Yizhar's presentation of space plays a double and contradictory role. On the one hand it represents the fulfillment of the central goal of a new Jewish art as articulated by modern Hebrew culture as a whole and Zionist culture in particular. Yet simultaneously, it also subtly and nihilistically undermines the humanist, nationalist ethos of this very culture. Yizhar indeed articulates the new Hebrew craving for reality of location perhaps better than any other modern Jewish author, supplying an element in which the Jewish historical imagination was severely deficient. However, the complex nature of his relationship to the Zionist ethos is perhaps best understood when seen in the context of the approach of the chief philosopher of the Second Aliya, the aforementioned A. D. Gordon, who had a great impact on Yizhar. Gordon was a proponent of the Zionist approach which sought the renewal of Jewish culture through shifting the habitual involvement of the Jewish imagination with text, memory and history to a concern with the immediacy of the elements, of the concrete physical environment. He believed that the central tragedy of the Jewish people lay in the fact that its protracted exilic condition had brought the nation to lose its "cosmic" orientation (i.e., an orientation that viewed human existence as taking place in the context of universal "nature") and so to form its identity only around a common heritage of history and civilization. As he defined nationhood primarily as a natural, almost biological, phenomenon that is fashioned and informed by native environment, for Gordon the loss of the "cosmic" ingredient in the nation's mental makeup meant that its identity was skewed and debased, and that the Jewish people was tragically relegated to a second-hand existence of mental deficiencies and economic dependence. Thus, more than anything else, the Jewish psyche needed a cosmic reorientation, a reengagement with the elements. Yizhar's narrative art can therefore be regarded as the uttermost articulation and aesthetic satisfaction of Gordon's cosmological crav-

ings. At the same time, however, this art also undermines the foundations of Gordonist Zionism, for Gordon advocates a consistent daily
routine of manual labor as the only way for a person to genuinely
engage with the elements, while Yizhar romantically rejects routine
of any kind, and ascribes to nature a transcendence that obliterates all
concepts of duty, need, intention, and will. Thus while the Gordonist
in Yizhar approves of Ephraim's "going back" to the alfalfa field, the
aesthete in him regards this backsliding as capitulation, as becoming
ensnared in a trap. This duality of approach developed a keen sensibility within the writer for contradiction and conflict, facilitating
his ability to intuit the dichotomies inherent in the Israeli condition.
Thus, it plays an important part in Yizhar's positioning as the chief
poet of "Israeliness", as we shall see.

4

Against this dualist backdrop of an intensely experienced space,
Yizhar's protagonists, always reflecting their creator, present a contradictory conglomeration of nationalistic Zionism and romantic individualism, and their passionate experience of the landscape contains
a similar dichotomy between commitment and flight, between a craving for the material and the real and a nihilistic yearning to indulge
in idiosyncratic and spontaneous emotionalism. The human drama
in which they participate is always one of conflict and confrontation.
The theme of strife is played on quite a few different registers, allowing
for a point-counter-point development of internal juxtapositions. The
first of these registers is the battle with the environment, with unforgiving nature which, "invaded" by the protagonists, attempts to reject
and destroy them. Here the contrapuntal polyphony of the author's
narrative art is organized around the opposition of two elements of
nature: nature as a spiritual norm of wholeness and even sanctity
versus nature as an unrelenting enemy which must be continually

battled. For while the protagonists are usually portrayed as an invading army intent on either domesticating the wilderness or fighting its habitual, autochthonic inhabitants, the Palestinian Arabs, nature is rarely presented as a neutral force, but rather as taking sides against the invaders. This does not imply that it is necessarily identified with the interest of the Arabs, as much as that it resents any concentrated effort to upset its own delicate equilibrium as a semi-wilderness that does not allow for more than a marginal human presence. It resents the Zionist will to change it, to press from it the resources needed for intensive human habitation, to harness it to the chariot of the Zionist project, making it feed and clothe millions of people that are too heavy a burden on its free, stony back.

Thus not infrequently the relationship between man and landscape in the stories is one of enmity and mutual distrust. Man, on his side, always attempting to overcome the wilderness, always intent on undermining the secret arrangements that the forces inherent in the landscape have reached in order to maintain stasis. The landscape, in its turn, unleashing these forces in its attempt to resist the elimination of this stasis. Yizhar's protagonists find themselves in a strange position vis-à-vis this inimical land. On the one hand, they are its children, born "on the crossroads, under a palm tree, beneath a sagging roof of an infant village" that did not offer shelter from the heat, the suffocating *hamsin* winds, the rains and the insects. On the other hand, they are the children of a besieged enemy, growing up in tiny farm-enclaves surrounded by alien elements, which, held at arm's length, are constantly pushed back with tremendous effort: "Only up to the fence was there some degree of cultivation, but from there on—thorns" (*Days of Ziklag*, 1958). Thus their lives are from the first devoid of gentleness and security, and informed by a sense of loneliness, of ecological orphanhood. The author's late and very revealing autobiographical novel *Miqdamot* (*Preliminaries*) opens with a horrific scene of confrontation between the protagonist as a toddler and an army of alarmed and angry hornets. The baby, left in the shade of a carob tree while his pioneer-father attempts the back-breaking task of plowing a piece of virgin soil that adheres with all the powers of inertia to its original state of wilderness, unwittingly touches a hornets' nest built in a burrow under the carob. Attacked by dozens of the poisonous insects, the infant has to be carried half-dead, convulsed with unbearable pain, in search of medical help. When after several long hours, a physician is finally reached, all he can say is: If he didn't die, he'll live. This scene can be read on several levels. Allegorically it can be seen as presaging the bloody conflict with the Arab inhabitants of Palestine. However, it can also be seen as typifying the relations of man and land as conceived in Yizhar's fictional world. It is a symbolical dramatization of the clash between human hubris and the permanence of the universe, to which a spiritual, even theological, value has been ascribed: The land is the Lord's and its position reflects a divine will, which one attempts to contravene at one's peril. Zionism, in this equation, represents human hubris with all its pathos, glory and tragedy, and its implementation breeds *agon*, contest, strife.

Another prominent register is the conflict with the Palestinian Arabs, who resisted the Zionist presence in their midst. This conflict was—and remains—absolutely central to all Hebrew culture and literature. From the publication of Ahad Ha'am's seminal essay "Truth from Eretz Yisrael" in 1891 until the present time, it has been the *leitmotif* of the Israeli drama. Many writers set novels, short stories, plays and poems to this backdrop. Military and paramilitary clashes with Arabs supply tension-filled moments as well as dramatic denouements to all the genres developed within the framework of a Zionist culture that progressively became more confrontational and absorbed in the life-or-death choices presented by the struggle over Palestine. However, one can safely say that in the entire Hebrew literature of the twentieth century no writer was more fascinated by this lethal struggle than S. Yizhar. If his very early short stories, written in the late 1930s, such as "Ephraim Goes Back to Alfalfa" and "Paths in the Fields", were still dominated by other aspects of the Zionist endeavor, from the publication of "A Night Without Shooting" (1940) the focus shifted, and the Arab-Jewish military showdown became the nexus of Yizhar's fictional world.

The author invested the better part of his creative energy into exploring it. Before writing a fictional work, he would research the military episode or battle he had chosen as the backdrop with all the meticulous care of the most exacting of military historians. For instance, he carefully pieced together every shred of evidence he could gather from the survivors of the battle over Hulda, the sequestered Jewish communal settlement that was abandoned under the pressure of repeated Arab attacks during the riots of the summer of 1929, before weaving it together with astounding loyalty to the verifiable facts in *The Grove on the Hill*. Similarly, the plot of *Midnight Convoy*, which focuses on the last military convoy that managed to break through the lines of the Egyptian army to bring desperately needed supplies and reinforcements to the cut-off and beleaguered Jewish settlements in the Negev, was based on a meticulous reconstruction of the actual event. The amount of research and factual verification that went into the writing of *Days of Ziklag* astounded military experts, who opined that perhaps no battle of the many battles of the 1948 War was as rigorously reconstructed and as minutely re-experienced, moment by moment, as was the seven-days battle over Hirbet Mehaz, which Yizhar then transplanted from historical reality into the huge novel whose plot it determined. Yizhar's fascination with the Arab-Jewish conflict manifested itself in complete historical verisimilitude, which formed the matrix into which he fit the fictional elements such as the protagonists and their respective streams of consciousness. Of course, those fictional elements were not disconnected from the conflict either. They consisted of the experiences of war—the fears, the dark premonitions, the many boring hours of listless inactivity, the dark élan of battle, the unexpected gushes of courage, the panic of being shot at, hit, or critically wounded, the loss of consciousness and the drifting into the emptiness of impending death—these are the sensations and emotions that interested the author more than anything else.

The relentless focus on battle creates the impression that Yizhar's fascination extends beyond the political and historical significance of the Arab-Jewish conflict per se. Battle seems to be the form of existence most appealing to his creative imagination and most conducive to the articulation of his sense of being. For on the one hand, it presents an experience which is set into place by history and informed by rules and fiats over which the individual has little, if any, control, while on the other hand it grants separate moments of a stormy and overwhelming sense of individual *being*; moments brimming with mental activity and visceral existential sensations. Thus it offers a unique model of existence: chaotic yet prescribed and unchangeable; deadly yet bursting with mental life; continuously and sequentially evolving, each occurrence unfolding as the unavoidable result of the events which preceded it, yet simultaneously broken into disparate unrelated units of experienced time, each forming a world unto itself. This duality appealed to Yizhar as exposing with sharp intensity the very essence of the experience of being in the world with its paradoxical, even absurd, comingling of oppositions: predestination and freedom, unrelenting exterior causality and the unexpected tides and whirlpools of a seething and uncontrolled interiority.

For Yizhar, the Arab plays the role of the ultimate "other" in this drama. As such, he is inevitably Janus-faced, a figure both bright and dark at one and the same time. On the one hand, he is perceived as an organic outgrowth of the landscape, its human representative. He therefore can at times be idealized, endowed with the grace and harmony of unperturbed nature, and identified with the most hallowed biblical figures. For example, in the beginning of "The Prisoner", the Arab shepherds are presented as part of an Edenic scene of idyllic hills covered by ancient olive trees and brilliantly illuminated by the golden light of the afternoon sun, "leading their flocks tranquilly across the unchanged fields and quiet hills, with the casual stride of those good times when trouble had not yet come" (p.66). They are figures in a holy template of flocks and shepherds "from the days of Abraham, Isaac, and Jacob" silhouetted against a distant backdrop of biblical villages "with [a] frieze of olives" gleaming like a bas-relief of "dull copper" (p.66). In comparison, the Jewish soldiers, who hunt and eventually interrogate one of the shepherds, are introduced as burdened with the modern machinery of warfare, and are not only mundane, shallow, sweaty, and graceless, but actually a dangerous alien element which, attempting to "penetrate" (p. 115) this "world of hills" (p. 116), is about to destroy it.

This, however, is only one side of the portrayal of the Arab village in the story—the distant, picturesque and idealized version. The other side emerges as the soldiers approach an actual village that has recently been conquered and evacuated. The narrator's impressions of the village as observed from close quarters are saturated with such an intense sense of disgust, alienation, and lack of empathy, that his very sentences, usually complex, well-rounded and mellifluous, suddenly become choppy, truncated and discordant: "A forsaken ant-hill, the rags and tatters of human life. The mustiness of don't-give-a-damn. A stinking, flea-bitten, lice-infested existence. The poverty and doltishness of miserable villages. All of a sudden their outskirts, their homes, their courtyards, their inmost sanctums had been laid bare" (p. 70). At this point, it is the Jewish soldiers who become the endangered invaders. Using this sink of iniquity as their quarters, they become contaminated, as if the surrounding scaly infestation gradually covers not only their skin but also their mind and souls with its ugly scabs.

The depictions of the Arab village are two sides of one coin, which is that of total alienation—an alienation which is equally manifest in idealization and demonization, and which allows the presentation of the Arab villager as both a biblical patriarch and a shred of "the tatters of human existence" within the compass of a single short story. The Zionist culture that Yizhar absorbed and gave expression to was that of the post 1929 so-called riots, which actually amounted to the first round in the Arab-Jewish continuous war. Before 1929, the dream of Arab-Jewish fraternization was very prevalent and influenced the image of the Arab in Jewish art and literature. It allowed for both an Orientalist stylization of the Arab (particularly the Bedouin) as a "noble savage", a man of courage, beauty, magnanimity, and stormy genuine emotions, as well as convincing realistic portrayals (such as in Y. Shami's masterful novella, *The Vengeance of the Fathers*, 1928). However, after the 1929 war, even the leaders of Labor Zionism, such as David Ben-Gurion, realized that the Palestinian nationalist movement had opted for an all-out showdown with the Zionist "entity", and that the two national communities in Palestine were irrevocably set in a collision course (Vladimir Jabotinsky and his followers had reached this conclusion a full decade earlier). Correspondingly, the Hebrew cultural image of the Arab changed: the earlier realistic-objective dimension shrank and almost disappeared as the Arab came to represent the all-but-abstract "enemy", a polymorphic figure onto which was projected the bright and dark aspects of one's own psyche. Yizhar's oeuvre as a whole is a perfect reflection of this confrontational culture.

5

Yizhar's aforementioned dualism is related to another brand of his thematics of strife. Lack of inner harmony breeds strife in its most basic form, that of internal conflict, and indeed such tension stands at the very core of Yizhar's work. His chief protagonists are always presented as agitated by some kind of intrinsic turmoil, which often is articulated in the form of a dialogue between two or more inner voices which express contradictory attitudes. Two of the 1948 war stories, "The Prisoner" and *The Story of Hirbet Hiz'ah*, illustrate this interior dialogue in its most heated and explicit form, where its moral and political ramifications are intentionally emphasized. However, the intrinsic dualism also pervades stories where no overt conflict or self-contradiction is evident. For the internal strife in Yizhar's stories emanates, as we have seen, from a deeply entrenched conflicted sense of being. This often, though not always, manifests itself in the interaction of the protagonist with a peer group or collective to which he belongs and yet also does not belong. The ambiguous interaction is not necessarily predicated on the objective circumstances under which the protagonist and the group he at least partly identifies with operate; and even when it is conditioned by such circumstances—particularly in stories where the protagonist is part of a military unit with a combative mission—the uneasy attitude of the protagonist toward his peers does not necessarily flow from disapproval of the group's behavior (though clearly it does in the two works mentioned above). Strangely, but very tellingly, this attitude can emerge at moments when the protagonist is wholeheartedly committed to the group's activity, and feels only admiration and strong emotional attachment to the members of the company who shoulder the burden of difficulty and danger which the activity entails. Thus, for example, Tzvialeh, the protagonist of *Midnight Convoy*, sings a paean of love for the large group of soldiers he has just watched marching under the weight of their heavy weaponry to battle and danger, intent upon the serious and possibly lethal business of facing the enemy, yet making no gestures of either doubt or self aggrandizement; but nonetheless, even while experiencing the rush of heartfelt identification and admiration, he is unable to hush the inner voice that keeps whispering that even now, "in the midst of all these things you have not forgotten your fancies and your wild and worthless dreams…even as the ground trembled you did not forget your trivial self" (p. 163-164).

The conflict between the acknowledged need to participate in the effort of the collective and the suppressed rejection of it as an irksome nuisance can be seen as the fundamental reality of Yizhar's work, both on the cultural and psychological level. As such, it has a nearly autonomous existence in most of the author's stories, regardless of their specific details.

Culturally, it can be viewed as reflecting the basic dichotomy between the Zionist ethos and the modernist spiritual and artistic *Weltanschauung*. The former emphasized collectivism, ethnicity and nationalism, and was based on an essentially optimistic view regarding the ability to change and greatly ameliorate one's condition through the full activation of will power. The latter focused on the individual as a separated unit, on the loneliness of modern man within an alienated environment, on his inability to escape the essentially meaningless limitations of the *condition humaine*. Yizhar, more than any other Israeli writer, straddled this divide, and was genuinely committed both to the Zionist ethos and to the modernist view of the human condition. He therefore could not avoid the dualism and the inner strife so rife in his work.

In this respect he resembles Y.H. Brenner more than the artist closest to his heart, U.N. Gnessin. For Gnessin, the early Hebrew modernist par excellence, fully and unconditionally adopted the view asserting the complete loneliness of modern man, and with great virtuosity evolved the artistic methods and devices that could best convey the existential experience of such alienation. Brenner, in contrast, though philosophically committed to a modernist-existentialist view of the human condition, was equally informed by the collectivist mores of the Russian intelligentsia and the nationalist ethos of the "New", post-traditional Hebrew culture and literature, which ascribed to the Jewish intellectual and writer the role of a latter day prophet, "a watchman unto the house of Israel", the custodian entrusted with looking after the national well-being. Alienated as he often was, Brenner would never renege on the duty of the intellectual to constantly conduct and articulate what he himself viewed as a collective *"ha'arakhat atzmenu"*, a term that can be roughly translated as collective self-evaluation or self-criticism. Thus Yizhar can be described as a writer and an intellectual who was constantly vacillating between the model of Gnessin (whom he admired and emulated as an artist) and the model of Brenner (whom he admired and emulated as a moralist).

Psychologically, Yizhar's dualism emanated from sources that become fully apparent only in his late autobiographical works written in the 1990s, particularly the aforementioned short novel *Preliminaries*. What in the earlier works seems to assert itself as an unquenchable thirst for personal freedom can retrospectively be understood as springing from a personality-deficiency ingrained in the writer's character from a very early age. In *Preliminaries*, the author traces the course of a breakdown of personality, which from early childhood undermines appropriate socialization and renders social adaptation of any kind a burden almost too heavy to bear. This deficiency is explored with exemplary moral and artistic integrity. The author reconstructs the conditions which defined his character when still a young child as that of the halfhearted outsider, the one who did not really belong, no matter how desperately he wished to mix and associate with the peers he liked. Little did it help that everything and everyone around him worked to make him deeply conscious of the need to integrate himself into the collective, as it was only through collective effort that the historical task of realizing the Zionist dream could be achieved. He describes the weakness, insufficiency and bitterness of an aging father, whose ceaseless conscientious hard work since making aliyah to Israel as an eighteen-year-old idealist never won him either the recognition or the modest financial security he deserved; the tormenting ambivalence of admiration and intense jealousy toward an older sibling, brilliant, handsome, robust, adventurous, happy, and obviously preferred by all and sundry, father, mother, comrades and adoring girlfriends alike; an awkward self-awareness of being physically unprepossessing and sexually undesirable. All these made for a tenuous, insecure and ambivalent internal self-image, which extended outwardly to the relationship with the group he yearned to join and yet also shunned. "Even when they are all together," the protagonist of *Preliminaries* remembers, "there is always one who is left on his own.... even when they all belong, there is always one who does not entirely belong. Or let's say he belongs yet doesn't belong, or not wholly, or not all the time, even if he is with them all the time." It was as if the protagonist was doomed to play the role of mere observer, watching others from the sidelines, recording their presence as if amassing some kind of knowledge or keeping a record that would enable him to bear evidence in some as-yet-unknown future. And therefore "it's as though all the time he is required to explain something about himself, to make excuses or apologize, instead of admitting, leave me alone, friends, let me be and don't wait for me." And yet at the same time he is torn by his own internal ambivalence, and something within him pleads "wait for me, I'm coming too, wait for me I'm coming too." [2]

---

2   All references are from Nicholas de Lange's translation of *Preliminaries* New Milford, CT: *The* Toby Press, 2007, p. 16.

This combination of cultural and psychological conditions can explain much of the vicissitudes of Yizhar's writing, from its very beginnings with "Ephraim Goes Back to Alfalfa", written when the author was twenty-one-years old, through to the surprising and very revealing works written when he was well into the eighth decade of his life. Among other things, for instance, they explain what may be referred to as the "unanimistic" attitude Yizhar adopted in some of his early novellas, such as *At the Edges of the Negev* and *The Grove on the Hill*. The term *Unanimism* was coined by the French poet, playwright and novelist Jules Romaines in his attempt to counterbalance the extreme individualism characteristic of modernist literature with a contra-literature based on the assumption that—particularly in the modern urban environment of a metropolis such as Paris—significant events happened not to the sequestered individual but rather to the group as a whole. These events are processed and acted upon through the *una anima*, the single collective soul, of the group. Yizhar was influenced by this concept, and wrote stories in which he attempted to capture the spirit of a collective in action, whether the group of workers drilling a well in *At the Edges of the Negev*, the group of settlers defending their farm in *The Grove on the Hill*, or even the group of soldiers desperately trying to hold on to the positions they established on the strategic hill of Hirbet Mehaz in *Days of Ziklag*.

However, Yizhar's mode of presenting the deeds and thoughts of dozens of characters is very different from Romaines'. Romaines posited that the "single soul" which unified the group, and, indeed, the nation as a whole (in his famous novels sequence *Les Hommes de bonne volonte*, written between 1932 to 1947, he aspired to display the workings of the urban French psyche as it manifested itself throughout twenty-five years of French social and political history, 1908–1933) could not be expressed through introspective narration. Rather, the comprehensive consciousness could only be expressed through a voice that in some ways was very close to the traditional omniscient narrator.[3] Yizhar, in contrast, did not let go of his narrative

---

3   This does not imply that Romaines' concept of the *uninamist* story was closely aligned with traditional nineteenth-century novel. Other than the omniscient narrator, it is free from most strictures of normative nineteenth-century prose.

forme maittresse, the interior monologue. To present a collective, he instead rapidly shifts the focus of the interior monologue from one character within the group to another, thus developing a "choir" effect. Yizhar's *Grove on the Hill* and *Days of Ziklag* are completely different in tone, structure and intellectual implications than Romaines' two great war novels *Prelude to Verdun* and *Verdun* (vols. 15-16 in his 27 volume *roman fleuve*) or Norman Mailer's *The Naked and the Dead* (another great war novel somewhat influenced by the unanimist concept). More tightly tied to the high modernism stream of consciousness fiction, Yizhar's war novel, despite its polyphony, does not offer, in the final analysis, a unified or collective view of the war. Instead it presents a conglomerate of many individual views, each idiosyncratic and closed within itself. Paradoxically, the loneliness of the individual and his sense of alienation from an absurd reality are arguably never more accentuated in Yizhar's work than in his vast war novel, which focuses on the activity of a unified military group. What is more, as one navigates through the high waters of *Days of Ziklag*, one comes to realize that the interior monologues offered *seriatim* become more distinct in style and captivating in emotional content the closer the respective monologist is to the habitual Yizhar protagonist, with his insecurity, internal conflicts and dreams of individualistic freedom. When the author "dubs" characters that do not share these characteristics, the artistic level of the interior monologue quickly plummets. The result is that many of the atypical characters are hardly distinguishable one from the other, and their respective monologues, too similar in both content and style, are eminently forgettable. Thus, even in his heroic attempt to tell the tale of an epoch and of the generation of youngsters fated to bear the brunt of the 1948 War, the author never really distanced himself from his initial modernistic-individualistic paradigm.

Even in the stories meant to produce a choir-like, rather than solo effect, it is the protagonist who stands at the edge even as he attempts to support the group in its collective effort, functioning

---

For example, the protagonists do not have to evolve personal relationships with each other or know each other personally; the plot is not strictly sequential and causal.

as an observer if not a severe critic, that remains at the very core of Yizhar's fiction. Indeed, looking at Yizhar's work as a whole, one can argue that the psychological dynamics of individualism and belonging which prescribe the centrality of the protagonist are the same as those which made the narration itself possible or perhaps even inevitable. For it is the distinct sense of being somewhat out of synch with others that not only produces the distance needed for observation and artistic description, but also creates the need for such creative endeavor as a compensatory procedure through which the alienated individual can counterbalance his sense of insignificance and marginality. In *Preliminaries*, where the author rigorously explores the sources of his own cultural and artistic mission, this compensatory aspect of his creative activity is squarely faced and acknowledged.

Paradoxically, Yizhar's enduring loyalty to his initial sense of marginality, of not belonging, or at least, to use his words, of being one who "does not entirely belong, or not wholly, or not all the time," strengthened rather than weakened his position as the quintessential Israeli writer. As much as it was frowned upon by ideologues and literary commissars, it endeared him to his avowed readers and enabled him to delve deeper than others into the depths of the common Israeli experience. Again, the late autobiographical works of the 1990s shed much light on this aspect of his cultural representativeness. There, particularly in the brilliant collection of short stories published under the telling title *Tzdadiyim* (the English "Asides" does not convey the full meaning of the word, which also means "peripherals", pieces not adhering to the center), Yizhar finally acknowledges the fact that his own loneliness, expressed in that of his characteristic protagonist, was not as unique as he had thought; that in fact the entire collectivist ethos with its triple emphases on nationalism, socialism, and vibrant, future-oriented, activism, had been to a large extent a façade under which a welter of loneliness, alienation, and a sense of personal discontinuity hid, or rather was forcefully repressed and denied—for official Zionist ethos and culture, like those proclaimed by most national and social revolutionary movements, was repressive and predicated on self-denial. In many of the *Tzdadiyim* stories, perfected the main narrative tool he was to use for the next two decades: the interior monologue as practiced by writers of stream of consciousness fiction.

In the second group of stories, written in the period between 1948 and 1958, the War of Independence absorbed the author's entire creative energy, and the stream of consciousness modality attained full ripeness. Yizhar focused on both the external circumstances and the internal mental experience of warfare, investing tremendous effort into crafting the large-scale novel which would become the definitive Israeli work of fiction dealing with military combat. He occasionally found respite from this heavy burden in lighthearted short stories written for young readers, hankering back to a seemingly happy childhood among orchards and farms, which were collected in two volumes: *Six Summer Stories* and *Barefoot.*

After the publication of *Days of Ziklag* the author, exhausted and somewhat disoriented, began looking for new topics and narrative modalities. He attempted to expand the approach he had developed in the stories for young readers by infusing the pseudo-idyllic memoirist manner with the seriousness, indeed, the sense of tragedy, which had now come to characterize his view of the human condition. The combination resulted in the short story "Habakuk" (1960), in which his staple narrative technique of interior monologue was replaced for the first time by the seemingly loquacious ramblings of a retrospective memoirist. The narrator, reminiscing about his earlier years, addresses a group of listeners-readers, telling them about a relationship he had when in the midst of the crisis of puberty with a unique, somewhat eccentric but entirely benevolent amateur musician, who eventually played an important role in his life. This musician ends up being tragically killed in a war in which he had hardly participated. In this story, Yizhar discovered a new narrative vein.

However, he did not immediately follow and explore it. Instead he took leave of prose fiction in an expressionistic novella *A Story That Had Not Started* in which he furiously mingled in a repetitive cycle interior monologue, dramatic reenactment of painful memory, and a highly emotional jeremiad against the mundane reality of a new Israel bereft of its pioneering idealism and naiveté. It conveyed, more than anything, the author's sheer impatience with the act of storytelling per se. With this novella or poem-in-prose, published together with "Habakuk", "The Runaway" and several other stories in the collection *Plain Stories* (1963), the author seemed to slam the door in the face of his readers, leaving Israeli prose fiction in the hands of younger writers such as Amos Oz, A.B. Yehoshua, and eventually Yaakov Shabtai (for whom Yizhar had the highest regard). Yizhar himself turned to an altogether different discourse—polemic, argumentative and at times pseudo-academic—dealing with matters such as the correct reading and interpretation of narrative, the impossibility of humanistic education as well as issues pertaining to the morality and immorality of Israeli politics and public life.

Upon returning to prose fiction in the 1990s, Yizhar came back to the genre he had experimented with in "Habakuk", developing it further. Innovatively exploring and fleshing out a special autobiographical manner, in which memoir, stream of consciousness, and an elegiac lyricism emanating from the amalgamation of vividly remembered moments of youth with the wisdom of old age, he produced a sequence of stories in which the origins of his own life-in-art were examined with brutal honesty.

The current selection represents all three phases in the author's trajectory. It includes the signature story, "Ephraim Goes Back to Alfalfa", a first publication of a very young writer which nevertheless clearly announces the presence of a master and contains many of the characteristic features of the author's more mature work, clearly displaying Yizhar's narrative art at its inceptive stage. It also includes "Habakuk": the author's first step toward his late style, and "Harlamov" (from the *Tzdadiyim* cycle, 1996), which exemplifies this style in its mature form, both focusing on the transcendence of music and its liberating potential—a topic of the highest significance for Yizhar's aesthetics and poetics. Representing the middle phase of the author's career is the novella *Midnight Convoy*, written as the turmoil of the 1948 War subsided but the gray Israeli "morning after" had hardly dawned. The story was thus written in a very particular historical milieu, with some initial distance from the battle experience allowing for a modicum of emotional restraint, but with the memory of war still so fresh as to hardly be regarded as memory. At this unique moment Yizhar wrote his most lyrical and optimistic story, a novella reverberating with the specific tonality of the time, the days in which the State of Israel, having just been born in blood and fire, took a first look in the mirror, pondering its own face. *Midnight Convoy* demonstrates the author's narrative art at its best and most characteristic, which justifies its place as the centerpiece of the current selection—and allows it to serve as an exemplum for exploring Yizhar's reputation as Israel's chief master of prose fiction. To this novella the balance of our remarks in this introductory essay is dedicated.

7

First it is important to delineate the extrinsic event which inspired the novella, for it served as more than a mere backdrop. As a matter of fact, the occurrence itself—the passing of the military convoy in the darkness of a moonless night on its way to the besieged Jewish settlements of the northern Negev—*is* the main topic of the story, and completely determines its plot. It took place in the summer of 1948, during an uneasy lull in the military activities of both the Israelis and their opponents. With the ferocious battles of the spring behind them, the two sides, exhausted and desperately needing both to re-organize and to strengthen whatever positions they had managed to occupy, twice agreed to temporary cessations of hostilities supervised by the UN. While the questionable lull held, each side was absorbed in preparations for the continuation of the war, which would resume within a few weeks. At this mid-point, the fortunes of the war had somewhat changed. The initial grave danger to the main Jewish concentration along the sea coast, which for a time, immediately after the invasion of Palestine by the conventional armies of six Arab states in May, had seemed to threaten the very existence of nascent Israel, had been overcome. The Egyptian armed column, which had reached the agricultural settlements and the towns adjacent to Tel Aviv itself, had been pushed back to the border area which separated the northern Negev from the southern coastal plain, and the entire area between Tel Aviv and the mountainous region, heavily populated by Arab villagers and town dwellers, was under Jewish control, with most of its inhabitants fleeing their homes to the mountains held by the Jordanian Arab Legion. Jerusalem was still under siege by the Legion, but the situation there had somewhat improved due to the trailblazing of a makeshift road which allowed the Israelis to replenish the starving city with the essentials, enabling it to keep resisting the besieging army and its ancillary local Palestinian forces. The Israeli strategists now turned their attention to the south. There, the Egyptian army, stronger, larger, armed with tanks and assisted by an air force—and thus more dangerous than all the other Arab armies put together—had established a well fortified line which stretched all the way from the sea to the Judean mountains, some units reaching as far as the southern suburbs of Jerusalem. This line efficiently cut the country in two, separating the northern Jewish concentrations from the Negev, where a few, sequestered Jewish settlements, all under heavy siege, were fighting for their lives. Clearly, the intention of the Egyptians was to cut off this vast and relatively empty area—in size about half of the territory of Palestine as a whole and the better part of the Jewish state according to the UN partition plan of 1947—from the evolving Jewish "entity", should it manage to survive the war, thus reducing the Jewish state to a miniscule enclave with little, if any, unoccupied terrain to accommodate the immigration of millions of Jews. This truncation of the prospective Jewish territory was also very much in line with colonial British interests, as the British were worried by the proximity of the Jews, then supported by the Soviet Union and its allies, to the Red Sea. The UN emissary, Count Bernadotte, had therefore already raised the suggestion of exchanging the entire Negev for the western part of the Galilee (belonging within the

Palestinian state, according to the original partition plan), already occupied by the Israeli army.

Defeating the Egyptian-British strategy was now the vital interest of Israel. The Negev had to be saved as part of the Jewish state, and for that purpose the Jewish settlements there had to be strengthened, replenished, and made ready for battle, so that once the temporary cessation of hostilities ended, the Egyptian army could be engaged from the north and the south alike, and eventually squeezed into an enclave where the IDF could attack from all directions. While the quiet held, the paramount need was to somehow cross the Egyptian line, if possible without undermining the ongoing *hafuga* (lull, pause), and resupply the Jewish forces behind it with food, medicine, ammunition, and fresh troops, without which they could not be expected to withstand the pressure of the Egyptian siege. This was the background for operations such as the one described in full detail in Yizhar's novella. The weaker links along the chain of Egyptian positions had to be found, makeshift roads surreptitiously charted within a few hours—otherwise the Israelis would be detected and attacked—and convoys subsisting of both units of infantry and trucks loaded with essential materiel had to be smuggled under the protecting darkness of the midnight hours. Such operations were kept to a minimum, and the configuration of each was unique, since similar attempts would certainly be blocked by the Egyptians. Thus the success of every one of them was critical.

Essentially, the novella is about such an operation. It opens in the late afternoon, as a group of soldiers, whose mission is to chart a road for an expected convoy, arrives at a spot that has been estimated as offering relatively safe passage. It is a large deserted area, a no-man's-land between the two armies, consisting partly of arable stretches, where the crops have not been garnered due to the flight of the local peasants, and partly of low but craggy hills, deep ravines and dry wadis—the characteristic geological formation of Palestine as it gradually and leisurely progresses from its sharp mountainous backbone toward its flat coastal plain. From the very beginning, the scene is enveloped in thick curtains of fatty dust, as the soil in the upper reaches of the Negev, though fertile, is very powdery. Its sods disintegrate under the slightest pressure, and the tiny particles are scattered through the air by the slightest wind, all the more so by the motion of heavy vehicles. It seems to the protagonist that this soil was made for the light touch of the bare feet of peasants or at most for the delicate hooves of donkeys, but not for Jeeps and trucks, which stir it, filling the air with a filmy, opaque substance that penetrates everything—eyes, mouths, hair, every crevice in the skin.

The poorly equipped group must rapidly chart a path that will make it possible for the convoy, particularly the heavily loaded trucks, to pass. It must be completed before nightfall. They quickly get started, surveying the terrain, which is quite different from what they had been told based on the fuzzy aerial photos available. Most chart the trail, which they mark by piling stones and connecting the heaps with white paper ribbons that are supposedly discernable in total darkness. The rest are sent on a reconnaissance mission to the outskirts of the nearest Egyptian outpost, where they are to be on the lookout for any suspicious activity that might indicate that the enemy has been alerted; if possible, they are also to mine the area between the outpost and the paved road the convoy is to use once it circumvents it, thus halting any Egyptian attempt to give chase and attack the convoy from the rear. Night descends. All preparations have more or less been set in place, and a protracted period of nervous expectation, as they wait for the arrival of the convoy, begins. At last, another platoon of soldiers, an assistance force, arrives, including a young woman who operates a wireless connection with headquarters. Eventually, the convoy itself appears. First march the infantry units—a few hundred troops—carrying their heavy machine guns and boxes of ammunition; then, arriving very late because of difficulties along the way, the heavy trucks finally emerge. Slowly and painfully they navigate their way along the makeshift trail, cross a deep wadi, and clumber with engines roaring under the strain onto the opposite bank, where they continue their slow progress.

At last the mission is accomplished and the caravan,

encountering very slight resistance as it passes by the Egyptian outpost, is on its way southward to its destination. Two trucks hit mines and are left behind so as not to slow the progress of the convoy as a whole, which must be far behind the Egyptian lines—and thus relatively out of the danger zone—before dawn. One soldier is killed, and several others wounded. As the convoy passes out of sight, the tension that kept the members of the group awake and edgy throughout the night is replaced by fatigue and half-sleep, with which the story ends.

Yizhar's choice of this particular episode as the topic of his most comprehensive war narrative before the *Days of Ziklag* requires exploration. Strategically important as the operation was, it does not make for an action-packed war story. A hazardous affair in its own right, it nonetheless was very different from both the battles that had preceded it and the ones that took place in its wake. Tzvialeh, the protagonist, even tells himself that this is a different kind of war, a "peaceful" war, so to speak. Yet it is important to note that even as he savors this moment of "peace", Tzvialeh is haunted by memories of the battles he has seen, which he forcefully tries to repress. One image, however, keeps obsessively reappearing, metonymically representing the horrors that he is trying to forget: a cadaver burnt beyond recognition, but for a single foot, still shod in a sandal with a rubber sole cut from a Dunlop tire, the Dunlop logo visibly embossed upon it. Though he speaks of a lull, Tzvialeh knows that it is fleeting, its peacefulness imaginary. The undercurrents of fear and danger are ever trickling through the depths of his consciousness—"tonight I am stumbling on a mine," he thinks. What is more, he is fully aware that the mission his group has been entrusted with is nothing if not a preparation for battles that will be every bit as ferocious as those he has just undergone. Toward the end of the story he openly acknowledges the reality of the situation: "No escape. It was naive to think we could have broken the siege with a convoy. Convoys are all well and good in a nice, peaceful sort of war—but they won't work here. You can't occupy territory with convoys, you can't break a siege or win the peace. To do that you have to die, over and over again. You're not out of it yet, my boy.... Always to have to die, always.... That's the way it goes. It doesn't matter whether you want to kill or not, to be killed or not—nothing can help you anymore." (p. 202-203). Yet despite the dark undertones, and the continuous awareness of the fragility of the calm, the fact that Yizhar chose a relatively quiet moment as the basis for his tale cannot be accidental. Understanding his reasons is an essential part of understanding this novella.

8

I believe that Yizhar's choice was guided by four different considerations. The first was thematic: in *Midnight Convoy*, he wished to explore the positive and uplifting aspects of the 1948 War. This is in contradistinction to his presentation of the war in two earlier stories, "The Prisoner" and *The Story of Hirbet Hiz'ah*, in which he scathingly criticized what he perceived as the systematic expulsion of the Palestinian peasantry. As the stormy polemics triggered by these two stories were raging, the author wanted to remind himself and his readers of the other side of the war: the defense of the Jews of Palestine from physical annihilation and the preparation of the foundations for the independent State of Israel. In *Days of Ziklag* these aspects of the war would drown in a boiling sea of carnage, and the war would be portrayed as the living hell experienced by those who fought and died in it. In *Midnight Convoy*, the focus on a maneuver relatively distant from the front experience, which has an obviously beneficial and life-saving character, offers another view of the war, especially in conjunction with the enthusiasm and naiveté of the protagonist. What is more, the wide strategic perspective prescribed by the attempt to save the besieged settlers of the Negev and together with them, the Negev itself as a part of the Jewish state, enables the author to view the war as a historic whole, to see it as the event which brought about the birth of Israel. This emphasis of the positive aspects of the war extends beyond the national into the personal, as we shall see.

The second consideration was stylistic, and had to do with pace and rhythm. Yizhar's meticulous historical accuracy dictated that the events he depicted needed to be closely aligned with the narrative pace he wished to follow. This particular historical moment allowed for an evolving, relatively non-dramatic tale characterized by a slow narrative pace and a leisurely descriptivism. While this might have disappointed readers who were looking for action and the heightened emotionality of choppy battle descriptions, it had its own rich compensations. It enabled the author to fully focus on his primary interest: the sheer experience of "being" in an open, uninhabited space. Rarely do we encounter in literature so sensitive and sustained a rendering of such experience as the one presented here.

As noted above, the terrain described consists of neglected arable fields and wild hills and ravines untouched by human hands. This combination elicits a dual response from the protagonist. On the one hand, it triggers a sense of sadness, as if he identifies with the "pain" of the earth whose plenteous crops are withering away. The wasted fecundity dovetails with Tzvialeh's sense of his own devastated life-force, his many emotions and reflections doomed, like the grains that have not been properly harvested, to serve no purpose and, left unused, to decay; for Tzvialeh possesses neither the social skills nor the emotional maturity that would enable him to channel his emotions and thoughts into constructive action or even to transmit them to a sympathetic listener. On the other hand, untamed, wild nature arouses in Tzvialeh the impulse to combat the open spaces and overcome the impediments with which they seem to intentionally block his progress. After all, it his task, his military mission, to rein in the wilderness and force it to serve both himself and his comrades. This dual relationship to the landscape creates a delicate ambiguity in the projection of space throughout the story.

Tzvialeh's great sensitivity to spatial impressions elicits from him a rich array of conflicting emotional responses. Starting with his disgusted sensitivity to the enveloping dust and its penetrative quality (rendered by the virtuoso descriptive overture to the story)—the dust seems as much a protagonist of the story as any of the human characters—these impressions lead to moments of the purest elegiac lyricism in which Tzvialeh projects onto the landscape his deepest sense of forlornness and unrequited yearning for sympathy. He etches into the landscape a self-portrait of sorts, a paradigm of his sensibilities and the harsh realities which confront and stymie them. Thus he attempts to personify the soil as a warm, delicate and embracing body:

> The soil beneath them was warm and chunky, and the hill's hump slouched on, forward, its peaceful folds trimmed with lacy fringes of gold—the oat-like wild grasses, woven between them, about a foot above the ground, transparent in a trembling halo of light, delicate golden-yellow bells, a fresh and heart-warming tremor suspended in the air. (pp. 101-102).

But other impressions must be acknowledged, for the delicate halo of the husks is truncated at the craggy and uncouth channel of the wadi. Then the field at night plays tricks with the senses and undermines Tzvialeh's self-orientation. It maliciously leads him into labyrinthine mazes, cutting him off his comrades, reducing his stature and self-confidence, waking in him an inner orphaned babe in the woods. Thus the landscape simultaneously represents a lovely, yielding femininity and an inimical environment with its intrinsic chaos, the harshness and ill-will of reality and the fragility and fragmentation of the self.

This ambiguity in the landscape is somewhat counterbalanced by a meticulous attention to vehicles and machines, which represent in this context the reliability and helpfulness of human invention and camaraderie. Hence the almost over-sensitive attention directed to cars of various types and uses, their speed and how they slow when faced with difficulties, their groaning noises, their vulnerability to mechanical failure, their awkwardness once the privilege of a paved road has been swept from beneath their wheels, and the great care and joint effort required for getting them back on track. To a very large extent, the drama of war is replaced in *Midnight Convoy* by the drama of exposure to open space, which can be both humanized and projected as an extension of the protagonist's interiority and slightly demonized and projected as man's enemy.

The third consideration in focusing on this particular historic moment is closely related to the second, and had to do with the artistic potential of the stream of consciousness narrative modality in the exploration of character. As we have seen, the landscape itself, as processed through the vivid impressions of the protagonist's consciousness, highlights essential characteristics of that protagonist. But the experience of space is only one of the many means Yizhar employs to thoroughly examine his character: The slow pace of the narration allows for the gradual emergence of a sense of Tzvialeh's personality. As a matter of fact, *Midnight Convoy* offers Yizhar's most intimate, close-up view of his typical protagonist, the habitual diffident, non-assertive young man, who "belongs" within the group he is affiliated with but at the same time does not altogether "belong"—a view that is here informed by the sensibility and delicacy which single out this novella as a whole. In Tzvialeh the author created nothing less than the most sensitive portrayal of his ubiquitous anti-hero, a portrayal which nonetheless is neither romanticized nor self-serving. Tzvialeh is projected as a very immature and insecure young man, who, deeply craving intimacy with other human beings, constantly experiences his own marginality and loneliness. More pathetic than attractive, he is a character with whom the reader can empathize rather than identify. The name itself, with its childish diminution, is not devoid of a glint of sarcasm (*tzvi*—a deer; *Tzvialeh*—a diminutive deer, a Bambi-like creature, naïve, easily frightened, in need of protection). The forces which formed him, why and how he came to be as he is, are not made explicit, just as little is told of his life before the war—most probably a life characterized by deficit attention and appreciation, leading to a lowly self-image. Everything known about Tzvialeh is gathered through the impressions and emotions that percolate through his stream of consciousness or through his interactions with other characters. Thus the slow pace of the novella allows for an immersion in the protagonist's immature subjectivism and interior restlessness. For instance, it allows a thorough exploration of his yearning for a father

figure. Obviously, Tzvialeh's actual father, mentioned once in passing as an elderly, benevolent but detached figure, did not provide a
steady, supportive presence, and the youngster is therefore starved
for a protective father-figure. This is expressed in Tzvialeh's interaction with the middle-aged Rubinstein, the commander of the unit
responsible for the preparations for the passage of the convoy. While
Rubinstein, in his low-keyed and down to earth manner, is completely
consumed by his awareness of the critical importance of the operation
and the need to do everything possible in order to ensure its success,
Tzvialeh is overwhelmed by personal emotions. He is constantly trying to curry favor, to be the good boy who is crowned with father's
approval, to at least remain, in so far as the tasks allotted to him
allow, in Rubinstein's proximity. Separation immediately awakens
in him a childish dejection, a feeling of being deserted or forgotten.
Rubinstein, for his part, does not in any way evince his awareness of
Tzvialeh's needs and attachment, but he is wise enough to keep him
near for the better part of the story. This partly explains the strange
sense of elation that characterizes Tzvialeh's attitude toward the operation as a whole and his own share in it in particular. Paradoxically,
this tense, difficult day may be one of the happiest ones in his life.
He realizes with much foreboding that the close relationship with
Rubinstein, prescribed by the combat situation, can hardly survive
the war. In a depressed moment, he imagines a future chance meeting
with Rubinstein and his unknown wife amidst a city street bustling
with Sabbath strollers. After a short moment of happy recognition,
followed by a formal introduction to the wife and a short reference
(for her benefit) to the war experiences shared with the anonymous
young man, there would be no common ground left. The meeting
would never lead to a sustained relationship.

Hence, Tzvialeh is aware of the fact that war, horrible as it is,
also possesses a flip side of human relatedness, and that peace can
be, in more ways than one, an anticlimax. As a matter of fact he
dedicates much thought to the possible disappointments which the
hoped-for peace may harbor. Tzvialeh hates the army and the routine
of camp life disgusts and frustrates him, as he lacks the social skills

xlix

needed to negotiate his status within a group of peers afflicted with boredom, repressed fears, and awakened lust. But peace will offer no solution: it will only throw him right back into the confusion and sense of failure that characterized his life before the war. It is only in moments of meaningful collective effort such as those described in this story that he can transcend himself. Thus Tzvialeh's fragile happiness assumes an important role in the story and strengthens the "positive" view of the war it imparts.

Gavri (a shortened version of Gabriel, but the name, thus shortened, also means "manly" "virile" in Hebrew) is the *alzon*, the braggart of the story, the antagonist against whom the Yizhar protagonists often measure themselves. Here like elsewhere he is the robust, heavily mustached and *kaffiyah*-adorned seasoned soldier, who has been everywhere, knows everybody, and regards himself as supremely savvy in all military matters (predictably he would have planned the entire operation in an altogether different way). Habitually, and here too, the Yizhar protagonist recoils from this character, his attitude is a mixture of genuine disgust mingled with a sense of inferiority and insignificance. However, in *Midnight Convoy* the repulsion is considerably minimized and softened, allowing Tzvialeh to confront his well repressed admiration for the dashing courage, resourcefulness, and social ease of the Gavris, without whom the war could not have been fought. For it is Gavri, of course, who is sent by Rubinstein on the fairly dangerous mission of reconnoitering the Egyptian outpost, and, if possible, also mining the path leading from the outpost to the road; and Gavri, together with the soldiers he leads, successfully carries out both parts of his task.

Here, Yizhar comes as close as he ever does in his early, pre-memoiristic fiction, to uncovering the hidden identity of the Gavri-like characters in his stories, which, starting in *A Story That Did Not Start* but achieving full sweep only in the author's late novels, such as the autobiographical *Preliminaries*, is revealed to be none other than that of his dashing, handsome and easy-going elder brother, who both in life and in his premature death in a motorcycle accident was given all the love, pride, and heartbreak of his elderly father, as well

l

as the admiration, love and hatred of his jealous younger brother. Like Esau in the biblical story this brother's portrayal was necessarily fraught with ambiguity. In most of his early stories Yizhar had to project this sibling-figure in essentially negative guises—an indication of the intensity of the pain inflicted by festering sibling rivalry. However, in *Midnight Convoy* this pain is considerably assuaged, and the Gavri character is therefore portrayed in a somewhat more balanced and positive manner than in most cases.

Dali (shortened version of Dalia) is the girl operating the wireless system, and we are told absolutely nothing about her. Even her face is never really seen, as she arrives at night, and remains shrouded by darkness for the duration of the story. Only the green or red eye of the apparatus she operates occasionally allows for a glimpse, revealing a contour, illuminating the movement of a hand pushing aside the long hair that falls on her face. Though her voice is heard, it is intentionally the mechanical voice used for transmitting short coded messages by wireless. The few words that Tzvialeh manages to exchange with her after much hesitation and ridiculously complex preparations are mundane, matter of fact, and desultory. They do not reveal any aspect of her character or temper. And yet it is Dali more than anyone else who dominates Tzvialeh's interior monologue. Nothing is more indicative of his emotional immaturity, for it is exactly the anonymity and inaccessibility of the girl that renders her the ideal focus of his adolescent eroticism. What Tzvialeh seeks is not a real encounter with an approachable woman but rather the repetitious wallowing in a welter of erotic fantasies, which, emotionally burgeoning as they may be, are never carried beyond a certain barrier of propriety. For instance, Tzvialeh, who is probably a member of an agricultural commune, is well aware of the way unmarried youngsters seeking erotic intimacy in these ultra-puritan little societies behaved. In the evening, after showering away the sweat of their daily toil and changing their clothes, they would walk toward the gate of the compound, pretending to enjoy an innocent evening stroll. Once beyond that portal they would find their way to the nearest grove or thick copse where they could enjoy, unperturbed, each other's company. Characteristically, sharp edges protruding and undermining the continuity and relaxed mobility of the reading process.

This does not imply that the story does not change registers, that it is not made to swell and recede in passages of crescendo and diminuendo. However, the reader is meant to be carried along the fluctuating tides and ebbs, following the protagonist in his confusion, hesitation, and oscillation between moments of forlornness and of warm camaraderie, to the unexpected vast upsurge toward a moment of triumphant emotional climax: the passage where Tzvialeh witnesses the marching soldiers, unassuming yet determined, devoid of military grandiosity, yet ready to meet their fate, whatever it may be. This is Yizhar's great ode, a narrative equivalent of Beethoven's "Ode to Joy" in the Ninth Symphony:

> One wanted all at once to rise up before them and state one's admiration, to praise this or that man walking his dark line, all of those unknown soldiers who kept on, whose only fear was of falling out of line—Some good word had to be found to fill the place of prayer for their survival—at least allow them to laugh, if nothing else. —And then it was clear that the best thing to do would be to join the marchers and go off with them, blessed and praised on your way to whatever fatal destination. For what is man but a gentle creature, devoid of any desire of his own for a march such as this, which he undertakes trembling with worry and want, though not reject-ing the burden but hoisting it upon his back and marching on, immersed in the rhythm and the sweat, too pressed for time to think about things and their ends. Diligent, anonymous, they passed on and on, in a single file of silence, one after the other, on and on, silent men marching in line—Something which could be perceived only in a blur, as it was greater than that which ordinary words can describe (pp. 162-163).

Upon close examination one can retroactively see how this cli-mactic paean has been carefully prepared and thoughtfully situated by the author. It is preceded by long passages of distinctly minor tonality, such as Tzvialeh's reminiscences of life in the military camp—brutal, ugly, and socially unbearable—or the long conversation between Tzvialeh and Ya'akov, a soldier he has just met, whose honest and direct responses reassert the horrific aspects of life on the frontline, which Tzvialeh himself consistently tries to repress. In this, the only real dialogue Tzvialeh conducts in the entire story, we clearly see the difference between the immature protagonist and the much more self-aware and straightforward soldier, who confronts his corrosive fears and confesses to having developed a set of superstitions. For example, he takes the sound of a braying donkey in a distant village before battle as a sign that he will emerge unharmed from the encounter with the enemy. When such a braying fails to materialize, he says, his ears strive to transform any noise they absorb into the hoped for "music" that for him is somehow connected with ideas of peace and normalcy, even as his worried heart fully knows the truth. This braying of a village donkey offers an intentionally orchestrated contrast to the Beethoven-like grand chords that follow it. And it is the donkey's braying, not the Beethoven-like choir, which supplies the proper closing note at the story's final paragraph; for, a master of Yizhar's stature does not bring a story to its closure with a festive paean accompanied by blaring trumpets. Rather he slides down from this elevation, resuming the halting and low-keyed music of Tzvialeh's alienation to produce a penultimate narrative section replete with anxiety—the possibility that the entire operation was bungled and will end in carnage and failure—and utter exhaustion, and finally arriving at a moment of renewed but restrained hope, a call for a refreshed and re-attuned receptivity to the wondrous reality of space and time: "And now you, son of man, pay heed to these hills, let your gaze extend till the very boundaries of the skies and the further expanses, until the limits of all life in this night world—do you not hear the donkey's call, call of peace?" (pp. 204-205). Having reached this point the reader experiences the musical satisfaction following the final symphonic chords, harmonizing all discordances and offering a genuine moment of tonal closure.

Ephraim Goes
Back to Alfalfa

TRANSLATED BY MISHA LOUVISH
FIRST PUBLISHED IN 1938

The door of the dining hall opened with a sharp screech and closed with a bang whenever anyone entered, the bright electric lamp attracted a swarm of busy moths into its glare, but the lazy breezes that came and went breathed a slight coolness and a sense of nearby trees. The spacious room was still half empty, and Gedalia—who was bent over the table-top with a soapy rag as he filled the warm air with his humming, accompanied by the scraping of moving chairs—was in a hurry to clear away the remains of supper. But those who were already seated at the clean half of the table were humming at their ease—some slowly sipping mugs of warm tea as they contributed to the performance by humming through their noses and casually drumming with their fingers, while others blew indolent, dreamy smoke-rings. A drowsy calm hovered over the four dark-green tables surrounded by their bright yellow chairs, over the tiled floor worn smooth by footsteps, and over the three light-colored walls embraced by a half-circle of windows, through which the coolness flowed in

And on the surface it seems that there is someone to rely on. And so? Yes, Ephraim, of course. "Listen, they're ringing the bell for the meeting." The bright peals rang out and reverberated, rejoicing and rippling, playing with each other's echoes, pausing for a moment at the height of the dense air and scattering laughingly in bright fragments which fell and melted away with a dying throb. And immediately afterward, the silence rustled in the distance, barely perceptible glimmers flickered over the orange groves on the slope, a sound of sweeping was heard at intervals from the cowshed, the skies were as arrogant as ever, and the cypresses bowed gently back and forth, and immediately afterward, tables were being moved inside, chairs grated, and a hubbub of laugher seemed to bubble up and overflow. No. It was not self-indulgence. But... she ought to understand, every job was hard—that was true, and after a week there was no difference between one and another. And when he said "to have it easy" that only meant... that was only to say... And, secondly, why not have it easy? Must things always be hard? Let it be easier for once. Let it be a little comfortable. Why not? Surely, after all, his wishes counted for something too. Why should he always be coerced, punished, obligated, submitting to demands forever? He would ask for a transfer to the plantations—say, to the old orange grove. There, at least, there was shade... Something soothing spread within him; the thread that had snapped seemed to be made whole, and everything appeared to be acceptable as it was, grasped in its true dimensions. When he lit a cigarette, his companion's face was dreamy, the shadows of her cheekbones were soft and warmly quivering. Her hands, clasped around her still knees, her dark-blue shorts, and her soft, light shirt were swallowed up again in the darkness, with that closed, distant melancholy which makes one want to be gracious and say something conciliatory and persuasive, or to divert one's attention and deal with something more pleasant. On the surface, it seems, all that is needed is to say just one word, the redeeming word, to point to this or that—and everything will be put right, and one can breathe freely, and both of them can burst into loud and friendly laughter... Now he had lost the thread again. Where was he? At the light touch, the one word, yes... A single rooster suddenly cried out from a distance and fell silent; the darkness quivered in the warm silence and moved secretly in the deep expanse, above all the objects and between them, barely touching the faint pallor on the horizon above the mountains, which had become heavy and close in the distance, saturated in darkness. From somewhere, the dim muffled sounds of a mandolin struck out feeble, lazy circles, which disappeared and reappeared in a melancholy, gentle reverie. From one side, the tin roof of the neighboring hut gleamed, and silver scales glimmered from the rounded masses of the dark grapefruit trees behind him, the blackness of which continued up to the rustling of the unseen casuarinas, and, on the other side, spots of light wandered in the still, tremendous expanse.

From the lit windows, there now emerged a grumbling mutter, gradually growing fainter, split for a moment by a shrill tone, a shout cut short and a grating chair; and a diminishing clearing of the throat presaged the voice which did not fail to come with great solemnity, and emerged in a smooth and level tone, in the confidence of habit, continuous, clear and complete, without interruption, except for the word "comrades", which always followed a pause for breath, and except for an occasional stifled cough. One very soon had enough of this voice, and one's thoughts wandered off again and started revolving in the same circles as before, while a hopeless pain, no longer even complaining, waited silently and patiently, as if casting up accounts in a perplexity expressed in a suppressed, unheard sigh.

"Well, that's how it is... That's how it is..."

And then, of its own accord, the bright image of the morning rises up—when Ephraim will leave the yard in the early dawn and go down to the alfalfa field in the valley, stepping in the same footsteps that the sand absorbed yesterday and the day before, continuing to tread in the rut engraved by the tractor wheels in this reddish soil, covered with the fine night dew, as the east, between the long-leaved eucalyptus branches, reddens and injects a blush into the greenish blue, while gray crumbly clouds evanesce on the cool horizons, their edges fluttering and falling away, and the whole land is filled with a quiet chill, and there is no wind. Then the same familiar joy will creep in, unheeding the first signs of the approaching storm, that joy of freedom, of open, easy breathing, of idle whistling combined with hopeful thoughts and restrained cheerfulness. And again the heart will presage something, responding willingly, ready to put everything else aside, longing and yearning for the brightening fields with the hardly visible copses, the duskiness of which makes one forget their isolation in the bareness all around. The stubble of the dewy fields will be golden, and some distant echo will reverberate, and the birds will argue with a joyful twittering. In the meantime, the road will turn back and meet the highway, on which a truck drives by exultantly, expelling to the rear swirling clouds of dust, and a cart dances by with a chinking of iron and boards. Someone passing by will say good morning—and then the reality will suddenly materialize and drive away all these transient illusions. A silent revolt, crying out within him, will drive him to rebel and not give up. Even his trousers look stiff and dirty, and his toe-caps smile insolently. And the path that leads to the alfalfa fields becomes strange and abhorrent and intolerable, the more the dew evaporates and the reticulated cracks in the dry soil disappear among the dusty briars, and everything that was so fine and beautiful grows ugly and appears dry and tedious—even the distant hills hide their chiseled clefts of blue and pale red with a turbid, impenetrable mist. Very soon, David and Nahum will start and acrimonious argument, so that you have to swallow the saliva in your throat, look pleasant and answer whatever they may ask—or even before they ask—and David says his piece and hints to Nahum that he has not yet changed his opinion. And then each will turn his own way, take their tools from the tin hut opposite, move about aimlessly and chat about this and that, without realizing that they said and did the same things in the same place yesterday. David will push up the peak of his crumpled cap and deliver his expert verdict:

"It'll be hot today, eh? Good and proper?"

"What? I'll look after the irrigation in the patch down below. Don't turn the tap on full…"

Nahum will answer inattentively, already wearing his rubber boots, carrying his hoe on his shoulder, and plodding off with a muffled thud at every step, bending with rustic thoroughness over the burgeoning rows, feeling with his finger in the soil and wiping it on his trousers, mending as he goes a breach in a wall of a furrow, until he crouches down in his place and stoops over his handiwork; and David rolls up his trousers, bares his hairy legs and hums the latest song that is going the rounds. Meanwhile Ephraim tackles the motor in the hut to make it start, grumbling as usual, because it is not oiled at the proper time, because barrels of paraffin have not been brought, because the mice have been gnawing at the sacks of seed grain, and a few other things, until the machine starts up and he joins David in his work and, at the same time, as he sings, chatting fraternally about whatever is going on and producing witticisms of his own to the joy of his colleague. And some creature inside him shrinks away to vanishing point, and only a suppressed resentment, an unpleasant, transient twinge, with a strange desire for retribution, is directed to the place that has been vacated. Then suddenly—that is, as usual—they hear the staccato whistle of the train, as it emits clouds of cotton wool, and melts away and disappears with a rush, carrying with it a smell of coal, and distances behind and horizons in front, until the thing that has died in Ephraim raises its head for a moment, jumps up and tweaks at the deceived heart and immediately disappears into its hiding place, as David says:

"Well, so that means it's time for breakfast already, and we're supposed to sit down and eat. What do you think? So you agree, eh? And where's our feller-me-lad? Na-hum! Ah! Hoy-tra-la-la-bim-bam-oy-oy. Now, what I've got to say is this: It's going to be a fine day today, and we'll be dripping lots of sweat. Ha-ha, what?"—and goes off to close the tap with a loftiness that means: Well, now we know everything, there's no point in a lot of talk.

And then, when Ephraim remains alone for a moment, that unknown someone openly takes up residence within mockery and disparagement: "Well, done, my fine fellow, very well done, eh?" And those buried dreams break out like wild, maddened herds, wailing bitterly and desperately: "Ephraim! How long! How long!—And when that someone, who keeps on smiling at him, will be strong—what

immediately forgotten, to meditate for a moment about Nehama and immediately return to the plan for the alfalfa field, to be swept away again by transient thoughts and feelings, to smile at the memory of a passage in a book he had read yesterday, and automatically to reach the stage when he would accompany David's singing with a burst of song. That was reality. Even if everything would suddenly sink and disappear. Even if a fog would again fill his throat near the gullet, and everything would be revealed, undisguised, in its nakedness, and that alter ego would weigh on his stomach and grin within his head: "Anything more to say, my friend?" He would feel a gnawing disquiet, and the world would grow empty: the hoe was superfluous and the irrigation unnecessary; he was at odds with himself, there was nothing to cheer him up, no anchor; the futile straws at which he clutched recoiled and retreated before the abyss, and they could not save him either… that, too, was reality. Definitely. And everything you had accumulated with hardship and toil was squandered in a moment for nothing; it turned out to have been futile and foolish, not worth a pin—fine fellow that you are. Where was a drop, a shred, a scrap, of all you had managed to do, to hold on to, to get comfort from, to accomplish? Anyway, why this pride, this self-esteem, this arrogant aloofness? But even such questions can be evaded. It's all familiar. The questions are familiar, and so are the answers. And in front of your straining eyes, screwed up against the strong light from which there is no protection, behind the sparse copses of parchment-yellow eucalyptus, behind the fields in the valley where the smoke rises from burning piles of thorns—you are embraced by the old, familiar mountains like a tremendous ring within which the roads are familiar, the hills are known and the dusty, dazzling silence is repellently familiar and boringly well-known. A distant sea breeze, the midday breeze, dilutes the silence, stirs the copses, subdues the smoke, and bursts in successive waves over the alfalfa, which turns white and shining at every sweep of the wind. The skies grow more incandescent, lower, nearer the ground; they are already low and burning. The sweat dampens your shirt, the wind cooling it a little, and your feet are too weary to stand. Your body is drawn to the ground that crouches cracked and dumb, wanting you to cower and fall on your face among the warm, crumbly clods, and not to move, not to stir, not to breathe and not to think, to be still as a stone, as a thorn-stalk hardened by heat and dust, to the end, until it passes over, until... The water overflows, and Ephraim leaps forward to confine it again to its channel. Somehow, you again feel at peace and tranquil: the shower in the evening, the clean clothes, the newspaper with a cigarette, and something vague beyond them, bear an unspoken promise and a consolation: it's only till the evening; soon the day will pass and evening will come, and it will be possible to start something and do this and that... These foolish thoughts pamper themselves with anxious love and care, to avoid being lost or damaged. And it is pleasant to listen to them and believe, although their song is old and familiar, and you have always known that there is nothing in them. Nevertheless:

"Soon it will be evening."

And once Ephraim has thrown this magic dust into his own eyes, as he does day after day, holding on desperately to this pleasant blindness, all internal frontiers are wiped out, all objections and misgivings thrust aside, and everything outside him becomes a matter of complete indifference. The body applies itself to its work—toiling as it has always done, and a creature that drops off and sleeps the sleep of the just, sated with weariness and hardship, moves about in Ephraim's rubber top-boots. The water flows in its channel, and the circle of the sun, which has no color but furnace-heat, beats down from above, burning up every slightest shade with its breath, and glowing with the gleam of quivering, boiling horizons; wheels of dust frisk and frolic on the tops of the hills, and a dreary dryness veils the brightness of the parched skies. And now the noon train drags itself away from the station with damp gasps, strenuous and vibrant, howling spasmodically, making the ground tremble, pushing on each carriage accompanied by its shadow, and then turning its back, a brown forelock waving from its head, diminishing and disappearing. And again they will summon Nahum and sit down in the shadow of the hut, wipe off the dripping sweat, drink a lot, look listlessly at the dry, warm sandwiches, and finish them with forced, but gradually growing appetite. A couple of them will pick up where he left off in the morning and appoint Ephraim as arbitrator. And as for Ephraim, who is stretched out at his ease on the ground—in another moment his eyes will close, even his body will be overcome by sleep (at that very moment when those important meditations are, of course, about to be grasped completely), the deep sleep that vigorously removes all cobwebs, such a sleep that the "Ephraim! Ephraim!" which reaches his ears to awaken him is so harsh and grating that he feels like knocking down whoever has awakened him and turning over on the other side, feeling with his eyelids the pleasure so cruelly interrupted, curling himself up for another moment of liberty, and closing his ears at once to any "Ephraim" that might come!

"Ephraim, perhaps we should go in, they'll probably be dealing with your problem soon…"

"Eh? What?" Had he really dropped off? What a thing to do! To discuss his problem—what problem? Oh, yes, the very same problem. But what had he to do with it? It was all one. It made no difference. Now, of all times, he was enjoying his sleep. To hell with it all, again they had woken him in the middle… What did they really want of him? Let them leave him alone at last!

"Ach, Nehama, what can I say? Perhaps we should give it all up… Never mind, let it be the same as it was…"

"Give it up? Why? On the contrary, make an effort, do something to change it. After all, you… you believe, in it!"

The night chill and Nehama's voice were suddenly close and familiar, but for some reason his lips were pursed in a petulant, obstinate grimace. His sleepiness had completely disappeared, and he breathed in deeply the light cigarette smoke. Everything had become serious, adult and sober. The dried moisture in the corner of his eye was removed with his little finger; his eyes, now cleared and his lungs, which had started to expand, quietly and warmly drank in everything that was throbbing in the dense dusk. Take away the weariness, and there you are: a new man! Ephraim as he is. From now on, after he will be working in the orange grove and feel fresher as a result of the change, a new lightness will vitalize his blood and there will no longer be any need to dismiss all those inviting follies that come to mind and recall so many pleasant, heartwarming thoughts. And besides…—a tremendous yawn, irrelevant and out of place, interrupted him and compelled him to stretch and twist his limbs: what a thing to do!—And besides, the time will come for everything that is hidden and secret, that may exist and may not; freedom and liberty will reign, a secret and limitless freedom…eh?

When he turned to Nehama, she was silent in the darkness, breathing softly, enveloped in a closed and proud indifference, isolated in a circle delimited by pride and determination to reject any out-of-the-ordinary glance. There was some kind of rebellious suffering, and repressed longing, and deep sadness in the heart, hovering in the shadows that surrounded her, though all that was lit up in the radiance from the windows was peaceful, motionless and self-contained, neither recoiling nor retreating, apathetically and indifferently mocking and pronouncing a brief and clear-cut verdict, until Ephraim felt like a child who had done wrong. All those foolish appeals he had just been making to himself were so pointless, hollow and irrevocably broken; he felt hurt and guilty. He gazed at her in perplexity again, and felt rebuked by her distant bearing. This noble and dignified silence, these clothes, so neatly arranged but looking so casual, breathing the fragrance of a clear and dewy morning, the bare, rounded, slim legs, these soft boy's hands, the dusky hair, fastened by hair-grips and flowing, warm and fragrant down her back, the eyes that did not surrender the dark presence of the dream—touched his heart, which seemed superfluous and too big for its place.

Bright stars twinkled in the velvety, softly breathing dusk, in the vast silence on all sides frequently rent by the jackals, telling their malicious tales in the harvested vineyards of the new wine that is finished, the grapes that are no more and the scented nights. His wandering glance paused at Nehama and withdrew behind his eyelids; even the memory of the good bed waiting somewhere, which he hastily tried to take hold of, was extremely weak and seemed to be a will-o'-the-wisp, a vain dream, offering no escape or appeasement. Well, that's how it was. And when Ephraim heard his own voice coming reluctantly from a distance, reaching his ears alien and strange, muted and low, he refrained from turning toward his companion, lowered his eyes and added a note of complaint to his voice, until his words were swallowed up in his mouth and he became inextricably involved in a confused stammer, and broke out finally in an uncouth tone, finishing abruptly with a kind of "What do I care? Even if it's like that, even like that, I don't care, on the contrary!" And all this unwillingly, in a mutter, with humble hesitation in a garb of defiance.

"Well, that's how it is, and what can I do? Didn't we once think of something else? Once we wanted lots of things, and what has become of it all? Things that today you don't even want to talk about—you'd rather put them out of your mind like your youthful peccadilloes. Who would suspect these fellows, as they are today, of the ideas and exploits of yesterday? Well, never mind. Human beings. One like this and one like that. And it's really best to go on holding your tongue. But now, look here, I myself, others too, all of us—tell me: are we really what we are because this is what we are actually like? This is what we ought to be, this is our real self, the thing that was latent in us then like a bud in the bosom of the leaf? I mean, couldn't it have been different? Surely it isn't reasonable, is it? After all, it all happened just like that, by blind chance, by accident! Just by chance. It's only chance that I'm here and I'm this, chance that I'm not there, somewhere else, that I'm not different and not like this... chance! And then we look for logic and law... necessity... you understand?

"And why should we go on holding our tongues instead of protesting and crying blue murder. How long should we hold our tongues? And why? Why shouldn't we say openly and clearly at long last: So-and-so is what I want, and so-and-so is what I don't want! Really and truly. I want what's owing to me as Ephraim and not what chance offers me, what is forced on me, whatever comes to hand... You'll say: an easy life? No. It's not that. But if it's to be hardship— why does it have to be in these ways, which aren't my ways? Why shouldn't all my powers be devoted to what really troubles me, to what is hard for me because I, Ephraim, am me? Why shouldn't we have the power to choose for ourselves out of what comes to hand, out of the flow of life, what we are really in need of, what we love; and reject by the power of our will whatever we don't believe in, refuse it and not let go, give in, or submit? Do you hear? And at least not to sing a hymn of praise to our impotence and call it humble modesty and an example to all... No! Surely every human being has a stature of his own, a character of his own, a pain of his own, and his one solitary and unique personality, and therefore he must have one road, strait and narrow, containing only his own footsteps, beginning and ending with his own being—and this is the only road that is his, the only truth that is his, and without that it's all capitulation and betrayal and compromise and procrastination? Suffering? Hardship? Let it be hardship—but my own suffering and hardship, with a meaning; let the joy be comprehensible, comprehensible and fruitful... D'you understand? Yes... And in the meantime, days pass and accumulate to make up a large total, and it gets late, and the circle becomes smaller, and the debt to yourself grows bigger and more oppressive. And after all, sooner or later, you have to do something, don't you? Do something one way or another. You can't leave things just like that... there are all kinds of voices demanding satisfaction after prolonged hunger—and how is it possible to go on in silence? No. This time I'll speak, speak openly with those voices that are complaining here inside because they've been suppressed—some of them silent and some loud, some fleeting and some constant, and some of them, you know, are the kind of voices that a man likes to have inside of him and cherishes in his own stubborn way, and now they are swallowed up in the tumult of everyday doing and working (you must understand: I've no objection to it—there's nothing greater than working... but I want something left for myself... d'you understand?) and disappear under the weight of all this toil and labor, among a thousand things, trivial and not so trivial... You mustn't feel that weakness and old age are creeping up on you... A change has got to come, an inner change that involves an external one. That's why I want to transfer to the orange grove... No. I'm not so innocent and simple as to imagine that the grove will solve everything, but it will be a symbol only, a sign, or something like that, that there's been a change. D'you understand? I've had enough of submission and surrender… D'you hear? Yes. I say work and toil—yes, yes, of course, but what about the individual human being? The individual in himself, who's a part of his work—what about the individual? What about me? Suddenly your eyes are opened and you ask whether in exactly the same way it mightn't all have been different. But that's not what I wanted to say; no, not at all, that's not the main thing. What I wanted to say is only that I'm tired, really tired, and I want to rest a little, to go to sleep… And I'm sorry… I'm sorry I spoke so much…"

Here Ephraim finished, not at all as he started; his voice was dry, low, exhausted, dying away miserably in the silence around, together with the cigarette butt that had been thrown aside. And she, Nehama, who had bowed her head so long as he was talking, crouching and shrinking into herself as much as she could with a fastidious revulsion which made her shrink into her body like a frightened snail, felt some kind of pain probe and gnaw within, insistently accusing, and it was hard to bear its censures, or the distance between this voice and her inability to help; it felt so strange and peculiar sitting like that on the sack, and she felt so sorry about everything—about the time, about the years that were passing and the things that were happening, about her friend, wrestling with his problems and arguing that he had held his peace long enough, and it was not clear what would actually be asked of her, it was not at all obvious. Or perhaps she should now tell her own story and also, heaven forbid, make her confession in a broken voice: Oh Ephraim, Ephraim. But what had she to do with all that? What she wanted now was to shower afresh, to change her clothes and feel cleaner deep down inside.

For some reason she could visualize, hovering in front of her, that room in the hut, peaceful and pallid with the narrow porcelain bowl in which buds on long stalks flowered and silently perfumed the air, and the curtain whispered silkily in the wind, rustling in transparent ripples, revealing the garden, the garden of fruit trees saturated in the milky, crystalline blue afternoon haze; and there in the corner stood the piano—how long was it since she had played?—and within the pile of music she knew that green volume of Mozart's Piano Sonatas, buried deep under the weight of the heap, safe from the hands of women pianists who strummed and chattered and enthused and thought everything was so charming, including their own playing and the various trivial ornaments on the piano.

At this hour, when there was not a soul in her room, when the garden was immersed in a radiant glow and the crystalline horizon was imbedded behind the tops of the pines at the peak of the hill—then you could strike the keys and listen to the superabundant notes piling up and freely separating with an easy heart, as the nimble, dexterous fingers skipped across the keyboard, without compelling you to think of anything at all; and everything that existed previously was forgotten, effaced, melted away, and you were swept away into other regions, where the echoes of this allegro of springtime sang exultantly, so clear and comprehensible—just to laugh at everyone else, and to rise to distant, lonely heights, where you were alone with yourself in endless freedom.

Why had she really stopped playing? And apart from that, did she really have to give him any reply? Oh, no. Only to be an attentive listener, a kind of small audience. She could also, if it was done softly, stretch out and straighten her legs, and it was worth realizing finally—indeed, it was high time—that the piano and the music and light room with its rustling curtain meant nothing whatsoever, and her childhood was irrevocably over. That was clear. As for the things her companion was saying (how long, oh Lord?) and what he was telling her about... But, after all, it was all one: "chance", "fate", "helplessness" and those words—after all she need not answer, only listen. To sigh, she thought, would be out of place. Or perhaps, perhaps after all she, too, should start lamenting on her own account about the strength that had vanished and passed away, about the inability to endure and always, always be silent, about the incapacity to smile in tranquility. All her pride would drop away, leaving her sapped by consumption... Hey, Hey! Wait a minute, my fair lady, that's enough! Is he still talking? Never mind. These roads are too slippery, my dear. Even broad and muscular men collapse here, even they. Isn't it better, my dear to strum the melancholy piano music of charming Mozart: how does he put it?—"Well, that's how it is."

They rose and turned to the room with its wide open lighted windows. Ephraim was tall and broad, his white shirt falling squarely over his short trousers, a fresh cigarette glowing in the corner of his mouth, his heavy hands stuck into his pockets; every additional step showed that the blood still flowed in his limbs, as they stretched and straightened, and there was still strength in these active muscles. The folly of looking back on the past is cast aside in one hearty expectoration, and with one more bone-cracking yawn he shot a smile at Nehama, who for some reason was raising her eyebrows and whistling quietly, something like a fleeting, evanescent smile on her pursed lips. One might have thought that these apparently invigorated steps concealed some hidden significance and a secret sign presaging steadfastness and vigor, if you like. When they entered the room, after a slight pause in the doorway to adapt themselves and their eyes to the light and sound, Ephraim sidled in, slipped between the chairs, got himself a seat and looked around, noticing by the way that Nehama had remained beside the door, leaning on the wall, her arms folded on her chest, her feet together, and not a place to take hold of from her sandals to her hair because of her self-contained pride. He became aware of shapes of faces; there were many in the room—some people were absent-mindedly concerned with their own affairs; some were sleepy, but made an effort to look alert; some, to their shame, had dropped off in public, with their heads hanging; others were seething with the effervescent words within which they were bursting to express, while others again were listening devotedly and diligently, swiveling their eyes from speaker to speaker. As for those outside windows, their heads dipped into the room and disappeared in turn, or hung on the edge of the sill with great concentration, as a smothered laugh or a rustling whisper broke out among them, and sometimes a hand holding a cup of water was extended into the room for some thirsty soul. Avigdor was on his feet, conducting the meeting, talking fluently, his bald patch gleaming, his shaven cheeks hale and ruddy, and refuting with his fleshy hands the arguments of his predecessor on the lines of: "Is it possible to deny what reason tells us?"—while the other, to whom the words were addressed, formed phrases in refutation with oral grimaces, finding his chair too narrow. Above, the electric lamp radiated a yellow light as clouds of smoke wreathed around it.

Was it not somewhat strange to come forward now, in these circumstances, with all those affairs of his? Wouldn't it be best now not to trouble all these people and to let them discuss and argue about everything except himself? And between ourselves, wasn't what he had babbled like a silly boy to Nehama absolutely enough? It would really be best to say no more, to leave the water to flow in the same channel, let everything remain as it was, and finally drive into his stubborn head the idea that renewal and a revival of youth were not inscribed in his book. He would have to get used to this law; that things happen of their own accord and could not have happened otherwise. There was no point in rebellion; revolt was futile and resentment pointless. Just be silent, humble and modest, welcoming present and future with a whispered "Amen". And what else? Only this: it's a pit about those beautiful, secret dreams that promised peace, that were an anchor to hold onto—and this is what has happened to them! And this too: that it's not easy to accept the lot of those decent, respectable people who will put up with anything and are content with what they have and hold; you'd better not think about the morrow: sun and alfalfa by day, weariness and waste of time at night, and then weariness and sun and alfalfa the day after tomorrow, and a long night of weariness and wasted time after that—many days, many nights, a long, close and crowded line swallowed up in undisclosed horizons. In any case, you must hold your tongue; you must not complain, or revolt, or charge with your lance at the peaceful, comely windmills. Isn't that so? But, no no and no again! It was impossible. There was no sense in being silent and humble. What was owing to him should and must be paid in full. There simply had to be a change—no matter what. Anything else was out of the question. Let it be childish, let the girl turn up her haughty nose, let these people say whatever they liked—what did he care? He wanted freedom, liberty, fresh nights, new work, with all its latent possibilities. How many shopkeepers

realize that this was just the opinion of an objective member and after all, we're all brothers, aren't we? It was sometimes a good thing to engage in "a discussion among ourselves" and to this opportunity had arisen, it really was and therefore he wanted to know, that is, to understand, if possible, what he, Ephraim, really wanted? Didn't he know, just like all the rest, that the orange groves had no need of additional hands? That is: anyone could work there when help was needed, while the fodder needed experience and skill, and not everyone was capable of working there... Now Ephraim was actually one of the few capable people, and he, Avramke, really appreciated him, and really he had no desire at all to oppose him or stand in his way, for all he really wanted was to understand, and in general, perhaps Ephraim himself would explain his purpose more clearly. And as for him, Avramke himself, he was ready, now as ever, to do his best and help everybody. Amen.

Peretz spoke immediately afterward, coming out alternately with "I think" and "I wonder". Was this the time for such an act? Wasn't it self-evident that such a step, in these days, was liable to be economically inadvisable? And he expressed his surprise: on the one hand they were trying to lower "the standard of living" and bring down the cost of milk-production, which was a difficult and uphill job; and on the other hand, to disrupt at this time, at this particular time, the supply of fodder by taking out a skilled and experienced worker, and introducing a novice in his place—how was it possible, what did they think? It was really extraordinary. He thought Ephraim's place was with the alfalfa and only there.

On the other hand, Shapiro was willing to understand Ephraim; yes, he understood and in parenthesis he added, he too had experienced moments like this, who hadn't? He was prepared to agree and consent to Ephraim's request, but on one condition, that Ephraim should come out with the name of someone to take his place without the farm suffering. And he was so pleased with this question that when he sat down a smile of satisfaction broke out on his face and his lips, as if to say, "That's it! That's how we talk!"

Dvor'ke was speaking now. She started off with great energy

and twice as much righteousness, until after three sentences she became self-conscious and confused and lost her tongue; and she hastily went back to what she had said at the beginning, and which had been so right and fine, and went on again, and went back again, until she got completely muddled and finished with "Yes, that's what I wanted to say," and wrinkled her brow, as if she was considering whether anything had been left unsaid—"Yes, that's all…" a brief look at the windows, one hasty glance at Avigdor, another general survey of the room, and she went back to her occupation of folding pieces of paper into birds and boats, and there was no one who could dispute her arguments: after all, she was working in the kitchen for the fourth year without a word, and Ephraim—why should he be spoiled in this way? These various cogent ideas met with support in various quarters, in a variety of styles and a multitude of original expression, drawn from the vocabulary of the newspapers, moving a few more comrades to speak out loud and clear and others to assume the expressions of rigorous judges who would show no fear or favor. Meir, the fellow from the cowshed, got up with a look on his face of "I have much to say, but I'm short of words", and his voice—which was always merry, ready to sing, quick to laugh and eager for one good joke—this time grew more and more serious as required by the subject, clad in weighty solemnity founded on reason and nothing else, and his left hand opened and closed all the time between his shoulder and his ear, while his right hand, resting gracefully on his hip, and his body, moving forward and backward in time with the rhythm of the words and the cogency of the arguments, completed this handsome picture, which he kept for these and similar occasions. Really, that Ephraim should make a proposal like this, there was nothing he had expected less. He was a simple man, and didn't know what was wrong with alfalfa. First of all, all kinds of work were equal; they all had one goal and one aim; secondly, on the other hand, this very job, with the fodder, the alfalfa more than anything else, was to some extent preferable to other jobs, and no one knew better than he the importance of feedstuffs. He believed that if Ephraim would realize that this fodder itself provided sustenance for cattle, yes, it was their main food, and that there was much more in it than the advantage to the farm economy—he was not spending much time on this particular point because it was widely known—if Ephraim took all this to heart, would he really be able to harden his heart and withhold their food? And apart from all that, since he had arrived at this point, he hoped that he, Meir, might be permitted to remark that from his own point of view, as someone who had been working in the cowshed—how many years already?—this was his fourth year too, yes, almost four years, in the same building, at the same work, without going outside, without a glimpse of the fields and the distances, without a chance to get sunburnt (here he pointed vigorously to the skin of his arm, on which the sunburn was somewhat dubious), with his days and nights split up—he had every reason to envy Ephraim, who had all these good things at his disposal, day by day and hour by hour—hadn't he?

Meanwhile, the one who was to be envied was sitting with his head wedged between his hands, sending up columns of smoke; he looked as if he was concentrating and attentive, and the features of his face, molded in light and shade, were set in that kind of frozen stillness that covers an unmistakable perturbation, till the tightly closed mouth indicated clenched jaws and gritted teeth, and the look in his eyes melancholy, focusing on and turning away from some single point opposite. A fine thing, wasn't it? He'd sown a single grain and reaped a hundredfold... What an awakening, what participation, what excitement and pontification, what a quantity of economic, social and educational moralizing! And perhaps it might also be possible to see in this room who was the target of this plethora of words, that hotheaded lout, indifferent to all economic considerations and stubborn as a rebellious mule, whom the entire community was eager to restore to the strait and narrow path with profound concern, unselfish devotion and dedication to a common goal—was it really he himself? What was it all about? What for? Well, never mind. Very soon he would no doubt hear. When the heat of justice abated, the radiance of confession would arise. Then it would all be clear: "Ephraim should leave and we stay?" "His place is with

the alfalfa and nowhere else." "This isn't the place for self-indulgence."
"We treat everyone with understanding." Favorable treatment for
everybody, but no favorites. Just listen: Ephraim actually ought to be
envied. And that's sad in a serious voice, very serious. And the grave
tone that is borrowed for such occasions leads up to an exclamation
mark. And heads nod from every side with a solemn "Yes". Yes, oh,
of course. Really to be envied.

Yes. The noonday sun has moved slightly westward, without
alleviating the heat. Overlapping heat waves ripple from horizon to
horizon, on the tops of mountains and hills, at the edges of the tree-
tops and the ends of the roofs, appearing here and there as watery,
glassy, transparent smudges, and mosaic of squares, some ploughed
and some untilled, some covered with stubble and the others with
grayish, stiff skeleton thorns, with squares of greenstuffs here and
there, climb up the sides of these hells with indefatigable perseverance,
until they melt into each other within the misty haze under the blue
sky; and on the other hand the mountain is packed with a medley
of rocks, with innumerable paths, rounded contours obscured by
shade, isolated smudges of bushes, disappearing village houses, and
a stony whiteness at its peak, which seems both near and far; and
the familiar scorching heat, which inflicts burns on the soul, flares
up increasingly as the sun declines toward the slope.

From now on, David and Nahum would go off to look after
the reaping, collection and piling, loading and transportation, while
Ephraim was left alone to go on with the irrigation, and even if you
blinded his eyes and stopped up his ears and extirpated his heart
and his brain, he would go on with his work to the end, without
forgetting the least thing, and with just the same success, for all the
time he would repeat to himself a host of high-minded declamations
about how good it is to be alone and how sweet to be solitary, and
had it not at first been somewhat uncomfortable to bend his back
again and to grip the haft of the hoe afresh with the same hard and
horny hands, he would have come out with those beautiful phrases
a moment earlier. Now was the time, he would say to himself, to be
once again Ephraim as he really was, when everything was open to

him, to express to the full ideas that had been pushed into the background, to examine the roots of many various things, to shrink into himself like a hedgehog, with his personality within and his prickles outside, and surrender to this silence around, just as his dreams had sometimes, somewhere, whispered to him, just as he had been so heartwarmingly determined to do in the days it was more pleasant not to remember, on account of the distress and the disappointment. Those days!

But perhaps, instead of sighing voluptuously, you will stop, my lad, and say frankly what there was in those days that make you so sorry that they have gone and are no more. What did you have then that you do not have now? Oh, those days! Illusion, illusion. Ephraim alone, bent over his hoe in an expanse of fields surrounded by mountains—that is the whole reality and nothing more. And when you consider the matter, you see that many years have passed by, alternations of summer and winter, without preserving anything but that purity of the past, virginity of the soul, that true reverence and innocent awe, the things that were sacred and humbly admired, and which now, as a result of familiarity, are still spoken of in a voice corroded by the smoke of cheap tobacco to arouse old sensations at no cost and give some flavor to the boredom of stale chatter. That's what people call becoming a man, a member of society. Of course. Go about among people and listen to their talk—sober, settled, adult, acquainted with "life", having a place, a "status" as they call it, that prestige which aims at nothing but what is most useful and most easy to the belly and the heart, whose outward appearance announces: We have seen and heard many things.

What do they talk about? About this fellow and that girl and what is going between them, about "tragedies"—that ambrosia whose flavor is always fresh—with head-shakes and meaningful detraction, about the hard "realities" of "life", with curiosity about the most intimate matters expressed in the language of those to whom everything is coarse and everything is known, with the faces of perfect saints, with interpretations of various hints, with heartfelt pity for anyone who is not like them, and explaining the moral to each other: We, you should understand, no mere nonentities, we no longer have any interest in silly childish trifles, but it's too early to go to sleep; perhaps we'll "arrange" a discussion, perhaps we'll have a debate, or just "have a good time together", maybe we'll sing a few songs, and perhaps we'll even get warmed up and start some dancing: "Hey the homeland! Hey my heart! Hey for labor! Hey the builders!"—we've had a successful evening this evening, now we can go to bed. That is what they call maturity. No one has been deceived. We all foresaw it in advance, and what we foresaw came to pass. That is life.

But what had it all to do with him? Once there was a different Ephraim, or perhaps it was all one long mistake, which he could not stop, could not change. The skies of parched blue, distant, blinding, caring for nothing; the mountains—if you like they are thinking sublime thoughts, but if you like they are just piled up in mocking chaos; and these fields are just earth, earth and no more. Ephraim's place is with the alfalfa.

There you have the comfortable drone of the afternoon hours, and row after row of fodder for the cattle, and the turbid water flows on, with bubbles of froth floating in the stream down the middle of the furrow, colliding, impinging on the sides and bursting, or sticking on the weeds, accumulating and forming a shoal until a wave comes along and carries them away. Here is loneliness. Here is silence. And what can you think about to distract your soul, to console it, to give it some food for hope? What can you hang onto, hold onto? A camel strides along the path, and by his side an Arab riding lazily on his ass, swaying from side to side, his sandals hanging on the tips of his toes, responds to your greeting, with a twinkling smile addresses one imprecation at both ass and camel, pauses and sways on. The afternoon hours drone on, the sunrays play on the bare side of the mountain, which grows partly dusky, with bright edges; the shadows begin to move and gather here and there; the groves, crowned with cypresses, reveal their dark, velvety green, folded into waves of dull green and greenish light; the clefts in the distant ridges in the east, outlined in red, show more clearly, and the cleft in the hills is reddish brown, a color that sings songs so close to your heart that you would like nothing better than to raise capricious clouds of dust in its soil and skip among its dry, crumbly cracks; even the clods beside you are separated by blue shadows; the light no longer pierces or burns, and you can finally breathe deep and actually feel that there is nothing in all this expanse of air but good oxygen, perfumed with the exhalations of soil and water and trees all around. It would be good to go home now, particularly at this hour, hands clasped behind your back, feet dragging along the reddish path, the dust glowing golden in the light, avenues of eucalyptus with circles of light beneath them, knobby, dusky cypresses, light, merry, blossoming branches in the dark orange groves, vistas opening above the hills and a silvery mist extending into the distance. And then—a shower, coolness, clean clothes, a sense of well-being in your limbs, tea and bread and jam, a glance at the newspaper, and this or that to do; everyone looks different, washed, at ease, a melody singing within and no need to bring it to your lips; it would all have been worthwhile, not in vain...But every postponement, every additional hour spent here, diminishes, spoils, taints and ruins it all in advance.

So a man becomes divided against himself, mocked at by gloomy nervousness; a foolish voice whispers: Revolt, defy them all—and a voice replies: Work, you fool, and stop all this nonsense. And a deep silence, a hateful silence, drowns out all the voices and makes everything meaningless; there is nothing to take hold of any longer, the ground is washed away from under your feet, and a murderous rage makes you raise clenched fists to destroy, demolish, insult, offend, annoy, to send it all to hell; because this is what it has come to, this is the end of all the dreams, and the loneliness within you cries beseechingly that you can no longer remain here alone, that it is unbearable that there is no one by your side, and you almost choke with loneliness, abandoned by your comrades. Don't leave me here, don't leave me alone, take me with you, among you, wherever you go—don't leave me alone! But it's all the same, as usual, as before.

Then, once again half an hour of silent work will come, speedy, honest work, obliterating everything else, devoted to itself, diligent and skillful, and a practiced hand gets on with the job in a flowing

rhythm: banking up and pulling down, releasing and collecting, breaking and raking, stamping down, scraping, weeding, digging, filling
up, and coating the water channel and the walls of the alfalfa bed.
Muscles are tensed, your body pushes against your shirt, your vigor
is skillfully directed and aimed, without a superfluous or inadequate
movement—ah, it is not for nothing that your work has won repute;
Ephraim with a hoe is a byword. And then it seems that you could
put up with it, that things are not so terrible, and in any case, you still
have both strength and ability, and a proud enjoyment of the work
itself, and a little steadfast freedom that still exists within its limits,
and if you have felt a little depressed about some things, that was
only because of this painful loneliness, wasn't it? If you start to admit
the truth, you go on to the end whether you like it or not, and you
must admit that it is not good to be proud and solitary, to give way to
illusions of inner tranquility, and it's a pity there's no one near to talk
to, to boast to, to let yourself go completely. Hail to the insolence of
"eat and drink and sleep", which, it seems, as people say, is the very
essence and purpose of "things as they are and have to be".

Empty talk! Just go back to that dynamic youth after a year
or two, and you'll find that everything has faded away, just disappeared—they've all become "grown up", "a part of society", respectable; they too gossip about "him" and "her" and the relations between
them; nothing loosens their tongues and relieves their boredom more
than tickled curiosity and scandalmongering; they have "business"
and "discussions" and "talks"; some of them, too, argue about their
"perplexities"—that, too, of course, in the same old way—and you
must never remind them of their "sin", that spark of life within them,
for which the weary heart, sunk in gloom, longed so much—and all
the vision dies away.

From now on, your eyes look out anxiously for the coming of
the train, after which there is only a little more than an hour left to
work—but still it does not come. White veils and transparent tissues
float in the skies; shadows lengthen and the heavens are shadowed with
a silent yearning, expanding, rising, their dome lifting, the deeps on
high swelling unrestrained with canopies of radiance and blue, and

an infinity of heights rises to infinity. There is nothing that is lost or diminished on the surface or in space, and every object has its song of body and color, and a secret mist moves between things, and the entire universe is covered in a down of radiance, and there is a great, wide space for this sadness to wander in, in the bliss of the afternoon sunshine, in the blue melted into gold and molded by the horizon, in the shining white scrap of cloud, in the hills that have turned into light-dust and in the greenery that prays. It is clear and obvious that the hour of the universe has come, it is plain and palpable that apart from this world of life, overflowing with radiance, there is no truth, no beauty, nothing—that this alone is all, and there is nothing above it; and you are distressed at your own inadequacy, your inability to express what has always been in your heart, ready to be said, because whatever you have to say is so coarse and second-rate, because you cannot penetrate into the very heart of this quivering and blessed reality, melt and dissolve in it like these insubstantial gossamer threads, which glimmer and disappear in a cloud of glowing chaff on every side. The shadows lengthen. The water flows in the channel. The alfalfa is inundated, one bed after another. So many longings are spread across the fields. Afternoon hours. Your cheeks are burning. The railway lines blaze up and into fiery scepters. Gnats and mosquitoes celebrate. A cart laden with hay grinds along, golden dust and shavings dropping from its wheels. Streams of lightning are shaken into many pools. Columns of smoke are absorbed in the distance. This man, who leans on his hoe like a drunkard, the water flowing at his feet, remains standing at the side, like an uninvited guest.

"Don't interrupt, let me finish!" Shmuel's impassioned voice drives like a wedge into the tumult which has arisen, for some reason, in the room. "Don't interrupt! What was it I wanted to say? Yes. It's absolutely clear to me that this kind of action will only be a bad precedent for many others. Is there anyone who is satisfied, who can get up and swear that he gets complete and total satisfaction from his work? That's quite impossible. It's obvious. And we musn't open the way for shirking. Just a minute! I haven't finished yet, let me finish. So it's perfectly obvious to me that if in the allocation of jobs somebody or other's personal inclinations clash with the elementary obligations of our economy, the economy must have priority. Priority over anything else. And we've got to bear the burden. It's obvious to me... The economy demands, and we give, willingly or not. The main thing is the economy..." (Why don't you conclude with "We're working for the future, we are suffering—our children will enjoy will enjoy the results!"?—someone, offended, says from the other side of the table). "And for the maintenance of the economy," Shmuel continues, emphasizing that he pays no attention to such little things, he has no time for them, "for the maintenance of the economy, there must be a man working at the alfalfa at this time, and the man must be there—with or without out-of-date philosophizing that we've forgotten long ago, and senseless bitterness," he could not refrain from retorting to the one who had spoken. "That's obvious."

"And does it have to be no one else but Ephraim?" cried the same one who had flared up, forgetting his thoughts of a moment before.

"Very probably. The situation is that you are the most suitable person."

"How do you know? It doesn't seem obvious to me at all."

"Comrades," intervened Avigdor, "please, please stop! We've no time for private conversations. Itzik, Itzik has the floor."

"We all understand you, believe me, Ephraim... If only we could arrange it some other way, wouldn't we do it? But how? Come on, you tell us! Lots of fellows, believe me, would like to work in other branches, I know myself that not everybody is satisfied with his job, but what can we do? We have to, and when we have to—we do it, and that's all. After all, it's not so terrible, believe me, and you've got to be able to take a firm grip on the plough."

Then David spoke, and asked protestingly what would happen if Ephraim really left the fodder patch, for he was the expert, and he was the most experienced, and he was the one people asked for advice, and he was really devoted to the alfalfa and understood the job, and so forth, and who would he leave it to now, and so forth, and during the four months he had worked with Ephraim not only had he learned a lot from him, and thanks to him he now knew the difference between alfalfa and clover, not only that, but he had seen no signs at all that Ephraim was "worrying" or "suffering" in any way, or that there was anything "not right"—on the contrary, and so on and so forth, and his voice was distorted with a lachrymose appeal "Don't blame me."

Then Avramke held forth again, and in his efforts to avoid annoying anyone, heaven forbid, and make sure he was not misunderstood, complicated matters until he was incomprehensible, and again there was an outbreak of chattering, very strange in connection with a simple question of work arrangements, and there was a tumult, until in an interval between the cries everyone could hear, from beyond the windows, the voice of a woman who spoke incautiously, without realizing that her voice might be audible inside, but when she saw that everyone had clearly heard her, she was terrified and stopped, and shrank back, startled, into the darkness, but her idle prattle floated in and filled the room completely, and tore away all the masks, calling the thing by its proper name openly and trenchantly, without any concealment or pious phrases: "He wants to rest, Ephraim, he just hasn't any strength left, poor fellow; give him an easy job, and what's the use of all the palaver?"

Immediately everyone put on a look as if to say: We haven't heard a thing. The very idea didn't occur to us. Ah, now it's all clear. Perfectly plain. And everything that's been said up to now makes sense. An easy job you want! At our expense? You—yes, and we—no! No, my lad! You'll live with us, and you'll bear the burden on your bent back together with the rest of us. No one leaves, no one sets himself apart, no separate roads for individuals. We, at any rate, won't allow it. Here, with us, no one gets special privileges. There will be no change just for one—we've all got the same right to changes, concessions, a meaning in life and a way in life, work and rest. Do you want to read? So do all of us, and there's a "Literary Circle" and talks and "Mock Trials"; you want music—okay, Shmuel will bring the gramophone and we'll all stretch out on the grass, listen quietly, yawn surreptitiously and go into ecstasies together; didn't we sing beautifully this very evening in idle, sentimental improvisation! And that's not all—there's a Ramblers' Troop, and Circle for Nature Lore and the Study of the Homeland, and a Cultural Committee, and a Library Committee, and a Members' Committee, etc. etc... —and as for general attitudes to the soul of man and inanimate nature, haven't we all read A.D. Gordon and know something about that too? But all of us together. No room for exceptions. And moreover, if you've got some talent, come along and use your aptitudes to make a circle for anything you like, so that we can escape from collective boredom and inarticulateness, but don't wrestle with yourself alone—that's hard to witness without protest. And if that's not enough for you, it's also hard to see Avigdor, traveling about on our behalf, going out on missions, while we stay here all the time. You talk about the individual! Why not? We've got the Problem of the Individual, the Individual in Society, the Question of the Comrade and the Question of the Female Comrade, and what else do you want? And in general, is there any shortage of bitterness and problems—it's all there, available, good and desirable! And surely, after all, there are fine moments among us, fraternity; all this is only a beginning, and how much toil it takes to create the slightest tranquility—hasn't the least indication of all this reached your ears? Who is it who talks about all this?

They were all still arguing. Short, sharp comments were being tossed from every side. Avigdor was banging hard and in vain with the nameless cup. A vein bulged on Avramke's throat. Shmuel was enunciating, one by one, "downright" statements which rolled out with guttural sibilation. Devorah was spreading her hands talking to Meir, who was nodding his head at every word she spoke—"Real talk!" Yes. And quite a few were talking with great seriousness and deep sincerity about some "heroic enterprise" in which they were engaged, and the realization of "the vision of the generations" which they were implementing "brick by brick and layer by layer"—as explained in every possible way in leading and other articles and sung in songs with or without dancing, and there was no hint of a doubt in their voices. What do you think? That's how we are: implementers of vision. Never mind that we're a bit like this and a bit like that—that's not

41

the main thing. You should see in us what is worth seeing: the heroism, the channel for latent powers, and the goal. "Comrades, this way we'll never finish, we'll never get out of here—it's getting late, tomorrow we've got to be early. Who's got practical proposals?" But these were not to be heard—there was much to be said and spoken after such a wide breach had been opened for such a seething, tempestuous stream. They talked to each other, with each other, without listening, only asserting. One was explaining the drawbacks of his job, and one was making comparisons between his own and someone else's, and the talk was copious and lengthy.

And what about Nehama—what had she to say? Ah, that Nehama. Her mouth was stubbornly compressed and she was still standing leaning against the wall, with a mingled feeling of wonderment and mockery, and it was clear that nothing escaped her eyes and ears. Why should all this fuss have been stirred up for his sake? Very soon they would be understanding him, and doing their best for him, and explaining "the situation" to each other, and "analyzing" that situation, and pointing to the "subject", and whispering under their breaths, and speechifying, until time for bed. If only he could get out of here now, go up to that very same Nehama; "Come along, lass, let's go out for a little stroll," with unbecoming bashfulness, to walk by her side in willing silence; to get out of the gate without the watchman noticing and pestering them with questions and warnings about "the grave situation" and "these times", to go down the path fenced with climbing vines, to reach the pine copse, to pass venturesomely through the threatening, dusty silence up to the wire fence lined with rustling thorn-stalks, and to look out at the mountain boldly thrusting into the realm of the skies and the whitish clumps of rock and the twinkling lights from near and distant villages; to follow the gleam of the wandering searchlight, to listen to the movements in the silence, and to feel that it is good to be at Nehama's side and that much has been forgotten because of her, even if she is silent, and he is silent, and all the world is silent. This is the time for foolishly whispering pleasant phrases, even if ordinary and conventional; this is the time for half-thoughts and fragmentary ideas, for smiling at many actions in which everything seems to have been said, for huddling into your coat and enjoying the warmth within and the chill outside, for feeling in the flow of time a fragment of eternity, and knowing that you must not break out and throw down the gauntlet, and for returning confidently, modest and humble, along the road by which you came.

It is warm in the room. A cloud of smoke is playing its tricks with the electric light, and through the window you see nothing at first but a black, solid frozen sky; but then, when you go on looking, the black melts into blue and lilac, and within the frame the cowshed roof materializes, a heavy, black entity, with the tips of the tree-tops, and above them mighty skies, on whose slopes you know that there are mountains, in whose heights burning stars celebrate in an eternity of silence pregnant with yearning and imbued with purity; there is coolness among them, a fresh, cool, caressing air between them, and crickets are no doubt strumming continuously in the fields. Hot here, full of dense smoke, stuffy with exhaled air.

And she, Nehama, what is she doing? Holds her peace all the time, just holds her peace. Has everything really been said? Surely you have something to say too, Nehamke. Say: There is no man who is born to freedom. Mortal man cannot combine labor with liberty and enact laws for himself. Say: We can move about only to the extent of the short chain with which we have been tied up to graze in the dirt, and there complete freedom until it reaches the limit and tightens round your neck; from that point onward—look, covet but go no further. I've got something to tell too: about a relative of mine in the town, a watchmaker. Dismantles and assembles screws and wheels, bargains and barters, haggles over prices, yawns and worries about sales and promissory notes, and in the evening goes back to his home on the third story in the suburbs, day after day, year after year, each day with its watches, each day in the dust of the shop. People flit across the shop window and one hour screws on to the next, even if it does not fit. Clocks run down, chimes are dulled… Is all this nothing at all, literally nothing at all? Don't be so silent, Nehamke, tomorrow the alfalfa will be waiting again; a new day, teeming with changes, will shine, without any possibility of knowing whether it is today, yesterday or tomorrow. What are you staring at, what are you looking for there? You too believe that the hunger for space and freedom has been sent down from heaven in equal portions like plates of porridge for the table, and that what is enough for the many is also enough for the one, including even that one who has nothing, neither will nor love nor practical talent for anything, but the yearning for freedom and the feet of a wandering gypsy to travel in happy lawlessness, to go anywhere in perfect freedom, subject only to himself, to his own authority, his own duty. And you are still silent... stubbornly, proudly rigid as before... Why, what is the sense of it, what is the use? Do you hear? Once, in ancient times, there was a dream about a fortified castle in the heart of the forest on the top of a lonely mountain, but that was a dream... It was only a dream, beautiful or foolish, but what now? Nehama, Nehama, now what, what will happen now?

Nehama is silent. There is an irksome feeling inside, a dreadful sense of alienation pervades the close atmosphere, and that feeling of complete isolation which comes down at one o'clock in the middle of the day or at midnight amidst a noisy crowd or alone like a stray dog, imposes a tempestuous rhythm on the wretched heart. Do you know these awakenings in the silence of the night? When the boards of the hut are pale, and the dusty ceiling contemplates itself and its shadows, and the clock ticks, with a metallic sound, requiems for dead moments, and there is darkness and silence in the windows, and your heart is paralyzed with dread, and everything is lost and everything is ravaged and despoiled, and there is no halting on the slippery slope to the abyss, and there is not a single living voice to help and break the loneliness, although beyond the wall there are people sleeping, living people, and you could shout and cry and call for help... It becomes clear that there was falsehood and deceit in everything, that only illusions concealed the dreadful reality, that there is a terrible mistake, for which no conscience can atone, in all that exists in the present... It becomes clear that all those acts and speeches and smiles were nightmare clowns, and shadows of a great fear; and one suppressed truth grips you chokingly by the throat: What are you doing here? What have you to do here? This time there can be no evasion, there is nowhere to go... The darkness around is heavy, oppressive and evil, and everything is strange—oh, how strange, incomprehensible, irrelevant, hard-hearted as a hangman, silent, silent, dripping into your soul, compressed by the regular ticking, and overflowing into the surrounding wilderness of desolation... And some kind of remorse arises, troublesome, oppressive and demanding, and you feel sorry about many things, trivial and not trivial, and it seems that whatever these people said was true and right, and like father and mother they meant it all for her own good, had it not been for her wicked stubbornness... Where did she get the impudence to judge her neighbor and criticize others in her heart? What right had she to demand anything, to disturb them—who are sleeping so well? Black. No escape. The boards are pale. And when at last you jump down onto the warm wooden floor and run barefoot to the door, something is released and unraveled in your heart; the two date palms beside the door rustle tranquilly and dreamily, and in the bakery they have already switched on the light, a warm and soothing light, and your foolish heart throbs at the isolated voices and the tingling life there, and there are stars above, in gleaming beauty, and a blue chill slips from the night itself, and the bray of an ass cuts across your fear, until a kind of dryness rises in the eyes and the heart, and a mocking smile peeps out and a blush emerges.

Then you wrap yourself up again in the sheet and sleep comes to your eyelids, and some nonsense kept for the purpose is taken out from its hiding place and given to your brain to think about so that you can fall asleep quickly, until in the morning you can get up and work in the hen-run in the usual, everyday way, singing serenely, jesting at your ease and chattering with your neighbors—those neighbors you cannot escape from even if you wanted to. All your efforts are devoted entirely to giving them nothing to hold onto, and no matter how much you smile to them there seems to be some distance between you and the others, who, on their part, feel a hint of resentment against you, and seem to be waiting for the moment when you too will make a mistake and that will be the end of this obnoxious arrogance—this life, ha ha, this life of labor, the handful of people who know each other to the point of nausea, the formula of freedom which is displayed for show on every side. Everything that is known and talked about as "a transformation of values", "the new human being", "the new experience" and the like has not rid them completely of a modest inclination for rosy and dainty things, or managed to obliterate a considerable talent for measuring, inspecting, taking in an entire situation, in all its details, at a glance, and afterward chattering in undertones about what their inspection has revealed; their repulsive examinations and interrogations in the shower, the comparisons, the analogies, the measurements, the knowingness, the allusions, the hints and the grimaces comprehensible to two and making the others prick up their ears, and then going out with a pious look on their faces, all of them wearing the same blue or gray shorts (even those whose bluish folds of flesh cannot take them), hungrily falling upon a child in the yard, or twittering something to one's "mate" passing by somewhere, clumsy, ragged and dirty, to disappear, after cleaning one's shoes on the threshold, into one of the rooms, with their couches covered with multicolored rugs and cushions edged with fringes or lace and a basket with flowers and something else laid carefully aslant on the floor, on the table or on the couch rug, and everything is in half-shadow so that it should all be really charming.

But you get accustomed to that too, and you stop feeling, pampering yourself and resenting it. But is that the main thing? Is that all that disturbs your rest? Apart from that, is everything in order? What is left to do, then, but to grit your teeth, to forcibly prevent yourself breaking out, in a drunken orgy, in the intoxication of unrestrained rejoicing, in the steps of a wild dance, in the unrivaled licentiousness of one sliding down the slippery slope to hell, knowing no limit or law, to the point of alarm and horror, of inhuman, primeval, bestial, inchoate cries of madness, in which God and the devil are combined in an impious rite of anarchy and a tremendous, primordial cry! What are the sufferings and afflictions of man!

Gedalia was now talking to the hushed assembly: "A comrade

who has worked for three years on end in one place has the right to transfer to another. But we have a case before us in which this rule can't be applied, because the farm economy will suffer. And I don't understand why such a big fuss has been made about such an ordinary question, and what is the point of all kinds of subsidiary questions, which whether they are right or not, are not relevant at the moment. You get the mistaken impression that things are really desperate here, that something essential is not in order, while we all know that this isn't so. You can never measure the importance of details, there's never a limit to criticism. So let's stop there and get on with our business. Ephraim will have to understand the situation as it is, and not demand the impossible at this moment. Another year, Ephraim another year, it's not so terrible. Your job is not one of the hardest, it's not one of the most boring. It's a job like any other job. In the meantime, let David and Nahum learn all about the work and get more skillful—and then you'll be able to do just as you like without causing difficulties. Time—perhaps I needn't tell you—passes, races on, you know; before you've managed to look around, a week has passed, the Sabbath has passed, and another week has gone; look, now we're ploughing and picking the olives, soon the rains will come, it'll be cold and muddy, the sowing will come and then the fruit-picking, and immediately afterward the reaping, and the grape harvest, and the heat—and the year will be over, faster even than we should like, ha ha, and besides, you should remember that nothing of what you do goes to waste, and there is no work that does not benefit the community, and in any case good intentions are at the root of it all..."

God Almighty, won't he stop? Another year, not so terrible; how does he know? Perhaps it is terrible, perhaps very terrible, and perhaps every day, every single day, is hard and terrible until it passes. And this goodness, these good intentions, what does all this wonderful goodness mean, after all? What do you get out of all this goodness, more than you would have without it? Look at that fellow; all evening he's been working, serving at table, bringing the food, taking away plates and bringing others, serving special rations for the pampered ones, full teapots here and empty ones there. Looking after this great fraternity of men of toil and labor, that's a good thing, certainly, very good, but it's not at all clear what it has produced: satisfaction, brotherhood? Couldn't exactly all that have been achieved more easily, with less boasting, even without so many supreme values: As far as I'm concerned, I don't need all this common good; I work because it's impossible not to work, because I've got to look after myself without depending on others, and without any more suffering and falsehood than there is already—after all, that's a good too, isn't it? And in the meantime, go on providing fodder for virtuous cows and lovable mules, and bring down the price of milk—surely that's something, in addition to the fact that the year will pass in a flash!

But all Gedalia's words had not yet convinced the assembled comrades, and now the way had been opened for arguments and problematical questions, people had to hurry and get things off their chests. Even Dov, who had ostensibly started with Ephraim's case and remarked that the community had the power to compel the individual to accept its verdict, could not avoid concluding with "Why does no one pick up the rubbish that lies about in the yard? Isn't it our yard? Why this indifference, this relying on some good person to take the trouble to do all theses so-called things? For instance, we've got flowers—how many people have volunteered to give up their free time to look after them? Let's have some more consideration, comrades, more warmth, surely after all we haven't all been turned into tractors and combines!" He also managed, by the way, to get off his chest the sufferings of the carter, who at all hours stands upright in his cart, his legs clad in a pair of old breeches, wrapped around and swaddled in rags, a worn soldier's tunic on his shoulders and a hat pushed down on his forehead, calling out to the "animals"—who stamp with their feet and shake their manes and gallop on with the cart dragging along like a wisp behind; then a light shines from every suffering wrinkle on his face, parched by wind and heat, and he holds forth with his hoarse carter's voice and sings songs about far-off days.

Those good people who were silent at the proper time, laughing when there was something to laugh at, dozing sometimes and getting excited when spirits rose, no longer knew who to listen to and what expression to put on; so in order to get out of their embarrassment they looked grim, pursed their lips in anger and declared that "This is really impossible." Some Yitzhak, whose whole heart shone out of his dark, stubbly face, who was always ready to laugh and produce crow's-feet at the corners of his eyes, he too had been offended by "lack of consideration", and there was an instructive example: that unnamed comrade who had run over and crushed with a tractor an unfortunate sack of olives lying by the side of the road, by the side and not in the middle—and the accused jumped up to defend himself in public; one argued and the other answered, and tempers rose, and the good-humored wrinkles were wiped out and disappeared. Then, in one of the pauses between outbursts of talk, there was one low voice that gradually silenced the buzz and turned it into thoughtful attention—Shlomke did not take his eyes off his cigarette box, and seemed to be talking to it alone:

"I have been sitting and listening for a long time to your talk... I often get a certain feeling, not very clear, and everything going on here in this room seems so strange and extraordinary that I don't know where I am. Just look at us: each by himself, each with his own affairs, each strange to the other, ignoring the other—no understanding, no attention, no sign of goodwill, and a feeling of loneliness—loneliness, comrades, so hard and unpleasant, as if we are really strangers, as if we had not been growing old side by side for years, as if we had not fed at the same table, as if we had never sung together. What has happened, comrades? Where does this estrangement come from? What for? One of us has asked for a transfer to another branch, and suddenly everyone's alarmed, and here we've been arguing about it for over an hour with such extraordinary passion... enough! Let's finish it. Avigdor, stop the irrelevant talk. It's late. Really. Let's finish the business."

Shlomke threw his box on the table and stared insistently at the assembled members. Avigdor, having been appealed to, put out his cigarette forcefully, and while the last wreaths of smoke were escaping from his mouth, and his hand, with its short thick fingers, was stretched out, concentrating everyone's attentions, ruled that, since Ephraim had heard this discussion and no doubt was well aware of, and agreed with the general and common view that had been expressed, therefore, in his humble opinion, they had now finished, and... But here Sarah jumped up and proposed that the question be put to the vote. This proposal was like a blast of wind on glowing coals, which whitened and flared up and scattered showers of sparks, and a flame danced and waved amongst them: how could it be—a vote?

"What does this mean?" broke out Nahum, who worked with Ephraim. "Is it really possible? To make someone work by the power of the majority or the minority? To work against his will? What kind of work would he do, what good would it be? And what feelings do you think would accumulate in the heart of such a man? There must be no vote here. This is purely a question of conscience, the conscience of the comrade concerned. He knows the position like everyone else, and he must decide without coercion—one way or another. And even if he decides the other way, if he chooses the way that isn't justified, we'll have to accept it as inevitable and get along somehow. Necessity will lead to a solution. We have done our duty by explaining and analyzing the situation; let Ephraim do his."

Sarah explained: She had never dreamt that they would vote on whether Ephraim must go back or not; but only to give him a demonstration of the general feeling, so that he could judge and draw his own conclusions as to what he should do in the light of the convictions of the majority as revealed by the vote. And this is what they should ask: Who believes that apart from Ephraim there is no one else suitable for the fodder growing? That was all she had thought, and heaven forbid that she should force work on anyone against his will.

"Ah, parliamentarism, is it a parliament you're making?" protested Shapiro. "What is there to vote about? Hasn't Ephraim heard all that's been said this evening, isn't that enough? What's the sense of all this formalism? I at least will refrain from voting, even if I realize that Ephraim is the only suitable man, to protest against this meaningless formality of futile voting, and compelling anyone to work against his will (that's the way! that's the way to talk here!)."

"What do you mean?" stormed Shmuel. "Hasn't the majority got the right to decide and demand obedience, and doesn't the individual have to submit to the decision whether he likes it or not? This is a new idea! The general consensus always obligates every individual to take a particular action, and he has to do it. That's obvious. There are no two ways about it. On the contrary, that was an excellent proposal."

Itzik wrinkled his brow; he was afraid this might be a one-sided proposal. In other words, what counter-opinion was there? For if there really had been someone else, would they have wasted so much time and given themselves so much bother?

"I'll abstain from voting at all," said Tzippora. "I shan't vote against, because there's no other suitable candidate, and I shan't vote for, because I don't want Ephraim to be in a dilemma because of me; after all you've got to take into account the individual's personal inclinations and not make him into a mere cork to stop up holes that the majority thinks have to be stopped up."

Behind the windows there was again a great deal of excitement, and after a while a faint voice could be heard twittering from that direction, saying: "Why is Ephraim silent, why doesn't *he* speak?"

...Where do these yearnings lead? Those Saturdays in distant winters, when the sun laughed in the skies and big-bellied clouds piled up on the horizons while some of them floated with their shadows over mountains and fields, and a cluster of tents was scattered in familiar disorder on the hill, and you took a horse and galloped over the open country, between budding cornflowers and a blaze of golden groundsel, and many-colored poppies and colorful sage and purple irises, and banks of wild radish and wild mustard, white and yellow—the entire space filled with shining patches, nothing blurred or pale, no mark or line to indicate limits or boundaries between the song of light and the color; the late morning breezes produced a cool and healthy shiver; there were puddles enclosed in luscious greenery, and brooks with damp sandbanks and smooth stones in them; screeching crows conversed about the last rain, and you met wandering flocks and barefoot children playing on their pipes. You

with every footstep and action: Well, man, you got what you wanted, you have what you desired—are you doing such great and wonderful things? And where would he get the strength, the ability, to bear the venomous, inner mockery that would trouble his rest? No, it was no longer possible. So what?

And to get up tomorrow with the morning bell, to go into the kitchen to drink and chew, to clear up the yard and set out along the path, tramping in the footprints of yesterday and the day before, already absorbed by the sand, to arrive with the shimmering of the rising sun and return in the evening glow, and, in between, the burning sun, the turbid water, Nahum and David going about their business, that's right and proper and you must bow your shoulder to the yoke—what kind of life is that? Is that possible? Do you still have strength for that? After all, you're only a man; there's a limit to anyone's patience; even a donkey kicks and rebels. To keep it all hidden inside, locked up in the prison cell of the heart, lusts and desires, yearnings and thoughts, always to postpone things for the future, when your luck would turn, and everything would go well, when the destined, longed-for place would be won, and until then a long stagnation and many acts which are good and useful for cows, mules and men—these finally reach their goal, these alone get everything with a prodigality which borders on waste, the choicest portions of place and time, but you must hold your tongue, with a "nothing has really happened" on your face and escape to your bed, son of man, to dream of reality and forget.

Very fine, isn't it? But what can you do? And how can you be saved? But, on the other hand, many other people are living just like you, under the very same conditions—what do they say? Why don't they waste away with longing for something else, and why doesn't what they have seem to them poor or insignificant? Or perhaps they are tired already, perhaps their desire is one that suits any place, and any place can hold them, or perhaps it is old age that is on the way? Or, on the contrary, satiation and excessive comfort? Idle talk! It's all according to the seed that was sown then: the flowers have budded, blossomed and matured—and now they are fading. The fountain of their vitality is exhausted. They have played their part. Others have to come. Fresh fountains must well up; while the one within whom everything has not yet blossomed, in whom something still beats and tries to push its way out, will be fettered against his will by the fear of change, the fear of the exceptional, of anything outstanding or out-of-the-way. You shall be with us, the same as the rest of us. Of course, it was not very proper to use such language about himself, but never mind, let it be. And although decent people do not confess self-love, which they call "egotism", narrow-mindedness and the like, feeling it shameful to be included in this category and insulting to be even suspected of it, nevertheless that makes no difference to the fact that a pain in the smallest fingernail means more to them than the soul of their neighbor, and that the fear of going bald is enough to make them hate the whole world. A man's self-love... But, on the contrary, try leaving every man made in the image of God alone to love him-self completely, with a complete love of a complete self—let us love ourselves and the world will be redeemed... Tut, tut, Ephraim, hold on, don't get excited, and come back to the point from your fool-ish musings: are you leaving the alfalfa or not? Don't demand what doesn't exist, don't give up what does, and don't always try to make a fresh start. But this foolish heart sometimes desires and sometimes does not—always at the wrong time; obstructs every decision, breaks every vow, covets what does not belong to it and burns with insatiable yearnings for whatever is not, believes in its folly that things are still possible, that what is distant and ephemeral as the breath of God is still conceivable; and for a song, for nothing at all, you're prepared to forfeit all you have, all this wretched, empty-handed posture in which you stand, impotent to pursue, achieve and cling to the tran-sient radiance of beauty.

And as for you, distant she, it seemed that the tempest you raised subsided into silence, and that after all it was possible to think and plan about some future that lay on the horizon of tranquility, about a change, about the orange grove, about the emergence of a new life, about one thing and another, and not about you alone. And now you rise again, once more as in days gone by, rise suddenly, shining, filling everything with your radiance, so that again I do not know what to do with these hands of mine, what I am saying, what is the sense of this chatter and tumult, and what will be the fate of all those futile plans that have been swept away in your turbulence and no longer exist. It was all lies, nothing but deception. All the soothing words were useless, and it would be better for everyone if Ephraim rested peacefully on his dunghill. I did not forget her, Nehama, I did not pass beyond her, but what I thought would fill her empty place did not come, did not fill it, and she is still within me as she was before, more than she ever was before. Once again those storms of sadness that should have been forgotten and wiped out long ago, again the unending, unremitting anguish, which insists, with savage fury and elemental force and a bitter imperative: Do! Do something, you wretch, do something! Don't stagnate! Fight for the last hope, for the distant shore which is all yours, even if you go down into the abyss! Listen, Nehama, what should have passed away did not pass, and what should have remained a complete whole has been split up into fragments. No, nothing has passed, nothing has been forgotten, and the same wounds are still bleeding, still bleeding... And what is a man, what are years and the passing time, if, as you sit like this among people engrossed in conversation, beside the everyday heavy green table bathed in smoke, you hold your breath and suddenly lose all contact with your surroundings at the sudden glimpse of a vision that rises alive and richly endowed with reality, at the revelation of a figure approaching, lifting her eyes with her enchanting, maddening indifference (ah, foolish heart!), looking around and looking away, her cool dress motionless and tight-fitting: passing by, her head bent, smiling, even giving and acknowledging greetings, and disappearing without turning her head. What kind of man is it whose imagination deludes him like this, and although he has not actually seen anything he is no longer in this world through the power of his emotion and that childish feeling which prevents him, for the sake of so-called pride, from turning his head after her—although this was no reality, an unreality in which you could clearly see her smile and the delicate crow's-feet that appeared in the corners of her deep-set eyes—God Almighty! those eyes!—and her legs, her slightly flexed legs. The room is not clearly visible. Of their own accord, the talk and the conversation pass around my body, which does not really belong to me. And this was no more than the faint spark of a memory of an elusive unreality. That was all. All, Nehama. And through this, through this alone, everything was destroyed and collapsed into misery. I don't want anything, I don't want anything in the world but her alone, to run after her, to follow in her footsteps, to keep up the pursuit, never to let her go… Now, tell me, Nehamke, how is it possible to do anything at all from now on, when she is not there? Not there. But Ephraim, who has not won her, is here; here is Ephraim, with all his foolishly bleeding wounds. She is not there. Distant. And you've got to go back to all those old things which only yesterday you wanted to get away from completely, which you hated with gritted teeth even when you were at peace, and today, when everything is lost and swept away, you have to return to the very same things, return and hold your peace.

So what's to be done Nehamke, what's to be done? Oh, it's sad, Nehamke, sad. Hard to be always alone like this. Or perhaps it's you, Nehamke, who haven't been blessed with overmuch happiness, standing by the light-colored wall, alone, silent, in blue shorts and a soft blouse, your warm hair fastened with its brooches, and a noble beauty, noble like the one beyond compare, emanates from you, more anguished and more speechless? Why are you silent among many people? Look, child, sister to my goddess who is more precious than anything else, you should not be like this, you should not bear by yourself this heavy burden with which you have been endowed, nobility, pride, sad obduracy and a terrible, unconcealed truth—share with me, I have much and yours will make no difference. Why should you and I pass by, each on his own road, glancing at each other, curious, wondering, ready to speak, ready to come closer, ready to meet, but with all our stubborn pride each plodding on along his own trail, neither willing to give up his own way, going on into the distance toward the mist and the haze? No, Nehama, there is nothing in my heart now, not even tantalizing illusions, not even plans for the future.

Everything is less, everything is common and ordinary, all is vanity. Every faith is a deception, every reality an illusion. I have to get back, get back into things, get right down to the depths and, from inside, call out for salvation. From inside the heat of the alfalfa, and not from the comfort of the orange grove, from the difficulties of a long and silent day, out of complete and perfect self-dedication to sufferings as they are, out of a great love for them, to emerge, burst out, and break open with my head a way to what I want.

Do you hear, proud she! People like us will surely go. People like us will hold their heads high and keep their lips tightly closed and their hearts hidden in their innermost depths—you will not see what is in it. This is the glory of life for you, distant goddess, this is your blossoming; the song of the seething blood and the enchantments of the desirous flesh, these perfumed nights that throw the past into confusion, these wines of desire that dazzle the conscience with shrill shouts of intoxication—these are for you. It is for us to go somewhere, to work in the field parched with heat, to pave the way for you, to be covered in the dust of your chariots—you, who are blessed with an abundance of life, who gallop past with a thunder of noble, spirited horses, with their swelling muscles that sing your pride. It is for us to whistle under our breath, to bow respectfully, to tread in the everyday paths from sunrise to sunset without a trace of the heart's cry to distant gods visible on our faces. For our tears, Nehama, there is no solace in poetic or sensual ecstasies. We weep, Nehamke, and hold our peace. Our tears burn deep, but we go on our way as before. Like the donkey whose master has tied him to a shaky fence, and he bows his head, hangs his ears, swishes his tail, and stands with his knees touching, waiting for nothing in particular and no particular future. Look, our souls are drawn like moths to the flame, toward the great confrontation, the idea of which pervades the flowing blood, the red, exhilarating, maddening blood—enticed by the fire. Our faces burning and reddening, our veins filled with joy and vitality, and immediately afterward, it's all gone, the vision is ended, rejected, and we are gripped by the desolation of things to come, more repellent than ever before, and then we have nothing at all to say. Then, as always, we are silent, we go out to the field or the chicken-house, waiting expectantly for a word from the stillness, for which we yearn from the depths of our humiliation; perhaps some hint will come for the old, perplexed longings, which do not know what sacrifice will be demanded of them and what offering will be accepted. So, Nehama, we go further and further away from both of them, from those who drink their wine like welcome guests of God believing in the sublimity of their emotions and the exalted intoxication of the soul—but afraid of our contempt; and from those who eat their bread by the green tables and sing tranquilly—and resent our pride. Both of them despise us and shrug their shoulders; when we weep, they think we weep because of them: the first because we are no doubt grieved by their absence, as they follow the call of beauty and we are left to loneliness; and the others because we do not have the weight to anchor in any waters or cling closely to any soil. True, true, we are alone and isolated, abandoned, no one to understand or sympathize, but always compelled to endure the odious within the odious, not outside it. You will not save yourself. You must go back, go back, immerse yourself in work, and from within the work itself, from the heart of painful experience, out of what is obnoxious in it and out of what is sublime in it—emerge afresh like the phoenix from its ashes. That is the victory, that is the determination and this is the pride. If anyone finds a long day in the sun too hard, he must submit to it until he subjugates it to himself. Admit the suffering and do not escape, but rise above it with love and courage. Truth, my lad, truth toward yourself. Isn't that so Nehama?

But even these are no more than hackneyed clichés, reeled off dozens in one breath and fit for those charming albums, signifying nothing but evasion and retreat. At this very moment, with a little stubbornness and recalcitrance, you can surely extricate yourself from the fields of hay and fodder; necessity—as some have said here—will produce someone else in your place, who is not crazy and sick with yearnings; you will regain some energy, a little vigor, to freshen your face, and find new beginnings once again. Well, what about it, Ephraim? Here they are waiting to vote, ready to vote on you in

were simply dazzling. From time to time they bemused the heart so that one longed for some happy word.

Distant shepherds somewhere beyond were leading their flocks tranquilly across the unchanged fields and quiet hills, with the casual stride of those good times when trouble had not yet come. It nipped at one in a fashion that presaged something very different. Nearby there were flocks grazing, flocks belonging to the days of Abraham, Isaac and Jacob. Somewhere in the vicinity the distant village slumbered, with its frieze of olives, a kind of dull copper. In the hollow hillsides the ewes were thronging together. There were mountains in the distance.

Our CO stared for a long time through his field glasses, puffing his cigarette and preparing his plans. Number one, there was no point going further. Number two, going back empty-handed was simply unthinkable. One of the shepherds, or one of the boys, or maybe several of them, would have to be caught or else something would have to be done. Alternatively something would have to be burnt, and then they could return with results, with real and undeniable facts.

This commander of ours was a middle-sized chap with deep-set eyes and eyebrows joining together. He was baldish in front and wore his cap in such a way that his forehead and what little hair he had left were open to the breeze. We watched him as he made his survey. He saw whatever it was that he saw. As for us, we could see a world of hills, all woolly with greenstuff and stony ground and olives in the distance, a world crisscrossed and bedappled with little golden hollows and dips of durrah. So entirely was it such a world that it infused a silence in one together with a longing for good fruitful soil that warms like a flame. It enticed one and made one wish for the toil that is accompanied by bending and stretching, it made one wish for grayish sandy dust for all that is required at the height of the harvesting; for anything rather than being a member of the rank and file while the commander was working out how he would fling us across this chunk of afternoon silence.

What was more, he was well-nigh ready and prepared. In the

shadow of a youthfully green tree we had already discovered a shepherd with his sheep before him, at rest among the growing durrah. A sudden circle drew tight within the universe. Everything both beyond and within that circle was concentrated on a single person, who had to be taken alive. The huntsmen were already on the way. Most of us were to take cover in the undergrowth and amid the flattish rocks on the right while to the left and moving downward the CO would set off with two or three others in order to encircle the quarry, make a sudden onslaught and drive him into the arms of those lying in ambush above.

We stole into the heart of the gentle durrah. Our heels trod on the chewed shoots and stubble that had been gnawed by those selfsame flocks. Our hobnailed soles kissed the dust, both brown and grayish. We took full advantage of the area at our disposal, the topography, the natural vegetation and the shelter to be gained from blind spots. Then we came bursting at a gallop down on the fellow seated on a stone in the tree's shadow. Panic-stricken he jumped to his feet, flung away his staff and ran like a fleeing hind, vanishing to the other side of the slope right into the arms of the huntsmen.

That was a joke, that was! Funny wasn't the word for it! But our CO was always on the job. He was already full of a bright new idea and that was really tricky and clever. We would finish the job properly collecting the sheep as well. He clapped his hands and then rubbed his palms together in genial self-satisfaction, as much as to say: "That's the ticket!"

Someone swallowed his spit and remarked: "There'll be goulash for us, I can tell you!" We all set to work cheerfully with the satisfaction of victors, and the prospects of a reward for all our labors. Now he became genuinely enthusiastic: "Get on with it, quick!"

But the trouble was, all this excitement had frightened the sheep. Some of them had raised their heads, some were preparing to run away, and some wanted to know just what those who were preparing to do something were actually preparing to do. Besides, how does one handle sheep? We proved to be a mockery and a derision.

Our CO made that quite clear, insisting that a pack of

schoolteachers like us and idiots like us were good for nothing except to mess up anything that was fine and good. Then he began with a *brrrr* and a *grrrr* and a *te-e-e-e, te-e-e-e*, and all the other noises that have been the basis of communication between shepherd and flock since time began. What was more, nothing would satisfy him except to have one of us go ahead as a wether, *baa*ing all the way along, while two more on either side flourished their rifles as though they were shepherds' staffs and burst into song as though they were shepherds keeping their flocks amused. Behind them another three or so were to walk in exactly the same way, in order that our energy and wide laughter might help us control our hesitant and somewhat confused stupidity, so that we would end up better and finer, in brief, as soldiers.

Amid all this confusion we simply forgot that on the other side of a rock down on the slope there sat, in between two rifle butts and two pairs of hobnailed shoes, a prisoner who was trembling like a rabbit. A man of forty or so he was, with a drift of mustache around his mouth, a stupid nose and somewhat open lips and eyes; except that the latter had been blindfolded with his own *kaffiyah* in order that he should see nothing. Though I don't know what the nothing was that he was not supposed to see.

"Stand up!" they ordered when the CO came over to inspect the spoils of war at close quarters and look him up and down. What they said to the CO was: "'Did you really think we wouldn't catch him? Of course we did! And how! There's no nonsense with us. Not a single bullet, but he understood he'd better put his hands up. That's certain sure!"

"You're good and iron!" the CO approved of them. "Sheep and shepherd together, just imagine! What will they say when we get back! Perfectly lovely!" He took a look at the prisoner and found him to be a little sort of fellow in a faded yellow robe, shivering as he breathed through the kerchief bound over his eyes. His sandals were trodden down, all of a piece, he had a hooflike leg, and alas-this-is-the-very-end was inscribed all over his hunched shoulders.

"Uncover his eyes and tie his hands together. He'll lead the flock ahead of us!" Our CO had had another of those flashes of genius which the intoxication of battle engendered in him so plentifully.

At that a spark of delight flashed from one to the other of us. Good. They took off his black *agal*, which is the rope of horsehair worn around the *kaffiyah*, otherwise known as the headcloth. They wrapped the *agal* around his hands, pulled it and bound and knotted it tight for a second and a third time. Then they took the blindfold off the frightened fellow's eyes and nose and addressed him thus: *"Nabi el anam kudmana!"* Meaning, lead the flock ahead of us.

I don't know what the prisoner thought to himself when his eyes saw the light, nor what was going on in his heart nor what his blood said or roared or what was going on frustratedly inside him. All I know is—he began gnashing and puffing at his flock as though nothing had ever gone wrong. Down he went from rock to rock through the undergrowth, the way shepherds always go down from rock to rock through the undergrowth, The astonished and frightened sheep followed him, while behind them and around them came our hoarse voices, our kicking legs and the buffeting of our rifles as we went down into the valley, carelessly guffawing.

So busy were we with all this that we paid no attention to several other shepherds who suddenly started up and vanished over the line of the hilltops, crowded as those were with golden silence and speechless melancholy. They gathered silently, driving off their flocks while managing to keep an eye on us from the distance. Nor had we noticed the sun which all this noisy while was going gradually lower, gradually growing more golden until suddenly, as we came around the mountain spur, we were smitten by a huge and dazzling wave of brilliance, glazed, dusty, glowing and flaming, so that it seemed to be a kind of silent remote rebuke, and a great outcry even more.

Naturally we had no time to spare for all that. We had to worry about the sheep and the prisoner. The former were bleating and scattering, while the latter was cringing and turning dumb. A kind of dull stupidity had fallen upon him, a sort of stupefaction in which everything was lost and in face of which all was beyond despair. He merely strode along, silent and unhappy, growing more and more bemused and stupefied.

It would take too long to describe how we moved through the valleys amid the hills with all their crowded golden silence, through all the summer tranquility; how the frightened sheep were hurried along in a fashion to which they were not accustomed; and how our prisoner continued to be as dumbly silent as an uprooted plant. Indeed, he was growing miserable to the point of mockery, alarmed and starting and quivering and tumbling over with the kerchief which was, of course, tied round his forehead, whenever he was given a sudden tug. He grew steadily more alarmed and startled, not to say ridiculous after a fashion, though virtually untouchable. And meanwhile the durrah went on yellowing, the sun added its silent pride, the dusty paths between the ends of the fields and the flank of the mountain absorbed our fit and proper paces as though they were silently bearing some additional burden. In brief, we were returning to base.

All the marks of a strongpoint began to emerge. There was an emptiness, a fine dust, a desolation. Echoes ceased abruptly. A forsaken anthill, the rags and tatters of human life. The mustiness of don't-give-a-damn. A stinking, flea-bitten, lice-infested existence. The poverty and doltishness of miserable villages. All of a sudden their outskirts, their homes, their courtyards, their inmost sanctums had been laid bare. All of a sudden their clothes had been flung over their faces, their shameful nakedness displayed, and here they were, poverty-stricken, withered and stinking. A sudden emptiness, an apoplectic death. Strange, rancorous orphanhood. In the heat of the day the place seemed to be squinting through a haze of dust, uncertain whether it was mournfully lamenting or simply bored or whether it mattered either way.

Over above, to be sure, they wandered about in the gray plumpish trenches, those citizens whose food was not food, whose water was not water, whose day was not day and whose night was not night, and may the devil take whatever they might do or whatever might happen, devil take what used to be decent and pleasant and customary, in short devil take everything. So let us stink good and proper and grow beards and talk smut and muck. Let sweaty clothes stick to unwashed bodies with all their sores and pimples. And let us shoot the stray dogs so that they also begin to stink. And let us sit down in the sticky dust with the smell of the burnt tires all around, and sleep in the muck and case-harden our hearts, all because nothing mattered.

The identifying marks of the outpost became clearer. We marched more pridefully. What magnificent spoils of war we were bringing with us! Rhythm entered into our feet. The sheep were bleating and flowing along in confusion. The prisoner, over whose nose and eyes the kerchief had been replaced for security reasons, was dragging his sandals and shambling helplessly along in his semi-blindness, generous and hearty curses accompanying him. Apart from all of which our satisfaction was growing and swelling, our genuine pleasure at this achievement, this real enterprise. We were sweating and dusty, so soldierly, such he-men. What words we could use to describe our CO! And it is easy to imagine the way we were received and how everybody roared with laughter and cheerful self-satisfaction, just like barrels with burst hoops.

Someone busting with laughter, the sweat running all over him, came up to our CO, pointed to the blindfolded prisoner and asked casually:

"Is that him? Settling him? Give me!" And our CO, still grinning as he gulped some water down, wiped off his own sweat and answered glisteningly:

"Just you sit down quietly over there, it isn't yours."

The gang all around burst out laughing to hear it all. Who gave a damn for strong point, for trouble, for the whole set up, for the whole snafu, for freedom and anything of the kind as long as we had all this? Oh, we were old horses. The harness did not gall us any longer. On the contrary. It covered any number of healed and unhealed sores and fitted well over the hollows of the spine which was no longer straight after the hard times we had gone through.

Then someone came along and photographed the whole kaboodle. When he went on leave he would develop the films and make photos of them. Someone else came up behind the prisoner, shook his fist this way and that with real appetite and gleefully crawled back among the others. As for a third, he simply didn't know whether that was nice or not, whether they ought to behave like that or not. He spent his time looking this way and that, seeking support in either direction.

And there was one who simply emptied a pitcher of water down his throat, gulping with flashing teeth and without closing his mouth, while meanwhile a finger of his left hand notified all and sundry that as soon as he had finished this gulping he would go on with his "that's the way things are." And there was another fellow in an undershirt who stared in curiosity and astonishment. He bared bad teeth over which many dentists had bent. Behind him were sleepless nights and narrow airless rooms and a thin and venomous woman and unemployment and party activities. All of them had labored and toiled in order to eliminate his everlasting, "Well and what's going to happen now? What's going to happen?" But they had all toiled in vain.

And then there were others who had regular jobs, and some who were on their way up the ladder, and some who were everlastingly helpless and incorrigibly unfortunate; and some who spent all their time at the cinema, or the Habima and Ohel and Matateh theaters, and who read the weekend supplements of two different papers. And there were others who could lecture you for hours on end about Horace and Isaiah the Prophet and Haim Nahman Bialik, and even about Shakespeare. Some loved their children and their wives dreadfully, together with the little garden by the home and the slippers indoors. Some hated favoritism and demanded fair and equal chances for all, and started yelling even at those things that scarcely had any scent of unfairness about them. Some were so furious at rent and taxes that everything decent within them had turned quite sour. Some were not at all what they were thought to be, while others were precisely and exactly what they were and the way people sized them up.

Now all of them stood in a cheerful ring around a prisoner with his eyes covered by a kerchief and who, what was more, chose this particular moment to stick out one of his thick hands, of which you could never judge whether they were dirty or not, or anything else apart from their belonging to a villager. And what he said was this: "*Fi sigara?*" His voice was noisy and creaking, and astonished them as much as if the wall of the house had started to screech. It immediately gained the applause of those with a sense of the ridiculous, and the restraining fingers of others who were sensitive to impudence.

Maybe somebody there even began to think of giving him a cigarette, but finally the matter was settled in a more military fashion. Two of the group commanders accompanied by an assistant commander came out of the H.Q. just then. They took the prisoner and led him off. Being blindfolded, he had no alternative except to rest his arm on the Group Commander accompanying him. The latter slipped his arm through the prisoner's and supported him firmly. In addition he said whatever had to be said to make him improve his hesitant shuttle.

For a little while it seemed as though they were both trying to get past obstacles without trouble. They helped one another as though they belonged together. So much so, indeed, that a moment before they reached the building this queer fellow croaked and repeated the words he had croaked before, "*Fi sigara?*"

Those syllables messed everything up. The fellow supporting him dropped the hand that he had almost been holding as they walked arm-in-arm. He shook himself free from all contact and raised his eyebrows angrily, almost insulted, as much as to say, "Have you seen the like!"

It was so sudden that the unprepared fellow stumbled over the step leading into the house. He tottered, almost falling on his face as he suddenly burst into the room. Startled, he tried to prevent himself from falling, pushing a chair away and pulling up at the table, helpless, heavy and almost in a state of shock at all the mishaps that had already happened to him and those that might next befall. He let his hand drop and helplessly resigned himself to whatever would happen.

At the table sat sternly official higher officers, solemnly waiting. The fellow's unexpected entry confused what they had already prepared in their minds, in the way of atmosphere and sentry at the door. The group commanders and others had to start pulling themselves together and organizing it all afresh. No wonder it annoyed them.

The man in the center was tall, with stiff hair and a keen, well-muscled face. To his left sat none other than our Section Commander, his very own self. Now you could see that he really was bald enough, and that the hair at his temples was turning white while there were still a few strands on the front part of his head. There was a crumpled cigarette in his mouth and he was sweating as he took it easy, the hero of the day. He was only at the beginning of his achievements, what was more.

A little further away by the wall, in demonstrative isolation, lounged a young fellow who was watching through lowered lids like one who knows a very specific truth and was waiting to discover how, in the last resort and without any possible alternative, that very specific truth out of all others would be revealed.

"What's your name?"

The tall fellow started his investigation very suddenly. The prisoner, still confused by his entry, paid no attention to the question. The chap leaning against the wall ran a wrinkle of certainty down to his lips as though he had expected that as well beforehand.

"What's your name?" the tall fellow now repeated, hissing the words.

"Who? Me?" the shepherd jumped and lifted a hesitant hand to the kerchief over his eyes. He pulled it away again halfway as though he had been scorched.

"Your name?" the bristly-haired fellow repeated once more, very clearly and with full accentuation.

"Hassan," croaked the other, moving his head in an effort to enhance his attention, in order to make up for his novel absence of sight.

"Hassan what?"

"Hassan Ahmad," he said more rapidly as though being shunted onto rails; and he nodded his head in confirmation.

"How old?"

"Can't say," he shrugged his shoulders, rubbing the palms of his hands together, wishing to be helpful.

"How old?"

"I simply don't know, *ya sidi*," he croaked through his fleshy lips, half-smiling for some reason so that his drift of mustache danced gently. "Twenty, or maybe thirty-two," he gladly contributed to the joint session.

"Well, and what's going on in your village?" the tall fellow went on with the same accented tranquility, a tranquility which was stressed and presaged the rage that would follow. It was a tranquility of petty and highly original cunning toward what comes, circling around and around from a distance, then suddenly striking straight at the main artery in the very middle of the breast.

"They are working in the village, *ya sidi*," the prisoner sketched a picture of village life as he sensed some impending evil.

"Working, eh! Just as usual?" The questioner took a tiny step along the spider's web. One of the numerous threads began vibrating and announcing the prey.

"Yes, *ya sidi*," the fly insisted on invading the entangling threads. It was absolutely obvious that he would begin to lie now. At this point he would undoubtedly lie. It was his duty to lie and we would catch him at it, the contemptible cur; and we would show him. Yet just as it was clear that we would get nothing out of him this way, that he would say nothing, so it was clear that, this time, us, those of us who were present, he would not mislead, oh no, not us; and he would have plenty to say.

"And who is there in the village?" the hawk retracted its wings directly above its quarry.

"Ah—eh?" the prisoner did not grasp the question, and licked his lips as an animal might.

"'Jews? Englishmen? Frenchmen?" The questioner went on like a teacher setting a trap for a pupil; just to catch him, just to find out and that's all.

"No, *ya sidi,* there are no Jews, only Arabs," he answered gravely, not in the least as though he were trying to dodge the issue. Once more he forgetfully raised his hand to the kerchief covering his eyes, as though the danger had already passed. The questioner glanced around at his comrades in the room, as much as to say: "You see! Now it's going to begin. That's how it is when you know how to get the facts.'

"Are you married?" he began again from another flank. "And have you any children? And where is your father? And how many brothers have you? And where do people get their water in the village?" He went on spinning his fine net of investigation, this tall fellow. The one being investigated labored and toiled to give satisfaction. He moved his hands in exaggerated, meaningless fashion, shifting his head about, stammering and stuttering and giving tiny details which annoyed the investigators and confused him himself. He had a story to tell about two daughters and a son, but the son had gone away and his sisters were not entirely not to blame for it, and had become sick and died and departed this world. In the middle of it all he thrust his thumb against his back ribs, and scratched there, up and down. He pressed all four fingers against the thumb in his endeavors, while stammering for the one word he wanted. Simply disgusting it was, for those listening to him.

There was a pause. The sentry at the door shifted from foot to foot.

The grimace on the face of the fellow leaning against the wall, and the way our bald CO stood beside the table, suddenly made it clear that it was not correct for the prisoner to have nothing to add. Nothing would help, blows were necessary.

"Listen, Hassan," the questioner now said. "In that village of yours, are there any Egyptians?"

Now he'll be talking. Now it will begin. Now he'll start lying.

"There are," answered the prisoner with disappointing frankness.

"There are ..." echoed the questioner with a measure of dubiousness that contained a certain dissatisfaction, as if somebody had given him something too early. He lit a cigarette as he began to meditate whether he should now move his castle or his knight.

Our own CO began striding up and down the room. He moved the kicked-away chair back into place, fixed his tunic within his trousers, turned his back on us and stared out of the window with obvious dissatisfaction. The chap by the wall also ran his hand over his face and gently pinched his nose. Breathing deep and presenting a shrewd countenance as much as to say: "You have to know how to take things in hand!"

"How many are there?"

"Can't say exactly, not many."

(Ah, now the lying begins. This must be a lie. There'll have to be some slapping about.)

"How many are there?"

"Ten or fifteen maybe, about that."

"Listen, Hassan, you'd better tell the truth."

"The truth, *ya sidi,* it is all the truth."

"And don't lie."

"Aye, *ya sidi.*" The prisoner did not know what to do with his hands which had remained spread out ahead of him. He let them drop.

"And there's no monkey business with us!" the tall fellow boiled over and added since it had to be added: "How many soldiers are there in your village?"

"Fifteen."

"A lie!"

Our bald CO, who had been looking out of the window, now turned his head. His eyes were smiling. He was beginning to feel the pleasure a man knows when he is due to enjoy something in another moment, and meanwhile there is satisfaction in restraining that pleasure for the additional sweet moment that will exist later. He thrust a cigarette in the smiling corner of his compressed lips and lit it. The five with open eyes in the room all exchanged the same secret, satisfied gaze. The sentry at the door shifted from one foot to the other once again.

"By my life, *ya sidi,* fifteen!"

"No more?"

"Ahadan. no more."'

"How do you know there are no more?" That was how the questioner dexterously proved there was no fooling him. Maybe he showed a trifle too much shrewdness.

"There are no more."

"What if there are more?" (What can anyone answer to that?)

"There are no more."

There is no saying where the kick suddenly came from. Flashing from its self-restraint and finally liberating itself slantwise, uncomfortably, for lack of the necessary distance for a real good kick, shaking up the prisoner who was quite unprepared with his covered eyes. He suddenly cried out with astonishment rather than with pain, and stumbled against the table. It all seemed so much more like an unfair game than a means of getting at the facts, It was something unexpected and unnatural, something that was not what was needed, not that at all.

"Talk up now, and see you tell the truth!"

"Ya sidi, by my eyes, by Allah, fifteen!"

The chap by the wall was clearly apprehensive that someone might believe the blatant lie. In his hands he held a long stick which he ran between his fingers with the gracious motion of a nobleman drawing his sword. Silently he placed it on the table.

Questions went on piling up. Swiftly presented questions. Without an interval. From time to time they were besprinkled, and more and more easily and naturally, first with one kick and then with another. Cold kicks, kicked without anger, steadily more skillful. From time to time they seemed not to be added at the right point. But from time to time it became even clearer that they were absolutely necessary.

For if you are out for the truth, then you have to hit. If the man lies, then hit. If he does tell the truth, don't believe it but hit him so that he shouldn't lie later on. Hit just in case there may be some other truth. Hit because it is a habit. Just as shaking the tree brings down the ripe fruit, so beating the prisoner gives rise to the maximum possible truth. Obviously that's how it is. If anyone thinks different, don't argue with him. He's a defeatist, and that kind of fellow shouldn't make war. Don't have pity, hit. No one has any pity on you either. And apart from that, these fellows are accustomed to being hit.

By this time they were asking about the submachine guns in the village. An urgent issue that, and it had to be thrashed out. It was impossible to take as much as a single step forward in this connection without using force all the way. Anything else might lead to the shedding of Jewish blood, the blood of our lads; so the business had to be cleared thoroughly. They chewed it up, over and over, again and again. They went back and chewed it from the other side until it began to stink, and they had no choice except to believe that he must be lying. Then followed the business of fortifications. They ordered him to describe the village defenses.

Here the prisoner became absolutely confused. He found them hard to describe. He could not go into abstractions or talk geometry or mathematics. He wigwagged his hands, he capered about on his legs, he hopped this way and that, he did his best to convince with waving arm. The kerchief over his eyes dimmed everything, made it all meaningless and confused. But in the room it was absolutely clear that none of this could be anything but sheer deliberate falsehood.

"You're a liar," insisted the examiner despairingly. "I can see by your eyes that you're a liar!" And he menaced the blindfold with his fist.

They were making no progress. The whole business was boring, and by now they were thoroughly sick of it. They had entangled themselves in a cold and clumsy cross-examination. Nobody was enthusiastic. There was not even any satisfaction in hitting him. So it became even more astonishing when the sound of a whistling stick was heard, coming down from somewhere or other on the prisoner's back in an alien, discordant thud; something being done as a thoroughly unpleasant duty.

All good and fine. Now came the artillery. The prisoner insisted that the barrels of their cannon were no longer than his arm, starting from the shoulder and finishing at the palm. He demonstrated the size with chopper-like blows of his left hand aimed at the very root of his right shoulder, and then exactly halfway down the right hand; as much as to say, from here to here, saying it devotedly and sacramentally, hitting again and again until he eliminated all doubt; without knowing whether that was enough or whether he would have to go on and on. And meanwhile a blind grimace entwined itself on his lips and around his mustache.

The questioning petered out miserably. The sentry at the door shifting from one foot to another at his post had been peeping out of the doorway from time to time. Maybe he was seeking something in the bright sky that differed from the sheer mess of this dirty room. Now he began to feel apprehensive. Something dreadful was about to happen and there was no other choice. For what could be left, after all, except to have them tell him to take the carcass along and finish him?

"Well, that's the way it is." The examiner stretched back against his chair, wanting to take a breather after all this nonsense. He crushed his cigarette impatiently, dropped it on the floor and crushed it.

"I'll finish him off," suggested bald-head as he flicked his cigarette through the doorway.

"An absolute dumbbell," decided one officer.

"Just pretending to be a dumbbell," said the other.

"What you have to know is how to talk to him," said the chap leaning against the wall, twisting his lips in recognition of a truth which they had presumably doubted and denied.

The prisoner had already sensed that there was an interval. He licked his thick lips, struck out his thick hand and said:

"*Fi sigara, ya sidi?*" (Got a cigarette, mister?)

Of course no one paid any attention to the idiot. He waited a few moments, then drew his outstretched hand back, thought the matter over and stood still again, an absolute donkey for you. And only to himself alone did he moan: "*Ahhh, ya rab.*" Meaning: Oh, Lord God.

Well, what next? Where to now? To the quarry slopes in the villages? Or maybe to some torture of the kind that opens mouths and restores truth instead of falsehood? Or was there any other way? How were they to get rid of him? Or maybe… Suppose they were to give him a cigarette and send the dolt back home? Get the hell out of here and we don't ever want to see you again!

Finally they phoned somewhere or other and spoke to the Assistant Boss himself; and it was decided to send him on to another camp (at least three of the fellows in the room disgustedly turned their noses up at this shamefaced, civilian, namby-pamby trick); a camp where prisoners were questioned and handled the way they deserved. With this end in view the sentry at the door, the same one who had felt uneasy all the time without knowing why, would go off and fetch the dusty Jeep and the growling duty driver who was annoyed at being called out of turn, which was so easily proved by so many facts and also by objurgations. Apart from which, as far as he himself was concerned he did not have the least objection to going off to some place where he could see human beings, but this was a matter of principle, sheer principle. And then another soldier also came and sat down beside the driver, since there was some job which could not be done until now in the absence of transport. He was now given this additional objective of accompanying the prisoner. And that was the way they would pass through the town, Spandau in front and prisoner behind. Burdened with these two functions in order to make sure that never under any circumstances would this trip be deducted from his leave (that being a separate account), he sat and loaded the machine gun.

As for the prisoner, after he had been pushed and began groping around and banged against the side of the car and was helped in, the only place left for him was on the floor where he half-lay, half-kneeled and crouched entirely. Two were in front and the former sentry behind him, his pocket bulging with the proper papers and travel orders and chits and all the rest of it. That afternoon, which had begun some time or other between the hills and the trees and the flocks, was now due to finish in a way nobody could forecast.

They were already out of the smelly village and crossing, from the wadi to the fields, then on through the fields. The Jeep dashed along bouncing on all fours, and stretches of the not-so-distant future began to be transformed into reality. It was nice to sit facing the fields as they bathed in an increasingly reddish light that comprehended everything in a sweep of tiny bright golden clouds, a light rising higher than anything; than all those things which concern you and me so much, even though they did not in the least matter to the driver or his comrade with the mustache beside him. They smoked, whistled and sang, "In the Negev plains a man defending fell", and, "Your eyes are bright with a green green light", one after the other. There was someone else on the floor of the Jeep, but it wasn't easy to know what could be going on inside him since he was blindfolded, beastlike and silent.

A fuzz of dust rose behind them, a smoky wake which wavered and grew pink at the edges. Irrelevant ditches and unimportant potholes in the road made the Jeep jump, while fields spread their arms out to infinity and gave themselves up to a twilight that was fuddled with forgetfulness and gentleness—and something so far away, so far away, so dreamlike—until all of a sudden and unexpectedly a strange thought jumped into his head and would not budge. "The woman, she's undoubtedly lost." For up to now it was astonishing where they could have come from, you understand; as though you were thunderstruck to think that here, right here beside you, something was happening; the same thing which in other circumstances is called by other names, and which is also known as Fate.

You'd better take a jump at once, one, two, and get right out from under this bad business. Sing as a second voice to the two in front, set out for distant regions in the twilight through which the sun was burning with a reddish-citron color; only you would at once see again what had so suddenly emerged through the astounding breach.

The fellow here at your feet, his life, his well-being, his home, three souls, the whole thread of his existence with all that was involved, were in your grip somehow or other as though you were some lesser demigod here in the Jeep. The man carried along, the collective flock of sheep and several souls in the mountain village, these variegated threads of life were twined together to be cut or grow inextricably involved, all because you were suddenly their master. If you liked you could just stop the Jeep and let him go free, and everything would cut up differently. But…just a moment. The fellow on the back seat of the little Jeep suddenly felt the spirit darting aloft within him. Just a moment: Let the fellow go?

Here we could stop the Jeep, here by the wadi. We could let the fellow down, uncover his eyes, face him toward the mountains, point straight ahead and tell him: Go home, man, go straight along. Take care about that hill, there are Jews on it. Take care and don't fall into our hands again. And then he would take his feet over and dash home. He would go back home. Precisely that. And listen, what a story! The dreadful, tense waiting, the fate of a woman and her children (an Arab woman!). Forebodings at the heart that wrestled with the decree of Fate, wondering will he, won't he come back, guessing what might happen next; and then everything solved satisfactorily so that she could breathe easily, he's condemned to life. Hi lad, come and let's let the fellow go!

And why not? What was to stop it? Simple, decent and human. So just get up and tell the driver to stop. No more fine phrases about humanity any longer. This time it's up to you yourself. This time it's not someone else's malice, this time it's your own conscience you're facing. Let him off and you've saved him. Today that alternative, that ominous, tremendous alternative we always used to talk about so nervously, is firmly in your own two hands. There's no dodging it now, not with Soldier, not with Orders, and not with Suppose they caught you, not even with What will the boys say. You're standing nuked, facing your duty. And the choice is all your own, nobody else's.

Then stop the Jeep. Stop the driver. Let the poor devil go. You don't have to give any reasons. It's his right and your duty. If there's any meaning or sense in this war, now's the time for it to be seen. Men, men, there was a man and they sent him home. Snap your fingers at all this customary cruelty and send the fellow away. Just release him. Hallelujah! That peasant, that shepherd would go home to his wife.

There could be no alternative. Otherwise years would pass

Now listen lad, do you weigh all these miserable trills and tremolos against a human life? How would you like it if you were crouching on the floor of a Jeep, if your wife was waiting at home and everything was destroyed, flying about like chaff, lost and done for, waiting and waiting while the heart burns away and you're not at home; waiting with tears, waiting with your fist, with humility, with prayer and protest...

He has already said all he has to say. He told us all he has to tell. And now what next? Even if he did lie, even if it was untrue seven times over, still, who and what is he more than a miserable nonentity, a withering submissive creature, a face wrapped around with a kerchief, all squeezed up and twisted, worthless, an empty frightened bag, fading away to nothing, abnegating himself, expecting to be kicked and regarding kicks as natural. (Take a kick at an Arab, it doesn't mean anything to him.)

And you, his guard, you simply have to let him go even if he himself laughs at you, even if he or somebody else regards it as sheer incapacity, even if your companions mock you, even if they ask you to prevent his liberation, even if they send you to the Chief Prosecutor because of it, or to a score of prosecutors. It still remains your duty and you had better set about it and escape from this swinish routine. Then there'll have been somebody who was prepared even if he paid for it to get out for once; to get away from the pigsties which rose so high and spread so far and wide while we were good citizens, and which have now officially and solemnly and by general agreement become the way of the world, the practice of everybody who wants to be worthy of the magnificent name of soldier.

We don't get any leave, we can't go home, it's hot here, filthy here, miserable here, dangerous here—so what? Let's take it out on the enemy. Let's do something. Let's knock off some miserable Arab. (Who asked him to start this damned war anyway?) Let's permit ourselves to do everything we were once forbidden to do.

Ah well, here's a certain Hassan Ahmad. His wife is either Halima or Fatma and he has two daughters and his flock has been stolen and he has been taken away somewhere or other on a bright

and sunny afternoon. And who are you and what's your life good for?
All a fellow like you is worth is for having all the black bile inside us
emptied out on you, and the hell with it.

Of course you're not going to let him go. That's perfectly
plain. It's just fine thoughts. It's not even cowardice, it's something
worse. You're a partner in the business, that's what you are. Hiding
behind that stinking "what's to be done, it's an order", just this time
when you have the choice and it's all in your own power, in your
very own hands.

The choice is yours. A great day it is. A day of revolt. A day
when you have the choice in your own hands at last, and the power
to turn it into a decision, to give life back to a misused man. Think
it over. To act as your heart desires. In full accordance with your
own love and your own truth, in accordance with the greatest of all
things—the liberation of a man.

Let him go.

Be a man.

Let him go!

Well, it's quite clear nothing will happen. Fly away, good idea.
You'll dodge, that's plain. You'll look the other way. Of course it's all
lost. I'm sorry for you, prisoner. He simply doesn't have the strength
to do it.

Yet maybe, in spite of everything? Right away, here and now.
It would just take this moment. Pull up, driver. Get off, Hassan. Go
home. Do something. Talk. Stop the Jeep. Say something now, this
moment. After all your aching and bellyaching all these long and
empty days, be a human being at last the way you want to be.

The fields were one vast shallow pinkish-gold expanse, all the
tens of thousands of dunams made up one single enchanted plain
without valleys, without hills, without acclivities or declivities, without villages or trees. Everything had been beaten down to one single
gold foil, one leveled expanse above which were scattered quivering
restless golden dust-blobs around a vast land of gold that stretched
on to infinity; even if it were possible that on the other side (where
nobody watches) amid the evening mists making their way down from

T he shawls of dust, twisted tight to the rear in a grappling coil, went forward on an occasional dare and knotted up the front view as well. At once everything was dimmed and grayed, walled up in a ball, thickened with dusty spinning, a choked and blinded enclosure—except when the wind gave in, not a minute too soon, and slackened a bit, venting the rest of its rage on that gigantic whirl of wake in back, waving and tearing at it, scattering it furiously to the sides of the road and deep into the fields, which were already as blanched as could be; for stubble and summer grasses, great clods and minute granules, had long since been entirely leveled into gray lumps, nameless and formless in the scorn of uniformity, fainting under this floury, weighty, compulsory veil.

Within, of course, no one cared much about his appearance any more, and what had with such pains been bestowed by loving mothers was darkened and dyed by this mass of grossness, which not only eclipsed each countenance but continued to descend and to settle, not ungently, distorting each one still more, but with a soothing innocence as of immaculate snow, which knows no favorites, whether flesh and blood or clods of earth. And it was not enough to swallow the dust with inexhaustible patience: one was obliged to go on, to get there, without falling into one of the dips of the wadi, which now came rubbing up from the left and later from the right and all at once you have to move as fast and deftly as you can to brake and circumnavigate the sharp angle of a gully, which in itself is really very simple and unassuming, and has merely found this a good spot for a plunge, so that even if small and insignificant you quite respectfully shy away from it and choose a circuitous route. Moreover, the hour is pressing, as usual, and you have no time to flirt with this willful and whimsical road nor to play catch with the dust, for an itinerary is an itinerary, even if only by guess in a heavy haze of dust, whereupon you continue your course here and there by heart—and besides, you can't even swear aloud, so clever is this dust.

Even when the vehicle stopped finally and was silent, it was worth waiting a while for the dust to disperse and settle, part of it sinking back flaccidly into its powdery bed, the rest keeping on vagabond in the wind, where, with a bit of luck, it might even complete its trick of circling and storming back to take a look at what was over there beyond the hills, and to dance a bit and be gay, until dropping far off in distant expanses to set up a bustling camp in the outlands—but the five travelers would not be delayed. At once they jumped out and at once their shoes sank into that same old floury jelly, vile in its limpness, but they emerged and climbed up the slope, which now turned out to be actually the side of a mound, at whose foot the car had halted.

As they climbed, they rid themselves of those wraps in which their faces were concealed, and, beating their clothes and shaking their matted hair, hawked and coughed to clear out what had clotted in their throats. They raked out their noses, dug into their eyes, picked their ears (which were ornamented with wreaths of dust suspended on insubstantial downy hairs), and as they clapped palm against palm, and palm against thigh, the first words were uttered

—monosyllabic imprecations   after which they began wonderingly
to regard their surroundings.

Actually, it was the same old thing. Fields of sorghum on every
side, unreaped, as usual. A few patches left fallow and ploughed, others sallowed with weeds, Struggling thorns on the slopes and midget
shrubs, ragged and dusty. Nothing else. No, that's it. The hills reach
as far as this point, and beyond them the mountains, rising high but
with something fuzzy and decayed about them, a mist of sadness
hanging over them, unclear, indefinite, like the end of the Sabbath
gazing down at the coming week of toil. No villages, except for those
two over there, their hue the hue of the soil, to remind you that they
were fashioned from the same dust (in the meantime they had also
been conquered and had returned to dust, so that only the shades
of buildings testified to their existence). They shifted their eyes from
the nearby hills to the distant hills, and pursued with their gaze the
meandering course of that sizeable wadi, which though low brought
law and order to the spurs of the hills round about, and to the criss-
cross of cultivation.

Already evening, everything deserted. Withdrawn into
silence.

But by this time the little man of the group had taken out a
map and unrolled it, and with it spread before him he pointed now
forward at the landscape, now downward at the map, explaining
that this here, at this spot: that's us. And that, there is El-Quf, and
here, just at this spot, over there, on that hill, yeah, that's Hirbet Um-
Rish, and here's the path, here—that's it. And from this point to the
road—three kilometers.

They took another look at the terrain. Not much visibility
straight ahead. And sideways, the little, furry hills slithered down to
the canyon. In one place, the canyon cleft the bank to bare the white of
its stone soul, and immediately set bunches of dusky brush all around
that the soul be not naked. Then silence was heard, spreading out and
flowering over the warm fields to the farthest limits of the cultivated
land, rising and falling in accordance with the contours, reaching
out to pour itself like a soundless wind over the desolation of rolling

expanses, until it became so broad and unfathomable that, without knowing when, and without any obvious connection with anything in particular, you suddenly began to feel like a lamb left behind, tiny and far off and lonely, or like a tamarisk tree in the wilderness. Fear sweeps in lightly, but worry spreads—there's enemy here somewhere. Someone unseen sees you square in the open. And you can no longer help hearing that old orchestra which now begins—properly concealed, of course—its old song in you, despite all that has passed and all you have learned: that song of the battlefield coming up close, silent song of the heart, unwanted but undeniable.

But the little one went on pointing forward and explaining that there were no difficulties in the last kilometer (except for the wadi in front of the main road opposite Tel Abu-Shiñ), and that beyond the road is not our problem: that's where Shmulik's boys take over. The first two kilometers or so are ours. "This is going to be a real dark night," said the little one, wrinkling his brow and the end of his nose, which he lifted to sniff the air and sky, as if seeking approval of his estimate of the darkness: "We have to get everything ready in advance."

Of all the five, the only ones who kept up with the little fellow on the map, on the ground and in his explanations were he himself and another rumpled, skinny guy. The other three turned aside casually to busy themselves with cigarettes, lighting them and muttering a few words, which developed into head-shakes and sputterings of smoke; but, although their lazy glances went no further than the vehicle below—that little Jeep waiting silently by the crossroads, as if restraining itself from another burst of motion and at the same time as if in a daydream—one of the three turned and lackadaisically inquired:

"Well, what about that road?"

"The road," replied the little one without turning, "is not in our hands. There's a lot of traffic there during the day, but at night, nothing. Just let's not do anything to get them worried, and let's not have any chance meetings with strange travelers. One lousy shepherd could spoil everything. There may be mines where we cross the road—we're not sure."

No, you're not even sure that the place where you're perched like a goat is not within some mortar's range, or set straight in a machine gun's line of fire. Nevertheless your mind has already begun to organize the place, getting things arranged. And what had been no more than abstract signs and marks on a map, or strips of light and shade, a kind of fantastic carpet done by a wildly imaginative weaver of air-reconnaissance photos, has begun to seem real in the lines of the fields, the windings of the wadi and the course of the road, as they went on until vanishing in the horseshoe bends of the gulleys, which were ploughed and kerneling sorghum; the red lines on the map became the contours of the hills, and the dotted lines were now one or another of those paths whose appearance and vanishment bore witness to the wisdom of their course, chosen by generations of learned feet crossing from fields to home and from home to fields. And the more you got things in order, everything set in its place, the better you began to feel, until it was about time to go out there and get started.

But you couldn't satisfy this guy. The problem, in his opinion, was the road, so why not start there, with the weakest link of the chain. And the others seemed to agree, for they, too, shrugged off their comfortable indifference and would have gotten to the heart of the matter, were it not for that little fellow, who was dressed in ill-fitting, faded dungarees, which would have given him the appearance of an inflated wineskin, his trousers draggling limply on the ground and making wrinkled rings about his ankles, while his bear-like hands would have been entirely engulfed in the ample dens of his shirt sleeves, had he not quick-thinkingly fastened a broad, revolver-slanted leather belt tightly to his belly, with the rest of the garment bunched up above this strip of corset like a full tire, thus doing nothing to diminish the roundness and extent of his belly; and had he not turned up his sleeves and doubled them back to a point below his elbows, displaying his short, thick, hairy forearms. But those were the arms that held the map firmly against the provocative and tricky wind, and the little fellow's opinion was held just as firmly. Without heeding the challenge of that partisan of the road, he dismissed all apprehensions in brief: the road is none of our business. However the way from here up to the road is no one else's business but ours.

No doubt that mutterer was a good fellow and even though he did not relent but went on muttering out of the side of his mouth about the foolishness of not beginning down there and saving the finish for here (so as to be sure everything was finished and done with), he obeyed and started down to the Jeep. But then the skinny guy, he of the wiry hair, had something to say; he had come to the conclusion that the route should be planned not along the crest of the hill, as was marked in advance on the map, but rather in the valley, a natural shield against observation and shelter from fire, in case the worst came to the worst, and it would be a good idea to look and see where that gully over there, for example, led.

This was too much for the descending grumbler: "So you want to run around gullies to see where they're going. Well don't, you can count on their getting to the Mediterranean." "Or to the Dead Sea," put in the fourth of the group, a tall person whose accent immediately betrayed his origin. "Or to Egypt," continued the descanter, who being mustached stroked the length of his pride with his left thumb, but a bit too quickly, moving first from his nostrils to the left, then to the right, so that it was understandable why, when in Tel Aviv he told stories of his patrols, he was regarded as a real wit: only now he had regained his good mood and, as he turned back toward the others, he threw them a sneer before mounting the Jeep.

"We'll look into that too," said the little fellow. "The line of advance will be this path, this way south. We'll use the gully if we can. And if not, we'll take the upper route. Now let's go!"

"Perhaps you remembered the lime?" the skinny guy said again, being apparently a man of stubborn views.

"No, but we do have paper ribbons," replied the little fellow who, sitting down efficiently and diligently behind the wheel, turned on the engine and looked around to see if everything was in its place.

"There's nothing like lime," said the skinny one, inserting one leg after the other into the Jeep: "planting piles of white stones, or sowing a white strip behind you."

"Like in the fairytale," said the one who had this far been silent; "when the children went on scattering seeds behind them to find their way home, and then the birds came and ate them all up, dammit, go slow or you'll get that dust up again!"

It was no use, neither the request nor its execution. The Jeep had hardly moved, circling easily away from the road covered with pulverized, floury dust, when enormous bubbles looked up from below and swelled into dizzying eddies which subsided almost immediately due to the sudden halt of the Jeep. The little fellow jumped out briskly and started piling up stones on the spot, and the skinny guy, catching on quickly, shifted the stilts that rustled in the expanses of his almost empty khaki trousers, and got out to help him, whereas the three others, who had not troubled to move, immediately assumed preoccupied expressions, looking carefully all around, in front and behind.

Behind them rose the mound of white, calcareous soil, thorn-gripped, with its high, wrinkled dome looking something like a pallid ulcer, its swollen roundness walling off the horizon, a possible ancient city in its entrails; but before them was only the gentle rise of a hill-slope, no more than a field ploughed last year whose borders were this year's sorghum crop. Meanwhile the dust they had stirred up in that half-minute drive dragged behind and slipped away lazily, its bowed, decrepit head collapsing along the length of the road, till the spot where it was swallowed up between two spurs that fell into each other's arms and shut out the world.

"Okay," said the little fellow, when they had moved off again: "let's go up and take a look. Tzvialeh and I will go down to that gully, and you"—he turned to the back—"start the marking with piles of stones like that one. Make it an easy road, as simple as possible, and clearly marked."

"What about the others?" inquired the mustached fellow, who liked work as long as it was divided up between as many participants as possible.

"They'll be along at eight," said Tzvialeh, the skinny one, "and we'll spread them out along the road. At nine the cover goes out to take the strong points along the road and to block it off. If all goes well the convoy will get here by eleven. We're just a little too late with everything!"

"If I had my way," said the mustachio, "we would have brought the convoy through now. Not before and not after but exactly at sunset. From a distance they wouldn't be able to make out anything, but we'd see enough up close, and we wouldn't need any of this muddling marking business. You only need guts, that's all. Right?" As no one was kind enough to agree with or contradict any of his statements, he repeated his proposal from the beginning, in full detail, enumerating on the one hand, the advantages of twilight, and on the other, the supremacy of guts, and how it feels to be a hero. He would have enlarged upon the latter had not the Jeep stopped once more.

"We get out here," said the little fellow, "and we climb up to the crest of the ridge by foot, and low."

Appreciating his good judgment and his knack of overlooking nothing, they got out and followed like a flock of geese, waddling over the hard clods and bending somewhat over the insistent ground. But he looked around at them and, while unholstering his pistol, cocking it and putting it back, said in his usual tone of seriousness: "What's going on! Spread out, load your weapons, and keep your eyes open—you don't know what's up there!" And that old song which habit had not yet spoiled, the melody of a battlefield so near, swelled up and died down again into an abstract entity, the existence of which one might not accept but was forced, nevertheless, to admit, and to keep on.

Then Tzvialeh, the skinny one, called out in his deep voice: "Ah, here it is!" and pointed to a narrow thread of trodden dust paling among the thorns and stones, which had seemed more substantial when observed from the top of the mound, and still more definite and real when pointed out on the map, not maybe yes and maybe no, as when passing it by with too high a step and losing it again as soon as you have discovered it. So in order to corroborate its identity, they made another pile of stones, and thus there came into being, in the expanse of the desolate fields, two points, between which some imaginary line ventured to come into being, the straightest between them and therefore the shortest as we all know, and the foundation of the route which was as yet unseen, but which had already won its existence: the route of the convoy.

It turned out, as usual, that the summit of the ridge was more distant than they had thought, and that a few hundred paces further up the hump stretched a tract of waste, wild with stones and thorn bushes spreading out over the head of the hill like a spiky hairdo, greenish brown; and that same path threaded its way into the thick of the brush (which here and there was knee-high, with reddish ground peeping through), infiltrating but lost in the end. The route would have to be diverted, apparently, to the edge of the patch (which made an easily remembered mark without the need for piles of stones), so immediately they gathered rocks, laying them upon the face of the boulder which had been, with admirable strength and skill, uprooted, upturned and put firmly in its place by that valiant mustachio, who after having worked and won, brushed the dirt off his hands, smoothed his moustache as usual, and said: "What's the result? That we're bringing the convoy through on the same side that faces the enemy!"—lit a cigarette with a dexterous flick of the match, which flared up with a whistle like an arrow from the bow, and exhaled a jet of thick smoke from his mouth and nostrils, as if his moustache had caught fire. The little fellow, who had spread a map on the ground and, squatting on his heels, was examining it, and the contours, and his compass, and the area in front of him as well, also stuck a cigarette in his mouth, held out his hand to mustachio in mute request for a light, and fixed the gaze of his deep-set eyes on the skinny guy, who was standing there diligently and obliviously picking his nose: "Eh, Tzvialeh, what's your opinion?" Tzvialeh understandably enough promptly recalled his proposal made down below to look for a road in the gully, and announced that it was still valid.

The danger of a conflagration was already hanging in the air. Crisscrossed for the fire were all the tactical principles for movement along bad roads in enemy territory, a subject upon which many things could undoubtedly be said and weighty arguments deployed—but time was pressing, and the little fellow nipped the argument in the bud by turning and going back with Tzvialeh to the Jeep to ride down to the gully, leaving the three others to their labors with sticks and stones, so that if no road were found below, their time at any rate would not have been wasted. Nevertheless, understandably enough, no sooner had the Jeep moved off than that stifled flame burst forth, as they rolled and carried the stones on the edge of the brush, and apart from the simple solutions apparent to any layman, other, surprising possibilities were raised—if only one had a little time for thought and were provided with a few materials and tools—bold and captivating solutions, with bridges or without, with tunnels or without, even with the aid of water currents controlled by electric power, if only one had the will.

Trying to avoid unnecessary jolts, the Jeep slid down to the gully at the foot of the hill. Then it butted into the sorghum field, scattering seeds from the ears bowed under their own weight, rocked on all fours over the crumbly clods of earth, and drowned amid the tall stalks and yellowing leaves—and immediately there was a sense of harvest and harvester and an indefinite sorrow went buzzing and fading away. After that they broke through and emerged into the open field, turned to the right, and thereafter tore along, picking up speed, as the furrows in this section ran in the same directions their wheels.

"Say, this road is great!" said skinny Tzvialeh, his hair streaming in the wind as if it was going to fly off; his neighbor at the wheel pursed his lips and nodded his head in assent, calling attention to what was still to come.

And indeed, the hills were closing in and narrowing the gully, and in this narrow gap they were again confronted by yellowing sorghum, which had been sown by one who did not consider it a little acre forsaken by God; they drove through to the edge on the boundary of the steeply rising slope, whereupon the gully swerved to the left, encircling the foot of the hill, and separated into a number of branches, no more than winding channels, which if one pursued them would only remove him still farther from the line of advance, and even if one were to turn back later on, slanting back through the valley in the direction from which he had deviated, it would be a long, as well as dangerous, detour—so it seemed they would have to give up the idea. The little fellow pursed his lips and looked at Tzvialeh, as if there were anything more to say, and the latter, who felt somewhat to blame, immediately bolstered himself with forced enthusiasm, and declared: "Let's give it a try. You've got to climb a bit, but afterward, there's no doubt about it, you go straight down to the valley after that junction of the channels and you're right on the road. It's perfectly clear to me!" But as he spoke so emphatically, he turned aside so as not to meet the little fellow's eye and his wrinkled brow, which was a quiet but very definite answer in itself. "Oh, all right," he reconsidered and went on: "It's too bad there's no time… it's perfectly clear to me!" "There really is no time and it'll be a pitch-black night," replied the little fellow, and he turned around in the furrows, crossed the fading yellow sorghum, waking a whole row of ears from their dreams of harvest, and sped back through the field to the broad road of dust opposite the mound, passing their own pile of stones, which at that moment began serving its purpose, and continued straight to the mound opposite, thus marking the first sign of wheels on the new route.

こぇ

After that, they all got up and went along the hill by the side of the tract of waste, and reached the peak; immediately a world of hills was revealed, and to the right that strange mound, which was like a baton lifted: the enemy is looking! They lay down flat on their bellies and scanned their surroundings, while the sinking sun filled the entire west with a roar of streaming sparks, tumbling as they blazed and scattered, and its reddening wheel, behind a bank of gilded dust, quivered incessantly, flickering and blinding. The soil beneath them was warm and chunky, and the hill's hump slouched on, forward, its slopes dividing on each side, flowing down gently in easy, peaceful folds trimmed with lacy fringes of gold—the oat-like wild grasses, woven between them, about a foot above the ground, transparent in a trembling halo of light, delicate golden-yellow bells, a fresh and heartwarming tremor suspended in air; but the halo of husks ended in the channel of the wadi which was thereafter ploughed along its entire length, with clumps of stones in the furrows; and further off, those stalks of sorghum were crowded with ripe and overripe ears, with always as some unfaded pale green here and there among the gold, and an unreaped sadness. Corresponding with this ridge but curving toward it on a slant were other ridges on both sides, crested rows of low sister hills, full of good cinnamon soil, warm summer earth, land of the free winds, eroded by mountain streams, mixed with loess swift breezes had brought, and brushed by torrents.

But only go a little further east, the entire flock of hills immediately bunched together and climbed higher, all disorder and division: the backbone of the ridge disintegrated, its vertebrae split and sharp, the rocks showing through like whitening bones. Everything there was bare and scarred; olive trees gripping the smooth bareness of the stone; narrow gullies massed with debris and bent by shattered boulders, and bushes of the purple Abraham's balm in the winding riverbed; and at last the horizon, bluish, marked by a hard line broken here and there by a smudge of copse, or a clump of village houses and deep blue shadows of drifting clouds.

On the other hand, to the right, as one turns to the west, the hills slumped over, bowing deeply in their expanse, and a little further to the right they ceased altogether, replaced by a broad, recumbent plain; there another world of fields breathed rays of warmth upon its belly, a plain of gleaming flickers in the afternoon, and in the evening a silent abyss of dancing, gilt chips, in the declining wind, in the silencing of the mischievous dust, all those gleaming, watery mirages whose course runs where none can tell.

They lay on their bellies on the top of the elongated hill and observed the hills about them. A great wide world. You breathe in a feeling that perhaps you were intruding into a domain not yours, attached to a land too large, too distant, alien. The fields were hostile to uninvited guests. The smell of their husbandmen still gripped their earth, that withered crone whose heart still belonged to those who had ploughed her. Thus this naked fear, twitching and fluttering like a kerchief fallen in flight. A wide world. Fields, hills. Scorched, dusty horizons reflected desolation. Perhaps you should have turned back and cleared out of here at once, and gone back home? You had this prickling feeling that you were not hidden, but very much exposed. No one knew where the trouble would start, but it will start. There's too much light on us here. (How much firepower can we get from three submachine guns and two pistols?) Dammit!

So eyes were drawn more and more to the right, to the enemy's posts, immersed in the western glow. Those illuminated columns of dust, burgeoned for a moment, were now transformed under the sunset clouds, the hues of the world and their load of longings and yearnings, and have become simply clouds in sunset—only at the very center of this scenery for a would-be drama dwelt the generalized entity called the enemy, in essence only a vague fear together with an express fear, and also a kind of curiosity as well as some other, unknown fear, and a misgiving as to whether it would not be worthwhile, after all, to make a detour so that you should not be discovered; not without a certain vindictive craving to get up and give it to them if they fall into your hands, or, at least, tease until they split. Dammit.

This sensation affected them so much that one of them, who had started to say something, began in a faint whisper. "What are you whispering for?" said the one with the moustache. "Whispering! You can yell, and even get up and stand on your head—there isn't a dog to hear you. What do you think, Rubinstein?" he demanded, seeking an expert opinion, as he shook off grains of soil and winkled out thorns that had stuck to him—"He's three kilometers away from the enemy and he whispers: pst... pst! What are you so nervous for?" But Rubinstein—the little fellow, of course—smiled and nodded his head: "There's really nothing to be afraid of here," said he. "Only by the main road when we get there—that's where we have to be quiet." "Oh, that's another matter," said the other, contentedly stroking his moustache, "but whispering here! Well, there's a limit!"

But that Hanan who had whispered a moment before (and one look at him, even in the twilight, was enough to testify that this was no Hanan—but plain Hans!) had not yet been delivered of what he had to say: "Wait a minute," Hanan continued, "tell me, now, how did we get our backside kicked up there?" "You don't know!" said the mustachio (whose trademark would very soon be swallowed up by twilight, and he would then have to be recognized by his big body and the white *kaffiyah*, an Arab kerchief which he wore hanging loosely about his neck, or, of course, by the very fact of his being no one else but that Gavriel—surely you guessed it was he and no other—of whom you have no doubt heard in one of the numerous stories describing one Gavrosh, or Gavri, or Gavrilla, or even Gavriella—depending on the subject, the hour and the taste of the narrator—who was always none other than this big mustachioed fellow standing there adorned with a *kaffiyah* wound, in various shapes, this way and that, round his neck): "You see that mound? That nipple? They went out to take it and the school building by the road. Everything went well until they started clobbering them with two-pounders and Vickers guns just like that. And that's how it was. Four of us caught it. And wounded. We were lucky to come out of it even like that. So what? Nothing. So they turned round once." "Poor bastards," Hanan shook his head, panting. "Dammit, we haven't got anything!" he added after a silence. "Artillery is what we need here," was Gavri's verdict. They gazed over there. Streaks of light shimmered as usual round the mound, like little flies round a sheep at sunset (just try to touch that sheep).

"That was the third time we got it there," said Rubinstein, raising his eyebrows and wrinkling his forehead deeply.

"Yeah," muttered Hanan, nodding his head as if something had become clear to him.

"Don't worry," said Gavri, very confidently, "every dog has his day!"

"To hell with them!" sighed Hanan from the bottom of his heart.

Of them all, only Tzvialeh lay still, warming his belly on

the soft, dusty, scented earth, fragrant with the dust of clay and he chewed a dusty stalk (with its chalky, not unpleasant, taste recalling some memory of childhood), keeping himself withdrawn from the conversation, and from the business of standing up and everything, going out by himself, slipping away with pleasure, silently escaping to the expanses of the great universe that gradually opened up all around as the sunset became a reality, steadily losing its strangeness and beginning to be grasped and understood. The sheep-like hills. The flat and crumbling ridges. The fervent joy of unlimited expanses. That friable soil, made up entirely of small, pea-like clods which were nothing but fine dust burnt by sun and wind into a flour of granulose clots, which—if you were to step on it or to crumble it in your palm to feel and enjoy its quality, or to put it to your nose to breathe the scent of the granary, the dust of harvest and threshing, the smell of bread and satiation—would disintegrate instantly into dusty powder, dissolved and dispersed. This is what went shooting out from under the wheels in streams of dust, this is what was so easily seduced by every riotous and licentious gust to dance off, capering higher and higher, in wide frolicsome circles, with chaff and thistles, twirling faster and faster like a top in the fields, and then becoming one big living thing in the empty expanses, and falling suddenly into silent, arid hollows, where it died with a minimum of convulsions—this was arable land which a single shower could liquefy in a viscid past, with a good smell of wet clay, the fragrance of moist soil, renewing youthful loves, and with another shower or two it would be all weak, treacherous, swampy mud, with depths here and there, enormous impassable areas into whose mire a world could sink, with unseen swelling udders; sucking and absorbent, the streams in the gullies, and winter over all, and the green of verdant vegetation. Until the coming of summer. With the very first hot spells, this will be a frowning, riven soil, clefts crisscrossing it with endless squares and cracked tiles, scaly, sharp-edged concaves, yellowing all. Only a drop here and there, oozing out of tiny flakes of soil, could join the insubstantial particles in warm, soft, crumbly, cinnamon-colored clods, which when the time came would carry the naked soles of reapers, who cut the ears of the sorghum behind them and pluck that last sesame, as well as the feet of cloven-hoofed sheep which sow numerous olive-like droppings and, later, legions of grayish thistles, carthamus and thorns branching wide, and ridolfia and fragrant fennel shading, and patches of carmel thorn spread out on the slope, and below, the screw bean, that miniature acacia, which, until it is covered by dust, infuses a touch of green into the brownness and, together with the gold of curly St. John's wort, proclaims the nature of summer, so that you have a hankering to walk here, to walk in these straight tracks, and to leave the path—any path—for the bare, naked fields, brownish, warm and golden under that oppressive furnace above, blue and reddish, burning and quivering with blinding flickers of light on high —to walk and sweat and rejoice and raise your arms to the full breadth of the wide expanses, and to be ever a small, invisible ant within the broad, empty fields. Oh, how many fields there are to walk in!

"Okay," Rubinstein got back to business. "Now we have to find where the path leaves the thorns," (the shorthand for all varieties of arborial growth being simply "tree", for all types of bushes, "thorn", and anything lower and greener, "grass", of course—a most economical and practical brevity). And that Hanan, Rubinstein thought, had better pile up some more stones at this point together with Tzvialeh, while the others go out to look for the rest of the trail and mark the next point, so as not to lose time. The hour of sunset was already approaching. The golden dusk darkened, deepening in color. The few feathers that remained above suddenly blushed, with a kind of enviable innocence, and below, the stones on the sides of the hill were gradually revealed, and rocks sprouted up, thorny burnets settled about each stone, like sheep around the trough.

After some time, the lost track was found awaiting them by the edge of the patch of waste. As soon as they reached it, it smiled at them and continued along its ancient path, a path of asses and plough-oxen, and silent tillers of the soil, who walked barefoot, rose early in the morning and labored late into the evening. It continued further along the contours of the hill, keeping to the shoulder of the ridge, which was distorted here by a slight curve, and stretched two arms to the west, as if in a deep, formal bow; then continued from shoulder to shoulder on the heights of the curve, skipping over the sources of the many mischievous rills, which spread out like a fan gathered together below in the single trunk of the wadi which, as it deepened in its westerly course, widened and became flatter, the hills retreating on each side, until over there, at the cleft between the concave ranges, it lay flat, a straight channel, at the end of which extended broad, darkening plains, into which it disappeared for parts unknown and vanished after a last little wag from side to side.

But if a man and his beast could easily make their way along a path like this, skipping here and deviating there, without even noticing the unevenness of the way, not so tonight: you're going to have to bring through five and ten-ton trucks, without lights, as rapidly as possible, with drivers who are not the best in the world and who have never, just as you had never before, been here, who have never even heard of the place, and who are in the long run nothing but one big soulful mouth of tired, nervous, grumbled cursing: I want to see the truck that can cross these crevices and boulders. So, what next? To the left, as you have observed, is no road at all. To the right—well that's already on the other side of the hills, right under the enemy's nose, within the range of any and all machine guns (apart from the enormous trenches typical of the flat places in the wadis), and we've got to get going, man, it's getting dark now.

Here Tzvialeh came up from below, with the radiance of the sunset gleaming in his hair as in filaments of wild grain, and he brought an idea. It was a simple one: a little lower down, to the west, the wadi became shallower, at the place where it emerged from the precipitous concave slopes; there we'll turn to the right (stretching out some paper ribbons) and that will be the crossing; we'll put up two piles of stones there and cross between them, then we'll turn left again and take the path we left behind at the point where it enters that sorghum field, and we should be getting started already. Of course he had already managed to get there and back. And if we have to sweat a little here and there with the hoes—it could be worse. We start from here and turn there. It's too bad there's no chalk.

Naturally, there was nothing to be said against simple logic. Rubinstein went to bring the Jeep from the rear, while the others departed to collect stones and pile them up. The slope was entirely covered with dry, villainous thorns, and small, treacherous clumps of stones; they descended in a line and pushed through the thorns to the slope of the wadi. The first veils of darkness hung in the air. Beyond the curve of the pass, the sloping spurs of the hill showed up darkly beneath the demise of sunset. An adventurous tickle lit them up in their descent. What a prospect—opening a road, wandering in secret valleys, in whatever was still hidden in the depth of night with heavy vehicles following at your heels or whatever had survived of your feet... It was hot, and beads of sweat stood out on the backs of their necks. One gap of laziness in the marking and the convoy is in for a hot spot. But no. You are filled with a desire to work and do a good job, so that everything will go smoothly. A feeling of helpful cooperation springs up, very like that of the union songs they used to sing, which one always wanted to imagine already a reality.

※

At first the wadi, as was to be expected, disappeared, and no one knew where it had gone. And when it was found, its banks were dug out like cliffs. He ran quickly along the precipitous edge, uncomfortably wondering whether or not they might conclude that he had misled them and blame him for the mishap, and he was already thinking of excuses for himself, although he had only just seen the place. The uneasiness hung heavily upon him until at once the place appeared, lying before him exactly as he had described it: perfectly shallow and open for passage. "That's my boy," cried Tzvialeh, "here it is!" And he hid his merriment with a complaint about the hoes, that deficiency called an "entrenching tool", much to the agreement of all. Well. We'll put the one pile here. The next one a bit further on. Those are trucks, five and ten-tonners, and drivers who are not the best... like that until here. *And they crossed the Jordan in its midst*—what Jordan but the wadi! So what do we have? From up there among the thorns (still lit up in the sunset afterglow) till here—a straight road, a single line. Now let's get with those paper ribbons. It's really something. A bit of white paper and you've saved a fumbling convoy, rescued a vast area from siege, given it bread and clothing and strength to endure—a bit of white paper! Good to work here, a war in which all you do is open a new road in the land—this is something else again! We've got to raise it a bit, so that they will see it clearly. This is where the Jeep will descend and be the first to cross over, a pioneer. And that, perhaps, is the true meaning of the word "pioneer"?—it's a good feeling!

"Well, how is it?" Tzvialeh greeted Rubinstein enthusiastically as soon as he got out of the Jeep, fresh from its maiden voyage during which it had navigated the crossing effortlessly. "Not bad," the other replied. "We'll put a man or two here to guide the drivers, another on top, another by the stones, another near the thorns, and we'll need two or three more between the road and over there—how many does that come to —say six or seven." "And do you think anything could go wrong on a road like this?" Tzvialeh would not give up until his handiwork had been formally praised. "No," said the little one, "it'll be all right. I don't know how many men we'll get to help." "But this crossing," Tzvialeh insisted, "doesn't it seem to have been made just for us?" "As long as one truck doesn't get a blowout just here," interjected Gavriel, who had come down with the other two, rolling out the ribbon of paper in silence, putting little stones on it here and there to keep it from being blown away, and though thorn-rankled they received continuous guidance and care from mustachioed Gavri, as they labored bent and straightened, in and out of alternate darkness and twilight. "Just let one of them stall," asserted Gavri, "and you can say goodbye to the whole business. They should have been going through right now! Enough light for us to go by and enough darkness not to be seen from a distance!" But this was already old news. They jumped onto the Jeep, which immediately started off the hill to return to the shoulder and take up the abandoned path, halting once by a large boulder which they pushed upright, burdening its heavy head still further with additional stone markers; and then with a surprising hop-skip-and-jump they reached the track, as it was about to be swallowed up in the sorghum field and the thickening darkness.

"Hey, it's another 'Burma Road'," [4] said Tzvialeh with a kind of sudden joy.

"My foot!" Gavri retorted at once. "This thing, 'Burma Road'? Were you there? I was there a little after it was opened. This is a super highway compared to what was there. You don't know what you're saying! What a job! Bulldozers, pneumatic drills, everything. Not like here, rolling a couple of stones this way and a couple more that way, and there's your road."

"But—"

"No buts. You are ignorant."

"I'm only saying…"

"Say, what's wrong with this guy, always saying something."

"At night… Using this road at night…"

"Oh!" Gavri conceded. "That depends on the drivers. There are all kinds of drivers. With this kind I wouldn't travel by day either…" He was silent, then continued: "Say, the best thing is to jump into your Jeep and off you go, and you don't have to count on anyone, and you don't have to worry about any ho-ho boys dragging along behind you like zombies!"

It was not dark, and you could still see the land swelling beyond the sorghum field. Lights flickered, and you could clearly see how distant it was, how many fields and lands there were between. Flat expanses, now pacified in the passing of heat, of the dust pranks, the work of man, all transitory details. The traces of pink faded and darkened in sudden leaps, as if one veil after another had in fact suddenly been dropped. Immediately you realized your home was not to be found in all these expanses which, broad and distant though they were, formed only a negligible part of the distance separating you from home—but this was incidental. For the job itself gripped you with enthusiasm. The smell of the night earth, and the atmosphere

---

4   Nickname given to a side-route opened by the army to beleaguered Jerusalem.

of the place, and the ripe sorghum made you forget that all these belonged to someone else and merely reminded you of those others which were your own back before all this, before it started. Again the smell of earth, and again the smell of straw, as if the whole war were a passing dream... They set to, and marked this spot as well, and in the meantime they tried to level the ground with their spades and with stones to plug up the hidden crevice at the beginning of the field. Then, with their feet dangling outside, they rode on, through the heart of the dark gold, somewhat melancholy sorghum, and continued along the easy path, which was, again, like the return from the fields in the evening and... Then they left the sorghum and the field became visible again. But here, it turned out, the hill had suddenly gone wild; the rocks stood out like dark patches in the dusk, and the adjacent slope was cut off from the left and plummeted to the bottom, bushes blackening every side.

They tried to go on, but immediately halted at a dusky spike of rock. When they retreated and detoured, a precipitous slope opened wide. They went back and detoured to the right, but every beginning ended soon enough in the same way, until they stopped these gyrations, and got down to scout around and look for a way out. The darkness was thickening rapidly. The range of visibility was coming close quickly to set up a narrow, circular prison. "To hell with it," said Gavri, "couldn't we have come out here a day before? I just love this 'last-minute' system of yours!"

"Listen, Gavrosh!" said Tzvialeh briefly but with meaningful emphasis. "We've already chewed our cud on that. And it's been agreed that we can't move around here a single minute more than necessary before the time comes, not do anything to arouse attention in any way in this area—that's the order (and besides, haven't we gotten kicked around enough and paid too much? It's time we learned our lesson, don't you think?)"

"When I tell you to start from the end and work your way back," the other persisted, still angry, "you come along with your maps and your snapshots—you can shove 'em. All I need is my eyes and my feet and my hands!"

"And your tongue too," Tzvialeh couldn't help retorting.

"The maps here," intervened Rubinstein, "are really not correct, they're not accurate. This wadi, for instance, isn't marked at all. And in our air photos a bit of light got in just here. But we'll scout around for a while and find a route. Another kilometer and a half to the main road. And only one or two hundred difficult meters on this slope."

"Not counting that wadi." And they were silent for a moment considering the seriousness and urgency of the position.

"Listen to me," said Gavriel. "Listen to me too, for once: let's follow the old track, roll a few rocks aside, straighten a few crevices, bring each truck through separately, just as slow as you like —but don't let's wander about in the dark. That track has been followed for hundreds of years and they didn't use it for nothing!"

"We'll look all around. There aren't many alternatives, with the mountains on one side and the enemy on the other," said Rubinstein.

And he started turning as he spoke. "We'll pile up stones every few steps and mark the way with the paper strips—we've no choice!" said someone—no, it was Hanan (that same Hans), licking an injured ankle.

"Bunch of chickens," snorted Gavri. "Satisfied with anything right from the start, the first thing you do is find any old piece of consolation. The road isn't a road, so you make a pile of stones and there's your marker, you're happy. The road's blocked—so you crawl round the side on your bellies and you're satisfied. You'll be two hundred years old before you die." This, of course, was food for a lively conversation, but Tzvialeh forestalled it by crooning to Gavri, in a fox-trot passion:

> It—could—happen—to any—one,
> My honey...

thus blasting a wonderful opportunity for a debate, whose contestants could have drawn upon sundry episodes, both from the history of

Jewish settlement in the last few decades, and from various concepts
gathered from flowery speeches and weedy poems, uttered while waiting for the tables to be moved back so that all might dance the *hora*.
But the darkness was thickening and the road was no road, and there
was no help in sight, and dammit they had to find something!

Tzvialeh turned aside and went rapidly down the slope on
those stilts of his that rustled in his trousers. After having descended
a few steps he was devoured in darkness. Immediately he stumbled
on some protuberance and was compelled to run so as not to topple
over. At one point he lifted his feet to step over some black spot
which looked like a hole, but was only some stupid bush, sticking
out its sneaky claw and tearing a flap of khaki from his trousers. So
he began to skip to the side of the slope over the pits of the wadi,
but slipping pebbles tripped him. When he had climbed back on all
fours to the bank, he could not find a safe footing, and raising his
eyes, it seemed he had gone further than he intended. He tried to fix
his gaze on the Big Dipper, but there was not yet enough darkness
to project its majestic radiance, come late this evening. So he continued still faster, jumping here and hopping there over what appeared
to be at once both a knoll and a hollow. It seemed he was lost. So
he was, gotten mixed up and just plain lost. Amusing in his babyish
persistence, he had gone on and on, as if to prove it to someone, and
in the end was caught in a trap. Retracing his steps he leaped into
the floury gully, where he felt as if he had been closed up in a tomb.
He went on stumbling, almost running, and shedding as he went
his baseless fabric of a vision. When he regained the bank, he found
himself standing in the middle of a field of sorghum. The question
was which field of sorghum. The hilltop to the right had retained
a degree of luminosity, and the edge of its hump was delineated by
a sharp shadow. He realized he was sweating and at the same time
breathing in a feeling of wonderment, a murmuring excitement rising
in him. Something which was in the multitude of days and events
forgotten —even the forgetting had been forgotten—was now about
to be grasped in an instant. And it was preceded by a special sort of
stimulation inhaled and filling his lungs. It was so clear, so transparent

and obvious that the funny thing was you didn't know what to say about it, even though you felt it flowing within you like the waters of the brook. He licked his lips. He was alone and solitary in the world, standing somewhere at the foot of a hill in a sorghum field, one man in the darkness who had actually discovered nothing, having had access to no particular source of wisdom. And at the same time he felt the presence of some thing or feeling, a wonderful sensation, spreading and moving, and at the same time so warm. He regretted turning back and finding the others again: it was as if he had gone far away and had arrived in a new land, a place for which he had always inexplicably longed. This was something of his own, hoped for. He shivered with the strength of a new vision suddenly perceived, and loneliness emerged from all sides to embrace him. But he recovered, scratched his nose, smiled a little to himself, and began to go back, breathing deeply. Immediately he remembered and looked around him. Say, there's a field here—he decided with unusual calmness and clarity—we can make a road here too. Something began singing in him, he could not tell what exactly, but he wanted to find it again, to continue with it, and could not. Embarrassed, and a bit ashamed, he jumped forward and started climbing.

"Hey," he called, in order to find his bearings, a strange and echoing cry in the thick silence.

"Who's braying there like an ass?" a voice replied from close by, and at once a dark thick splotch appeared, the identity of which was unmistakable: "What's all that noise? You picked a great place to start yelling."

"Sh-sh," said Tzvialeh, "don't shout, I've found a road."

"Around the world and back again?"

"No, perfectly simple: straight down from here. A turn here (we'll have to mark it very clearly), afterward another one, and you go on into the sorghum down there." It was warm at this height, and it was not clear what all the excitement had been down below. In the distance the last of the dim orange flickers expired. You wanted to say something friendly, to be immersed in work to the point of oblivion, bound up closely with all the others, who couldn't imagine how good it was to be with them. The rumbling of the Jeep approached and as if the end of a tunnel had suddenly opened up before them, here it was, right alongside. One of the figures in it said: "Well, up to this point you can get through somehow."

"Somehow won't do," replied Rubinstein at the wheel. "You have to get there easily. And how is it further on, Tzvialeh?"

"We'll make a miniature Castel[5] here," replied Gavriel contentedly, and it seemed as if they were all united and working together, each supporting the other, each understanding the other, as if they were singing together, and there was no need at all to talk about it.

Some time passed before they had learned what sort of place this was (though by daylight they were sure to be, as usual, quite surprised), and had set up not a few piles of stones, and had rolled away some boulders, while arguing about the arc of a curve which a good-sized truck could make without turning around completely or slipping down the slope; and they unrolled the paper strips, dug here and there with their little spades, and made a trial trip with the Jeep to demonstrate various principles of road engineering. It was clear they had accomplished nothing, for to take out small stones, and uproot and roll away large ones, was not enough. You remembered the size of a truck, its length and breadth, not forgetting its weight; then you reexamined the fruits of your labors and turned away dissatisfied. You started again, working your little spade double-time—and the only apparent result was the sweat which gleamed upon you. Meanwhile the dusk was getting thicker, more oppressive.

At last a great, dense darkness materialized, the stars emerged cautiously above, and the spirit of peace rose to the horizons, waiting for the hour of its emergence, when it would make its way silently, beyond the barkings of distant dogs, far past the distant brayings, over and above the chirping of occasional crickets and the great and empty fields, silent and darkling over the face of the entire night, that young night, warm and good for love, which had just begun. It did not take you long to recall the big gate of the kibbutz, made of crossed iron bars (the lowest two pried apart for various purposes, the

5   A fortress on a hill along the road to Jerusalem.

nature of which was left unexplored, for various reasons) suspended
on two enormous iron beams, which, in a moment of nervousness,
had been enveloped in coils of barbed wire; and how the gate could
be opened just wide enough to allow two people to slip out on their
way to the fields, a young, anxious, and enviable vision (when you see
others leaving, and arousing some discomfort when it is you who are
slipping out, for who knows if there isn't some wise-guy back there,
peeping at you full of understanding, the generous results of which
will be apparent tomorrow on the face of everyone who looks at you),
swallowed up in the darkness, with who knows what awaiting them
there. A warm, young night.

But there won't be enough time to finish the job. There's
nothing to do but wait by the mound on the far side of the road.
They assembled alongside the Jeep. It was decided that Gavriel take
Hanan and the other fellow (perhaps we forgot to mention that his
name is Ya'akov, a first-class scout, nimble as a fox, and a fine fellow,
except when one of his unpredictable moods clam him up so that
not a word can be pried out of him) and start out from the sorghum
field, by now so darkened that it was indistinguishable from any
other sorghum field, to find the path, which was supposed to be a
little to the right (or a little to the left), and follow it to the road;
there they would stop a while and examine the broad wadi stretched
before the road and size up the situation, noting the possibilities of
blocking and mining the road, what places should be held by ambush,
by which route to approach the enemy's strong points that would
be seized. They were to observe, as far as possible, what the enemy
was doing in the area of the mound and along the main road, and,
above all, to mark out the route enemy road. This was a place of
possible unexpected trouble, yet it was the place where your pon-
derous convoy had to be brought through quickly. And when they
finished, they would come back here, to guide the covering force
when it arrived, and the convoy when it arrived. Whether or not to
post a man or two there, beside the road, and all other questions,
he would solve once on the spot. The password, they remembered,
was: "tonight—ours".

They reached out and groped in the piled-up interior of the Jeep until each found his soiled coat; although it was warm, they put them on, because you never knew what might happen, and besides, one felt an urge to gird oneself with something when going out to battle. Their shapes were immediately altered in the darkness, became more clumsy, lost something of themselves and put on something that was not theirs. They picked up their weapons, securing the magazines. "Wait," said Gavriel, "let's not forget to take some crackers and a few cans of juice." The earth of the field and the sorghum stems produced a scent that was long since known and enjoyed, like the scent of a field and straw stalks at night. They trembled a bit, perhaps a shiver of cold. "According to the map," said Rubinstein, "it's a straight, easy route. The hills are always on your left. Don't climb them. The road is a kilometer ahead of you." "Everything's under control," said Gavriel, twisting round to tighten his belt. This was Gavri's finest hour. Not his was this enterprise of spades and hoes, of big stones and small. Not for this had his mother borne him. "Just don't get fancy and light a cigarette beside the road—there, anyway, it's not like —" spoke up Tzvialeh. "Relax, boy," said Gavriel. "Any more good advice?" "Sure. Details later." "Awfully nice of you. Anything else, Rubinstein?" "No, that's all. The usual schedule. If those guys only get here on time." "Okay," said Gavriel, "so let's go!"

Stones grated, stalks rustled, shadows moved off, and straight away everything was engulfed, only the pallid, dark field and the black skies remaining, adorned with string of stars. The Jeep started up, turned around and began to climb. "Can't see a thing," said Rubinstein. They looked out, one this way and the other that. "Not sure if this is our route." "Wait a minute, I'll go ahead"—and Tzvialeh jumped out and sniffed in every direction. Immediately he was gripped by that sweet, languid feeling—"We're lost"—which confused things for a moment. The Jeep snorted behind him. There was a kind of hovering sadness, and you were tired of flight. He closed his eyes for a moment; circles revolved in front of him, and of his whole being nothing was left but a single tiny point which moved further off and fell into the abyss, endlessly falling—he shook himself and awoke, stepped on a few paces and collided with a heap of stones. "Hey," he called out, "it's here!" The Jeep came rattling up, its window shining faintly. He took out his handkerchief and signaled it nearer, until the Jeep reached him. Rubinstein was enthusiastic about this great discovery. "Let's fold down the windshield," he said. So they loosened the two screws that held it on each side, and both of them, with a soundless effort, pushed the windshield down to the hood of the Jeep, fixing it fast. Back inside, Tzvialeh leaned forward, his hands resting on the hood in front of him. "A bit to the left," said Tzvialeh. They made a difficult turn, and went up to the ridge of the hill, from one pile of stones to the next, the thin paper ribbon, faintly white, running beneath them, vanishing and reappearing in turn.

They navigated the Jeep from one heap of stones to the next, trying not to swerve from the previous wheel-ruts, thus deepening them and etching them clearly, Then they saw before them the yellow of the upper sorghum field, with its upright, waxy ears of grain like unlit candles, which again issued the fragrance of straw at night and the smell of dust. Now they were already at the far end, trying not to bounce over the blocked channel, starting their descent down the slanting slope to the shallows of the wadi at the designated crossing place. This of course, on reflection, led to a definite feeling of satisfaction in traveling over a route which you yourself have created from nothing, and which is now an accomplished fact, an effort that has succeeded, a goal achieved.

They went sideways round the stone alongside (better push it back another inch), passed between the two stone-pile markers at the crossing, traversed the gravel of the wadi, turned sharp right, and climbed between the dry thistles, angling toward the bare rocks above. But when they had attained the top, hoping for wider horizons, they were greeted by the rapid onset of the dark, silent as a black river. A dark land all around. Light is what everyone is afraid of. If there were any human stragglers left anywhere (hard to believe!) in the midst of the crouching, infinite darkness, they could only be waiting anxiously for some evil opportunity, their weapons in their hands. Rubinstein halted and turned off the engine, rose, and standing on his seat, observed his surroundings. "What's up?" whispered Tzvialeh. "Nothing. You can see the main road from here." At that moment a green flare sparked up in weak, spectral light, then burst overhead and split in scintillation, so that the pallid, flat outlines of fields and hills flickered and darkened, till once again that black, opaque river began to flow thickly, during which silence the report of the flare's detonation reached them strangely, necessitating a considerable will to overcome the urge to get down and hide. "Did you spot them? That's where they are," said Rubinstein, "just as we thought." "At least three kilometers, right?" "Yes, just about." "Won't they be able to distinguish the noise of the convoy when it comes?" "I don't think so, but if they do hear it, and even if they understand immediately what it is they're hearing, they won't start anything till dawn. That's how they are." "As long as someone on the lower road doesn't notice earlier, and warn them." "Yes, the road will have to be well covered."

This road—which, of course, was not even a road, but only a narrow path of crushed stones upon which no traveler would deign to ride, but would avoid or attempt to by swerving to the side as far as possible into the ditch in order not to be bounced about upon its craggy surface—this was the wreck of road which marked the boundary, the only remaining hole in the siege wall through which today's convoy must be drawn. And furthermore, whether you succeed with this convoy or not, those fellows will have caught your scent and tomorrow or the day after they are sure to occupy the route and set up posts on Tel Abu-Shin—so the hole would be closed and the country completely cut off, nothing left free for passage but the heavens above and this narrow path, and that's a fact. Listen, this convoy must get through tonight, no matter what. Do you get my meaning? Thus splendidly crowned with this important and patriotic consciousness, Tzvialeh swung his head round to another rocket, a red one, which burst in a shower much further off, beyond all the furthest of the western hills, tracing the profile of the distant horizon, and silently going out. So they went on, each occupied with the complexity of his own thoughts, until they raised their eyes and looked, and a second bump confirmed the previous one; they had deviated from the road. Where could they be but in that same rocky patch. They pulled up and reversed with such a jolt that they immediately climbed up onto a bank of stones behind them and had to use the Jeep's special gear to get back down, whereupon they had to struggle to follow a somewhat roundabout path until they emerged again at the boundary of the patch, which was the plain marker they had previously set for this section of the route. They had no alternative but to go back and put up additional piles of stones to mark the marker. When they had finished, and were ready to go on, Rubinstein turned and pointed: "Look there!" It was behind them far off, a little, quivering pool of yellow light, moving slowly; you were still wondering what it was when it jumped up and turned, sending forth a beam of light, after which it continued to float past slowly in the distance. "A car!" whispered Tzvialeh with suppressed dread. "Uhhuh." "On the main road?" "Uhhuh." They peered, straining their eyes at the slowly moving blotch. "A patrol?" asked Tzvialeh. "I don't think so, they're just going about their business." Now the light reached the place where it had previously turned and again became a beam for a moment, with an apparent increase of speed. "If they suspected anything they would dim the lights," Tzvialeh tried to comfort himself, speaking to Rubinstein, and the other replied: "If one more car like this takes that road in another two or three hours, there's going to be a war out there, and perhaps in the whole country." The light disappeared behind the hump of the hill and they waited for it to emerge again. It seemed to take longer than necessary to cross such a short distance. Had they gone away? A cricket began chirping in the brush, its screeching shrill. Then the spot of light, like a long puddle, returned, glimmering as it floated on, flickering for a moment now and then as it bounced along the uneven surface of the distant road. Another rocket, a green one, flashed up, stabbing, then burst and went out. For some reason, that oppressive feeling came back again. It was your uneasy conscience, though this perhaps was no more than your consciousness of being a stranger here, far from anything that was yours, and not close to anything belonging to this place. They climbed in and sat down, both silent, then made their way down along a path the shape of which could no longer be discerned.

⁂

Parking the Jeep at the foot of the mound, they tramped through the layer of dust that had drifted from the main road, and then were climbing the slope again. You could light a cigarette and disperse the confusion of your thoughts with a long puff of smoke. "What time is it?" said Tzvialeh. "Eight," said Rubinstein, after drawing on his cigarette over the dial of his watch, raising a reddish gleam on the tip of his nose and a passing glimmer in the pupils of his eyes. "Already eight," said Tzvialeh. His voice was instantly swallowed up in the warm night without leaving a trace. Everything was silent, as if asleep. In the sky, lingering over the already blackened land, dim, pale remnants of blue were still visible, but vanishing. They had stopped and now sat in place, breathing tranquilly. The taste of dust switched its itch over their noses, the backs of their necks and the palms of their hands.

After a while, it became apparent that time had passed, you wanted to say something, but realized that in fact there was nothing to be said, for mere words effortlessly spoken were not the trouble (except, of course, when the listener was a certain girl, the very fact of whose presence and attentiveness incited you to talk, to chatter with enthusiasm, until it dawned upon you that you were not only quite profound but also more handsome than you had thought). So what. But once you had taken notice of the silence, it became self-important, impolite and superfluous to the point of unpleasantness—but still you could not find a word to say. Your claims were refuted before they were uttered, so that the situation began to be oppressive and irritating, as you became aware of the fact that this silence was no longer simply a state of non-speech, but had taken on solid substance, its weight growing more painful by the minute. You wanted to speak to someone, to make some observation, or maybe to sing. At least you

121

can let out a good yawn, man, to give assurance of there being no bad feeling, only an ordinary harmless sleepiness which has overcome you and will pass. But even that can't be had. The silence shall go on and not be broken. What about the other guy—he should be the one to open up and speak. It's too bad this isn't a threesome with somebody else, someone more talkative. But maybe the little guy hasn't noticed anything out of the ordinary: who knows what he's thinking. He's interested in deeds, incapable of thinking about anything that can't be said aloud in front of everyone. That's his type. Good guy, good to go out with him, to find reassurance in his fatherly confidence, to obey him and try to win his praise, to please him, like the wise son whose father is bound to be glad. Even if at the same time there is, as usual, an impudent impulse to rebellion driving you to scoff at the guy and the things he says, defying him like a lawless wind.

When are they supposed to arrive? And what time is it now? What if they haven't even left yet? They were supposed to be bringing more barrels of oil with them. They should have sent a winch out with them. We won't even have any decent mechanics in the convoy. They weren't released: whoever goes back to headquarters won't be seen again for weeks and months. He won't get out of there, because that's just the kind of mechanic they need there, they'll keep him at headquarters by hook or by crook, and besides the trip back by plane is a matter of priority and taking your turn. So the convoy would be coming without mechanics. They should have cut the number of vehicles to a minimum, taking only what's most necessary. No clothes at all—why take clothes? What else could be left out, fuel? Spare parts, ammunition? Everything is essential, but the absolutely essential doesn't consist of much. Dammit, this is really a siege. What's that line—*None went out, and none came in, straightly shut up*? Talk about Joshua and the walls of Jericho. There isn't even anybody to get angry at. What a job it was to find this place, on the dividing line between the plain and the hills. They don't suspect we're here. Tomorrow they'll take another look at things, and that'll be the end of us. Nothing will be left open but the skies. Either that or another offensive. This mound, how do you take it? Have we enough guns yet,

S. Yizhar

or tanks? So that means another little night operation. Once again poor meager David against mighty Goliath. Very soon there will be nothing left of David. We've got to get through tonight!

He put his knees together and rested his chin on them, his hands clasping his scorched ankles. He breathed deeply, in silence. It was warm. The sky wasn't black, only the ground, flooded with darkness. The silhouette of the nearby hill was visible—soft, hunched up, like a soft, feminine shoulder. Maybe in the long run it's better not talking.

But Rubinstein got up to listen to something intently, then relaxed and yawned, let out a long sigh and said, as if carrying on from where he had left off (who knows what's really in that fellow's mind—it seems he was actually thinking all the time): "It's late already, what happened to those guys?" "You think we've suddenly become a bunch of punctuals?" said Tzvialeh, settling his chin back on his knees. "Afterwards," added Rubinstein "everything turns the wrong way, you get a big mixup and that's the trouble." "As usual," muttered Tzvialeh. But how good it would be if you could find, and knew how to say, something between the two of you, something that would sound not at all like your known and accepted self, but more essential and important, something entirely different, with a heartfelt meaning for the both of you, something that would not only make a bond between the two of you sitting there dumbly in the field, but would also capture something of the dark's intangibility and make it more intelligible, that dormant, dumb, indefinite realm in the soul, whose existence you sometimes do not even realize. How good it would be to attain a moment of light, or understanding, which would immediately lead to an awakening and a silent consent to all that had forever been covered over; joy in contact both shy and curious, an opening of gates and an emotional closing of the eyes, which led to a certain recoil, of course: that familiar recoil which is a fear of a strange tread upon your own private, personal ground, that revulsion away from the possible violent uncovering of what by nature should be hidden, delicate and enigmatic, its survival dependent upon dark silence, lest it wither, for which reason, whether arguable or not, nothing but

123

silence is fit and proper (excepting, of course, that night with the girl, Nava's her name, to whom you poured out your enthusiasm while she gazed at you in wonder)—although sometimes, somehow or other, one suddenly and unpredictably pulls out some precious private word from that delicate and enigmatic realm described above, and as in a miraculous inspiration makes it real, utters it, touches it with every sense so that it will not be the same as what has always been said, in order to proclaim this time a true friendship, which should be created eloquently between the two compatriots of this expansive and empty night, sufficient to express that something, fine and serious, which would give a different color to all these things, and subsequently to all those other simple things that are to be spoken and done from moment to moment and from day to day. "Yes, as usual," said Rubinstein, and the silence returned.

You feel a shiver, your heart shakes. Just your imagination (or the cry of a night bird). To hell with that. Who better than you should know that even if it were clear to you what all this was about, and especially if you were able to accomplish this miraculous deed of contact simply and well, the whole bit would not be anything, after all, but the musings of a fool, rarefied sentiments which you would be better off without, or at least shouldn't be suspected of, a fellow like you, who is thought of as very successful. If you shut your eyes you'll be asleep in a minute. You feel time marching on the spot. You grow impatient. And then something begins, deep inside of you, wailing mournfully. Good God, what have you to do with all these things? What do you care about all this? What business is it of yours? An obscure fear begins to whittle at your thoughts —what kind of beginning is this (I'll step on a mine tonight, that's for sure)? Rubinstein spoke: "It's half past eight already." But why answer him? A red rocket leaped up, flared, hung still, burst and withered at once with a pale, futile, impotent attempt somehow to change the stillness and the circumstances. But that same disquietude quivered in the air, releasing the shapes of your nightmares which now loomed above you. Unhealed scars opened in an instant, and you don't know whether you are sick or afraid, remorseful or dying to flee. You observed the clear image of a foot clad in a sandal, all its details defined. They poured gasoline on him as he lay by the side of the path, legs astraddle and arms outspread, and they set fire to him just as he was, instead of taking the trouble to bury the body, but the fire died down before it had been completely burnt, and you could see, sticking out of the charred heap whose shape was that of a recumbent man, one unconsumed foot, intact, though somewhat blacked, and clad in a sandal. Where are those bastards? "Rubinstein—maybe we should go out to meet them? Are you sure they know the way here?" "I imagine so. Ovadiah is coming along with them." "It'll take some time to put them in their position," Tzvialeh grumbled, even Rubinstein seemed to be angry: "What kind of a business do they think they're running!" A sandal with black straps, crudely made, its sole fashioned from an old tire, so that when one walked in it, the stamp "Dunlop" was impressed in the sand, a twisted zigzag of grooves.

Funny about this Rubinstein character. In an hour or two both of us are going to step on a mine, with this convoy. Or an Egyptian patrol will knock the hell out of us. Or some shrapnel from their twenty-five-pounders, or six-pounders, or whatever they have, 4.2 inch mortars blasting away four rounds at a time. If I get hit, he won't leave me, Rubinstein. Not because it's me, but because you don't leave someone in the field. Especially when you've been in the same unit with him for a time. It's only natural. He'd jump in to pull me out of the fire, and I'd certainly do the same for him, if it came to that; I wouldn't let go, I'd drag him out, as if he were everything to me—and in a few months, or maybe a year, after the whole thing is past and gone (how's that for imagination!), and we two are still alive (doing who knows what in the morning!), we would meet somewhere and call to one another a big "Hey!" and shake hands, really happy to be together and a moment later, after the noise of greeting had died down, we would find there was nothing to say, only embarrassment, and dwindling mumbles, and we'd feel strange, or almost strange, and the best thing for each of us would be to find a reason to go off on his way—after which Rubinstein would point back over his shoulder and explain to his wife, for this would be a Sabbath afternoon, in a city street, and strolling by her side Rubinstein would reply to her curious, inquisitive look: "Oh, that's Tzvialeh, I forgot to introduce him. We used to be together, back in the army, swell guy—what times we used to have!" and at once confused, even before he had begun, he would attempt to relate his memories and feelings, but would fall silent, thus bringing to a conclusion all that fraternity and friendship, friendship of fighters, of life and death, of my life for yours. How could such a thing melt away and crumble and be nothing! It wasn't clear but that's the way it was. But—hey!—what's this—there's something here, really!

Rubinstein looked up as well. "Ah, they've finally got here," he said, getting up and going down to the road. So that tremor of unrest in the air was none other than the noise of the approaching trucks. Your eyes, having adjusted themselves to the conditions of darkness, like to imagine that they can see more than just a yard or two in front of you in the pitch-black dust. It'll be interesting to see if they find the road. It won't be so simple. Hell of a job. But what are you crying about, sourpuss. What's wrong with you? Shut up, you trembling soul of worry—hey, did they whistle? No, that was Rubinstein whistling from here. Somehow or other, he had taken up that jerky song that spread like the plague and now everybody was singing it. So this guy really can be in a good mood once in a while—he even seemed happy. "Well," said Rubinstein, when Tzvialeh had climbed up and sat down on the Jeep's fender, letting out an inconsequential yawn. "If they're only half an hour late, it won't be so bad." "Wait and see, the night isn't over yet," grumbled Tzvialeh. Thinking about the others back there the dark became full of thoughts, as if they were denizens of another, better world. As if they weren't flesh and blood like yourself, but made of a different and rarer material. For instance their girls, they tell you about them and say some of them are unbelievable. The approaching vehicles grumbled more and more annoyedly. They could be heard bouncing from time to time over the uneven road, and then the sound of the roaring engines would change its pitch, the drivers would switch gears and continue to wrestle with every rut, pressing onward in the darkness. In another minute a black blotch appeared, suddenly, only a few paces away, and it seemed they, too, had noticed them only at the last moment and halted abruptly. "Rubinstein?" someone asked hesitantly, *sotto voce.* "Hi!" Tzvialeh answered. "Who's that?" continued the low voice, and someone jumped out and came up to them. "Hello Tzvialeh. What's up?" he said, shaking off the dust as he spoke: "Man, that's a hell of a road. You've got some dusty darkness here, man." "We've been waiting for you Ovadiah," said Rubinstein. "Well you know how they do things. Hurry up and wait until it gets dark, and it's a pretty dark darkness." "You didn't use your headlights at all?" "We did, once. In the big wadi below the village. We'd gotten off the road and they told us about mines. You know, over there." "You did? Well," the little guy was not pleased—"and how is everything going over there?" "Okay, But what a bunch of drivers they've found. Where do they get those one-armed clowns? Wait'll you see them, Rubinstein!" "How many men have you brought?" said Rubinstein, returning to the subject. "Three, counting us," said the new arrival, pointing his thumb to the Jeep standing behind them with the windshield lowered, and to the several heads which emerged, protruding silently from the framework of its body; "and behind us is Yehudah'le with the G.M.C.—about twenty men." "Not enough," said Rubinstein. "What do you want from me. I told Long-neck—" "Well, okay. We'll manage somehow. Smoking is permitted down here, but put them out when you get up there."

"Say," said Ovadiah, "we brought a transmitter with us; you'll have contact with the convoy and the base. When's the first check-in, Dali?"—he turned his head to the Jeep at the back. "At nine," replied one of the shadows in that direction, whose voice, its timbre so unexpected in these circumstances, immediately aroused such an astonished curiosity that you felt a need to turn your head and peer at the shadow with wondering eyes. "That's good," said Rubinstein. They thoughtfully produced cigarettes, and when the match flared, only for an instant in the shelter of an encrimsoned fist, he took a hasty glance, hoping to distinguish something, but caught no more than a few blurred and shapeless forms, already lost again in the darkness.

the same time his foolishness became fully apparent to him though he was unable to act, raising his hasty eyes to take in something of her back, so that he saw the broad, baggy, shapeless leather jacket round her shoulders, and how she was sitting with her chin resting on the back of her hand, and how only her hair—perhaps from the glow of a cigarette, or the light of the stars, or who knows—held a slight, silent gleam upon it, revealing that this was one of the other gender, differentiated from the rest of those milling about. One girl can bring a lot of glamor to all this, just be being here. As long as she isn't of course one of those—Tzvialeh, alarmed, cast a severely critical look into the depths of the darkness. Damn all those Shulahs and Tzipkehs, those Orahs and Habubahs, and all the rest of them that sit and purr over the radio and make themselves real sweet, little animals who think they are who knows what, making eyes at you and pretending to be accomplished at the art, or leeching on to you never to let go, or sticking up their silly noses, their loud laughter suddenly souring into sheer poison tempered after a while to a lethal boredom—better leave them alone!

The bulky jacket enveloped her completely, concealing everything in its disregard for her true size. But here was the actuality of a girl, the reality of a body, warm and white, so that suddenly your heart was stirred remembering the softness and delicacy beneath that coarse and bulky garment. The memory of a single knee came into focus in all its details, a slightly elongated kneecap, full and globed, the knee of a young, maidenly, ripe leg, tensed in fresh skin of slight, marble-like luster and the length of the line from the calf's whiteness not sharply curved, whereas the arch of the calf swelled toward the smoothly concave inside of the knee. And the nearly perceptible muscle of the thigh's other side rose up between the easy dimples upon each flank, between them a mere hint of something bluish and intimate, almost nonexistent; but these depressions disappeared in their rise to the velvety softness of the top of the thigh, delightfully downy, smooth nakedness, all of it warm and round and soft—but suddenly he felt uncomfortable, even ridiculous, and like a boy caught in the act, tore himself away and went off.

"Tzvialeh!"—this time someone was really calling his name. "Hey, I'm coming," he replied, trying to give no evidence of that gay stream within him which had suddenly become a flood. Rubinstein was explaining how to receive the men and distribute them along the road, as well as the place to park the big truck so as not to cause a disturbance and where to move the communications Jeep so that they would be able to work. Immediately they started carrying out the plan, with a growing tumult. The strangeness of the place had already taken heel and all the silences had dwindled and gone, and now were waiting somewhere else, moaning like a sullen dog or a muted violin. With its engine wailing, the big truck tried to comply with the plan, and executed tactical advances and reverses in the dust (whose unsavory but almost forgotten existence was thus recalled), while the Jeep was making hasty attempts, leaping energetically with the dark forms in it, and climbing a bit up the slope of the mound, where its crew had already jumped out and encompassed the driver with a wealth of useful advice. Nevertheless the first marker, the pile of stones indicating the beginning of the road, seemed to have disappeared. Tzvialeh moved off, listening to the anxious, unsettled hubbub—he wandered about a little in the stony field, raising his head every now and then, sniffing about and above and in the creviced shadows made by the humpy hills; he had already started scratching the back of his neck in bewilderment, when he came upon it exactly in the right place. "Tzvialeh? Where's he gone again!" "Not gone at all. I'm over here. Come on straight toward me."

It's easy to talk about driving attentively so as to follow the wheelruts in a field, but what about when you don't see either ruts or field or at all? In the evening some kind of straight line from pile to pile had still been visible, but no longer. Tzvialeh came back and stooped over the hood of the Jeep, waving his white handkerchief to guide Rubinstein, who, as he bent sideways to improve his view of the ground, almost fell out on it. The Jeep moved forward slowly, and behind it, in double file, walked the men in an even thicker darkness, as in a foreign and distant land, but they placed their confidence in the Jeep and its guides, for after all someone ought to know something moist with loneliness. At the site of the second marker they left one man, explaining what was before him and behind, and the signs of the sky as well, assuring him that they had posted him here not to test his courage under stress, but only to show the convoy the way. The man neither argued nor grumbled, simply asked what he was to do in the meantime, and how he would know when they were coming back, and whether there was a password, enduring in silence any remaining doubts. Thus they left him and continued on their way, but immediately went wrong and found themselves among the bushes of the rocky patch, upon which they made a laborious retreat, wasteful of time and talk, thereby lifting the spirits of the man posted alongside the nearby marker, who eventually claimed that he felt quite at home. So they went on, deepening the impressions of the wheels in the soil, dropping off one man here and a couple there, and explaining everything patiently to every one of them. To those posted at the turning point of the wadi they suggested that they accompany each vehicle on its way down, with the aid of the paper ribbon glimmering like a brook below. Then thorns and little stones. A rock suddenly shot with a clatter from under their wheels. They crossed the gravel of the channel, turned left, climbed the slope at a slant, detoured round the stone that had been displaced, and bounced perceptibly over the crevice which was supposed to have been filled in. Two men were left at this point, with full instructions as to repair, the others looked back: a silent abyss flowed over there in the valley, in the darkness; and the lighter sky, gleaming with stars, stars of love and longing and sensual desire, was both near and far. Only about eight men remained when they crossed the track in the sorghum, its pale gold glints flickering here and there, one complete ear of corn alive in a mirage-like, interior light, as it glowed toward decay. Hot stars in the sky, and here it was cold. "Dali," they called her—that would be Daliah. She ought to be cute. Good legs. Hair combed back. The rest was hidden by the coat. Everything was humming and quickening like honey bees for love. An attentive regard would reveal the stars not inlaid in the topmost level of the heavens but with still greater heights above them, for they hovered in their hosts in an intermediate level with a whole enormity of sky beyond them. But in these myriads of acres of land was not a single spark of light. They left the sorghum field. The winding descent was directly ahead. From here the main road could be seen by day. Now, in the darkness, Gavri and the other two are crouching somewhere in this panther-like and threatening night.

Ovadiah came up, and it took quite a while to post the next man. Even then everything seemed complicated and difficult. This was a matter of big trucks, monsters which tolerated nothing but a proper road, or at least, a straight, flat line, so that all this plotting and planning seemed useless, as if one were trying to train an elephant to walk a tightrope. Wouldn't it be better to admit that it was impossible, and save all the trouble and toil? They took pains to explain to the men the great importance of their task to the convoy, the operation in general, the whole nation, and pleaded for their patience: they were to give individual attention to every descending vehicle, to go down with it, to give it their personal escort, soothe the drivers with helpful directions, signal, wave their handkerchiefs, mark out their shirt sleeves with white paper, used envelopes, or, if they had them, scraps of newspaper saved for a certain purpose, taking constant care, dammit, not to show off, so may they thrive and succeed. But still they felt disheartened, and so kept on, by foot and Jeep, broadening a curve here and there, and arguing in a whisper, feeling their way at one point by brief match-light, and taking advantage of every flare that flew up, with the ultimate conclusion that, given more time and visibility, everything could be much improved, perhaps even another route found somewhere. Ovadiah even claimed that the vehicles, after all, were not the main thing, never had been and never would be, but the men, hear this now, the men who guided the vehicles, and trucks and trains can't take the place of our boys' brains—"Rely on them!" "And what about the drivers?" "First of all, who asked you? And secondly, it'll be okay." Rubinstein was busy collecting anything that was white or light-colored and putting it down on both sides of the route, paper and rags, stones and thorns. But Tzvialeh's doubts remained unalleviated, solemn-hearted.

to mind a certain room on the second story, as seen from the street, from beneath the canopy of the fig trees: one whistle from below, and in the clear, tranquil square of light a silhouetted head would appear, calling down "Tzvialeh? come right up!" and it was Sabbath and clean and cozy....Unconsciously he began whistling, and when he noticed, immediately changed the tune and began chirping the one Rubinstein had whistled before, that jerky tune. "That tune got hold of you too?" Rubinstein leaned over to him. "It keeps running through my head,"—(so tunes too, as well as convoys). When Tzvialeh reached a certain tremor in the melody, Rubinstein joined in and hummed along, beating time lightly with his left hand on the wheel.

They joined the two who had been posted by the cleft and instructed them how to fill it in properly, since they had been trying before at the wrong place. They bolstered them with repeated reminders and warnings, until a flare flashed up to settle their doubts about where the enemy was located: they were at least three kilometers away. "Then they won't hear the noise when the convoy passes?" one man interrogated them, his spectacles glistening and they explained that by the time the enemy understood what it was all about, it would be all over. "Isn't that a bit, you know?" demanded the man. "Well, that's the way we are, you know," Tzvialeh replied, and they went on down the slope.

The feeling of the real beginning of what would come became more intense. What had so far been maps and photographs, arguments and speculations, was now spread out on the ground and transformed into a reality; it was the men, coming and going, just being there, that made it real. The fellows in the wadi were glad to see them, happy to be doing something, and so were those on top. By this time the field possessed an intelligence, no longer a shapelessness wandering confusedly in the wild. Yes, just let there be no mines by the main road, and everything will work out well, maybe even without casualties, and they would all return to their homes, this time without having to wait, without this terrible and vain waiting. But here was a different kind of war, a war in which you make a road, one might say a sort of peaceful war, simply creating a road! "Rubinstein" —Tzvialeh was startled at his own voice and did not know what he should say. "Uh?" replied Rubinstein. "This—" said Tzvialeh: "I was thinking, do you think it will come off?" Rubinstein turned to him and nodded his head. Then you felt you wanted to be a real friend of his, who would know what this man liked most and give it to him, or at least talk to him about it, one who could tell him something to make him happy, so as to be sure, to be sure… "Yes," said Rubinstein and turned back toward the darkness, looking for the path.

No. There can be no more holding back. You feel your heart is almost full. You feel the growing flood within it, the gathering strength of that undefined desire for the freedom to go out and find that radio operator whose name you don't know, and as the desire became clearer, you went up and spoke to her, without an introduction or the usual sort of line, many words of love, which would woo her into utter devotion, with caresses and embraces and kisses. To come and embrace this girl and bestow upon her all of what you are, not letting her alone to see or hear or move, except as in the rising tide of your love, in the storm gathering with gusts of the early rain, or the north-east wind in the winter fields, a strong blast of joy, which can never be properly controlled or adequately understood. Thus you were blinded, as if on a night of bewitching moonlight, the world drenched in a smooth and shining golden glow, transformed all the while into something finer and more perfect, covering over all blemishes, a special radiance, smooth, clear and quite uncomplicated, banishing with its touch every trivial day-to-day aspect of your being, so that no more would you be bothered by any conceivable apprehension for the future—there would be nothing but you and she, only you and she, you and she alone. There you are, distant storm, faraway darkness breaking over the horizon… And if she would not respond at all? Or if she were to complain that you are just a hopeless fool, and to resent your arrogant finesse and your crass molestation, or whatever else she could find to blame? Then again she might not think any of these things, not think anything at all, and only be swept away together with you—Dali—this ardent joy would fly up in her, too, glowing with an experience in which there are neither thoughts nor everyday things with usual connotations, for love could give voice to so much more than those trivial preoccupations, be free, rising like a hot day in spring: such were the sensations of two lovers, clinging to each other, beautiful and young, and everything so free and wide, with the prediction of a possibly great romance...

"So far everything's going according to plan," said Rubinstein from his place at the wheel, his eyes peering into the darkness. "Yes," said Tzvialeh. "In the meantime Gavriel is also busy looking things over." "What?" said Tzvialeh. "Gavriel," said Rubinstein, looking at him. "Yes," said Tzvialeh. "You're not listening," smiled Rubinstein, looking at him. "Yes," said Tzvialeh inattentively. It was easy to put his hands between his knees, to huddle up in silence, swaying with the shifting motion of the road. He shut his eyes so hard they trembled, and when he opened them, breathing deeply, they were somewhat moist. The rocky patch loomed darkly on the right, its rocks showing up lighter. This was no longer the first time that everything in this place seemed familiar. What if one were to try to leave the path, going off to the left or right, where would he come to? What else could be here? What do you know about the things that are taking shape and growing out there, a little further on in the darkness. A flare went up accompanied by two shots, with a third after a slight pause. What's that? Gavri? Was this the beginning? (We should have told the men on the slope about him.) "Did you hear, Rubinstein?" "Yes." "Maybe, it isn't anything after all?" "Apparently it really is nothing," said Rubinstein, after halting and raising his brow as if listening to distant music. "Maybe someone shooting at a jackal or something," said Tzvialeh, more to seek assent than to express an opinion. "Perhaps," Rubinstein shrugged his shoulders and drove on, in what looked like a tacit conspiracy of silence and dissimulation.

※

Switching off the engine they left the Jeep to tramp through the floury dust of the road, climbing the slope of the mound in front of them; there they found a different sort of bubbling, life lit up a little with noise and laughter, sparkling cigarettes and figures moving to and fro, seeming quite at home. In addition to the previous truck, which cast its ladder-lined shadow along the side of the road, the shadow of another, anonymous vehicle could now be discerned, that of the unit of scouts who were to conduct the battalion upon its arrival, and who were at present to receive, at the request of Natanchik (whose dust goggles, pushed back on his forehead, gleamed and gave him the look of a pilot or maybe a diver, something daring at any rate), "all the necessary details" from Rubinstein and Tzvialeh. Meanwhile, waiting for those details, some of them were lying relaxed in a circle, others were wandering about and mingling, while the rest occupied themselves with crates and accessories, a lantern, properly dimmed by a shield of newspaper, supplying them with light. Two men, who were bending down nearby so as to scan a map, or so it seemed, were in fact in the act of attempting, with little pocket knives on a sheet of newspaper, to cover slices of bread with circles of meat which they had extracted from a tin. So it was as if cargoes of gay assurance had been unloaded here and piled up high. The young sports reclining in their circle of pleasure were, of course, playing catch with jokes, each burst of laughter a sign that one had been caught and another thrown: "Now I'll tell you one! Wait a minute, hey wait a minute—this is great, I'll tell you one!" In the midst of one such burst of applause someone was crying out in a shrill supplicatory voice, only to be silenced and obliterated by another voice which commanded greater confidence. But a bit above them the darkness gathered, forgotten as a faded beauty, and the stars twinkled away on their own, sloping down to the west, engrossed in their own affairs.

Another outburst of responsive laughter aroused him to approach, his smile at once spreading independently, ready for the tickle which would add one more loud laugh to the chorus of brays, while he bent to search out familiar faces among them, thus promptly treading on someone's foot, bringing the laughter to an abrupt halt, after which that face turned toward him, wrapped in goggles, which gave it the expression of a bulldog, and remarked: "You ass, where are your eyes?"—immediately adding "Who's that guy trying to push?"—bringing to an end his gropings on the edge of the circle. So he left them, but over there, out of the way, a reddish eye stared at him from a Jeep, and a hoarse whisper, like the crackling of dry grains split with occasional honks and squeals, emerged from a communications set, beside which sat an enigmatic figure, apparently the objective of those voices which were sent forth sporadically, though not without due respect, whenever something worthy of notice was found. He approached her circuitously, the whispering set between them. Her head was bowed, and the bright reddish eye shimmered on her hair, a thick curtain of which dropped from time to time by its own weight onto her temples, arousing her to that swift, light movement with which she lifted it to its place behind her ear. Rather than taking notes from the radio, she was tapping, with the tip of the pencil in her hand, the rhythm of a song seemingly humming in her head, while her other hand manipulated the knobs in anticipation of some foreseen event. At last a ventriloquial voice was heard, its speech indistinct and punctuated by wasplike chirpings, but she resumed her ministrations within the playing shade of the set, casually pushing back that falling curtain of hair once more to its place, and moderately shrugging her shoulders. And indeed this was the way, with that same arch of hand and gesture of twinkling fingers, working with such airy casualness, with such detailed and dexterous attention, so typically blasé, as the girls at home were wont to be; so that something long lost had in a minute been found, something mysterious explained until one has better understood, and at the same time been aroused by a curiosity to know more, from a closer range—(whereas strangely enough none of the gestures and movements of the men, not of any one of them, recalled anything, either from home or from any other place, for all their doings were so simple and usual, there could be in them no surprise). When presently the voice fell silent, she spoke into the mouthpiece to periodic replies come out of air, in the end glanced at her watch and switched off the set, whereupon all became still and dark.

"Anybody got a match?" she said from her place. "Here, let me"—Tzvialeh jumped forward, his heart and his lighter snapping to be opened; flicking the lighter, he shaded it with his other hand against the momentary dazzle of flame and raised his eyes to her, whose delicate line of nose could be seen, and arched brows above an eyelid with lowered lashes, just the tip of her chin and a glimmer of her neck's smooth whiteness, then it was dark again. "Did you come with them?" said the girl, as if in compensation for his politeness, blowing out smoke and waving the light of her cigarette toward the ring of jokes. "No, I'm in Rubinstein's unit," Tzvialeh replied, inhaling. "Oh, then I've got a message for you." "Yes?" "The companies are already on their way; in half an hour the convoy moves out—I got it a minute ago. What should I answer?" "When's the next contact?" "At half-past. Every half-hour." "I'll ask Rubinstein in another minute." They both inhaled deeply (were they friends already?) "It's really dark tonight," she said after a while and looked up at him. "Like a crow," said Tzvialeh, snatching a glance at her as she raised her eyelashes, pushed back the falling sheaf of hair, and nodded slightly. "Where are they, the Egyptians?" she asked, sticking her hands into the pockets of her wide coat, where she found a handkerchief which she put to her nose. "They're over there. About three kilometers away. You can see from their flares"—which display of knowlegeableness brought an undeniable strain of boyish pride to his voice. A roar of laughter drew both their glances to the recumbent circle. She stepped down and approached it, "Hey, here's Dali," said one of its voices, intoxicated with laughter and gaily confident. "Come on over here, sit down with us and we'll sing something." Nice guys, thought Tzvialeh—actually they're all nice guys even when they act like a bunch of delinquents and pretend to be hard, they're still nice guys. All these dirty jokes, of course, are only kindness in disguise. Tzvialeh was proud of this universal love of mankind of his. He took in a long drag of smoke, and with a hop of his heel and nod of his head made himself ready to join in whatever they would sing, and it was really nice.

"Tzvialeh!" Rubinstein then called. "Yes?" he replied, surprised and not exactly wanting to know. But at once he recalled Gavri and the three shots a while ago. At the same time he was unwilling to leave what had been beginning here, though it now occurred to him that, actually, the girl had hardly paid him any heed, almost nothing had happened. He turned and went down toward Rubinstein. With his every step a strange cloud thickened within him, bulging wordlessly. He felt weary, an emotion which found no outlet. Discarding and stepping on his cigarette, he saw a foot clad in a sandal emerging from a heap of ashes whose shape was the shape of a man. To hell with it, you damn dainty —but he did not finish the thought, for there was Rubinstein in front of him, chatting as usual with two or three fellows, with a sense of calm justness that was disturbing. A cricket suddenly started chirping, its shrill twitter so near that apparently a stone's threw could kill it. Damn this Rubinstein! He doesn't give orders, doesn't raise his voice, only asks quietly, though actually it's the same thing. But why the hell does it have to be just now. The urge was to play contrary, to annoy him for the fun of it. If all freedom had been canceled this still remained (do not obey! be perverse, yes my boy, lead the revolution, be brave, be proud, be that volunteer charging forward in defiance of fire and danger—that was okay; but this interfering with his private life, telling him how to do things—that was another matter! No! Because at this you wanted to wail like a dog being strapped and you ached to bite and bite! Maybe this wasn't the way to take things during a war—but who the hell was made for war!). "What's up?" Tzvialeh grumbled aloud, sullenly. Sticking his fat nose into a man's life, who asked him. "What's the matter with you?" asked Rubinstein, whose wondering was quickly discarded as he explained that the men had to be taken down to the last slope, where they would contact Gavri, their mission being to guide the convoy to the positions on the road at Tel Abu-Shin. As he himself had to stay here to get things organized, Tzvialeh would take them in the Jeep. The box of food was to be brought to Ovadiah. That was all. (All? To hell with him—let them crawl over there on their bellies, who cares!)

Afterward, while they were trundling along slowly in the Jeep, groping for the wheel-tracks, and none of the attempts of the other occupants to start a conversation with Tzvialeh had extracted more than a miserly yes or no, there having been no success regardless of which of the various openings were used, such as "This road is a piece of shit," or "How do you manage to see anything?"—or "Doesn't look like there's going to be a moon tonight"—and statements of like nature, which were however followed by more spontaneous remarks, such as the opinion that "he must have a needle up his ass," whereupon they left him alone, and turned to singing in a low voice, in quite good tune, a song which did not end but which was gone over again and again until the night and the hill's coldness and the wildness of silence brought them to a hush. It might be expected that, given conditions such as these, the driver would have no thought to spare for anything but driving and keeping to the road, but this was true only for the first hundred meters. Thereafter hands and feet and eyes continued dexterously to do all that was required of them while your thoughts went out in search of untrodden paths, skipping off and breaching every barrier, with riotous cries, running amok, until at last they gathered together in calculated imaginings. First you opened the big gate of the kibbutz, making sure no one noticed her or you, although you pretended, of course, that it was nothing of any importance, and you went off by the dirt track descending to the left of the little wood. Walking beside her you wanted to start talking at once, but you put it off, sensing that the time for talk had perhaps not yet arrived, and, actually, what was there to say? So you tried whistling quietly. The path narrowed and she was walking ahead of you. From behind, you could see two chestnut braids (for it was still daylight, drawing toward evening, after work and the shower), pretty braids resting on a white, shoulder-pinched blouse of bell-shaped sleeves, and within the skirt of blue, a shapely waist and violin thighs, while sandals held the slender legs, the oval calves and firmness of youth. She had folded her left arm behind her, three fingers clasping her right arm, which dangled at her side, (the free little finger squeezing a crumpled handkerchief), and thus she stepped lightly, her head turned a little and bent, serious and thoughtful, perhaps whistling quietly too, or perhaps restraining her lips (a few freckles were sprinkled about her nose), being as she was somewhat self-contained, though she gave the impression of seeking something extraordinary, more beautiful

and special than the everyday world could supply, something pure as
the virgin yearning for that which had sprouted but not yet opened,
so that you were obliged, by the simple fact of being with her on
a stroll, to know a great deal, to have read a great deal beforehand
and to make intelligent comment now, or to be wisely silent, and
never clumsy, for your worth was being weighed all the time on the
sensitive scale of a girl whose will to love was all innocent, as a plant
facing the sun, and now, venturing with you upon this pastoral, she
was to be loved mutely, from a distance, which would widen her
eyes with wonder...

The man at the first post halted them, asking the password;
inspecting the faces of each of them, he seemed willing to hold
them there for as long as he could with his grumbles about what
was not in order. They crossed the rocky patch, passed the men on
the thorny slope across the wadi and between the two markers; the
guides were leading them, their white handkerchiefs flourished more
for their own sake than for the road's; they climbed up the spur, the
rift in which was by now almost entirely filled in; they entered the
sorghum field, glowing dimly in the dusk. It wasn't easy to determine if Dali, already far behind, was really a pretty girl, and how she
recalled, in the glow of the cigarette lighter. A rounded chin. What
did you know about her? But then, what did it matter? After all you
had a right to make your own mistakes. So this was it: run up to her
and tell her with all your eagerness—come, my Dali, let us go forth
into the field—although not always had it seemed possible. But now
it seemed most definite, so much so that there were no more worries about who she really was (as long as she didn't turn out one of
those dumb Tzipkes or Habubahs who stuck to you like leeches!)—it
seemed sure she would be different. You felt certain she would know
how to forget herself and get excited at the proper time, get really
high—dammit, I'm going to step on a mine tonight! And of all that
she is and has been given by God I shall have no part, nothing at
all; she won't even know I existed, at the commencement of love,
eyes shut, unconstrained. Now! And, dammit, it was good to love,
to be in love, once more, as once was—to be filled with it's so good

to be with you, in the midst of all day I dreamt of you, living that all day I was burning for you, feeling cause it's great you're here, I'm nuts about you—to be singing with you're wonderful cause you're you, like this, everything about you, and when I know you're going to be with me the world is different. And that desire, that desire all mine, to show you, to take you off walking, hearing you and seeing you, laughing at your side, looking at you from the side and from within myself where is nothing but love for you, to be your strong adorer, until, in due time—for what could be finer than two people on a stroll, side by side and yet walking each by himself, embraced, an arm of each around the other? Yes man, this was the renascence to which one awakened, like, who knows, like a fig in the first heat wave of spring, the deep, juicy green bursting from within the hot dryness of air that intoxicated all under its weight, heavy with ripeness, me and my doggy dreams—"Hey you!" someone was saying to him, "don't go so fast, our bones are fragile!"—nudging his shoulder for emphasis.

❧

But they had already reached the winding route down the slope. And the fellow who was standing there, apparently Ovadiah, came up to them at once. No, they haven't come back yet. Yes, they'd also heard three shots, but from the other direction. No, no car had passed along the road. In any case, they hadn't seen or heard one. Absolutely quiet. Positively. Great, you brought the food. Yes, it's cold already, getting colder. Momentary flutter of a distant wind. Yes, the winds are blowing, winds of the fields. Smell of harvest and crops. That's the sorghum down there, no doubt. Big melancholy fields. Sleeping in the barn, the straw tickling, stacks of sheaves, one breaks an ear into grains and chews them. Dew. Awakening in the middle of the night, tremendous, gleaming skies, big lights ripe as fruit, no barriers at all between things—and Dali, sleeping in a world of straw stalks. In the morning, paths had been sprayed with wet gold, dew dripping from the leaves—just think of it, just think of it, my boy, that's all there is to it; up early in the morning, the water faucet bursting with laughter, feeling excitement, enthusiasm, making love, loving, work, going out to work. What?—"How far from here to the road?" "From here?" "Yes, to the road." "Not much." "What do you mean, not much? How far?" "Well it's about, a little less, let's say yes, a kilometer, less than a kilometer," said Tzvialeh and made up his mind to pay attention to what was going on. "So are we going over to take a look?" Now he was completely awake: "What's this about going over? You guys take it easy. All we need is for you to start roaming the roads, you on this side and they on the other. They'll be here in a minute." "What did we come here for, a sit-down strike?" "Take it easy, that's all. Don't you guys know how to sit down and take it easy?" "Hurry up and wait," said one. "Hey," said Tzvialeh, "who's the wiseguy?" Ovadiah appeared, the voice of pacification, and Ovadiah proclaimed war to be in the long run only a brief moment of battle, whereas the tasks of preparation and organization were prodigious. Everything was dependent upon organization, said Ovadiah sagely, to execute the plans so that everything clicks at the same time and in the right order, said Ovadiah, and he also said a few more things.

They gnawed at the hard, dry biscuits and sucked from the slit in the can of fruit juice. You still wanted to know why they hadn't returned yet, what was taking them so long over there? Everything here is ready and waiting, but over there, beyond the road and the big wadi, only the darkness knows what's going on. Time's getting short, the escort units will arrive soon and take up their positions along the road. How can we send them over there when we don't know anything about it? And there's still a good long way to go beyond the road, and the night waits for no one, and there's a good chance we'll get shot at from some place or other, a skirmish or two and you don't know what your chances are. He threw away the juice can, refused another biscuit. There was no end in sight. Your entrails have begun to collect signs of danger—something definite would have to be decided, and now. A minute ago he had contended that they should not go out to meet them, and now this seemed, if one might say so, ridiculous (though not entirely without foundation).

They could get more and more tangled up until they'd never get out of it. But staying here was also an endless mess. Had anything really happened to them? When the convoy comes there won't be time to hesitate and consider: it will have to go on through at once. Hold it up and you'll never get it through. (The serpent within you nevertheless hints that that is what will happen after all, your version of the destructive urge that begins its temptations at the very moment of crucial decision; forget about the preparations, let's go back to where we were, and tomorrow or the day after we'll try again, perhaps we'll succeed...we are not strong enough to support a failure)—treason! If we don't get through tonight, it's all lost, the ultimate stupidity of failure—if they close this hole we can all kiss ourselves goodbye. Gavri, the great adventurer playing around wherever he wants and doing everything except for the one thing he's under orders to do: to come back and report. A guy like that shouldn't be sent out to scout. Has anything really happened? We have no choice—we're going down to the road, but not by foot, by Jeep. That's the best way (idiot, stay here, you'll step on a mine!). In the Jeep it'll all be over in a minute, there and back. To hell with those mines—whatever wills Allah. Now, right now, without any more arguments: "Everybody back to the Jeep—we're down to that road."

"Say, wise up and have something to eat," said Natanchik the scout. Ovadiah put forward a logical line of opposition, but his arguments seemed out of date by now. When he concluded his dispute with a plea that they at least take a machine gun with them, he sounded as funny as somebody's mother running after him with a sweater (and the only trouble was your having to break off that excited film of imaginations: you weren't even allowed to think; your mind could be a world of beautiful visions—stuff them on a shelf, buddy, they have nothing to do with that man of action whose job is to lead and protect a convoy). Down they went over all the convulsions of the road, from one man to the next, the last one pestering them to take him along too, out of his villainous boredom, assuring them that from a practical standpoint it did not matter whether he stood or went off with them, but in the end loneliness covered him, left behind. They entered the lower sorghum field, on the right of which the hill's wall thrust its upper edge into the sky, while that well known, lonely and troubled sense of the unknown descended upon them; using no path they crossed the sorghum field straight to the right attaining the abandoned track, which was supposed to cut by in this vicinity in its approach to the little wadi which ran down to the big wadi beside the road, if only they had not gone wrong and reached some dark place, some land of slopes and rocks, bushes and thorns, in which there were no more straight lines and directions, a chaos of the lost, a dreadful warning to every eager adventurer setting off without a second thought. Rubinstein would never have done this. Don't think about Rubinstein. That star marks the south, and that's our way. End of the sorghum field, what next? "You sure you know where you're going?" Natanchik, who was seated alongside, voiced his misgivings: "I don't see any path." "You'll see it in a minute," Tzvialeh comforted him with confidence in advance, trusting to luck. Perhaps the others had taken the wrong route and gotten lost, and that was the reason for their disappearance. It was getting cold. This was your responsibility. The sight of a body in a corner of a field stretched inertly on the clods was still vivid in your mind, the figure of a man twisted in a coil of death. And where were the two others? Now they're here: one flat on his back and the other with his limbs strained as if he had been wrestling and felled in the fight. And then the picture changed and a foot came into focus, clad in a sandal, an intact but bodyless foot clad in a sandal whose sole had been fashioned from an old Dunlop tire—hey, wait a minute! This is the path! Well, in that case—what the hell were you worrying about—the path's here! Beyond the hill were darkness and the sparkling skies. But this path is great. So I wasn't wrong after all. The convoy will get through, the path has been found. What's that?

"Say this is a good path, a real road," said his neighbor. "Of course," said Tzvialeh. "I can see you've put a lot of work in here," said the other. "You bet," boasted Tzvialeh with joy in his heart. As far as I'm concerned, said Tzvialeh to himself, most things in this world seem dubious to me—due to confusion perhaps, or inability—but with this convoy it's going to be different, going to keep on straightforward despite the doubts, the faltering confusion, and it will get there safely. I'm going to remain my own self and for all that the convoy is going to get here. A man should never be afraid to dare. This is the place where the road is supposed to be—what about it? Where is that hill behind us? If we get caught in an ambush now, that's it—although we can claim we don't want to play because we didn't take a machine gun. But beyond the road will be, of course, the mines, where it crosses the path, or before that, in the bed of the big wadi. What is it?

Tzvialeh halted at once, all four of them listening. Something was out there, no doubt about it. "Ssst"—the whistling whisper was heard again to the left of the track, from the channel flooded with thorns. Every pale rock on this slope might also be a man aiming a rifle. And those black spots—there was a rustle in the thorns, something was really perceptible there, black and looming large—a man emerged and stood up straight, came up to them and said quietly, "Someone there?" His heart died a bit, but Tzvialeh pulled himself together. "Hello," said Tzvialeh, "who is it? Ya'akov? Hey, what's up, Ya'akov?"

"Nothing," said the other quietly, "is the convoy here already?"

"No, we came to see what had happened to you."

"What happened to us? Nothing happened," said the other in the darkness. And it was all very strange. It seemed as if they were hiding something, holding something back. But Ya'akov explained that they'd had a rough time in the wadi where they had made a few signs with stones taken from the shoulders of the road; they had also done a bit of searching for mines (their method was simple: cover the whole area by foot and if you weren't blown up, you knew there were no mines. There was no point worrying about anti-personnel mines: they were big enough to be seen and there were no signs of digging)—in addition they had looked around on the other side of the road. They'd inspected the positions at Tel Abu-Shin, and there was nothing there at all. They had also gone down the road to scout around further—Gavri didn't want to come back before they'd examined everything. Now he had gone off again with Hanan to the bridge over there, to see if it was worthwhile lifting it. "They left me here, to sort of cover them. Nothing is doing here. There were a few shots over there, don't know what. When the flares light up, it gets even darker here in the shadow of this hill. I heard you coming from a good way off. Want to see the wadi?" So it was that this distant and dangerous place became just a place like any other, neither as distant or dangerous as had been in the cogitation of one far removed. "Here, have a sip of juice," said Tzvialeh to Ya'akov, generously as to a brother or friend.

The wadi was a deep pit, quite narrow. The descent into it slanted down one slope and emerged in a slant at the opposite side; this diagonal course the men had marked, pushing aside a few flood-driven stones at the bottom of the channel. Still it was not easy here, so close to the road—all we need is for some truck to get stuck in the middle, not the ideal method of crossing dry stream beds. Oh, and maybe in spite of everything a better crossing could be found? But here was the road. This was it—crushed stones flattened by a roller with only goodwill in its heart, and churned up again by trucks without the least bad in theirs. These two hills were the strong points; between them the path ran whitely, marking the border. This was the dividing line between two separate lands, from here to the sea on the one side, and to the mountain tops on the other. This was the last breach, all the rest being closed, the only surviving bridge. And this silence of bare, limestone hills recalled that moonlight night, when you had walked at home, along the gravel road, its destination concealed by the mysterious pallor in the air. That was when everything had been more beautiful, with the outline of a slender, delicate profile, hair shining with light: for this was the adoration of beauty from a lover's heart—lay off, man. Stones worn with the steps —who's that? Who could it be but Gavriel, with Hanan (Hans, Hanan for short)— we have met upon the road at the border's edge. Smiles. Conversation. Coughs. Everything looks different when there are people. A gentle rebuke. A growing feeling of fraternity. A sense of friendship between men working at night, a closed circle of companionship. Seven men in the heart of the land, a different land. There was more to it than could be seen at first glance, this restrained merriment.

❧

Afterward Gavriel and Hanan went off with the other three to reconnoiter the route to the attack positions, while Tzvialeh and Ya'akov returned to the Jeep and crossed the wadi (damn shame we can't fix things up here—it isn't good enough as it is), where they remained, each sitting in place, silently. Here it was different, completely. It's one thing to be with the men, these men, in the open field, at night, in action, and another thing again when you think of how it is in camp, in the rear, the base, those damn huts and the parade ground and everything else. Disgusting mess of boredom—they should all go to hell. Those damn polished tables in the mess hut and the waxed floor, filthy beneath its smoothness, and the sticky tableware and the big, oily, sooty pots in the kitchen, and the twisted image of those miserable cooks, flushed with sweat, foul and peevish, and the roaring primus stoves that screeched, scraped upon the floor as you pumped them, and the meals and the noise and the meat torn into portions by a fork and a piece of bread, and the soup, chill and slimy—whatever your finger touched carried a print of sand and grease—and the mobbing and the long lines and the pushing and the grumbling, everything smelling of shame and resentment, marked by deceit and unfairness, the indignities which had been heaped here by the world—and suddenly you have been blessed with officers in your midst, sporting rights and privileges, their voices and strides as of another breed, whereas you have only the big, long dreary barracks to remember, obscene even as they were swept and washed, and the tattered, stained mattresses, the card games, the gags undisturbed by the sour smell of those asleep in the dark stink of their closest garments, bundled in piles of blankets, their outer clothes lying there, carcass-like, at their sides; so you wished you could fence off a plot of privacy in the midst of all this, a kind of personal paradise of your own, and you persisted in this dream despite the moldy hug of ragged bedding, your dream of private habits and private filth, your native right to be inexplicable, a creature of its own caprices within the vast, meaningless and dreary business of this world; and the tedious winds blowing unceasingly from the walls, from the penciled sketches and inscriptions, identical all, and the walls were stuck with jutting nails at which clothes and discontented eyes grasped in their climb to find a hold on the smooth, sooty ceiling; and the flies, and the emptiness as viewed through windowpanes never entirely undamaged, with the remains of spidery rancidness upon their cracked stumps, between which an occasional errant breeze made its way. At such a time you might glimpse a landscape, sunlight and clouds, or a tree moving in the wind, and you would feel a scream of insanity rising in you at this reminder of the world which was different, of a life that was more than this perpetual meanness.

So you broke out, to the sun, the trees, to the grassy soil, to the human spark not yet extinguished in you, which you intended to preserve. But you had no pass, and no transportation ticket, no permit of any kind at all. Those were the long, yellow days in which you fought over black bootlaces at the commissary, waging murderous arguments with the clerk, the secretary, the adjutant, the sergeant-major. Meanwhile time stood still. You felt that what you wanted and had asked for was only your right: after all something was due to you in all this mess, they owed you something for all this, and besides, you had set your heart on it, in obstinacy, deliberate stupidity, sometimes just for the sake of being insubordinate. So there you were standing on the road, waiting for a lift home, without a pass. And by the time you had to come back, dog-tired. Then there were programs, shows, screeching in the showers, lining up for a shower, lining up for a shave, in front of the latrines—no paper! Then there were movies: hey, a movie tonight! And singing. Or another great event: the barber's come! Hey, everyone, the barber—I'm first in line! Come and get it! Then those aimless visits to other units, soda at the canteen, jokes, stories about broads, yeah, all the dirty little details, and also sad songs. There wasn't a girl in camp without a

pack of yelping hounds at her tail, she of course a mixture of panic
and shame and surging pride. But always there was the howling for
one reason or another, and the apple-polishing and the ass-licking,
whether you wanted to or not, whether obeying with a smile or
saluting sulkily, your obsequiousness was demanded. But then there
was volleyball: bang—great shot! Do it again—great shot!—and
those rumors. Always rumors. They say—dammit when's this thing
going to come to an end! So you stood by the gate, looking, looking, and you quarreled with the MP's. Home. Get out to the fields,
to your work, to something, your wife, your kids—to something
your don't need a pass for, which you do under no orders, though it
itself will be your order of life, your difficult mission which can be
accomplished better and more quietly, when everything is different,
and the men —hey, I'm still here. Right, here in the silence of pallid fields, the fraternity of comrades in a night action. This Ya'akov,
what do I know about him? What do I care about whatever he is on
the outside? It's just good he's here. So we sit and think in silence
—perchance to dream? No, he's staring at the stars. "Are you asleep
or just looking?" said Tzvialeh.

"Just looking," said Ya'akov, drawing his collar closer to his
neck, for it was getting colder. "Wonderful sky tonight," continued
Ya'akov.

"Yes," replied Tzvialeh, a rank taste in his mouth.

"What are the names of those stars, do you know?"

"Not me."

"Neither do I," said Ya'akov, clearing his throat a little. The still-
ness rustled. The thorns by the side of the track were tall as the Jeep.
"Once I really wanted to know, to study," Ya'akov spoke up again.
"Nothing came of it." Just another variation of the same biography.
What difference was there between you, only the name.

"What do you do, on the outside?" said Tzvialeh.

"Me? Nothing. I work."

"What kind of work?"

"Plumbing, construction, things like that."

"Married?" (Mind your own business.)

"No, I live by myself. But I've got a girl in Tel Aviv."

"What do you plan to do when you get back?"

"When I get back? Who knows. There've been three times in these past few weeks alone when I thought I'd never get back. I was sure this was it."

"Were you on Tree Hill too?"

"Uhuh. You too? It was, where I was anyway, it was crazy, I'm telling you. Dodick was right alongside me when he got it. Did you know him? Three wounded, one of them lost his foot. A three-inch, poor son-of-a-bitch." Again the stillness rustled and they gazed at the pallid hills beyond the road. A feeling was in the air, that it was late, time for them to be getting back. He fidgeted and swallowed his thirst for a smoke.

"So you believe in fate?" Tzvialeh said.

"Well, I kind of started to believe. I didn't know I was like that. But suddenly it seems that lots of things we always laughed at are really different. They're not so—you know. I started thinking, what's a man, after all—I've never talked to anybody about it yet—a man—and there's something above him too—I don't know how to say it..."

"Are you religious?"

"Don't be stupid. I was only talking about ideas you get sometimes, suddenly. Religious—if you mean prayer book, synagogue, kosher, the answer is no. With me it's thinking and not religion."

They were silent. Tzvialeh's thoughts returned to that big wadi, which was in need of improvement, and also to the fact that it was already time to hurry up and get back. That Gavri was always disappearing. He had almost forgotten the man sitting beside him, conversing, when the latter spoke up again, and it seemed that in the interim he had found the words he had been searching for: "It's just an idea, a thought you get suddenly," he said, coughing a bit, "some kind of understanding. You've been left alive and you want to say something about it, that you don't want to be alone, and you don't want to be afraid. There's that girl you have at home, and life hasn't given you anything yet. Up until now it's all been just an introduction, not the thing itself, not life itself. When you go out at night

and the whistling starts, and the shells, and you want to live, not be
hit, then comes this feeling that if you believe, and don't tell anyone
else, the shells won't get you. You'll run in between the bullets and
come back alive. You just believe. Believe, that's all."

"Uhuh," said Tzvialeh wanting to say more, something com-
radely, but he could not find the words, so he repeated, "That's
right."

"Sometimes," continued the other eagerly, "sometimes I'm
ashamed, it seems childish. But as soon as the bullets start flying, the
same old story comes on again, all at once, jut like that. You feel it
coming, you feel you've got to believe, it's inside you, in your belly.
You want to run away, or hide behind something. At least to believe
nothing will happen. Another self, a different man comes out of you,
or gets into you, and he's different. And you have to make sure it'll
be all right. You have to believe your luck is looking after you, that
you won't get hit, that every single thing you do, standing or lying or
crawling—that's the thing that saves you and keeps the shrapnel away.
That's the way it is. Do you feel like that too sometimes, Tzvialeh?"

"What," said Tzvialeh, with an uncomfortable urge in him to
change the subject: "me? I don't know."

But Ya'akov had apparently not yet finished, and the others
had not yet returned (damn them all!). So he went on talking, and
even though you really wanted to listen, you didn't want to hear these
particular things, a subject not to be broached. "I'll tell you something else," said Ya'akov: "when we start out, the first thing I do is
to look for signs that it'll all be okay—it sounds funny. I've got to
hear a donkey braying, that's the sign it'll come out right. If I hear
that, I'm sure. If I don't hear it I get nervous. That's what I've got to
hear. I'm so excited waiting for it I get worried, so anxious to hear it
I begin hearing it as if it was really there, beginning to sound. I hear
it beginning every minute, how the sounds come one after the other,
going up and then down and down again till they stop. And at the
same time I know I'm fooling myself, and there hasn't really been any
braying yet. And that gets me angry. Here it is!—I think. And then,
no. Now, now it's coming, I think again. And again no, not yet. But

it's got to be soon! In some village there in the distance—have all the donkeys just got up and gone? I'm listening. I just listen. We're getting near the place, and I haven't heard it yet. What to do? I want to stop and wait, not go on till I hear it. The whole world's just one listening ear—and then, all at once, there it is! It comes. I hear it. You understand me?—I hear it. Wow, what a relief—I thought I'd never breathe again. Now I know everything's going to be all right, nothing is as terrible as I'd thought, the world is just doing what it always does. When a donkey brays at night, that's a sign of peace. The end of the world won't come tonight, there's still hope. That sound is like a voice speaking especially to you. And when I hear, it's for all the others, too. That's what I believe. Sound funny to you?"

"Well, have you heard it tonight?" began Tzvialeh, at once regretting his crudity; however someone else interfered.

"Hey, what's the uproar over there?" a deep voice interrupted, and they trembled at the fearful discordancy. "Oh, Gavri! So you've finished already?" said Tzvialeh hastily, trying to cover up the awkwardness in which he was caught: "It's very late."

"Not very," said Gavri, with great assurance. "Meanwhile you've been sitting here like a couple of old maids tattling on everybody. Now tell me what you were talking about."

"The usual crap," said Tzvialeh, "you know, just talking. Jump in and let's get out of here."

"They won't admit it, the slippery bastards," said Gavri. "We run our ass off on these hills and here they are selling all our secrets. Now don't deny it—what were you saying about us?"

All seven of them crammed into the Jeep. "This Jeep's like a camel," said Hanan. "Drags you along without a complaint." "Show me a camel that doesn't complain," replied one of them. They moved off, lurching over the bumps of the track. "I'll tell you what," said Gavri, "the Jeep's like a camel, and we're its ass, ho ho!"—thus exhibiting his characteristic vigor and eloquence, a man bothered by blocks of behavior in his judgment and universal condemnation of others. "Listen," said one of the men, "it's great what we're doing tonight—breaking the siege." "So far nobody's managed to break it," said another knowingly. "It'll be terrific if the convoy gets through," waxed the first. "But the whole plan is wrong," intervened Gavri: "first of all, why midnight, why not during the day? Afraid their spotters would see us? Take my advice and send out one truck an hour, every hour one truck. Nobody would suspect, we could spread them out, hidden in the bushes and wadis. And then, in the evening, the minute the daylight fades, they start out—and make it! "They would," agreed one, whose admiration for Gavri steadily increased, a phenomenon not unperceived by the latter as he continued: "Secondly, such a simple thing as lime, without which no one knows where the road is. But with lime you can see everything." "You sure can," said the same supporter. "Third, reconnaissance, before the convoy arrives. Especially for mines," said Gavri, alluding not obscurely to that field in which he was expert and the others helpless without him. "Or, for example," he continued, "they could have painted the back of every truck white, and then on the road, one behind the other, nobody could go wrong. You'd think they'd know what was waiting for them here—but they left their brains behind." "As usual," agreed his admirer: "we're always all screwed up and that's why we get screwed."

Such was the inspiring aria, Gavri's solo accompanied by firm chords of assent, which pleased their ears as they drove over the track and reached the stalk-broken sorghum at their previous crossing-place, entered that breach only to be bumped and butted by the stones and clods of the wadi-bank, the Jeep groaning under its heavy load; to the left rose the hill like a wall with its top in the heavens (without whose help I don't know how we'll manage to get them down here to the bottom) but below a puddle of darkness and sadness had gathered, whereupon they reached the first post, whose guard stopped them, saying, "Hey what's up? We were getting worried, what happened to you?" As there was no reply, he said, "What are we lying here for anyway, just waiting all the time?" The Jeep responded with a wail of increased effort and started its climb up the winding path, while Gavri did not swerve from his criticism of the apparent aptitude of those organizers who had calmly marked out this appalling route of descent, without consulting him or heeding his advice to keep the

old path: "The men who took that old trail," said Gavri propheti-
cally, "didn't take it for nothing." Once on top they left three men
with Ovadiah, their task being to guide the soldiers who were due
to arrive; meanwhile they had the fortification of a few cans of juice
and a few crackers, as well as Gavri's advice to lie down in some furrow and light their cigarettes under cover of their hats, hiding the
flame from the other guards, so as not to make them jealous, for if
the others were to see it they too would light up a smoke and the
whole area would be one big cigarette, glowing away and revealing
all—you had to be careful with those National Guards, a bunch of
idiots from whom could be expected nothing of value.

They danced over the fissures in the road and entered the yellowish sorghum above, bent with the weight of ripe ears, every stalk
rustling under the rumbling Jeep; leaving the sorghum, they skipped
over the filled-in cleft, the men stationed beside it approaching hastily, to observe and be observed, but they too were left behind as the
Jeep circled past the fallen stone and descended to the flat part of the
wadi between the two markers, after which the whitish paper strip
appeared and was followed up to the flat summit of the hill. So once
again you have come back to a girl's smile, to that special way of
pushing back the falling mass of her hair, of turning her neck as she
bobby-pinned the unruly locks, her curved hands and fingers moving
with the silent dexterity of the casual and the calm—now these various attitudes of hers began to take clearer shape, shining and luring
one's hopes to a different horizon, with nostalgic longings, with a sigh
of yearning. This was the fragrance of a being more beautiful, more
perfect in its purity of line, comprising warmth, knowledge, delicacy,
as well as the desire of a utopian heart which only a man of great
worth could attain: fragrance that tantalized, aroused and shattered
with the images of beauty it effused—all the beauty of fields and hills
and skies—that maiden fragrance which turned curiosity to passion
and passion to madness, till you feel you cannot breathe, your throat
clogs at the slightest thought, the merest transient recollection of a
bent knee, the back of a neck, the line of a waist, the slender ankle
dimpled gently as if by a master craftsman, the white throat, wise

look, smile which bespoke a promise of contentment, until you were lost in all these things and images, nothing remained of you but a mist, which was probably no more than the obscurity of weariness, of your desire to sleep, were it not for that one fiery spot within you throbbing, craving and radiating like ripples in a pool.

Wait a minute, what's this in front of you? Looks like a group of men—what are they up to? These must be escort units setting out, we'd better get over to the side and make room, they're here already. There are the first of them, the front of the file is already passing, a young fellow, half his head lost in helmet, his windbreaker coming squarely down below his waist, which was girt with a pistol belt; Gavri, whose friends are everywhere, no matter what the darkness, suddenly called to him; "Hi, Shuki, you're looking great!" But the other, solemn at the head of his men, gave only a kind of smile in reply, the implications of which were blurred by darkness: "Hello, Gavrosh!"—and continued on his way ("That's Shuki, the CO, great guy!" explained Gavri briefly). Next came the walkie-talkie man, his antenna waving before him like a bug's with a thick, continuous rustle spreading from its top: suddenly, not losing step, he put the microphone to his mouth and uttered something in a ventriloquial voice, singsonging away until he stopped, and once again the thick rustle swished out around him as he passed. Next was a tall lad who found it difficult, being long-legged, to keep in step with the man in front of him, and after him came a man whose spectacles gleamed, and another after him, until all was combined in a line of men passing, bereft of any personal expression, their weapons jutting above their shoulders. After the termination of the leading unit came, so Gavri explained, the first platoon headed by its chubby commanding officer breathing hard with the exertion of the march, throbbing with energy and importance, his helmet hanging at the back of his head as he chewed its strap; after him were two machine gunners who shifted their weapons from shoulder to shoulder, and then the riflemen, carrying, in addition to their weapons and packs, those boxes, of which the inventor's mother should be cursed, along with his wife, sons and daughters, too, if in addition to his other inventions he had succeeded in spawning his evil seed in the land. Silently they passed by, their coats rustling, their feet stumbling upon stones here and there in their zeal to remain in line. This was followed by the next unit, then another, at whose appearance Gavri, the all-seeing, bestowed louder hellos and softer, as befitted the person and his office, explaining hurriedly and adding brief comment as to the importance of each man, the nature of his particular talents, and the basis of his rightful fame. The men paused for a glance, hurrying on. The mortar crew passed, bent under their load, puffing like steam engines but accepting no pity. It was a long, silent line—but then one spoke up and said: "Hey here's Gavri, the ass-kisser, got a soft job as usual!"—only to be swallowed up in darkness before Gavri, raging, could call after him: "Hello, who's that, who's that, you, Haimo? Is that you, Haimo, the hero Haimo, our great hero, Haimo, we've heard so much about you, Haimo"—unmindful that the man, whose name was perhaps Haimo, had already passed out of hearing, where he no doubt was continuing to whisper his slanderous disclosures to his neighbors down the file, which kept on ceaselessly, without a break. Then one of the onlookers suddenly whistled, excited by something. A unit comprised entirely of midgets appeared, almost children (woe to your poor mothers, not knowing who will return in one piece from this night). There they went, one after the other. Another company commander passed and at his heels the whisper of the walkie-talkie on the back of its bearer hurrying not to lag behind. A human chain setting out in the darkness, on its way. This was the quick march of the night, armed, heavily equipped, energetic rhythm, power in perfusion, and one wanted all at once to rise up before them and state his admiration, to praise this or that man walking his dark line, all of those unknown soldiers who kept on, whose only fear was of falling out of line, a laudatory tribute delivered in proper speechmaking style, continuing, damn it all. The men of a demolition unit passed, their packs on their backs; they made a big noise about Gavri who encouraged them with words of counsel, sundry intimations comprehensible to the expert alone. Some good word had to be found to fill the place of prayer for their survival—at least to allow them to laugh, if nothing else. But Gavri was not one to stop before earth and sky had been filled with his sonorous presence, and then it was clear that the best thing to do would be to join the marchers and go off with them, blessed and praised on your way to whatever fatal destination. For what is man but a gentle creature, devoid of any desire of his own for a march such as this, which he undertakes trembling with worry and want, though not rejecting the burden but hoisting it upon his back and marching on, immersed in the rhythm and the sweat, too pressed for time to think about things and their ends. Diligent, anonymous, they passed on and on, in a single file of silence, one after the other, on and on, silent men marching in line. About two hundred have already passed, maybe three hundred, or—could it be—four hundred, keeping to their long line, one group after another, each with its gear and its silent faces in the night march. Something which could be perceived only in a blur, as it was greater than that which ordinary words can describe.

Suddenly you are disappointed in yourself, for being as you are. And when you remember how in the midst of all these extensive preparations, all the labor here undertaken, the all-comprising endeavor of these two hundred, or three hundred, or maybe even four hundred men and their efforts, an endeavor which extends above and beyond their private identities, displacing all those factors of their existence which do not have direct bearing upon this immediacy, thus bringing to naught the affairs of each as an individual, each with his own home somewhere, and his unique soul, all trivial and tedious now—how in the midst of all these things you have not forgotten your fancies and your wild and worthless dreams: if only there were at least something of reality in them, something actually to be found somewhere, and not these frivolous, disembodied vapors which were more nothingness than existence, whose content, if there were any, though it puzzled you not a little, was essentially devoid of meaning. But even as the ground trembled you did not forget your trivial self.

The men came, on and on. For a moment you discern an individual face, but swiftly it has become but a continuation of that line being swallowed up in the darkness. It was good to see such an exhibition of strength. A vision of former marches came pitifully to mind, squads with sten guns charging, so precious in their meagerness. But this time everything is going to be all right. Tonight, the convoy will get through. The siege will be broken, the road breached, we're going to make it! Just so nobody gets blown up (when he cries out, the fact that he is not at all nameless will become clear, and that he has a home, and that justice has been unalterably perverted in the wounding of this known soldier, so definitely named and valued). The lads came on and on. As solemn as if to a ritual, they marched to battle, these anonymous men. Small they were, and bowed under the weight of their weapons, breathing hard and moving on, trying not to fall out of line, keeping up the file of man after man, unit after section, a constant flow of humanity. At last, when the line came to an end, space was empty. It seemed strange to go back to the Jeep, to start it up and move off. Without a word, they made their descent, continuing as they must until they reached the mound, and stopped. Here, in the meantime, everything had been transformed. Trucks gnashed their gears and tried, wailing their indignation, to find their proper places on the rough ground of the darkness, so that somebody, whose hoarse voice upbraided them as he struggled to bring order and civilization to this blind and cacophonous jumble, would be satisfied. Everything had been transformed here, and now actually had the look of a permanent camp, or of a settlement established overnight. Storm lanterns shone here and there in the small channels, deemed by those bending down beside them as sufficient to ensure proper cover under the conditions of blackout. Men with white bands on their wrists were moving about by the big, floury road of dust, and these were no less than genuine MP's taking charge of all, and soon to demand your pass, so as to leave nothing of the former wildness of the deserts. Someone was sitting on a car and in front of him a red eye, of which he repeatedly demanded in a monotonous voice: "How do you hear me?"—after which he would emit, at intervals, a series of sharp, muffled whistles, while his instrument replied to him in incoherent human syllables which had perhaps been uttered from within a barrel. The glowing tips of cigarettes moved, and dust rose, the stubborn and malodorous dust, clinging dumbly to everything and elevated above all, as a species of dim, smoky canopy, which when one of the drivers erringly turned on his headlights for a moment, so that the entire field, with its bustle of movement, suddenly flared up in a golden light, giving it the appearance of something in a children's story, was revealed hovering over all, a scintillation of golden dust, embracing and enveloping and blocking the view with a whitish, shining, turbulent circle, like a spell of witchcraft.

But where was Rubinstein in all this mess? And where has my Dali gone? Gavri was already everybody's old buddy and everywhere he greeted friends and acquaintances who knew of course that he had come back from a reconnaissance mission, and that if the convoy were going to succeed it was thanks to Gavri, everyman's hero, whose exploits had already been related here and there, in a whisper, not neglecting the visit to the Egyptians an hour ago, from which he had returned after having made such fools out of them that you would burst your sides with glee just to hear about it, for even after the bastards had fired two or three shots at him, he had continued to take this pleasure at their expense, incidentally noting all the details of their position, to the last jot, thus ensuring the ultimate success and security of the convoy.

Then Rubinstein suddenly turned up and told him that the convoy had already set out, but one truck had overturned in the wadi by the village and blocked the road. "Sss," whistled Tzvialeh, "what a beginning!" And then he said, "Did anything happen to anyone?" "Nothing happened to the men, but the road is blocked." "So what now?" said Tzvialeh, though no definite answer was expected. Dammit. At once you were reminded of those cursed commands to retreat at the approach of daylight, when you have to leave, to withdraw, because you haven't succeeded in getting organized, something hasn't come in time, a tardy company, a platoon lost, or a change of plans, an agreement to a momentary cease-fire, or something of the kind— that despicable but feared order to retreat after you've been crawling all night and in the end arrived, the firing has started, there are even bodies lying here and there, the wounded are groaning while you cannot reach them, but you grit your teeth and say finally: "To hell with it, we'll get through, no matter what!"—and then those orders, "retreat", "operation canceled," "no attack tonight", all those orders which enrage you to rebel, and at the same time humiliate you so that you feel trivial and foolish, disgusted with your comrades and with your own life, with everything, especially this war, as well as everything else under the sun: now once again you would have to sweat out a beginning, once again all the torments of getting control of yourself and your fears and thoughts and luck, all over again from the start, and all because of that retreat. Unspeakable night. Night of evil, barren and malignant. Idiotic night which had been turned back—just a truck gone off the road. To have to wait until they get it out of the way, till the winch comes, while here everything's ready, everything in its place, ready to go—better run away from the start than go to the men and tell them: "All off, operation canceled."

"Well, it'll take another half an hour, or an hour," said Rubinstein, producing a cigarette and showing in the flash of the lighter swollen bags under his eyes in the shadows of his eye-pits, a weary and aging Jew. "It's not so terrible yet." That's the way it is, already willing to give in, the old bastard. He ought to be cursing hell out of them, he should be running from one man to the next, down the mound and its twisting paths, stirring them up, shit! They should be shaking their fists, screaming and swearing together. "Yes," said Tzvialeh, and immediately felt a great weariness, wanting to stretch out and lie down in absolute motionlessness, as if he did not even exist. "I'm going to dig up some chow," said Tzvialeh, turning away; once by himself he found a crate, something upon which he could sit, hunched up with his feet raised, they too resting on the crate, his hands holding his knees together and the whole thing weighed down by his chin,—so he sat, secure for a while.

And so it was that his thoughts returned to Dali, who had not been seen of late. You haven't seen her, but don't worry, you're as dear to her as the snows of yesteryear. She's not looking for you. Who really needs you? How different it would be if there were in the world a Dali all yours: you would come to her and embrace her and kiss her and make pretty speeches, and to hell with the world One girl all yours, dammit. What distant and mysterious refuge had she found for herself, right in the middle of the road? Suddenly the whole of your marked route was recalled: from the main road, the northern highway, until this point beside the dusty mound. The intersections and the possibilities of shortcuts to be dared by adventurous drivers seeking the easy way, who left the road to brave detours over untrod stretches, and were rewarded by being the subjects of a vigorous dribble over the furrowed fields; the wadi with its steep, earthen banks, where they had to move cautiously along the excavated channel, especially where the channels drew so close to the road that only a thin strip of track remained between the two gullies. That was the place, apparently, where that damn truck turned over—left-handed drivers! And further on, the clefts and scars in the road over which you skipped and slipped until you reached a sloping bridge, which was higher than the road at both ends, so that any one entering upon it or leaving its causeway had to be warned in advance, otherwise he would be bumped as he drove onto the bridge and banged and shaken as he drove off the far side; but from this point on one could continue smoothly, the route was easy, flattened by many wheels, so you enjoyed the hard, straight road with the yellow expanse of sorghum on either side. But not for long: a little stream had come creeping toward the road to take a look, just an innocent look with no ulterior motive, and only incidentally had the bridge, which once spanned the stream, come to an unfortunate and lowly end at its bottom, the ground having fallen from beneath it, on both sides; such were the painful results of curiosity, although the bridge despite its fall had no intention of being idle, and managed to attract the road, pulling it through a serious of turns until it crossed the channel spirally at the lowest point, with a dizzy dance and dive, a joy to every valiant driver, who could change gears here and push with his foot and slam with his hand, twirling the wheel like a yo-yo; afterward there was a stretch of deceptive trail and then the plain opened up again, like a racecourse, at which you, too, wanted to open up and whiz past the plain on your left and the plain on your right up to the foot of the mountains, the hills to the right, enveloped in dust, to race through that glowing gold to the sea beyond, but you have already reached the outskirts of a village of mud huts, at the entrance to which a concealed trench (such were the remains of Arab fortifications) invited your caution; there, cramped between faded walls, you had to push on noisily through dust completely transformed into floury powder, and promptly turn left, by the side of a small wood of eucalyptus (planted in an old quadrangle of clay bricks, in which a ditch still held its water till the end of summer), pass alongside a few tamarisks of flattened foliage, and observe in passing the faces of yellow soldiers peeping out at you from their momentary refuge in that sagging, tin shanty shaded with tamarisk branches, which with the aid of a few perforated cans had been made into a shower, the waste water stagnant and greenish about it, and wasps, and washing, and naked male bodies, their genitals, and more dust, a schoolhouse, rotting mattresses, one wheel-less armored car, victim of a mine: now you were already at an abrupt slope which broke off into the wadi, and a cleft hidden by a heap of dust came rushing past under your wheel—this was another of the Arab defense trenches—and no matter how careful you were, you could not avoid that severe bump extracted as a toll at this crossing; now coils of barbed wire testified to mines and the approaching front, and on the slope of the hill and in the gravelly bed of the sprawling channel, studded with Abraham's balm and elecampane. Your noise rose obnoxiously as you ground your gears, though in the end you attained the right bank of the channel, there to choose between two roads, each as bad as the other, their fault being the ironic result of that hearty welcome with which they had greeted previous trucks, whose passage had so deepened the wheel-tracks that later vehicles, no longer welcomed, risked splitting their belly on the ridge between the ruts. Afterward the horizons opened out again, and tripping past the abandoned Turkish railway embankment the road turned firmly to the east, following which no bump or jump, no matter how fierce, could cause you to swerve your eyes from that tower rising ahead of you, surrounded by roofs and trees, like a farmhand leading a flock of geese in a little green meadow, orchards and sprouting patches at his every side—a sign you've already covered half the road! But it's only half the road, and you've done it in daylight. Imagine how it will be at night, in the dusty dark, with muffled lights, with drivers who are definitely not of all-star quality, and who are further handicapped in that they have never seen the road, this road about which they couldn't care less, either for the road or for the fields or for the whole damn convoy—all they want is a little peace and quiet.

※

Now he unlocked his hand, freeing his knees, and hauled up his chin from where it had been anchoring his weightless legs, and straightened up. This was not weariness, or a wish to sleep, though you were wearied by the struggle not to be indifferent. Although you made no effort to listen, it was clear some vehicle was being guided, and had apparently slipped backward, for the voice directing the driver uttered only one continuous croak: "Forward, forward, forward nice and easy!"—and at once you could distinguish the wail of this particular truck from the noisy buzzing below. Could you hear a donkey braying with all this racket? —though in the long run we have very little to say or determine in all this, like leaves in a raging stream. Out of nowhere you hear that a truck has overturned. Out of nowhere you catch a shell. It could happen to you. "Hey!" croaked the guiding voice below: "You made it," upon which the slam of a door drew after it a rush of returning silence, filling in what had been chipped by noise. For some reason it now became clear, all at once, that there would be an end to this war, and those who somehow had remained alive would eventually return, each to his place, where he would find that, as far as he was concerned, nothing changed, everything had remained almost exactly the same. Only once was a man young, and now you were still a man but no longer young. As such you would return. You had not learned to be different, no new man had grown up inside of you, as you had been so were you still: no cleverer and just as foolish and, above all, no more successful than before. Moreover the world would go rolling on quite happily without you, even with all due reverence for your unique and precious soul, there was no doubt that the world could do without you just as it now did without the thousands who have already become no more than a memory. Furthermore, who promised you that the war was obliged to give you something? What justification did you have for the grumbling and dissent, the disappointment and sulking, who could be blamed, his name screamed aloft in shame as traitor? Who gave a damn?

So forget it! This was probably just the feeling of midnight coming on. The stars above have changed their attitudes. What's happened to me? He suddenly felt a strange but definite need to find Dali and have a talk with her, what about didn't matter, it was just a feeling after all—but most definitely to have a talk with her. Guided by these good intentions he got up and went to look for her. But she was not to be found. Neither was Rubinstein. Strange, where were they all, what had happened in these five minutes? Suddenly he found those long-sought words which would tell her, all at once, all that was in his heart, the simplest sort of phrase: Hey, I like you a lot! He would just smile and say it, like a light breeze. It would be so fine to come and say all at once with all his heart, just like that: I like you so much! You hardly know her. Actually you don't know her at all. Perhaps she's not all what you think, and you have only been imagining. But there was not imagining in this itch of yours to go and tell her. This was your frivolous, mad, but very real wish. Moreover she really was like that, was as you wished her to be, she was as she must be, for you had decreed, that was it, was she, and now you would reclaim her. For God has suddenly brought you together, funny. What will she answer when you come and tell her, with all your heart, simply like this: "You know, I like you a lot!" Will she turn her eyes to you for a moment and say: "Hi, how's it going?"—then turn them away and busy her fingers again with her knobs and wires, the end of a love affair. But that won't be all, I won't stop. I'll say: Seriously!"—and she'll reply: "You don't say. Seriously!"—as if flicking her finger to remove a speck of dust from her dress. But you will keep on fervently trying to save something from the disappointment of humiliation: "I really do like you." "That's nice," (she will say) "anything else?" Damn it all, why should it have to be exactly like that! She might, let's suppose, say something else, something good, even if it were not spoken with any particular emotion, even if she were not to return your enthusiasm, not for example falling on your neck; suppose she were to say something like, "Oh really?" indistinctly, or something else—who knows what she might say—and to smile a little. This would be a smile as to a friend, not outspoken, but they would laugh a little in the meantime, so as not to be embarrassed, thus improving the situation somewhat, although there was still more room for improvement, such as for example if you were to go up and say, "Dali, really, you're great!"—upon which she would gaze at you, astonished. You wouldn't know what to say next, but neither would she. For a moment she would gaze, then lower her eyes. Or smile for a moment. Or, dammit, this is too much. What kind of sentimental bastard have you become, man? Where is everyone? What's going on down below? If I knew something special, something really important, a fact, or a piece of news, or something I could tell her, winning her complete attention for that great, special, important, and interesting item, I would go over there and tell her in practical, businesslike fashion, straight to the point, without affectation or any display of feeling, nothing personal, no passion, nothing. Dammit what's happening to me! Hey, what are those Jeeps doing here? Two machine guns to each and a crackling communications set, its eye glowing red or green; white, Arab-style kerchiefs—*kaffiyahs*—a spirit of exciting events returned with the smell of gas and dust, awakening your will to adventure; pulling yourself together you came back to something you had almost forgotten. Tonight we break through. But this fleeting wind was immediately stifled by a doubled and trebled rain of dust, which choked up your nose and chiding you, after its fashion, for your having neglected it of late, whereas it had only been napping briefly. With a grimace Tzvialeh escaped into the field beyond this turbulent, constricting thickness. But here in the field were all those Jeeps, racing about to find their positions, passing one after the other at feverish speed, until at last they calmed down, switched off their engines and fell silent. Immediately human voices broke out, young voices, uttering big words, coughing and whistling and chatting with friends in the seventh Jeep further on, and it was obvious that these were bold men, proud of their virility and the vigor of their Jeeps, and their hair-raising adventures, and their contempt for everything you held dear, for indeed what was there in the world but these heroes and their exploits which all men must hail. These were the great and terrible friends of no one living except themselves, these were the instruments of retaliation, who had attacked and taken, flying by night and galloping by day, who had at the last minute saved the day, whose appearance was lordly, complete with awesome moustaches, a forest on their foreheads and chins, quick to devour all men and skillful on the female track, springing at their scent, no matter how distant—though each of them kept his mother's picture in his breast pocket and refrained from peeping at it out of shame in front of the others, who would doubtlessly rebuke him for not putting a hot pinup in its stead, which he did not, because actually he had no girl. (They had been drafted straight from home and school for what was described as a three-day mission, now half a year old.) Then the men from one of the Jeeps started up a song, and those of the next Jeep, jealous, began another for the fun of it, leading to a battle of shouts and arguments and loud laughter, sputtered by coughs in the chilly air (Mummy would have been singing them a lullaby just about this hour!)—glowing cigarette tips waxed like the firmament and wheeled in the dark, until after a short fray one song outsang the rest, and subsequently was sung by all with that particular enjoyment and emphasis befitting a new song just learned, worthy of being sung again and once again. Next they wanted to sing something else but couldn't find the proper song at once. So in the meantime they sang a sad song, and then still undecided, another sad song, till their voices ran wild spoiling the song and inspiring them to request someone, one Abby, to take things in hand, and his boy, Abby, obliging enough, took off on that crazy jingle which had relentlessly enslaved every tongue and ear, till the mound and the dust and the road and the Jeeps were caught up with the song, singing away in voices thick and hoarse, whistling, humming or just crooning, so the song passed from wave to wave, from guard to guard, as far as Tel Abu-Shin and perhaps even further.

Suddenly he bumped into someone, and it was Rubinstein, who looked up at him and said: "Tzvialeh, where have you been?"

"Very funny," cried Tzvialeh. "Where have I been. And what about you?"

"I've been right here all the time," said Rubinstein innocently.

"So have I been here all the time," Tzvialeh retorted with the same intonation.

"Strange," said Rubinstein.

"Amazing," said Tzvialeh. And they shrugged their shoulders, smiling at each other, after which the facts of their position were discussed, beginning with the revelation of the convoy's approach. It had already reached the village, and now the Jeeps of the commando unit would continue with it, guarding it front and rear. Gavri would go with them and come back about daybreak, if every thing went as hoped. Our duty was to ensure that everything came off according to plan in this area. And that meant—said Rubinstein—"being everywhere and keeping your eyes open."

"Sure," replied Tzvialeh, his glance already darting about in search of a different sort of conversation. He had almost begun to ask Rubinstein if perhaps he had seen someone somewhere, when his lips failed him, so he said instead: "It's getting pretty late!"—whereupon Rubinstein said, "Yes," a modest summation of his considerable concern. "We've got to make it," whispered Tzvialeh to silence his own apprehensions, as if they could be put off. The numbers on the clock were reaching their peak only to grow smaller, then not so slowly to run back up into the coming light of dawn. It was already time to be getting up and racing in front of the heavy trucks, clearing their path of every obstacle, ensuring them a smooth road, well marked and secure so that there would be no doubt of their successful passage. But everything was dependent on time, treacherous time. They haven't gotten here yet, and still ahead of them was the labyrinth of that village, that precipitous descent to the valley, the agonizing adulations between the rows of mines and in the gravel of the valley, and afterward the climb up the opposite slope, in the darkness, no one knowing where he is or seeing anything further than the shape of the vehicle ahead of him. As if it were just another jaunt in a couple of cars, whereas it took a damn miracle to get this convoy together and on the road. You need trucks, but nobody is going to give you his precious truck to ruin. So you start making the rounds, getting some by persuasion, some by force and the rest by sheer larceny. You get them all together, only to find that almost all of them are unfit to travel. So you repair them. Then comes the time to load them, but you don't know what comes first, what to take and what not. So you get everything organized. Of course you avoid no quarrels and spare no complaints and even go to headquarters to raise hell, until at last you find the little man with the magic key who solves all. Except for the matter of drivers, who has drivers, who has spare parts…what do you think we are, a bunch of damn sorcerers? But no sweat kiddo, we're going to make it. Actually we have no choice. There's no time to go back, or to break up and quit, or for anything at all but to get through. Just so they come, let them come on and get here.

The convoy must be climbing the hill now, a unit of Jeeps preceding it and another following, up to the top of the hill and then down diagonally to the wadi, back up through the sorghum, and back down the winding slope to the wadi, where the going would be somewhat rough until the main road—but that's all! That's the plan. Now just let them come, and we'll get down to business. One boy had brought along a harmonica with him, as if on a hike, at camp during the summers as they used to be. Somehow harmonica music always got you going, although it seemed to be getting a little too merry and noisy. Lay off. Just so they get there.

"Say, does anybody have a match?" Wait a minute—that's Dali! Five paces away from you and you've been looking for unicorns in the wilderness!

"I've got a light for you," said Tzvialeh, fiddling with the screw of the lighter and shielding it with his other hand, finally serving her a brimming cup of red flame. Here she is, she whom you have wrapped in desires, come out of patches of light and nighttime expanses to initiate some mysterious rite. "What's up?" said Tzvialeh, trying to be suave as he nodded toward the radio.

"Nothing," she replied, bending again, enveloped in smoke over her notebook, with its dots and dashes, her pencil moving rapidly under the small, reddish lamp which made a tiny pool of radiance despite the world of surrounding darkness.

"Received anything special?" (Perhaps she doesn't know that you have the right to ask?)

"Just something for Shmuel over there," she replied, tracing a circle with the tip of her finger to define the whereabouts of over there. Her voice was low, resonant. And now it was even quieter, himself having added nothing.

"Cold tonight," he blurted, before it occurred to him that this was not the ideal way to start a friendly conversation.

"Not so bad," she replied lightly. Well how could you be sure this line hasn't already been tried tonight, before you, just the same kind of stuff, already all used up and done with. You're just a miserable mimic, impressing no one. But on the other hand—"I mean compared to how it was during the day," he said, rubbing his nose.

"Uhum," replied Dali. What next? "But the worst of it is this dust!" he said, a new horizon opening before him. "Horrible," she agreed, without raising her eyes from the hieroglyphics in front of her and upon which her pencil continued to scribble—as if for example he were a single fly not worth the trouble of a swat. Very nice. (Just so they get there!) Now what next? You must have something up your sleeve. Now is the time, man, or never. What has happened to all your profound sentiments all at once just like that? So to hell with all profound sentiments all at once or never. Suddenly he was startled to find himself blurting out: "Dali"—in such a way that she immediately raised her eyes to him bewilderedly and said "Uh—what is it?" (So tell her something, you dumb ass!) "Nice to hear that singing," said Tzvialeh. "Never mind them!" said Dali, going back to her notebook. (What next? You've already talked about the harshness of the weather and the hatefulness of the dust and you've tried your hand at music, a subject which would be better left alone in the future)—"Why, don't you like the way they sing?" "What?" said Dali. "I don't even know them." "A harmonica at night or camel bells, those are the kind of things it's always nice to hear again." Bravo! Now you're talking, man. It shall be known that you're not just another one of those usual, coarse bastards who jump right into it with their jokes and their wisecracks and their paws, smelling of sweat, unwashed for days, stinking of liquor and cigarette smoke—that the land is not devoid of men of taste. "Sure," said Dali, still engrossed with her pencil and paper. "They sent the whole message backwards!"—tracing and crossing out with her pencil, so distant, so fine, so self-contained, unattainable even as she was sitting within reach of your hand, bathed in the alluring reddish light while the radio chuckled in a whisper alongside. Dali, what can one find to say to you? Dali, my darling! "Oh-la-la," said Dali, "are those guys mixed up!" Then you felt a sudden pang of sadness as if you had suddenly seen things, in one clear glimpse, for what they really were, a sadness unconstrained by trivial cares, powerful and all-encompassing enough to smite you with a choking hand upon your throat. (Just so they get here!) For a moment he closed his eyes and felt the sickly taste of dust on his lips.

"It's too bad you weren't here during the day," said Tzvialeh suddenly.

"What's different by day?"

"You can see the hills and the mountains over there, and that plain."

"Mm," said Dali, "and that's the route the convoy is supposed to take?" "Over there, to the south."

"That's the south? Then over there is north?"

"Sure! Look, there's the North Star, and that's the Great Bear, look over there!" How could you point out a star to someone without laying your other hand on her shoulder. Apparently where there's a will there's a way.

"It's funny," said Dali, "I'd be afraid to go ten steps here, I'd get lost."

"Well you have enough to get lost in here," said Tzvialeh, "it's endless." A special channel of awareness was opening up within him, a silent cry of adoration, a dark yearning which needed no eyes to guide its object. It was she who possessed the creamy warmth, hidden and fragrant, which should be held and caressed, with a murmur in her ear, until you were hers, and you could sing to her of an end to all wars and dust and noisy crowds of packed and pushing soldiers, you could sing of something else, broad fields and hills, that would be given to those who had such a Dali, who adored her just for being as she was—a world of true peace and beauty, rich as fertile, rain-soaked soil, of fresh, peaceful verdancy, and the little things in life that, having neither tongue nor time, sing a ceaseless praise of their own, Dali, Dali (no doubt about it, I'm going to step on a mine tonight. Just so they get here). "Yes," said Dali, pulling at her cigarette and finishing her scribbling, which act allowed her at last to sit up straight in her broad, bulky coat, to shake away her hair and made herself comfortable. "There's plenty of space here." Then she raised her eyes, drawing at the cigarette, the dim light revealing a strong, individualistic eyebrow line. She looked at him, and a deep calm, like that of a field after rain, descended on Tzvialeh, who, breathing deeply, knew that his skin was quivering like a horse at the touch of a caressing hand. A minute or so passed. "What's happened to you?" asked Dali.

"What do you mean?" said Tzvialeh, breathing deeply.

"Cat's got your tongue." He stood upright, slim, in front of her, gazing at her enveloped in darkness. He was calm and at peace but anxious. He knew his hands were very cold. He wanted to say something, all the fine things that could be said in a whisper, that had been waiting for such a moment, if only there were courage— "Guess it has," said Tzvialeh, moving his lips mutely, and tried to smile. Dali smiled a little too. It was if they were now enclosed in some sort of circle, while an unoppressive silence quivered in the space of the night, clear and high, like the treetops stirring without wind, a gigantic, unexpected pause between them. Then Dali exhaled and, stubbing out her cigarette on the side of the Jeep, almost said something, but didn't, turning to her set with a glance at her watch, because it really was a certain time, time for her to ready her voice, poke at the knobs in front of her, and begin to speak mechanically into the mouthpiece. Tzvialeh set off at a run down the slope of the field, as if someone were already impatient and waiting for him there. He wanted to shout something, but only laughed a little and again started to looked around for Rubinstein or anyone at all who might be there among the trucks and the men where he wandered, darting up and down, then halting to pause and think a moment, after which he set out and actually discovered one man with whom a conversation could be started, so there they were laughing and clapping hands together in excitement, as Tzvialeh said to his companion: "Dammit, I can't wait anymore—when the hell are they going to get here?"

※

But it was only after midnight had come and gone, at one in the morning—when the men had finally found a more or less comfortable position for the night, all fastidiousness overcome as they chose their beds and blankets, for anything would do as long as one could curl up in it and take an undisguised nap without further resistance, thus putting to an end all yawns and chatterings and fake looks of wakefulness, for there were some who already had a sour taste in their mouths from the naps they had been taking on and off as a minority right, while others having long since forgotten where they were and why, now found their ultimate destiny in a cold, crumbling sprawl of inertness—that a sudden breath of energy blew up, and a tremor shook about the mound. At first they only listened, unwilling to admit this disturbance of their repose, but the clumsy movements which followed could not be denied, as they became more lively with some formulation of purpose, conversations having already been started, and shufflings turned into definite changes of place, now accompanied by exclamations and wise replies and no lack of laughter, until it was apparent that one would be able to adapt himself to the importance of the moment. A grumbling noise of traffic approached, ever nearer, seemingly without beginning or end in the midst of that great darkness from which it burst forth and was ejected. Another moment, and a half-track was already shaking the ground with its roar, lumbering up to the mound, its chains screeching, and someone on top of it from out of the exhaustion of dust and darkness and impatience shouted something indistinct, confused and eventually destroyed by the noise and dust, so that the shouter deemed it best to halt, though immediately afterward his voice was again heard, those obstinate shouts. This time someone had apparently understood the meaning of his cry and replied with a shout of his own, so that things took on an aspect of strangeness and broadness and immortality. The first truck had already come into view from behind, which aroused the dust to further efforts in its mimicry of an all-containing, all-drowning ocean, until scarcely a breath was left, though this was actually appropriate to the general bedlam, everyone going and coming and milling around, disappearing each with his secret purpose, or cunningly lighting one of those myriad matches which revealed in a drop of flame a sea of dense, writhing, colorful dust, from which voices emerged only to die down again, the only constant sound being the screech emitted by the braking wheels of one of the furthermost vehicles.

Suddenly a whisper passed through the crowd: Avraham has come—referring to a man standing in a half-track and leaning over its side panel to talk to someone below. Though it appeared no one knew exactly what this highly acclaimed Avraham had done to earn his fame, everyone knew that if it were actually Avraham who had come, no doubt could be retained as to the importance of this convoy, obviously it was even more important than you had thought; moreover the presence of such a distinguished figure dispelled all doubts as to its success. At once you felt rightfully proud of this Avraham, with whom you were to participate in this great enterprise. You were inspired by the spirit of devotion urging you to request permission to go forward and join him in the half-track, to be side-by-side with him in the kernel of events and at danger's core, forgetting or perhaps momentarily disregarding the well-known fact of the half-track's activities and duties, namely that its presence at the head of the convoy was solely for the purpose of setting off mines and crushing them under its weight, with a resultant minimal damage of split driving

but as Tzvialeh recalled, one had already overturned, and how could they lose another one too? However it might be, there was a feeling of disappointment as the roar of the engines died down, although from the sound of the curses you would never know it; in addition, those who had been prepared to move on as they were now found it possible to arrange things more comfortably, while others discovered that they could even stretch their legs, or let their heads fall back in a brief snooze, while the more hearty gathered by the maimed truck to watch and sympathize.

Tzvialeh knew no one in the convoy. And his patience had been stretched more than he realized, perhaps because so few were aware of how much there was still to do and what was in store for them in this second and shorter half of the night. To hell with that tire—I would have left them here. Risking the whole convoy for one truck! We've got to get going—Tzvialeh boiled inwardly—got to get it over with, finished and done. Those guys at the guard posts are probably sleeping already. And those posted alongside the road, how can they wait so long, cold and lonely, and not fall asleep? Meanwhile we're making so much noise here, who knows how far it carries? Let's get out of here, get it over with! He jumped off the Jeep, but his knees began to buckle with weariness, so he changed his mind and went back to his place. The smoke was burning his throat. Would anything really happen during the rest of the journey? Avraham. You hear a lot about him, all kinds of stories—(What a racket! Nobody's going to hear any donkey tonight). Well, let's get started. If I know them they can't find the right wrench or the screws are rusty or something else is broken. But with a Dali like that you could, anything at all. So what's going on? Moving at last— yes! Here's Rubinstein, now let's go? Everything's okay, good old Rubinstein, the calm and practical one. We're off. Are they following us? Sure they're following. There are the Jeeps, the half-track's iron voice comes clear—we're off! Barrels of fuel, clothes, food, munitions, water-pump motors, medical supplies—boy, what a welcome the convoy will get. It's too bad I can't go on with them till the end, when they bring all these supplies to their final destination—what a welcome they'll get! Now where's our track?—after considerable effort it was found. Suddenly it gave the misleading impression of having swerved to the side, and the illusion tempted you for a moment to continue in that direction and get lost (madness!). You had to pull yourself together, arouse your self from time to time with a look in all directions, in order to keep your wits about you and see the way clearly. This climb will be rough for the heavy trucks. To the rear Jeep followed Jeep, the rest of the convoy swallowed up in darkness, nevertheless proclaiming its existence in a querulous, muffled grumble. Bending down one could see the truck's antenna floating erect above the bluish horizon, clearly visible. "Hello, Jonah Two, come in, come in"—this is it!

Suddenly there was something ahead, twisting, vanished and then there again, which shortly turned out to be none other than the handkerchief of the guard at the first marker. "So it's for real this time?" said the man as they passed him joyfully and with great interest. "This is it," Tzvialeh replied proudly, like a commander entering the city at the head of his victorious legion. Hey—halt! What's going on? The convoy has stopped, what's the trouble? Rubinstein jumped off, but before he had gotten far the trucks roared, and one could hear men calling "Move out!" one to the next, and so they did. Until once again they halted, because the others were not following. One of the men sitting on the top of the load of one of the trucks in the middle of the convoy had gotten the idea that something was going to fall. Not wasting a minute he beat on the roof of the cab and the driver stopped. The next truck managed to brake to a stop a split second before colliding with the one ahead, and so it went down to the end of the convoy, each truck screeching to a halt; meanwhile the man sitting on top of the preceding truck, seeing how things were going, cleverly banged on the roof of his cab too. All at a halt, the guilty ropes were tightened. But the drivers had become suspicious. They couldn't see a thing, not even the back of the truck ahead. A few of them decided to station a man on one of the front fenders. The others, deeming this an improvement worthy of notice, did likewise, so that every front fender soon had its watcher, perched aloft and trembling with progress, their eyes on the wheel tracks as they guided their drivers with broken syllables emerging from the handkerchiefs about their mouths. So the convoy continued, inching forward, until the next snag, encountered immediately, bringing all to a halt. Hurry up and wait. Once more you had to go back and find out what had happened in one of the distant segments of this long, blind caterpillar. Then the gears grated again, and the big dark trucks swayed from side to side as if sailing on crests of waves which seemed to be lifting and moving the heavy loads effortlessly; only their roar betrayed them.

Now they were passing along the black rocky patch. One could see the horizon. A pale green spark appeared in the sky, chasing a faint echo of escaping shadows. On the move. Groaning, the trucks moved slowly (what did they remind you of, trucks on the move?)—little by little, but moving. Rubinstein suddenly swerved aside and motioned to the next Jeep to keep going. The Jeep passed, its three men dark in the obscurity of its interior, grinding on. The next Jeep passed, its radio chattering, a pale gleam in its green eye, then the third Jeep and then the half-track came up, clicking its metals as its wheel belts groped to find soil, took hold and pushed on, the cabin rising and sinking like a gander. Next came the first truck, covered in dust, a man lying on its fender and another, just a head with a cigarette peeping out from the cab, looking, watching. From the unending line behind, other heavy creatures emerged, announcing their existence with a muffled, powerful roar. Wrapped up against the cold were the men in them, each a son to his mother and father, faceless, nameless, shapeless. Then Rubinstein turned, racing the Jeep through the field and passing the convoy to reach the top, as if this were really a road, whereas Tzvialeh had to grasp at anything within arm's length, just so it could serve as anchor as they skipped and bumped and eventually got back into place, before the slanting slope to the wadi began. He felt a spasm of victorious laughter in his stomach. This was a real convoy, much more than you had imagined upon being told at sunset of some convoy that was to pass here at midnight. The men on the edge of the slope were waving their handkerchiefs. "Go slow here," Rubinstein told them, pointing to the rear with his thumb, so that they should pass the warning along to those behind. The men bent into each truck, saying "Go slow" in a night whisper, which was followed immediately by a change of gears, sometimes executed in expert silence though many ground out their discomfort, as if not a mere spoken phrase had confronted them here but some real entity which plucked upon their nerves, changing the rhythm of their progress to the tune of caution.

But the slope seemed too steep and slanting. All we need is another truck overturned. The Jeeps made it, the half-track had already passed, and now the first truck started its descent. Over the thorns was stretched that thin strip of paper fastened down with little stones, looking pitifully thin and pallid, though this was merely the deception of appearance, for the paper fulfilled its mission successfully, being clearly seen. Tzvialeh and Rubinstein parked the Jeep at the edge of the crossing's flat surface to watch the trucks in their descent. The first big-bottomed truck, its brakes screeching on and off, crawled down on its belly, swaying slowly, blind and wailing, its advance observed by the driver, whose head protruded from the open door, and by the man on the fender as well, while two men walked in front, waving their white handkerchiefs (this is where the lime should have been!) —so the big beast was brought down. From time to time a projecting lump of rock shook the truck so that every onlooker was quite shaken, but it was only air, bursting out somewhere like a cork being drawn. And then the truck halted, bent over sideways, for the driver had stuck his head out and most of his body too, looking down and saying: "Maybe it's better over there, to the right?" "Not on the right, don't turn," yelled Tzvialeh—"keep going straight!" so the truck released its brakes and, pushing its clumsy bulk forward, swayed a moment and stopped opposite the crossing. "I can't make it!" cried the driver from his cabin, leaning out to look. "You'll make it, you'll make it—just take it easy!" "These guys are nuts," said someone, but such defeatism was not to be heeded. "Hey you," Rubinstein called to the driver: "Keep going straight, this way, keep going until this point, then make a sharp left and you're over." But the driver had his doubts. He climbed down from the height of his cabin and got out to size up the situation with his own eyes. (Maybe we were too sure of ourselves, dragging ourselves out to this place—this isn't a road, cried a voice inside Tzvialeh.) The driver lit a cigarette, paused a moment before putting out the match, and looked around. In the flickering light he stood revealed, one man in a faded leather coat, his back bent and his face wrinkled, a knitted cap on his head, one of a thousand truck drivers, each with his own wife and children, his home—this particular one now coughing, spitting profusely and hawking again. "It's not so bad," he said through his stuffy nose, and climbed back to his place, adding "Gimmie some room and I'll get there." He put his foot down hard and the engine picked up, sneezing deeply, faithful as a dog; then he changed gears, released the clutch and accelerated slightly, straightening the wheel, but the minute the bouncing front wheels began to sink into the gravel soil of the channel he spun the wheel to the left, his whole body thrown into one quick movement, after which he again accelerated and leveled out, waiting for the rear wheels to catch up and take their plunge into the channel to his left, and when they finally did he accelerated even more and turned even further to the left, as slowly as possible, until it seemed he was at the point of total collapse, the long drawn-out groan of the truck soon to disintegrate into a whimper, but lo, the groan grew to a roar in a sudden increase of power and there it was, that swaying truck, a swagger of pride, climbing up the other bank far up the path. "Great!" Tzvialeh shouted after him: "you were just great!"—and went back down to do the whole agonizing act over again with the next truck.

All concerned, the guides walking ahead with handkerchiefs and those on top with their calls and cries, were straining every nerve to get their trucks through, helped also by the fact that none was alone, each but a link in the chain of the convoy. Each passing vehicle deepened the ruts of the road, leaving an even clearer mark; moreover those placed in the middle of the convoy had no time to pay attention to the obstacles of the meandering road—actually they could not even discern them, following as they were each at the tail of his predecessor, so that there was no time to think of anything else. They kept on, skipping and bouncing, encouraging one another with the curses of the determined, till with a last squeal of strained springs each finally crossed over. Then Rubinstein took off upon another bold and dangerous dash to reach the head of the convoy in the upper sorghum field, although this enthusiasm was almost terminated unexpectedly by one rut which they noticed only upon smashing into it, but the Jeep's special gear, after a considerable struggle, got them on their way again, the only damage being that to the tip of Rubinstein's tongue, which had almost been severed. They drove speedily along the channel, paying of course no heed to any of these transitory evils, their only concern the waste of time, and in the face of their aggressive fearlessness the channel, being nothing, was of course, by a mighty hop, skip and jump, now more amusing than terrifying, eventually crossed a little further on, after which they attained the sorghum, where, cleaving their way through the waxy stalks of dim, quiet gold sprinkling a shower of grains about them, the path was found and the daredevils and their charger literally thrust themselves between the half-track and the first truck. Oh God now we have to get over the next slope. Now that we've eaten dust we're going to have a sip of the wine of paradise, just one or two slips on this descent and it's all over with this convoy, not to mention the siege which won't be broken and who knows what else. Only a kilometer away from the main road you could destroy the convoy without any need of mines or ambushes, the only enemy your own fumbling hands. Well we're just not going to let it happen!

❧

First Rubinstein sent the three Jeeps to the main road to cover the road and the wadi and report on the situation. Then he ordered the half-track to wait by the side of the route, ready to save the situation with its winch, while the driver, being cautioned, prepared his front cable for an emergency. Then the truck approached, the first of the long line. Ovadiah raced about among his men, shouting down from the top of the hill, loud enough to wake the dead. He was weary after a whole night's labor with light-colored stones and pieces of paper gathered from all the countryside and from the pockets of his men, in which was discovered a hoard of letters, newspapers, crumpled bus tickets and the like, now distributed by a generous hand as markers along the route, but that was not all: there was also a tiny bonfire, camouflaged by stones, flickering at the edge of the second bend, the difficult one, and what more could a good man do (in spite of which it was still not enough)? The driver in the leather jacket climbed down, came up to them and asked: "This is what we have to go down?" "That's right," replied Ovadiah. "So get a horse," said the driver jokingly while his fingers performed some tricky twistings with a twirling key chain, winding it up to the very end, then spinning it out again to the other end as if in some miniature rope trick, then repeating the whole thing, taking many encores, a typical truck driver. "Nope, you're the one who's going to go down." The driver shrugged his shoulders in silence and you felt like some loudmouthed brat. "Can't do it?" Tzvialeh ventured to ask nervously. "Huh," said the driver. "How's about letting me turn around and go back home?" "What are you talking about?" said Tzvialeh, feeling himself on trial in a tight spot. "That's what I mean," said the driver. "You won't let us go home. So what are we going to do? So let's get on with it. What else can we do"—as if to encourage Tzvialeh. "Make sure everything on your truck is tied up tight," added Rubinstein: "we don't want anything to get lost." "It's all in good shape," declared someone from the top of the truck, gazing patiently at them with a glassy, bovine stare. "Put it in first and down you go!" said Ovadiah, anxious to get started and be useful. "Any more good ideas?" said the driver jokingly as he spun his key chain. He walked a little down the slope, took out a cigarette and lit it, then lifted the match, together with the chain of keys twinkling about his thumb, and held it above his head to light up a little of the way, though only the cracked hand of a workman was shown, after which he spat once again and returned, stooping a bit, to his big truck, which was waiting there bulldog-nosed, knowing nothing of what was in store for it. In the meantime the trucks behind were gradually being emptied of their men, and soon one could hear the voices, coming and going, of the restless and the curious, investigating and explaining all, the problem being, according to some, a roadblock of some sort; others whispered that mines had been found, but all the while the flares, now closer on the right, continued to cast their glimmer, arousing a vague, hasty urge to lower the head between the shoulders, where it was somewhat more hidden, for the bad smell of failure was in the air. Half past two in the morning.

Ovadiah went up to the cabin of the first driver: "Ready?" "Ready," the other answered and set his engine roaring. "Follow me, straight behind me." "Now you just step out of the way and let me drive." "I'll guide you." "You think I'm a boy scout? I don't need a guide." "Well then I'll just show you, so you can see—" "Listen, who's the driver, you or me? Now get out of the way and let me get it over with." "Do what he says," said Rubinstein with a smile, "leave him alone." Ovadiah, offended, walked away, intending to stick his hands in his pockets and make it clear that he'd had enough of this game, but this was immediately forgotten as the big truck, with its five pairs of wheels, tilted a bit and started down, the wheels revolving slowly, devouring dirt, the clumps of gravel crushed in their wake, stamped flat underneath, and in the air rose the smell of exhausted petrol, but suddenly the entire truck quivered to a halt, as if something had happened to its guts, for it began wailing shrilly and went back in its tracks, there to brake and start down again, having this time reserved sufficient space for the turn, a wide arc which the front hurried to describe while the back moved more slowly upon a smaller perimeter, thus the whole rounded the first turn and then, with no particular effort, the second, trampling all the papers and stones, those decorations that Ovadiah had arranged with such devotion and diligence, the poor little bonfire being swallowed up and extinguished among the wheels, but slowly, heavily, the vehicle moved on, with a loud creak from the crates on top and one chain grumbling bitterly, and a near scream from your own breast when it seemed as if the truck were going over, though as it developed this was only a list to starboard with the third and final wave, after which it was finally there, yes, in the lower sorghum field.

"Whew," breathed Ovadiah, straightening his body which had been drooping steadily in accordance with the truck's descent. "That's the first one!" said Tzvialeh, looking about to find someone with whom to shake hands. The second truck, full of barrels, emitted a muffled rumbling like distant thunder at every jolt. All we need is one shell in those fuel barrels, Tzvialeh began to think without finishing. Or a mine, he started again. Dammit, we've got to make it this time, this was a prayer from the depths of his heart. The truck had noisy brakes which screeched an instant of agony each time they were called to duty, so that the descent was danced to a staccato of bitter dissonance, screech by screech, bit by bit. Nevertheless, it did not have to reverse at all, rounding one bend after the other, the first, the second, the third, whereupon it halted all at once, its barrels thundering, waiting for someone there, who finally said "Okay," so that it could continue into the expanse of the sorghum field. Then came the third, whose driver asked for someone to walk in front of him and tell him whatever he needed to know, and in addition placed a man on each fender, voicing his discontent with this journey in such darkness. Even by day, he said, he would not go down a slope like this, his was a truck, not a damn mule, he added, whereas in a place like this, such was his opinion, only mules should be used, as any ass would tell you, though all the while he did not stop, despite his lengthy and heavy words, inching forward down the slope, apparently accelerating and braking at the same time, until the men on the fenders felt the sudden lurch of seasickness. At the second bend he simply announced that it was impossible. It couldn't be done. So they came to guide, advising him to go backward a bit. But he would not consent to shift into reverse until they had put a stone in front of each of his wheels: the guides were more than willing, and gathered around the truck to shout "Hey-ho! Hey-ho!" and to push sportively at fender and bumper, a great help, though the truck finally made it after which, with a stirring noise, it circumnavigated the curve, and its driver found this an opportune moment to step out of his cabin and explain to the whole entourage that he had arms and ammunition on top, and that he had no intention of fooling around, this was a serious business, but the rest of his speech and all that was still on his mind was heard only by his own crew, willingly or unwillingly, for the others had gone down to bring the next truck, the fourth.

And that one made it, too, laden to overflowing with crates and bales of clothing; so did the fifth, which had two real clowns on top, with ropes in their hands, which they employed to the amusement of the guides as whips or lassos, however they fancied, anything was good for a laugh. Next came an extra large truck, the driver of which announced that his brakes were sick, just sick, so that the only remedy was to take up a pile of stones on your shoulders or belly, each in accordance with his style and design, and go along step by step beside the wheels of the truck, setting the stones under the wheels and quickly pulling your fingers away, two operations which must be executed simultaneously, or else, as someone explained, the truck would ride over both stone and hand. This one went down too, revealing in passing two stretchers tied to ladders on its side, reminding you of something you would have preferred to forget. But it was already clear that the convoy would traverse this descent with such success as to arouse suspicion: fate could not afford such generosity, and the only question was when would the trouble start. They no longer waited for each vehicle to complete the descent, but began bringing them down all at once, one after the other. There was even a moment to look up at the skies, and suddenly to remember that in spite of all there was a night in this world, and distant hills, and an enemy, and a convoy, for which this route had been made, and it all seemed strange, almost irrelevant to this tense and intricate labor, guiding trucks down the bends of a road not worthy of its name. Climbing once more, after having done so too many times, to the top of the road, you were just a tired dog. Now they were going down with a certain order, mechanically. Every driver was told the right thing at the right time, and he, being no more than a link in a chain, could do no more than accept orders as if they were holy writ, following them to the letter, turning the wheel and stamping on the brakes, while the men on top of the truck dozed, having relinquished any hope of understanding what was going on below, reconciled to anything

Now what next? Rubinstein? There he was, standing silently, wearily hanging his thumbs upon his belt, his middle-aged paunch in front of him, staring into the darkness. What could you say to cheer him up a little, to give him a taste of friendship? But it was better to say nothing. Nostalgia filled the night as the stars slipped westward, about to glide away and disappear. A band of jackals took this as their cue and began to wail, complaining of hunger and cold. Three o'clock. Really? "It's three a.m. already," said Tzvialeh. "That's right," said Rubinstein. (What was his first name actually? Aharon? Yankel? Berl?) "The night's almost gone," said Tzvialeh, "Yes," said Rubinstein. "But we sure did make it, didn't we," said Tzvialeh, trying to open a friendly vein, but Rubinstein made no reply, and a glance at him was enough to discover that he had only shrugged his shoulders. "So what next?" said someone who had just come up, and not just someone after all, but Ovadiah. "So that's all?" "Let's wait a little," said Rubinstein, pulling his thumbs out of his belt and digging in his pockets for his cigarettes. They smoked and looked ahead in the direction of the road. The pulse of green and red flares continued at its regular rate, as if become a permanent function of the night. Here we stand like some mother who has just sent her son off to war, counting the minutes and watching the signs, only dreariness in her emptied house. Oh yes, war! It was cold—somewhere there was coffee. A warm, lighted dining room and a cup of hot coffee. It'll be bedtime soon. Meanwhile that lovely girl has aroused you—there she goes, over to the doorway, maybe you should get up…

What's up? Only Ovadiah speaking: "In the meantime I'll get the men together," he said, and Rubinstein silently nodded his assent. Then someone came at a run: "Rubinstein?" this someone said (but it's a girl, look it's Dali! Wow! How did you manage not to notice her when she was sitting here all the while right at this spot, near enough to hear you call her name if you had only thought to call? Wondrous and wondrous!) But what had happened? "Rubinstein?" she repeated. "Is that you? Listen, one of the trucks is stuck in the wadi by the road. They can't move it. They want to know what to do." So it's happened. You knew it, even before it happened you feared it. "Where's your radio?" said Rubinstein. "Here," she pointed and started walking toward it (now you see how she looks when she stands, the dainty sway of her hips as she turns—as if this were the time and place)—immediately she entered her temple, sat down and began that ceremony of repeated invocations in a monotonous tone, a cryptic litany whose design was never clear, although in the end she asked to be connected with someone denoted as "Sunbeam".

Immediately an echo emerged from the dark depths of the instrument and proclaimed that it was indeed Sunbeam (who, it was obvious, was but a novice at these rites, though he tried to appear otherwise). Rubinstein asked what he had to ask, and Sunbeam replied. It was revealed that in no less a place than the bed of the steep wadi just before the main road a truck had broken down and refused to budge. They had tried towing it but nothing doing. The cause of the breakdown seemed to be one of the axles or something which had been twisted so badly it could not be set back into place. The question was what to do now. But Rubinstein had already decided: "Leave the truck where it is. Unload it first." It wasn't easy to conjure up the expressions of those on the opposite end, but they promptly replied "Okay." But it was not okay yet. "And don't stop. Go on and get across the road," said Rubinstein. "Get across it fast," his hands speaking no less than his voice. Keep going, keep going, don't waste a minute —Rubinstein pressed them—get across that road! Let the Jeeps in the rear take care of the unloading—they'll take the most important stuff. (What's the trouble down there? Then they should take only the motors for the water pumps. Leave the clothes behind. Just leave them there. So what if the truck's in the way—push it out of the way, dammit, pull it, blast it out of there, you've got to get going!) All right. All right. You're moving out already? Good. (Don't stay on the main road. The worst possible place. Get off, immediately. Don't waste a second.) Keep on going across. That's right. Good. Keep on going across. (What a place to pick, the wadi! Who was to blame? Everything was so well organized here—this damn road can drive a man crazy!) Yes, said Rubinstein when the voice spoke again: keep going, keep going. And hold your contact with me, don't switch off (but what about the batteries, grumbled the radio operator at the other end). Hold your contact with me and don't switch off, ordered Rubinstein (it's a good feeling to have someone take all the responsibility, make the decisions and give the orders). "Hello Jonah One, hello Jonah One," said the muffled voice: "We've crossed the road and we're going on." "Hello Jonah One, Hello Jonah One," said Rubinstein. "Keep going, don't stop. Over."

So that's it. Too bad about that truck. That makes two, counting the one that overturned back there. But we haven't had any casualties (you don't know what's still ahead of you—nothing is finished yet. But it is finished. What else is there? It's really all over! You can say your prayer of thanks). And what about the other positions along the route? Dali operated the set with capable hands. She was in her element, this was a task she had mastered, every detail, so that for example when Rubinstein had to speak she would move aside so as not to be in the way. Then you yourself were caught up by an impulse to perform some deed of heroism in her presence, to be an example of extraordinary bravery. Just say the word and I'll jump—"This is A Company," explained Dali, turning up the volume on the set while another voice from the depths of the radio confirmed the convoy's announcement that it was entering the area of that company. "We're counting on you boys," said the convoy to the company with a smile. "We're all yours," replied the company to the convoy, with a left-handed salute.

Three-fifteen. They opened up a pack of crackers, and although these barely-edibles had already just about ruined their gums they tried to chew them again, filling their months with dry, insipid dust: it would have been a task for a steam roller though it was eventually loosened somewhat with the aid of spit, enough to be swallowed. Whereas all you thought about was: how marvelous to break bread in her presence! You could put out your hand and touch her, stroke the slender hands emerging from the voluminous sleeves of that windbreaker whose form is chaos. But it's my joy just to see you, Dali. What else could there be in this wearing mixture of worry and panic and eventual satisfaction carried on the invisible waves of speech. But the radio was talking again: something had suddenly gone wrong with another truck, which was now being towed. (What's the matter with them? Out of the frying pan....!) That's the way it was in a night convoy: you say you have to get through quickly and here you are driving in first and second, stopping every minute, climbing over boulders and leaping ravines, unbelievable things, and only that inexplicable will to keep on keeps you going. (Suddenly you remember the convoys of children, those nights when the children had to be evacuated from the kibbutzim: that worry seemingly without end, the mothers straining their nerves to keep their self-control, that sickening tenseness as you follow the progress of the convoy, its cargo of little children, through a fearsome emptiness which could be filled with explosion any minute, while some of the kids are sleeping and others peering out, asking questions, uncomfortable, miserable, scared as could be, their every word having taken on the ultimate weightiness of a last testament, a farewell to the world, but you must continue your passage through the dust of the dark, strange, perilous fields, not knowing what will happen—must keep on without stopping.)

No, of course they can't stop there—it's too near the main road. And how did they like our route? We told them it was a convenient beaten trail, a good dirt track, but how did it seem to them, who used it?

Although the dust and the stink of petrol have all but destroyed your sense and smell, nothing in the area having escaped that rare mixture of gas and dust, you seem to have a special faculty sensitive only to Dali, her own private fragrance, young and warm and nightlike for love, arousing in you a need to cling, to touch lips, close eyes and luxuriate in pleasure. "The Jeeps guarding the rear have crossed the road." Hallelujah! Now the whole convoy is across the road. Onward!

Rubinstein was leaning on the fender of the Jeep. Then he changed his position, resting his elbow on the hood and sticking his fist in his cheek. Then he bent his head, resting it in the bed of his elbow, curled up in a pygmy shrink, and at last closed his eyes and breathed deeply. A weary man. But here you were, with Dali, alone together. The great, clear night was full of unidentified whispers and tremblings, and you could feel your heart beating in the veins of your throat. Or perhaps this was only your apprehension. However it might be, you felt rather sad. Won't you run your fingers through my hair, Dali? (Ugh! Such dust!) Won't you whisper softly, "Tzvialeh", caressing the name until my breath is gone in this great wide world so gently breathing. No more convoy. Now comes the precious moment of quiet, in which dream and reality merge. Three-twenty. Two hours to daybreak. Not even that. When does the sun rise here? Suddenly the radio's whisper was broken by slight crackles, which ceased immediately. Dali rubbed her weary eyes with her fingertips. But then you heard something you wished were only some trick of playful sound, though your heart sank in pain. Shots!

Really? Yes, shots. Rubinstein! But now there was an explosion; a thunderous roar arose from the hills on the other side of the main road; a pillar of flame rapidly dwindled and disappeared. A mine! The worst of our fears. "It's a mine!" cried Tzvialeh. Rubinstein sat up. Dali put her fists to her breast and looked back over her shoulder. What can we do? We've got to get down there! Where's the Jeep! "Let me speak to them," said Rubinstein briefly. Dali pulled herself together and held the mouthpiece closer: "Hello Jonah One, hello Jonah One, message for you, message for you, Jonah One, over." But the radio's only reply was a continuous crackle, not a word uttered. Again she repeated her adjuration, and again the set crackled without speaking, although one could discern electric splutterings. The shots grew louder. Not a doubt of it. You could already hear machine gun bursts. Really hitting it up. What had happened exactly? An ambush? Damn it all. Where were the covering forces above the road? Damn this waiting. The radio has nothing to say. So let's get the hell down there! Dali tried again. Her voice was somewhat muffled. No one heeded her messages, no one reported the strength of her signals, not a sound, nothing at all. What happened, dammit, have we lost the whole thing in one blow? But they're still shooting, really whooping it up. You feel sick to your stomach with all that food you ate. Why aren't you down there with them in the fight (while another cowardly voice within you praises your good fortune at having stayed here). But they've really caught us. How are we doing down there? Damn this waiting. Then someone was coming at a run, Ovadiah, yelling: "Rubinstein, what's going on?" But it was clear that he had better be silent, so he was, looking enquiringly first at his colleagues, then at the horizon over there. Bursts of fire. Has someone gotten it this time? (But only if he isn't a friend of mine!) Two brilliant flares burst on the other side of the enemy (a kilometer and a half, two, to the west), hung in the sky, their dull, yellow radiance descending, until they faded into nothingness. Who surprised whom, we or the enemy? So it wasn't an ambush, then. (But in that case—just so it isn't Gavri, or Ya'akov, or Hanan, or Avraham—no, not Avraham—and not the driver with the leather jacket and the knitted cap, and not)—why are we sitting here like this! Now the radio opened up its voice, but the words were interrupted and jumbled by sharp squawks, rattling like dried peas. "Hello Jonah One, hello Jonah One, report my signals, report my signals, Jonah One, over," said the set (instead of immediately shouting out what has happened, who's been killed and where the convoy is!). "Hello Jonah One," said Dali calmly, "I hear you, over." "Hello Jonah One," said the set automatically, "Truck number seven hit a mine. I repeat: truck number seven hit a mine. Several wounded. I repeat: several wounded. Scouts have gone ahead." Then the voice asked how they were hearing it. "I hear you, over," replied Dali, swallowing deeply and unthinkingly stroking her cheek. "They're shooting from the hill opposite the post. The Jeeps have gone out in front, the Jeeps have gone out in front, over." So this is it. Several wounded. How many wounded? Who? But Rubinstein's only thought was of the convoy. Asking again for Sunbeam, Rubinstein ordered that unknown in the bullet-filled distance of death's danger: "Leave the damaged truck there and carry on. Do you hear me? Get moving, get moving." (Why was it that only the seventh set off the mine, after the six in front of it, and the half-track and the Jeep in front of them, had passed safely? Seems it got out of line or—just luck?) "Leave it there and get moving, do you hear me? Keep going! Over." Now Rubinstein wanted to speak to

Shuky of A Company, and Dali uttered her adjurations and caught the childish voice of A Company's radio operator. Damn it all, right on the main road, they couldn't have picked a better place! "Where are they shooting from?" asked Rubinstein. The operator with the childish voice explained that they were shooting from the opposite hill, only rifles. The Jeeps were attacking them, and apparently they had begun to retreat. The Jeeps would chase them and try to make contact. "Hello Shuky," said Rubinstein, "don't chase them, don't chase them. Do you hear me? Keep firing after them. Keep them busy. Keep firing and cover the convoy. The convoy must keep on going. Do you understand?" "I understand." "And keep a watch on the road." The other replied that the road was already blocked and mined. (God bless good old Gavri! Just so he doesn't take some stupid chance now.) Then Sunbeam was speaking again from the convoy and asked if the damaged truck should be destroyed to prevent it from falling into the enemy's hands. "No," said Rubinstein, waving his hand and shaking his head in denial. "No. Do you hear? No, no. Over." (It was obvious: the Jeeps had to come back this way in the morning and a burnt truck would be too much of a sign.) Suddenly someone was firing from that hill, now what? Where are those asses who are supposed to be covering, what have they been doing all this time? Reclining on the hillside in the sleep of the innocent, instead of scouting, keeping on the move and giving cover! Well, however the fates decree. It was probably only some poor Bedouin: Allah picked them out a ripe target for their thievery, but our Jeeps' machine guns told them something else again.

But immediately his uncontrolled imagination ran riot, continuing to depict in full detail that nightmare of tanks and armored cars coming violently at them from within the walls of the enemy stronghold; crossing all the lines, they gained the road and were approaching at full speed, to attack you, deploying and opening fire with six-pounders, two-pounders, 20-millimeters, Vickers, dammit! At once telephones were ringing in all the command posts, guns were alerted, target indications, ranges and figures passed on, the first spotting shells came whistling overhead, followed immediately by a veritable bombardment, while the convoy crawled along at a speed of two or three kilometers an hour, loaded to bursting with ammunition and fuel. We don't have a chance. Perhaps we should call it all off, retreat? Rubinstein, retreat? All the signs are against us, one breakdown after another; we've got to get out of here, while there's still time, back to our own side, before they block the road, trap us in a crossfire, encircle us, destroying—we have got to get out of here. For the moment the road is open, soon they'll report more casualties—take it easy.

Again the radio emitted the hoarse voice of the convoy's operator, who reported one killed and two wounded, adding that the convoy had continued on its way and the Jeeps advanced toward the hill. He asked if they should wait for them. "No, don't wait, don't waste time, just keep going, keep going," Rubinstein told them, gesticulating with his hands as if he were addressing someone in front of him. One killed (only one!). It was probably one of those riding the fenders. I probably don't know him. Now the Jeeps were reporting: they had chased away the snipers and were now asking permission to continue their pursuit. But they too were held back by Rubinstein: "Don't follow them. Go back to the convoy." But they had to return to the truck to unload and carry away whatever they could. "Just do it quickly," said Rubinstein. The convoy must go on. The convoy must continue, keep going, keep going! (Who knows what's better in the long run, to keep going or to return?) Now the radio had resumed its empty crackling, while some unknown event was taking shape beyond those hills, some scene involving men active and tense of whose doings you knew nothing at all. And that one killed, his family, those he has back home, don't know yet. They think he's still alive. Although maybe one of them is dreaming some nightmare this very minute. Or a shutter has suddenly slammed, or a crow called outside. It happened so suddenly, the way it always happens. Poor guy—though he's not the one to be pitied. He's out of it now—it's them. For them it's only the bad news of the war. "Hello Jonah Three," a hasty muffled voice broke in, from the Jeeps: "there may be more mines around the damaged truck. Should we make a search?" Man, not so nice, not so nice at all. Maybe they've landed in a mine field. Where you don't even want to walk a step, not to budge an inch. Mines! Hello Jonah Three," said Rubinstein, "keep away from it, don't go any nearer, go back and don't leave the road!" You're all ears, but there's nothing to hear, no explosion. It all happened so quickly, only a minute ago they were here, still intact, everything ready in perfect order. The quiet was unbroken. Tzvialeh wanted to ask them more, to press them to speak, to keep telling what and how, just to keep telling. But if they don't want to say any more, okay, so don't say anything, just keep going, keep going, keep going, just let them keep on going! What were mines doing there anyway? To secure the main road? But why from that side exactly? Just a bunch of some Bedouin? Strange. Hadn't you seen some spots, like black tents, at about that point? But, they might have been just bushes, and maybe that's all they really were, only bushes. They should have gone to check, but there were orders not to move around. Who is the innocent and who the guilty? To hell with it all! Nothing but silence. The flares were going up at short intervals, a sign of curiosity and suspicion. Did this signify that the enemy as well had been surprised? Or did it? Although what did it matter now (just so they've already gotten out of there!). Our road, begun only tonight and already done with—the last chance of an opening has been closed. Now there's no way but war. No escape. It was naïve to think we could have broken the siege with a convoy. Convoys are all well and good in a nice, peaceful sort of war—but they won't work here. You can't occupy territory with convoys, you can't break a siege or win peace. To do that you have to die, over and over again. You're not out of it yet, my boy. Hey, who are those guys? Ovadiah's group. Now they'll start nosing around with questions. No, they're quiet, too. Everyone feels the tension. Just say one word and they'll be ready to do anything to help—that's all they want to do. Good men. It's cold. Whose ill fortune was it that descended upon all of us? Mine? And at first everything went so well, too well. This coldness is that of an alien land. Always to have to die, always. Always.

The convoy was further away now, swallowed up in the dark. There were more fields of black, many other fields, and nothing was sure yet. Eight kilometers farther down the way Shmuel's fellows are supposed to be waiting for them, to celebrate the end of the winding journey. Our midnight convoy—what a way to have to end. Now there won't be anything else but fighting. No escape. What a wonderful prospect, more damn war. As if what we've had already is not enough. On the other hand, if it begins it has to come to an end some time. Just so it will end one day. So that we may know at last who is alive and will continue to be. The way things are now, nobody is sure. Maybe this time your turn has come. Just so there won't be any more wars! Although we have no choice now, this one has to be fought. No escape. We've got to push them back out of here, those bastards. Without the help of anybody else at all. You can despise the indifference of the world, if you wish, but you'll have to fight. There's no doubt about it, and why complain. That's the way it goes. It doesn't matter whether you want to kill or not, to be killed or not—nothing can help you anymore.

Where are they now? Nothing but silence—maybe they've taken the wrong road. But that's asking for it: stop looking for bad signs. Why should they go wrong? Gavri's leading them. Conceited bastard, but he knows his business. Tomorrow will see the spinning of tales and legends. Tomorrow. One killed, poor guy. Suddenly, he's dead. And the wounded. The convoy will get through, it must. Actually we were afraid there would be even more casualties. It must get through. What's that?—only Rubinstein, lighting a cigarette. So maybe we have finished, after all. It was his plan and he saw it through, everything on his shoulders. But it seems we've finished now. That man is tired. But we can't leave yet. We have to sit and wait. Wait until the very end. Until the convoy gets there and finally reports: We've arrived. If only that report would come over now! And until the companies return—that's easier. And until everything is really finished (Gavri is supposed to come back in the morning—they'll set an ambush! Don't come back, Gavri, don't come back!) "Will they manage to get back by morning?" said Tzvialeh. He realized that he had broken a long-held silence, thus instantly alerting everyone in the area, certain he had something urgent to say. He could feel their tense expectation now, as they waited for a reply. But Rubinstein only said, "That depends." And after a moment's thought, added, "We have to go back to the mound. By daylight we have to get out of here, there may be planes in the morning. They won't find anything here." He thought further, moving his fingers as if calculating a problem, and said, "Contact the base and tell them to send the winch to tow away that truck in the wadi. We may still have time to do it." (He's got the mind of a fussy gardener, this Rubinstein!) So that's it. But I want to stay. Don't want to go back before... I won't leave this place. I'm tired enough to want to go home no matter what, but I won't (maybe she'll stay too). So, it's settled, we're staying, we'll go on sitting here in the cold, in the dew that has begun to form and moisten the ground, this ground of ours upon which we sit, knees hunched up, waiting for them to come back. Those are our brothers out there—we can't leave yet. "Well," added Rubinstein, turning to Ovadiah, "take your men, collect the others on your way back, and wait beside the mound. Tzvialeh will go down and bring us the Jeep."

The night was still deep and black, but its melody had changed. It was colder, dew fell. You had not yet closed your eyes. You felt sad, but alert, as if purified by a sleep of dreams. You felt yourself pierced by an inexplicable sorrow (which might be only hunger). There was this sense of being very close to something, the nature of which was soon to be disclosed, and afterward there would be light in the world. As he turned to go down, the radio opened its voice again. Everyone stopped in mid-stride, waiting and listening, while the ventriloquial voice said in its usual fashion: "Advancing, nothing to report. Advancing, nothing to report. Over." And Dali replied, not with a song or prayer, but simply: "We heard you, over."

So Tzvialeh went down along the track, with its deeply imprinted wheel ruts, crushed clods, clumps of stones and little weeds, proceeded along the three bends and reached the dim sorghum field below, the wall of the hill rising above him, its upper edge in the skies, where different stars now shone, in a different composition, their song and their shining changed. In the midst of the sorghum, a few paces further on, a cricket started a song of its own, or perhaps it had been singing all the time but they had paid it no heed. The echo of events momentous and loud had been taken up by the fine soil, the good soil fit for seeding. Then you found yourself remembering a body carried on a blood-strained stretcher to a large truck, which swayed in its journey over the rough road, while the one inside, he too was swaying, though he had no road any more. Tzvialeh was struck by that special awareness for which one often strives but never can attain, and it seemed to him as if he were on the verge of something too exalted to be put into words, for indeed it was, in these wide open fields, the very threshold of life and death, something of the truth of existence, which, though quite simple, was entirely beyond comprehension. Immediately he felt colder, gripped by fear, a dark dread. He moved on again and reached the Jeep. The seat was damp, as were his clothes. He forced his foot to start the engine. It was life, the movement of life, that had choked him. Breathing very deeply he gained speed and drove up the road, the Jeep's power awakening and flowing through it. And now you, son of man, pay heed to these hills, let your gaze extend till the very boundaries of the skies and the further expanses, until the limits of all life in this night world—do you not hear the donkey's call, call of peace? So let's get on back to that lovely Dali of ours.

Habakuk

TRANSLATED BY MIRIAM ARAD
FIRST PUBLISHED IN 1963

I

Well, I have been meaning to tell the story of Habakuk for a long time, and always kept putting it off for one reason or another. But today I'll begin without more ado.

The beginning of Habakuk is rather well known, and it's very simple too. Like this—

Ah, but it seems I must stop here, even before I've begun, and give warning to any of you boys who cannot bear sad stories, for I'm not at all certain this story won't be sad. Its beginning is bound to be a little bit sad, and so is its end—inescapably so—and only in the middle, maybe, it'll be a bit different and not just sad. Anyone who has reservations about sadness, therefore, well, he's been warned here and now, so let him leave off before we've begun and go in search of something that'll make him happy, and more power to him.

Well now, Habakuk. Though of course not the Habakuk of:

awed and enraptured and with an intimation of sacredness in my heart, from Jean Christophe and Uncle Moshe's. As far as Jean Christophe is concerned, you can read it and see for yourself. But at Uncle Moshe's they had a gramophone. A wonder box, highly polished and with an outlandish air about it, did my Uncle Moshe have, and it had a peculiar kind of smell, foreign like the fragrance of an English pipe or a rare wine. And it shut with a kind of latticed lid, and it had its place on a special stand in which the records, too, were kept; and if you'd go and turn the handle stuck in its side and put the pick-up arm gently on the record—then its notes would break over you; and if on top of that you'd bend down and place your ear against those lattices—then the notes would swell and reverberate and make you forget the whole world and create another whole world for you, a new and unknown one. All you had to do from there on was to change needles for each new side (as, indeed, was printed there explicitly: Use each needle once only! —a warning we adopted for our own use and applied to various occasions), and turn the handle some more, and pick a time when Uncle Moshe was not having his siesta—then oh then you could listen, endlessly ("Hast thou found honey? Eat so much as is sufficient for thee lest thou be filled therewith!" Uncle Moshe once quoted Proverbs at me when, coming home, he found me still by the gramophone just as he had left me; I smiled noncommittally, though, and told myself: "Hast thou found honey? Eat it all up!"). I just couldn't listen, couldn't tear myself away, and even the paucity of Uncle Moshe's records did not hold me back. On the contrary, I could listen to the same record over and over again, till everything, every last detail, had sunk down deep and been embedded in the core of my being, fused there with the swaying of the eucalyptus branches beyond the window, merged with the flickering dots of light, tied up inextricably with the smell of the smooth box and rippling with the stillness in the large room (empty except for Kadya, the maid, padding barefoot about), and with the splashes of scarlet shimmering on the red tiles where the sunlight fell.

As a matter of fact, Uncle Moshe had plenty of records, but nearly all of them, alas, were of cantors. Those he loved and would listen to when overcome by a homesickness for times and places I knew little about; all kind of drawn out prayers and psalms and litanies which would elicit nothing but a mocking smile from me and from my friend Yishai. Yet besides this disdained treasure of cantors there was the smaller and the more wonderful treasure that I was at liberty to cherish. There were fragments of Tchaikovsky there to wring your heart, and scraps of this and that opera, Caruso and Chaliapin and Galli-Curci, and in addition there was Sarasate's "Andalusian Romance" which I could whistle, so high and shrill as to frighten the ravens in the topmost branches and make them complain loudly, and so as to astonish the gang, who would stop what they were doing and give me a scandalized look—me walking by whistling with my gaze on the clouds and my hands in my pockets, my shoulders hunched and the sound coming from between my pursed lips like a violin in my ears, and like a rusty kerosene pump in theirs—so they would point a finger to their head as a plain mark of their opinion, or even pick up a clod of earth or a pine cone and throw it at me to help bring me to my senses and make me behave like a normal being: *Uskot, inte el thani*, they would shout at me the cry of an Arab carter scolding his horse—Shut up, you there!

But Uncle Moshe's treasure included Beethoven's Violin Concerto. Ah, what do you know! And to that I would listen with my finger stuck between the pages of *Jean Christophe*. Yes. In those days I had never yet seen either an orchestra or a conductor, nor was I familiar with the various instruments and I could only guess what they were and what they looked like. Not that this prevented me in any way from being enraptured, of course, and from finding a thousand thrilling and wonderful things in the music which no one would ever have imagined were there; nor did it prevent me from taking it upon myself to conduct—with two hands and ten fingers and stormy tossings of my head and flourishes of my whole body— fervently leading the great Beethoven and his magical musicians from glory to glory, up to the exultant moment of triumph——and on, humming short phrases and tiddle-dumming others with one foot beating the rhythm like a dozen drums, and being moved to tears, and to joy, and to

great and colorful flights of fancy beyond anything their creator and
begetter could have imagined or thought possible, beyond any time
or place, and beyond supper time—till somebody in the household
would weary of me and the noise of my music and my odd caper-
ings, and would scold me and pack me off with a "Come, that'll do
for now!"—and I would rise as in a trance and trudge home through
the sand, between houses framed in casuarina and tall eucalyptus
trees, singing, blissful, unaffected by the being sent home, dreaming,
romancing, gesturing, and there would be no containing my heart
that yearned for faraway places and marvels and secrets, for the not-
here, not-thus, and for beyond all this, beyond all and any of this
here, beyond every given thing, now, like this. No.

Do not be surprised, therefore, at what I asked Habakuk (I
believe I still politely called him Mister So-and-So then, and he
grinned and said, "My name is Yedidiah," with an emphasis on the
name as though he were quoting it straight from the Bible, and
as though it were some unfamiliar Adaniah, Yozabad or Yediael!),
while still exchanging my first words with him I already asked: "And
Beethoven's concerto, can you play that?" and I whistled the famous
theme to make sure he'd know what I meant, and also to make him
realize that I was an old hand and knew what I was asking, even if
at the same time my expression must have shown an awareness that
I was asking the impossible, asking for rain from a clear sky, asking
with such plain and obvious doubt in my voice—the which he, nevertheless, ignored, to say with astounding simplicity:

"Yes."

"Yes?"

"Yes. That is, I'm no Heifetz, but I play," said this balding, big-
nosed fellow with his nasal twang, as though he hadn't said anything
extraordinary.

"Oh!" I said and fell silent.

"Really?" I said when I could speak once more.

"Would you like to hear it?"

"Would you play?"

"Why not?"

"When?"

"Why not now?"

"Now? You mean right away? Do you mean now?"

There and then casting to the wind everything that that same "now" had initially been meant to contain, my going that had been aimed at some task, some necessary thing to do, necessary beyond all doubt—forgetting all about it without a moment's hesitation.

"Come on, then!" I cried, ready to grab his hand and sweep him along. But he started out with his odd lurching gait, his bob and bow with each step, smiling broadly, making me forget that he, too, was turning back from wherever he had been going, altering his course for my sake and abandoning some worthy and necessary purpose which he had been pursuing prior to our meeting, leaving it unaccomplished—everything was canceled and abandoned, his pursuits and mine, and we walked off together to hear Beethoven on the as yet unproven violin of Habakuk, whom I called Yedidiah then with some hesitation on my part but with obvious pleasure on his, as though I were calling him, say, Adaniah the Priest!

We did not have far to walk. In fact, we didn't have to walk any distance at all, only to turn around and enter a yard through a battered wooden wicket hanging on its last hinges, skip down the two high stone steps, cross the yard and then, instead of climbing to the wide portico and walking through to the front door, veer off to the right—not for us the main entrance—and along the wall and, yes, to the left again and across the path hugging the house, over worn, wobbling flagstones, turn left once more and down a flight of stairs to the low entrance.

I stopped at the door.

"Down here?" I asked.

"In the vast depths," he confirmed, "Yes, down here I live," and smiled at me.

And we went through the door, which wasn't locked, and were inside a room whose small windows floated just above ground level.

So this then was the room which I'd soon be at home in, a habitué familiar with all its nooks and crannies and all its accessories.

Not that there was much of those latter. In fact, there was hardly anything inside that room. This new friend of mine had nothing. He was not weighed down by anything. Such was Yedidiah, or rather, Habakuk—he had nothing. At any rate, nothing but what his room contained. And the room contained nothing. A table and chair, a bed, a few packing cases (serving various purposes: cupboard, bookcase, pantry), all of it pushed up against the wall, into corners and out of the way, so that there was a large clear space left, bare except for the music stand jutting out in the center of the room like a raised hand waving pages of music. In addition there was a tin container crouching in a corner and adapted to contain a paraffin lamp, when it turned into a stove, or a "furnace", as Habakuk called it ("Whose fire is in Zion and whose furnace in Jerusalem!" he grinned one wintry morning, proud of his ability to find apt quotations from the Bible for every last thing). A kettle would be put over the holes punched in the top of the tin, and slowly the water would come to the boil, and tea would be made when tea would be called for, between one thing and another.

But all this emerged only later, of course. There was none of it that first morning but: "Sit down," said Yedidiah and pointed at the bed covered with a gray army blanket. He opened his violin case and, moreover, took out a violin (for there is a story about a man who opened such a case and came out with a hatchet!), and he took the neck of the violin in his hand, and it transpired that his hand was white, with long fingers, tapering, nails like nut shells, and he took out the bow and strung it, and swung his violin in place under his chin and tuned it.

"Beethoven: Violin Concerto in D Major," he announced ceremoniously (pronouncing the "Beethoven" differently from the way I used to in Jean Christophe) and, tapping his foot one, two, three, he began to play. His fingers quivered on the strings, his hand flourished the bow, his eyebrows worked their way up, way up the height of his forehead, and his forehead contracted, and his brown eyes looked straight in front of him and his chin bulged atop the wedged violin.

But the sounds emitted by his violin's belly did really and truly bear a faithful resemblance to those produced by Uncle Moshe's gramophone in the red-tiled room, though it would be wrong not to mention right at the start, without detracting from the man or his beloved memory, that there was something pale in the playing of this new-found friend of mine, and not only for the lack of an orchestra but also, I am afraid, due to a creaking here and there and a jarring now and then and a note gone a little wrong, so that the particular brilliance that would dazzle you when you put the record on inside the polished box was wanting here. And yet it didn't matter. For I was absorbed, lost in this man and his playing, fascinated by the very reality of notes being produced before my eyes—a man standing here and making his violin sing; not some hidden mechanical device but the product of these hands belonging to this man here, these hands bringing the wonder to pass; and despite the fact that the man was big-nosed and balding and brown-eyed like a dog, here he was singing fervently in this basement of his that contained nothing, nothing but him.

2

And so his foot tapped out the four drumbeats, and at the fifth the woodwinds joined in and sang two phrases, and the drums came back and from there on the violins' strumming kept their beat, and then the second theme broke forth (so there were two themes, were there, and not just a flow of countless melodies following one upon the other...). And apparently there was a transitional passage too, between one theme and the next—like this, and then the violin made its entrance. Majestically. It came and climbed and surged and soared rapidly to its towering heights. And staying with that theme, the famous one, and then on and away, passionately—Habakuk drew his bow back and forth over the strings, the fingers of his left hand flying and flickering on the strings. And then, suddenly, the musician made a sideways gesture with his chin and wrinkled his brow at me, as a sign for me to turn the page—but I did not know what to make of his sign, and he was obliged to interrupt his playing and turn the page himself quickly with his bow-holding hand. I did not yet know the meaning of that sign, just as I knew nothing about the notes on his pages, and just as I marveled at the words introducing a new movement, never thinking that *"allegro ma non troppo"* wasn't some sort of inscrutable incantation to be understood by none but the initiated, but meant, simply: "fast, but not too fast", "fluent but not hurried" or some such thing. A little later he had to stop again and explain to me, ignorant me, such a rudimentary thing as the meaning of that obscure "D Major". And it wasn't at all easy to get to the bottom of it and walk this valley between major and minor, or to look and listen and make out all the minutiae of the scale, and place the finger on each ascending "sharp" and trace each "flat" down to its precise spot—and move on and deeper into this wondrous valley and actually feel the spirit expand and grow richer and everything around get clearer and brighter as it opened up wider and wider, and we go on and up and down, from low D to high D and back, and we fetch paper and draw sweeping scales on it, and beat out a rhythm with one foot and hum and sing a phrase, high and happy. And we pick up the violin again and he fiddles a snatch, bits from here and from there, by heart and from the heart and in plenty, the greatest and purest, the most simple and glorious of music.

Oh, how dreadfully ignorant I was of all this. I am ashamed to tell—such utter ignorance. I knew nothing, nothing. I was nothing but a lad from down there, from the plains. A lad loving the almond trees in bloom in winter, hankering after the hum of the water pumps in the summer orange groves, forever daydreaming, in and out of season, simple and naive as a bird on a bough, a cone on its pine, and knowing nothing, not even that he does not know—a sort of plain, white, simple circle.

And thus several great and weighty matters were explained to me, and we arrived at the larghetto and went on from there to the *rondo-allegro*—and we enquired briefly into the construction of the

concerto in general, and Beethoven's concerto in particular, and such
novelties as the innovators had introduced—taking exception to all
those triflers and new-fangled tricksters of the present day—and what,
as against these, those others, the geniuses— had written in their diaries, and what he himself had written in his diary, so that meanwhile
I found out that indeed, people do write things in diaries, day by day,
and we could open the exercise-book and see—and on such and such
a day we found an entry written there, and it was just exactly what
we were looking for: a neat and complete phrase, complete, too, with
allusions of the kind that make you crave for an explanation: "The
world is full of gods!"—such and no less was written there on one
page, in carefully drawn letters deserving equally careful study and,
more than that, unlimited admiration, which I proceeded to bestow
upon him liberally, and with all my heart.

And in due time it was noon, and then it was afternoon
already and he, with his violin in one hand and bow in the other,
smoothed the wrinkles of his mobile brow, and asked would I do
him the honor of sharing his meal with him, a plain and simple meal,
a mere appeasing of hunger with a bowl of soup, which he could
prepare in a twinkle, a soup made of nothing but vegetables, yet
thick and tasty and good and containing, what not?—tomatoes and
onions and carrots and pumpkin and peas and pods and greens and
golds and lapis lazuli, nourishing as anything when dished up with
lots of bread and good cheer, one heart, one plate, one spoon— so
how about it?

Said and done. And while the soup stood simmering on the
makeshift stove, light and joy trickling through its holes, we drifted
back to Beethoven in his heyday, from Opus (q.v.!) 55, which is the
"Eroica", to 57, which is the "Appassionata", and to 59, which is three
famed quartets—up to Opus (ditto) 73, which is the celebrated piano
concerto, the "Emperor", and including Opus 68, which is the "Pastoral" Symphony, which is the Sixth; and these are happy matters
and inspiring, and they open up wells of emotion, and they make for
bright eyes and induce an urgent need to hum snatches from here and
from there, and a wish to do things in this world, great and burning

and sky-high things, heart-conquering things that bring tears of joy and gratitude to the eyes.

Yes. Ah yes, of course. And afterward we sat down in peace and brotherhood and ate that soup, as promised, with soft fresh bread, and its flavor was thick and buttery, even though rather oddish—and yet, if there had been a piano in that room we would have left everything then and there and gone over and played it, played one after the other two great, two stupendous, thrilling works filled with the fierce rapture of youthful love, like Orion on a bright winter night— the "Appassionata" for one, and the "Waldstein" for another—and until then, and for lack of a piano, that big-nosed fellow blowing and breathing through the steam of his thick soup, sat and sang the principal themes at the top of his weak voice, trusting to me and my lively imagination, and gesturing with his narrow-jointed, thin-fingered, long white hand to indicate how one thing proceeds from another and how passion mounts and scales summits, up, up to the god-like heights.

3

And it was well into the afternoon when we suddenly discovered that the time had come, or had perhaps even gone by, when we must stop and rush out and apply ourselves to various urgent affairs, postponed and forgotten and now coming back to mind like a horde of impatient, clamorous creditors. "Time's passing!" I said close to despair, though still unable to tear myself away.

"Time is always passing. Space is fixed but time passes," said he, lofty but obscure, gently laying his violin in the case and returning the bow to its place.

"I didn't manage to do a thing," I complained, getting up to go.

"One manages to do what one has to," he told me then. "One can't do more, just as one can't do less than one has to." Weighty words he uttered, words like these, without my having any idea how to apply them. "And you are young still," he added with a toss of his high forehead, "There's everything you can manage to do before you yet. You've only just begun," he said, and smiled at me. "How old are you anyway?" he asked, and I became aware of the approach of something new and unknown, something very special and very strange, beyond our sphere, as it were.

I told him. But he wasn't satisfied. On what day, he demanded, and what hour was I born?

Why the hour? What did it matter? By the way, I have an idea that my mother used to say, when telling us her once-when-you-were-a-little-boy stories, that I was born at sunrise, I think it was, though...

The words weren't out of my mouth before this friend of mine, this odd Yedidiah—whose face suddenly took on a new expression, lit up as of a man crouching over a fire—this odd one stretched out a hand and picked up a sheet of paper and deftly drew a circle on it with one swift stroke of his hand; a curious-looking booklet filled with figures appeared out of nowhere upon the small table, and he began leafing through it at incredible speed, found what he had been looking for and hastily marked a few dots inside the circle he had drawn—a blank space as yet, a breathlessly blank space seeming to await events; and he started mumbling and muttering incomprehensible phrases, obscure expressions among which I seemed, however, to catch the names of the better-known stars, without being able to catch their significance or present purpose—names like Venus, Mars, Saturn and Jupiter, as well as the lesser-known ones like Uranus, Neptune and Pluto, and maybe some more names or terms or god-knows-what that appeared to surround his diligently bent head like a halo—and he was completely absorbed, joining dots with a sure stroke, never wavering, as though no doubt could exist, adding here and there some extraordinary mark the like of which I had never seen before, in or out of a book, nor ever heard of, like some secret language; and he was creating all manner of curves and angles with the touch of his pencil and then making some of them run to squares and triangles, and all the while he ignored my questioning face as well as my actual questions, only making sounds of surprise and admiration like someone who has suddenly come upon a magnificent view from the top of a hill; he blurted out exclamations, and from time to time he looked up as though great and wonderful things were being unveiled for him. "Really?"—"Is that so!"—"But that's marvelous!"—"Incredible!"—and more of the kind, not to mention his "Terrific!" and "Fantastic!" and a host of other superlatives; add to that his eyes which, time and again, would be raised with a faraway look, far beyond the here and now, then would come back for a minute to rest upon my puzzled self (standing there somewhat apprehensive, and hiding in self-defense behind a forced smile), then back again to their encounter with the unseen and unknown. And I had already reached a point where I was wondering whether I hadn't better take myself quietly off, when the man waved a long white finger in the air as though calling for attention, as though on the point of speaking out, revealing great things—and I could almost feel my flesh creep, and stood transfixed, spellbound and fascinated by him, him gazing now toward his faraway distances, now at me, and as it were comparing what he saw there with this one before him here, or as though surprised perhaps to find that whatever he was seeing there was actually identical with this one here or with what he would turn out to be—the moment thickened and condensed, soon, very soon now it would burst, here now, it was coming—and the man lifted his finger, the magician's finger, and his face lit up: "See?" he addressed me suddenly in a somewhat stifled voice—"Look here: d'you see it?"—and his long white finger seemed to sprout out and point at a section his pencil had cut in that circle of his, and at another section, which later he entitled: "Here, this 'house' here"—he said with inexplicable excitement—"A beauty!"—he said and raised his eyes— "But this 'house' over here is rather dangerous, or it would be but for this angle here," he said and burst out laughing—at the frustration of the Arch Fiend's attempt, apparently—"This is an excellent angle. You can put your trust in it, never fear!"—he said and looked at me like a doctor reassuring a frightened patient. —"The only thing that's still in doubt is this square here..."—he said, and his whole forehead wrinkled in a frown. And once more he arched his crooked eyebrows at me, peered at me, or through me, and I was an open book, plainly, there for him to read.

"What is all this?" I quavered.

"It's you," he said, "and these are your stars. Everything's written here!" he solemnly declared. And I didn't know whether to put on a disparaging smile or a worried frown, whether I should come out with the first witticism that would occur to me or swallow it all and keep my mouth shut. Fate itself seemed to hover in the air over our heads. And anyway, it was obviously impossible to laugh it off. I shrugged a shoulder. I must have looked rather wretched. "Venus and Sun!" he sang out, for me to appreciate the achievement to the full. "Here they are playing now!"

I glanced over his shoulder, cautiously, to see for myself, as though peering into an abyss:

"Where? What's all this?" I said reluctantly, feeling like a naked man among the clothed.

"Your horoscope!" he threw me a magic formula. "Written in the stars," he added with a big, friendly smile. "It's all written in the book of heaven. A man is born under his stars, inescapably. Man is, and the world is."

Thus he explained the matter to me, only obscuring it the more. And it all remained very vague and not a little frightening, even though extremely tempting to jump up, if that was the way it was, and take a peep through that window giving on to the terrible place, where one would fain look though it is forbidden, and where if one does look one will pay for it heavily. I did not know what to do or say. And perhaps, I thought, I had better put on my man-of-the-world face now, and scoff at all this as silly nonsense and childish games, a world removed from two-and-two-are-four.

"So you read the stars?" I said, not knowing what else to say.

And at once I felt as though, for some reason, I were tottering on a brink, or as though something that I had always held in a firm grasp were slipping now, and I must pull myself together and

come and gather ye together, a day of trumpet and alarm, the day is coming, don't ye tarry, oh you there, come from here and beyond, come up and be not slack, all ye who desire, all ye who have faith, all ye who love—come hasten ye, come ye hosts, ye armies, come marching, all of ye, here, now—my God, my dear God—here we are all of us before you, here we are, ready. When I grow up, when I am I, if I shall be granted to become what there is in me, if indeed it is there within me, when I shall know things, shall be able, shall stand on my own legs, then I shall call out, hands spread, shall call out with all my power—to be attentive, alert, to be ready for anything, ready to leave everything and go, responsive to the slightest gesture as players to a conductor, spellbound, bewitched but awake, so as to rise and go, to his kingdom, the kingdom of beauty— and he shall reign triumphant, sole ruler, and we shall come to him, there, don't know where, stand there transported, our bodies humble but our eyes raised high…

5

And one day, when our little group had once more gathered, and it was raining outside and the stove, that "furnace in Zion", was dripping gold from its pores, and each of us curled up in his corner, huddled in his coat, and the room bare as ever, containing nothing but the few odds and ends pushed aside, and us—Habakuk the Prophet placed some pages of music on the stand, turned over a few and found the title and pointed at it with the tip of his bow and said nothing but: "Sonata for Unaccompanied Violin, by Johann Sebastian Bach". And he lifted his bow with a sweep and drew it over the strings once, harshly, and began playing and did not stop till he had played it through to the end, the whole Sonata, movement by movement. And no one opened his mouth or dared speak. Only afterward did one of us take courage to beg in a whisper: More, once again, Habakuk, once more, please!—But Habakuk hung back, this once.

Tired, perhaps. His brow was furrowed and his lips were tight with thought; his eyes were not upon us.

"It all begins peacefully," Habakuk said into the silence around him, "Like this:"—and he picked up his violin and played to show us how.— "And soon the terror sets in..." he muttered and played to show us how. "Everything is tossed. Nothing keeps still, keeps fast. A fearful wind..." he whispered and played to show us. "What will remain of all this?" he whispered, his eyes closed, not turning to us. And nobody tried to answer. Very silent we were. And the room filled with our silence and his words. There was nothing in the room except the beating of hearts and the listening to his voice.

"Now what do we have here?" said Habakuk over his violin. "In the Book of Isaiah, Chapter 19, we have its like: 'Behold, the Lord rideth upon the light cloud...'" he said, not to us, not opening his eyes, and played that phrase about the Lord riding upon a light cloud. Everything is right. Everything is proper, calm, before any test, before the trial. A light cloud in a clear sky.

Who can imagine the gravity of what is coming, of what is contained there within the light cloud, how suddenly the darkest of all should issue forth from it.

"And He shall come into Egypt..." said Habakuk, his arm raised as in dread, and the idols of Egypt shall be moved at his presence..." Rising and descending scales. Chords running, pursuing each other. Wave upon black wave. "And they shall fight every one against his brother, and every one against his neighbor; city against city and kingdom against kingdom ..." The holocaust grows and spreads. Even the most stable topples. Wilting, as a flower discarded or as a ravaged feast. What now? Is there no sign of salvation on the forehead of the Seer?

"And the waters shall fail from the sea, and the river shall be wasted and dried up. And they shall turn the rivers far away, and the brooks of defense shall be emptied and dried up: the reeds and flags shall wither..."

No. No sign. Even Nature is relentless. There is no escape. Where, what then? The bow twists and plunges, the strings lament.

"Where are they? Where are thy wise men and let them tell thee now…"Ah, what taunting mockery. Swept by the fearful current, losing all foothold, their last defenses shattered, and what was even yesterday the image of everything good and pure and valiant is now exposed in all its vanity and meanness, powerless to withstand the great test, the day of trial. And what is left you then? What is there for you under this overflowing scourge, in this perverse spirit, this fear and horror? What star of deliverance? Oh, who shall tell, who shall know, who shall see that far? You, Habakuk?

(Did Bach really write all this at the time? Just like this, the way Habakuk is reading and playing it for us now, with unusual force, sweeping and pulling us after him relentlessly and heeding neither a squeak here and there nor an occasional shortcoming in his performance? Or is Bach only in brackets and is it Habakuk come to prophesy on his own and as he played, lo, the Spirit of God was upon him?….)

"In that day…"—What day? Whose day are we reading of and in whose book of fate? Whose fate will it be to be killed beside the bridge in his twenty-eighth year? And whose to perish of a malignant disease with half his life unspent? And whose to live a humdrum, mediocre life till ripe old age, whose to become entangled in a plot and whose to be tripped by a snare, who is destined to climb the mountain and who to fall at the foot of the mountain hit by a stray shell? Oh, leave off and don't ask questions now. This is no time for questions.

"And it shall be afraid and fear because of the shaking of the hand of the Lord of hosts which he shaketh over us…"—And how long, how much longer? Will the land mourn forever? And shall every thing sown wither, be driven away and be no more?…

Whither, Habakuk? Oh, do not be so hard with us, so inexorable! Give us a sign. Prophesy and tell us about after the great and terrible wrath. Do you know? Can you tell? Do you see an omen in your stars? What is it that a man must be? What is it that we must be so as to make the world good, and make us care? Look down at us sitting at your feet—have you no message for us?

"And the Lord shall smite Egypt," plays Habakuk, "He shall smite and heal it…"—rising and descending (not always without some unpleasant squeaking, from sheer inability to play better). Perhaps that is it: ebb and flow. That it is never just one level line but that it flows, all of it, rising and sinking, being drowned and saved. Is that it? Look up, children, look round you, isn't that it? (producing a jarring dissonance at times, bracing himself and then continuing onward). Look, then, and see whether the light of day does not always follow the dark of night, be it even the darkest of nights—and after winter, is there not the spring? Evil is not eternal. No, but back and forth, wave upon wave. Remember that and don't forget. Oh. Please, Naomi, please try and smile at us here, with our bent heads and drooping hands. Yehiam will be killed, Ya'acov will die, that stray shell is still waiting for Habakuk too, others will stay alive, will live this way or that, as best they can, for good or for ill, becoming shopkeepers, becoming teachers or clerks, becoming successful, building a home and begetting children. Or is there perhaps another way? Not theirs? The way he is playing now—in awe. Raise your eyes to us, Naomi, your eyes that shine like Sabbath candles, look at us, take each one of us; draw us into the goodness of your light, you who guard the house and gather its four corners together: will you forge us a dam? And will you set us on the way? And already it changes, no more just prayer, but prayer and first glimmer of light, prayer and first hint of change, and now its sounds clearly: "And they shall return even to the Lord, and he shall be entreated of them, and shall heal them."—Oh, let us return. Who knows what is awaiting us at the next corner. Who knows if not another such fearful journey. But "In that day shall there be a highway"… There will be. There must be. And the light cloud will be nothing but an ornament in the sky from now on, an ornament and not an omen. And nothing ill will be borne upon it. No evil will be lurking behind the light smile. A cloud will come and vanish. That is all. Come and go. And there will be a blessing in the midst of the land. Amen. Amen and Amen.

And why are all eyes staring at the floor? And Habakuk, what does he say? No, he says nothing. He has finished playing, lowered his violin, placed his bow on the stand. He does not move. His face is tilted upward, as of one who has seen far things. Everyone is silent. Bach and Isaiah and everyone. An infinite echoing, reaching no shore. As within a large bell that has just stopped ringing. For a long time no one speaks. It is cold in the empty room.

At last Habakuk says—not to anyone but straight before him and scarcely audible:

"Naked and barefoot
And freezing with cold
And awaiting him
Always
Amen."

And, drawn together over this, no one dares breathe. A slight shiver passes down one's back. Someone wipes the corner of an eye. None of us can find anything to say that will be right, that will live up to this moment. We must go away. Let's go, boys, let's go home. Those of us who have a home. This one here, Habakuk, has none. No home, no possessions, no family, not anything. We shall go away and he—in this bareness of his, always. A violin he has, though. And the distant, evasive stars—they speak to him. And boys come to him, boys in their blossoming. And one shining-eyed girl too. What else? What else is there? What else is given man? In addition to music, to stars, and to the beauty of boys with one girl among them? And who doesn't love her? Everyone does. Whether they tell her so or keep it in their heart and do not, yet. She is our hope. She is our light. My light. My soul.

Rising and leaving. One by one. Good night, Habakuk. Good night, each. A tentative smile. He does not respond. Upright beside his music stand. Beside certain pages crossed by the violin's bow. And outside, pine trees rustling in the wind, and the smell of pines. Buttoning coats. Clouds come and go. Heavy clouds. A great rain is going to fall. Run boys, run. Come, let us run, you and I. Will you give me your hand and shall we run together through the wind and the rain?

6

Well. . . And then afterward... But now I have lost the desire to tell
what happened afterward. A sadness has come over me. Indeed, I
warned you boys at the start this was going to be sad, remember? In
fact, I had an entirely different opening in mind, but it turned out
this way. So let it stand, I shall not begin to make changes now.

But you, my friend, will want to know what happened afterward to this man Habakuk—he of the violin and stars—and how his
story ends. Well, the truth is that I do not know. We drifted apart,
after a time. We lost sight of each other and there was nothing except
an occasional sending of regards through a chance acquaintance. Like
stars whose orbits cross once and part again, who knows if ever in
eternity to meet again. But I did hear of his end. Hard and bitter
it was, his end. And I have hinted at it more than once throughout
my story. And I have hinted, too, that perhaps alone among us he
was not surprised by it. He could see over and beyond the stature of
ordinary things, those among which the rest of us dwell.

Though it is just as possible that he did not, that this particular
secret was not told him by the stars. It is possible that they preferred
to conceal it from him, for some reason, to hold back any sign, and
that his end came upon him like a sudden blow, like an eagle swooping
down upon its prey. And that it caught him unprepared, like us, like
all men, and unasked—terribly unasked. Who can tell now whether
it happened this way or that. If I knew where those diaries of Habakuk were now, then perhaps I would find out more. And perhaps
it is written there even, if indeed it was revealed to him from above,
perhaps it is there—the hidden purpose of a man's dying in mid-life.
Yet if we were to look in vain, what then is left but that a man may
die without purpose, that one evil thrust will suffice. Who can tell?
Ah, the angels fly high but man unto trouble is born.

As far as we were concerned, at any rate, it would never have
entered our minds that it would be he—that among all of us it would

be he for whom the shell came. He, who would not hurt a fly—and we, members of the Haganah underground to a man, and commanders in the Palmach storm troops in the not so distant future, we who spent nights secretly learning to use weapons—we did not consider the shadow of any such possibility. We did not, but the powers of doom, those that the stars know all about, they acted the way they did and placed their messengers in such positions that it all became inevitable. And it all was, and it happened.

I have no idea at all where, for instance, on the afternoon of that fateful Friday, the stars were.

Apparently they broke up and they stood at hard, stiff angles, and in one corner of the earth a war broke out. And it happened that there was sent a number of laborers to an embattled kibbutz in order to dig trenches, and among them was Habakuk. He was not a fighter, nor could have been one. He had never in his life borne arms nor learned to hold a weapon and, since he was rather too old for it as well, they made him a digger of trenches. And on that day, at noon-break, the laborers lay down to rest on the lawn in front of the communal dining hall, talking, one imagines, about the impending cease-fire which was to go into force that very evening, a cease-fire between the two warring sides. Only a few hours divided them still from the haven of peace when there suddenly came a brief little last-minute shelling, completely insignificant were it not that one shell, suddenly, found its way and chose to come, to fall, to hit that lawn by the dining hall and to explode amidst the laborers resting there. Habakuk was among the killed (Habakuk—though no doubt they didn't call him that, nor knew that he was he). They picked him up and buried him on the slope of the hill, in the shade of the pine grove. And there, along with all the other Palmach lads, he rests in peace.

And that is all. Or maybe just this. You know that there is a Memorial Day, when all the comrades of the fallen make a pilgrimage to the graves of their dead. There is a ceremony, things are said, and then people scatter and each seeks out the little mound where his friend lies buried—silent with thoughts of "Where are you now, and we, where are we?", and listening to the strange quiet, to the rustling of the pines on the slope and to things unsaid, things that were and things that might have been were it not that. And mothers sob, and girls draw a shawl over their head and young men pluck at their moustaches, ill at ease. One lingers a bit still, one leaves behind a flower or a green branch, and turns to go, parting again, each to his own, back to the land of the living and all its hubbub.

And that, to tell you the truth, was how I had wanted to begin this story, with some kind of melancholy opening, like this: Among all those at the cemetery dedicated to the war dead, among all those graves of young lives mown down in their very blossoming, on that pine-covered slope—one grave, I fear, remained unvisited, unasked for, and that is the grave of Habakuk (who wasn't one of the boys—though he loved and cherished them most truly). Who and what this Habakuk was—thus I had intended to say in that opening—that is what my story is going to be about. And may this story—thus had I intended to add—be as a candle to the memory of an unusual man. Such and suchlike sad words had I meant to say at the beginning, but then things turned out otherwise and I didn't.

But the way things have fallen out, I feel that I cannot now leave off and go my way before I, too, have stood there by this mound, head bent, silent and listening. And afterward, perhaps, I shall gather courage, and lift my eyes to question my strange and wondrous friend. My heart is somber. My heaven seems empty. But still my eyes are raised, truly they are. Ah, Habakuk, you who can see so far and so much higher than any of us, you who can look the stars in their eyes—can you hear my voice? You, wherever you are, say if you have found out there, beyond, tell us now, at this hour, when we are drained, when all our wonted wisdom is spent, is useless, and we are sick and weary and unable to bear this dull, flat, compromising nothingness, and in our agony we steal a look, sideward and up and even unto the stars, so high and so very unspeaking—let them tell, then, if they know better: What is it? What is demanded of us here? What must we do? Where go?

Habakuk, Habakuk, oh where then must we go? What should, what must we be? We who are left here, above, in the land of the living, having the sun, and our soul left us for prey—where must we now? Oh, what? What do you say? What do your stars say? Where?

Say, speak to us, be not silent, not now, speak. Thou that seest in the stars, thy companions hearken to thy voice.

The Runaway

TRANSLATED BY YOSEF SCHACHTER
FIRST PUBLISHED IN 1963

Things haven't always been as they are now. Not so many years ago, this entire farmyard in front of you was teeming with life and lush foliage. What didn't it possess? Beyond the shed there were flourishing fruit trees: apples, plums, quinces, and others. On that long patch grew potatoes, richly green stalks set in reddish hummocks; and we had sweet potatoes too, and maize and beans and what have you. The vines reached as far as the wall of the house, the end vine creeping and climbing right up the wall to the roof, and the grapes hanging in long clusters from its leafy bosom like the dugs of a suckling nanny goat. And all these wretched-looking orange trees—which now are saved once every few weeks from the withering thirst—used to be blooming, healthy, and dark green. Once there were flowers preening themselves in every corner, with the sprinkler going day and night.

The henhouse used to stand right here, in the center. A few years earlier the donkey was stabled there—actually it was a wooden shed which had been put up specially for him. There had even been a plan which was almost carried out to get a white goat and to fix a patch of green fodder specially for her; and there was already talk of the milk and all sorts of fine and famous cheeses which we would be getting from the pink-eared goats then in fashion, the ones they used to call "Romanian" for some reason or other.

The henhouse and the chickens are a story in itself that I'll have to tell you some other time. It started out as I said, as the donkey stall and tool shed, till once they shut two chickens in there for the night which grandmother had bought for a festival and which somehow had escaped being slaughtered. They were Arab hens, very speckled, and no less ravenous. Later they were joined by a brightly colored rooster in all his glory. and then one of the speckled hens was brooding, and soon there were a few chicks hopping about all over the place, despite her rebukes. A night jackal, I believe, finished them all off (or was it a day hawk, or perhaps a bloodthirsty marten)—because everything was wide open then and our farmyard, lined with cypresses along one border (only knee high, and every morning we would shake an army of snails off them), stood all by itself out in the open country. There was the settlement behind us, the orange groves in front, and to the right and left nothing but brambles covered with snails. And it was always a little empty, and a little out of the way a bit wretched by day and a bit worrisome at night if you were sensitive. But it was an exceptionally beautiful place, wide open for endless running: for those dashing to fetch something from the store as their bare feet were scorched by the hot sand, for the scampering of the darting lizards, for the meandering of hordes of snails, for the streams of flowers in springtime.

Just opposite our house, between us and the sea of orange groves, our neighbor Aryeh had set up his farmyard a little while back. With them everything was different, for to begin with they had horses, two of them, two white horses. We never had a horse. We managed to come by a donkey—a big black one, to be sure and that's as far as we got. But horses we never had: neither horse, nor mare, nor foal. And, you know, folks that have horses in their farmyard are always different from folks that don't have any and have never raised a horse in their yard; they go through life differently, have a different smell, and a different look in their eyes. Haven't you noticed that? I myself have always loved horses, but always from behind a fine screen of wariness, which is one more reason for loving them from the sidelines, without in any way detracting from my wonder and admiration—as an onlooker and not as part of them.

At any rate, our neighbor Aryeh, just opposite, had two. That's his house over there, and there's his yard, wide open on every side, too. Two horses he had, and a brand new concrete stable with a new wire fence all around, and he made his living from those two. White they were, pure white, the whiteness of smooth marble; strokingly white—for anyone who could bring himself to go right up to them and put out his hand to stroke them (their skin would quiver at your touch, and you felt how strong they were underneath that smooth, ripply skin. So strong!) White, but also a tiny bit flecked. Their tails and manes were always flashing with fiery sparks, and when they waved them they would catch fire like a brilliant burst of flame. Rich, heavy tails and long, flowing manes; one of them very much so. Long manes glowing with fire when they flew. That was the pair of horses he had, our neighbor Aryeh.

When the time came for us to clear a yard around our house, which till then had no yard, when the time came to put it into shape, clear it up, get it ready for the autumn planting—father strolled across the sand one evening to have a glass of tea at our neighbor Aryeh's, and the very next day, very early in the morning, just after our raven had woken us up—those horses, the two white ones, were already over at our place, and our neighbor Aryeh too, with a dirt-leveling sled; all the excitement of a new reality, a warm vitality, filled everything with the hub-bub of vigorous activity. There and then, without any preliminaries, the horses set out to dislodge the crust of sand that had been hardening since the beginning of time. But they were hemmed in by the narrow confines of our rectangular plot of land, and no sooner had they started out than they had to be reined in and turned back. No sooner had they put a foreleg forward to break into a trot than the bits were tugging at their mouths and they were pulled back on their traces, with the cries of "Round there! Round!" and "Whoa! Whoa!" they would be pounding their hooves, and the plot would be too cramped to contain all their latent power. They would turn round and go back, with the harness swinging, the chains rattling, and their master cracking his whip—not to hurt them, of course, but merely to stress the educational principle involved and to show off both his daring and his flawless professional touch. The sled, in that same superb swing, would tip out its accumulated load of sand, and the horses would already be dragging it back with a mighty stamping of hooves and a creaking of the freshly oiled harness straps exuding a pungent smell of sweat. Weeds, couch grass, thistle covered with snail shells, crusted clods of reddish soil—all were carried along in a mighty sweep, leaving behind smooth, moistly naked swaths redolent with the chalky odor they had so long been storing below the surface. The earth had been turned inside out, revealing its kernel of smooth, damp red loam.

All of us were there, not a soul was missing, and we all looked on while our lone house was being surrounded by the fresh damp soil for the first time since creation—presaging great events that were to come, laying the foundation for the new, good order that was to be established, the beginnings of what would culminate in a lively rhythmic cycle of well-ordered planting and sowing within the boundaries of this enclosed rectangular patch of land that was becoming more clearly marked with each moment that passed.

And suddenly there was the whole plot, completed, line after line of countless strips of moist glistening red loam smoothed by the passage of the sled; where the sled had tipped its loads, the earthy hummocks offered a tempting invitation to play. When a boy warily plunged his hand into their fresh moist depths, into the bosom that was so easy to knead and so delightful to crumble, he disturbed a host of tiny soil dwellers, slugs and worms whose world had suddenly collapsed when they were rudely uncovered and ousted from their hidden retreats. Some lay twitching on their backs, their legs wriggling helplessly, crying out to the heavens; others, exerting all their tiny strength, hastily squirmed and scurried away to safety, all except those that had been mangled and squashed and flattened against the glistening clean strips of red soil (like the jackals you see at night in the rushing headlights of a speeding car, you know, crushed and lacerated and smeared onto the road, with their pinkish insides exposed). This was on the one side, and on the other was a finished rectangular plot of crumbled earth emerged, charged with future promise.

That's how it was at our place and opposite us, not too far away, at our neighbor Aryeh's recently established homestead which like our own stood surrounded on all sides by the great wide openness. One farm yard and just another and patches of earth, redeemed from the sealed anonymity of a sandy crust overgrown with thistles and insignificant flowers so that the good order might finally prevail, for the benefit of future times, toward that day which was sure to come (about which we sing in our songs), when a closely populated settlement shall spring up on this spot (So be it, Amen) and courtyard shall touch upon courtyard, and tree upon tree, snug and enclosed. But until then, in the meantime, there was the good, stable smell of newly dug earth, fresh and stimulating. Even our raven, astonished, kept cawing, cawing loudly overhead.

And so it went on till breakfast time. By then, the plot looked so changed you could no longer recognize it. The only pity was that there was nobody else here but ourselves to admire it. Everything so new, gleaming, shouting. It was no longer the same farmyard of two or three hours ago, when the age-old wide-openness came right up to the doorstep, and the house seemed set in the middle of an ocean. Our neighbor Aryeh kept vigorously at work, taking huge strides with those long legs of his, again and again tipping over the heavily laden sled, whistling and firmly guiding his two horses, which, no sooner had they set out to clear a swath, were reined and turned round, with "Whoa, whoa! Turn there!" As if cutting into a cake, they sliced through the hump of earth near our doorstep—it had been there since the beginning of time and went on smoothing everything down, burying the upper crust and the litter of lime and cement that had been lying around ever since the house was built under the fresh pile it was pushing before it, leveling and clearing the land immaculately, turning up a new covering layer of red soil, moist, crumbling, soft, and fragrant.

Everything was going fine like this, when our neighbor Aryeh brought it all to a halt in a sweeping access of vigor. He wiped his glistening forehead with the back of his huge hand, his big feet encased in their heavy boots halted their pacing, and he reined in his two horses—which, while they had been tramping back and forth had been swishing their long, flame-flecked tails and pulling the little toy of a sled with a child's load of sand on it. He stopped; and they, we, everything stopped; and we were left very much with a what's-going-to-happen-now feeling. Father suddenly remembered and tore himself away rushing off to work, though you could see how very much he would have liked to stay on and see what came next. Others also became aware of their respective duties, of the compelling necessity to drag themselves away finally and rush off wherever they had to go; still they stayed on a little longer to watch just-this-and-that's-all. Later, they would cross over to their own yard, which lay isolated amid the wide emptiness that stretched right up to the edge of the orange groves—there to eat their breakfast omelette with plenty of salad and to drink enough coffee to slake their thirst. In the meantime, the sled would be unhitched and the two white horses tethered where they could browse a little (only they mustn't drink, not when they are hot and sweaty). They would be back before long, and by midday they would have left behind them a well-ordered farmyard, completely cleared and leveled out, a good thing both in itself and for what was to come, and ready for the autumn sowing—and then let all the experts in the world come along and say whether they'd ever seen or heard of anything finer than this. Our raven, perched on the old pole that had been there long before anything else and which no one was known to have put up, gave a loud caw, then another, and then took off with much flapping of wings for the tall, aged eucalyptus trees in the old settlement.

That's what our neighbor had said, and he was as good as his word, for everything turned out that way. Nothing could have been simpler, and yet it was all so marvelous (how lonely and deserted our farmyard was going to be without the horses after they had finished and gone back to their own yard never to return), with the fresh, festive smell of soil filling the air and mingling with the strong smell given off by bold white horses. Had not all of a sudden…but I'd better tell what happened in the proper order.

The first white horse, the proud one, had just been unhitched and had straightaway lowered his head and started cropping at the grass. Then the second white horse, the tall beautiful one, was unhitched. Dilating his nostrils, he breathed the air as if savoring the smell of the gentle breeze that came from the sea, and his skin gave a quiver as though touched by a hand. Then he lifted one leg slightly and moved it forward a little, quite casually, then took another step, his head raised and his ears tautly pricked up. And all of a sudden… ah…all of a sudden he dropped his head abruptly, like an eel reentering the water, stretched out his neck, and threw his two forelegs forward in a quick prance, as though cavorting playfully. The bridle chain slipped out of Aryeh's hand for a quarter of a second, no more than that, and the horse slipped the halter clear over his head. By the time Aryeh had caught hold of the chain again and given it a startled tug, muttering an oath (he had been struck dumb till then), the chain was no longer tied to any horse, and the horse was free of halter, bridle, chain, or anything else—was, in fact, utterly free of everything. In that same quarter of a second he had pranced forward another few steps, placing a sizable distance between himself and us, and halted there listening, as if to hear whether he was being called from somewhere. There he stood, erect and beautiful, and again it seemed that he would now breathe freely and be at peace, and calm down. But suddenly—O Lord!—perhaps because one of us had carelessly made some abrupt movement, or perhaps for no reason at all—suddenly he reared up, tensed his powerful frame against the solidity of the silent earth, and bounded forward like a shot, plunging away into the distance: in a surging flurry he took off and was gone. (It tore at your heart, this sense of his lost presence, this something that was now irreparable, the feeling that you could do nothing about it: it's-happened-and-can't-be-put-right.) In a surging flurry he took off and was gone, in the briefest possible instant, and with a suddenness so sudden that all that remained was the hollow shell of his presence of a moment ago, the recent pounding of hooves, now reverberating a thousand times louder than one was prepared to expect—a hollow shell of his presence whose slender connection with the runaway was now severed, as if this were all that we had been left with, the only tangible thing that we could claim as our own and hold on to, though it held nothing but the shame of emptiness: a force that had been violently severed.

He took off. It's only now that I can call to mind all the details. At the time I was too stunned, but now I remember exactly the powerful tensing of the body that came before that explosion, the tautened muscles which suddenly broke loose. I can see it all now, but then I saw nothing till after he, who had just been there, had taken off and was gone. Can you grasp what it was like? A sudden flurry and he was flying away. It was beautiful, I tell you, more beautiful than anything you ever saw, than beauty itself, so beautiful that it's hard to describe. As beautiful, say, as laundry fluttering on the line in a sharp winter wind, only the laundry is strung on a line, while he was as free as the wind; or as beautiful as a ship with pennants flying, only a ship plows through the water, and he was flying. And he got away.

What was going to happen now? What could happen? The sense of surging power left behind by the runaway sent a pang shooting through your heart, and also the feeling of what-will-happen-now; and his great beauty, streaking away like a flash of lightning, and the urgent sense of things that had to be done. Look at that neighbor of ours, Aryeh, standing there with his huge hands empty, his big feet empty, and his mouth gaping. What is he going to do now? What about his livelihood, and the wife and his two small children; what is going to happen to them? And what about the orderliness of his team of horses that had been disrupted and shattered? A broken-up team, one horse short. And what was going to be done about the remaining horse, the mateless one, which was now to bear the full brunt of Aryeh's awakening from his stupefaction? Suddenly roused, our neighbor rushed at the other horse which stood motionless, head raised, looking into the distance; he lunged at the bridle chain and furiously tightened it a notch, at the same time giving him such a kick in the belly that the horse reared up on his hind legs and whinnied in outraged surprise; whereupon our neighbor hit him with his fist and with the slack of the chain, cursing loudly from here to the back of beyond, without knowing whether the curses reached out as far as the runaway, who had vanished from sight and could not be seen in any direction, at any rate not in the direction we were facing. He had simply taken off and was gone.

How far would he flee? Who could go chasing after him? When would he calm down and stop? Would he come back before nightfall? Could anything be done about it? By now, he must have got beyond the orange groves, on the other side of all the fences and acacia hedges, beyond the system of allotted plots having title deeds and owners. By now, he must have got out into the open, those wide far-off places where there's nothing at night but emptiness and ravenous jackals and preying hyenas and other horrors.

After crossing the flatlands over by the Arab village, would he head for the sand dunes or break through to the south and keep on till he reached the desert? To the desert, probably, and beyond, back to his native land, the birthplace of his pedigree. His ancestors were calling him, his blood surging, back to his origin, to his stock, to his free existence. Free from all that had trammeled him. There he was, running, whinnying in a world of his own. Running, running alone. Beyond all law. He no longer belonged to anything or to anybody. He wasn't mine, he wasn't yours, and he wasn't his; he wasn't anybody's or anything's. He simply wasn't. He belonged only to his own lone, running self out there in the vast openness, his own solitary flight. The people he passed on his way would stop to gaze at him in wonder. More than one would crave to own him, would admire his rare beauty, would wonder where he came from, whose he was, and what he was doing there. But nobody would be able to answer. For who knows? He no longer belonged to those who know. He was out of their hands, beyond the reach of the knowers and of their knowledge.

Beyond the reach of their hands, the hands that stroked and also struck. Outside the limits of the farmyard, far far away. Outside belonging, and the things that belonged. There was only running, stripped of everything else. Apart from that, nothing...absolutely. Don't you see? By running...he...freed himself....yes...free...Of the whole world, and yet of nothing. Beyond the fence...Unchained, unbridled, unhampered. A white horse running in the desert plain. What's so surprising—wouldn't I have run like that?

We all remained standing there, like idiots, if you'll pardon the expression. The first to make a move was our neighbor Aryeh—he held the bridle of the remaining horse in one hand, and the slack, shamefully horseless chain in the other, the empty chain that held nothing but his disgrace. Violently he flailed the ground with the empty chain and said to hell with it, and other hard words which weren't for children to hear. He took a couple of long strides forward with great resolution, as if he now realized what he had to do and where he was going. Three strides he took, then stopped and just stood there, with nothing. Nothing, apart from his own strength and his big angry hands, nothing apart from his farmyard and his stable, his curses and his whip, his ability to tip a sled over, his love of good order, and the empty chain. He was like an idiot, if you'll pardon me. If that was the situation, what now?

They gathered round him for a council of war. They quietly walked over to stand silently beside him. Then everybody started offering all sorts of suggestions and good advice. As for me, I couldn't move. I could still see the whole thing: how all of a sudden he had pawed the ground and whirled away, his tail whirling, his mane whirling, how they suddenly caught the light and burst into golden flame, and then he was away in a blaze, his tail stretched back taut, far far away, and he was gone, vanished, except for that first sound of beating hooves which had stayed behind as a thing complete in itself, unattached and unbelonging, an ownerless thing that lingered on with us, undispelled, unallayed, all-pervasive, everywhere. That glorious flurry of sound had remained behind like a self-inflated bladder, unburstable, unchanged by the passage of time. It was like the surge of a takeoff, like a plane rushing headlong into flight, leaving us with a rich, wonderful awareness of its vanished presence; while he himself, who had brought all this about disappeared, was far away from everything, far beyond the outer limits of the orange groves. (Years later, when I happened to be in a plane that was flying low over these same orange groves, I looked down at the familiar place and was amazed to see how narrow this green belt really was, how sparse and scraggly, how utterly insignificant. Before, it had seemed to be not only a whole world in itself, but the very end of the world—the world ended with the orange groves!) By now, he must have got past the irrigation ditches, out in the wilderness that is never watered, the desert that is never plowed, the wide-openness that is never sown, where there is nothing but its own sprawling wide-openness.

The others were at their conference, and I, with the horse. Like me, perhaps, was the horse that had remained—-his bridle chain was clutched firmly in his master's hand; his heart, like mine, must have been with the runaway, judging by his pricked-up ears and his very pink nostrils, so distended that you could see the red inside—"My God, simply dashed off and bolted," I could hear his heart saying— "Suddenly dashing away into the open spaces and gone (Where to? Where to?)."

From this spot you could see no further than the orange groves. They were so to speak the edge of the world, the earth's quayside, bounding the sea. If somebody, Mustafa the watchman, say, could go out there at the right moment, or Yusuf the well-pump mechanic, or somebody else, and seize the runaway by the mane as he stood hemmed into some corner of the hedges, or quietly browsing on a patch of sap-filled weeds that had sprouted since the last watering; and bring him back, shuffling ludicrously on hobbled legs, his neck lowered submissively, his ears drooping.

True, yonder are the orange groves, darkly green and leafy, with the well pumps throbbing ceaselessly like so many hearts. But there's also a world beyond; you can't ignore it. Ah, well I know how far you can gallop once you get across beyond it all. Just turn me into a horse and I'll gallop out there, itching to get away into the open, beyond all that's so neatly fenced in and protected beyond the boundaries of the world's edge.

What happened next? Nothing. They were still at their conference, discussing what was to be done now and, of course, who was actually to blame for the horse's getaway. Who, the devil take it, had let that culprit tear loose and take off, curse him! By and large, our neighbor Aryeh admitted that it wasn't the first time that the runaway had bolted, and that at least once before he had taken it into his head to break loose. And what's more, the fit had seized him when he had been in full harness with all the trappings, and he made his getaway, may fire consume his bones!—with all his gear, in the middle of a job, straps and chains and halter and girths and ropes and all, even with the plow that had been lying on its side for a moment's breather between one furrow and another—over yonder it had happened, when they were plowing between those trees there—once, he had simply made off with everything while they were taking a moment's breather, just like that, simply dashed off! Only that the plow, which was off duty and trailing in undignified looseness on its side, got snagged on a tree trunk and held fast, holding him fast too, keeping him forcibly anchored there in spite of himself, against the furious lurching of his flight, and in spite of his straining and kicking, his neck arched back, his hooves churning up clouds of dust, in spite of his champing and biting and whinnying so wildly that all the horses in the world stopped in their tracks and whinnied back in reply. He was caught, and no nonsense about it; rebellious, kicking, whinnying, biting, and rearing up on his hind legs—angry yet subdued and all the while he was being soundly thrashed, with strap and chain and a hastily snapped-off branch, and in addition to everything else, with hand and stone in a vengeance bordering on madness. He was beaten into submission once and for all, so that it should serve as a lesson to him and to all other rebels, thrashed so hard that people came running over from all directions to put a stop to it and to beg for mercy on his behalf. That's what happened to him, and that's the way he ended up then, oh yes. No, no, you wouldn't have believed it of him when you saw him day after day, would you? so white and innocent, a nice quiet goose, you'd have thought.

I was sorry for our neighbor Aryeh, so sad he was and so empty-handed. A single horse is nothing but an indignity, the humiliation of a team of horses reduced to a single horse. All who stood there were silent. Somebody must have gone to the police, or somewhere. You've got to go somewhere. Somebody ought to be informed. It might be a good thing to call in a tracker. Some of the Bedouin are extremely good at it. But not me. I—where could he have gotten to by now? He must be far beyond the ends of the world.

I tug at Aryeh's sleeve.

"Ah," he says to me. "What do you want?"

"Nothing," I say.

"Did you want something?" he asks.

"No, nothing," I say.

"You wanted something," he says.

"Nothing, only to ask a question."

"You leave off!" he says. "Can't you see what's doing?"

And then he says, "What did you want to ask?"

"Nothing," I say. "Only where did you get that horse from?"

"That's a fine how-d'ye-do! What d'you mean where did I get him from? That's a new one! I just had him, that's all. D'you think I stole him?"

"No," I say, "But where did you get him from when he came to be yours?"

"That's a nice one!" he says. "He's mine, of course, d'you mean to say he's not? That's a new one. Whose is he if he isn't mine? Yours, maybe?"

"No," I say. "You don't understand. I'm asking how he came to be yours."

"Now stop bothering me," he says to me. "Just what is it you want right now? That horse is mine. I bought him and he's mine, and that's all there is to it. What more d'you want?"

"Nothing. That's all. Only....did he want to?"

"Did *who* want to?"

"The horse."

"The horse?"

"Yes, the horse."

"Now look here, what is it you want? What d'you mean, did the horse want?"

"Nothing, Just…did the horse want to belong to you?"

"Did he want to? Who? The horse? A fine how-d'ye-do! Who asked him? Now that's a new one! You there, what do you think? Whether he wanted to or not, he's my horse. Just lay off now. Don't you start bothering me now, d'you hear? Can he want at all? A horse? That's a new one! Here's another one come to mess things up!"

"But maybe he didn't want to…"

They began to scold me from all sides: "Leave him alone, boy. What are you pestering him for? Leave off, now. That's enough."

"All right," I said. "I've finished. I only thought…"

"Now quit it." Our neighbor Aryeh was good and angry and said very sharply, "Just don't think. Go home and bother them there, and leave alone now. Right? You can ask your questions there and eat your food there, and everything. And just lay off of me, d'you hear, if you know what's good for you. That's all. A fine thing when every pants-wetter comes pestering you!"

So saying, he tugged at the bridle chain of the remaining horse and turned away and left our yard—which was just now taking on its new appearance, exuding a moist freshness toward the sun which by now had risen so high that nothing obstructed its direct rays, neither tree, nor branch, nor grass, nor fence—back to his own farmyard, fenced in with new wire meshing, back to the newly built stable, all poured concrete and iron bars. And nobody knew how things were going to turn out now and what was going to happen to all the beautiful starts that had been made so bravely and with such high hopes. He went back tugging heavily at the bridle chain, and the horse trailed after him swishing his white flame-flecked tail. (Perhaps he wasn't the man to keep horses; perhaps he should have owned instead a couple of reddish mules, shaggy and donkeyish!)

What came of it? this is what came of it: the runaway got away and the stayers behind stayed behind. And all of us were left without a thing to do, only with sad thoughts—and the runner was out there, wherever he was running. The sun had risen quite high by now, and the sea breeze was blowing in strong playful gusts. But nothing stirred; everything remained motionless, purposeless, but out there, where we couldn't see from here, something was running. Whatever was not stirring here was running out there, running like a deer, running like a lion, like the wind, running free. And on account of him, everything had stopped dead here.

Ah, there's so much space for running over there! What would you know about that? If only you knew, you wouldn't stay on here another moment; you'd be twitching to tear away at a gallop. It's so wide open for galloping out yonder, away from this place here. Ah, yes, just to gallop, plain and simple. There's nothing simpler and more straightforward. No obligations whatsoever, no need to arrive anywhere, nowhere particular you have to get to, no duties to perform or what they call "objectives," no time limit, nothing at all like that. Can't you see what that means? Don't you realize? No? Well look here: after all....everything's wide open on every side, to the right and to the left and straight ahead and all around, and this sense of being free encompasses you totally, the warmth and the blue and the gold. What more can one wish for? Always there's this gentle breeze coming in from the sea, fluttering like a lively girl's dress even if it's a bit dusty. Of course, but it's a fragrant dust, with the grasses and shrubs nodding their heads in approval as it puffs by and skips away, charged with the warm, bluish oxygen. Out there at last, you can start galloping to your heart's content, to the full stretch of your imagination, and you no longer have to follow any set path or road, keep to any rut or groove or anything of that sort. There's nothing to stop you: it's just wide open, open and warm and vast. You don't have to get anywhere, reach any place; all you do is just gallop. So go galloping, young man! Gallop, son! No restraint and nobody to stop you. No accounts to render and no regrets. You just live your running to the full. You become everything you have ever wanted to be deep down inside you. Out there, whatever has been quivering inside you, whatever you have ever longed to be, to attain, comes into being in that wondrous running. Nothing to stop you. You won't stop in the noonday shade of a thick-branched sycamore to rest among the heat-weary sitting underneath it; you won't crouch down to munch green grass, or sip a drop of water; you won't encroach on our neighbor's plot or whinny to your mate. There's only you, wide open to run your race under God's warm sky stretching before you in utter perfection. And beneath that sky, the earth stretches in warm, dusty reaches, and at last there is breathing space for anyone who craves to breathe freely. That's all there is: a running field that is boundless, a vast openness, shoreless like the sea, the ocean, the sky, like the limitless sky itself.

I don't know what else there is to say, and there's no need to, either...why all the talk?....It's only that he is out there racing, he is out there running, singing as he runs, singing out to the world, and maybe he's not singing at all, and it's his running that's singing his song to him, as he swallows up the distances, his drumming hooves stirring up a light dust in the gold of the warm fields under the warm golden sky out there, outside, outside, outside....

Ah, do you know what it means to run! If you've never run you can't know what it's like. Just like somebody who's never been swimming can't know. Once someone *has* run he knows how it feels and he keeps hankering for more. How all of a sudden you are in the open. All of a sudden you're in it. Wide open, and everything is permitted. Wide open and you're in it. All of you inside the possible. Suddenly you are lifted into the possible, like...what shall I say?...like someone plunging into the sea and he's in it, surrounded and swallowed up by it. All of him becomes what the sea is. All self becomes the sea's self. All that's specifically *he* becomes one with the vast specific, which encompasses him effortlessly, endlessly. If you understand what I mean. I myself understand it. One moment I do and the next, I don't. It isn't at all something you can understand or not understand. Hell. No. It's *being* rather than understanding, that's it. Like....I don't know...actually it is like being in the sea with the water all around you, and you breathe the water in, battling to keep afloat on your back whether you want to or not. And it's all the same to the sea—your caring or your not caring doesn't affect it the least bit; it remains changeless, not even scratched, not even the faintest smile. But *you* care. Oh yes, to you everything matters. Your heart beats are now absolutely different. All those heartbeats of if-only-I-were change into heartbeats of here-it-is-at-last, and this-is-it. THIS IS IT. And you say: O God, let it go on, don't let it stop! (Because deep down within you there are always those shadows flitting across your heart, shadows of doubt and disbelief. It can't be—they say to you—you'll see it can't be, it can't last, you'll see it won't last, you'll pay for it before long, you'll see how soon you'll pay for it—and they give you a thousand reasons why, those hovering shadows. It would be much better if you could look away from them before they get a hold on you and effect you. Come, let's ignore them.) And what now?

What now? You keep running, of course. O Lord, at long last here it is. This is it, and you—incredibly—are in it my son, part of the running, swept along by the if-only-I-could which you have always yearned for. Do you know what that means? What it means to get there? But it isn't getting there—that I am talking about!—on the contrary, you never get there. There's no such thing as a point or line you arrive at, that you reach and stop at, as if "there" is a kind of place you come to and say, "So far" and no further!" Nothing of the sort. There's no such thing out there. On the contrary: yonder's the place where there is no destination. It's the place where everywhere you are is your point of departure, the place you start out from. It's just like….how do I know?…it's as if somebody had run out of dry land and had come to the sea, and one starts anew. You cross over and start from the beginning. And you're in the new, and in what is beyond it; in the different, the newly begun, the beautiful with an air of this-is-the-first-time, in the all-encompassing, the flowing.

O Lord, how he broke loose and ran! Ran like the best of dreams. Ran, broke free, free as the fullness within him, leaving everything behind—all of us: me, you (you too, my friend!), everything. The old, the necessary, all that is held to a single plot of land, the commonplace which comes and goes mechanically, dented and used. All the "this-is-not-what-we-imagined" which was vanished. All that has been left behind and saws away as it pleases—but now, finally the beginning starts, the opening—that *isn't as yet* that is just now starting off and will be and will arrive and is all involved in the possible, amen, all in the "maybe, yes," in the maybe this time. O Lord, why not, perhaps this is the time; perhaps this is the possible. Perhaps yes. Perhaps yes. Maybe we can do it now, O my God, maybe yes.

But what is there after all in these desert plains. What is it you're so happy about?

Ah, listen, listen. It's all wide open out there. Didn't I say before that it's all warm and open? That yonder stretch the open spaces where you run and run, where there's no *to* and no *until?* You must know, realize it to the depths of your soul, that such a place does exist, and it's not beyond the mighty hills, either; it's there, for anybody who wants to go there. Away from all the highways and byways. There's the real wide world rich and beautiful. The whole wide world rather than some measly road. What do you want a road for, when you've got the whole world to roam in with no road. What would you rather have? Suddenly you come across patches of meadow, and suddenly there is golden growth which has never been reaped; and suddenly a simmering with summer bee buzzes toward you, a summer-simmering bee; suddenly there's will-o-the wisp in an orange flash; suddenly there's the violet and blue and rich gold of thistles and briar and gorse, which are not thorny at all, but richly endowed with an opulence that is fresh and colorful and genuine, luxuriant and plenteous, profusely flowering, unattached to any owner or ownership, except the god of the meadow, perhaps. And all at once there is the bold twitter of larks nestling among the clods of earth, and the cutting flight of some birding; suddenly a brown moth or a snow-white cabbage fly flits toward you with a silent flapping of wings, or a pair of them, male and female, mincing round each other in a fluttering dance of courtship; and yonder suddenly you see a file of bustling ants intent on their diligent labors (and all the time dust clouds shimmer on the smoke-blue mountains to the east enveloped in a haze of blue and pink). And there are always white smoky wisps of cloud scudding somewhere, faraway, gliding across the silence of the fields. The silence is complete, golden flowing, warm and windswept, yet its skirts are flecked with specks of color—a murmuring lace work, together with the scent of honey and the cloying fragrance of mint, are sprayed sometimes with insignificant, sparkling drops, a sudden chirp or twitter, which only underscores its perfection, and it makes you itch to run on, faster and further and fleeter, on and on. Ah, always to be afire and never extinguished. Always to want and never to be satisfied. Always to set out and never to arrive. To be alive and not sluggish. Free and not bound. To be like the dolphin slithering through the wind-tossed sea, or soaring free of heart like the falcon into the wind, with the blue airy abyss below. To be at one with the incessant chirping of the cricket, always a single span above the earth and never quite touching, chirping endlessly, back and forth like a perpetual saw. To be swept along in this flowing movement, this running, to be carried aloft, to beat upward and fly—beyond all fences and all enclosures and all allotments, and all duties and obligations, out into the wide open. Ah, yes.

But where to? How far can you get?

Where to? How far? What a question! How do I know? Who knows? Who *can* know? At any rate it's not just a matter of "Let's go over there, and prostrate ourselves and return". Nothing like that, or "Let's drop over for a while and come right back," or the bloodless, cowardly "Be right back" sign of shopkeepers, or "Right here, just around the corner." No, it's nothing of the sort, and don't you think so. Where to, you ask? Out into the sun, of course, straight into it. Where else? In through its wide-open glittering gates and into its golden blaze. Where else if not into the sun? Into the sun, the sun, without ever coming back. Hallelujah.

What's that you said? Ah, I don't know myself. There's him running, running, that's all. And what else? Ah yes, the soil. Care to hear something about the soil out there—it's just take a moment—about the soil that never moves on, but is always stirred by the flurrying wind? It's beautiful soil, so brown and warm and dark, and always there's a whitish veil fluttering and frothing over it. A whole wide stretch of soil, a bit crumbly to the touch, perhaps like the good feel of a handful of warm soft-shelled nuts, which, when you lick them slightly, give off a tantalizing clayish smell like the coming of the first rain. Crush it gently, and it sifts through your fingers like the fine powder of white flour, wonderfully clean except for an odd flake of old snail shells, a tiny chip of gravel, a worthless speck of mold, or a shred of a rootling—darkish flecks in the rich brown. And what else is there on that stretch of soil? Not much. Nothing in fact, at first sight. But before long you notice that there's quite a lot, and in the end you realize—if you love the place—that there's everything there, that it's the beginning and end of everything. There's the warm brown, to begin with, and the warm gold too. There's the dense dusty-gray thistleweed that clings to your ankles, its golden starry flowers held prisoner by their thorns. And down there is a patch of wild corn, unsown by man, born of the wind and the rain. And further on are other pallid fields of select and pampered wheat, surging waves of sifted gold beaming their foaming love to the wind. But more than that—far far more—there's simply the brownness of it all, the plain brownness of it all, stretching out on all sides to the rim of the horizon, unadorned and unaffected, without any preening or primping; the brownness of wholesome soil, with all its dust and cracks and ruts and what-have-you—the beautiful brownness that captivates you and takes your breath away.

And have I mentioned the plants?—the carrot, the cow parsley, the ammita or others of their kin: the carlina and fennel and sorrel, some the yellowest of yellow, and some the whitest white. And not only them, there are others: the matted mesquite, indicating a deep layer of good soil underneath; the cress whose flowers are tearful like Leah's eyes; the shellflower, tilted under its abundant load; the oxtongue which suddenly shows its deep calm blue; the Spanish thistle, luxuriantly golden. And the edges of the fields fringed with bushy silybum that has long since faded in the spring; and gray-white binweed, and its rose-tinted bretheren; and the safflower, of course, no end of them. And the leaping grasshoppers and hopping locusts, and the eternal rasping of the cicadea, the one-stringed lyre of the fields.

But tell me, whatever happened in the end?

In the end? The end of what!

That runaway horse, the white one. Have you forgotten?

The horse? ah yes, Yes of course. He was caught in the end, caught and brought back. You thought he wouldn't be caught. Did you? go on! The way things go in our world, he had to be caught. What else did you expect? Runaway horses get caught, if not today then tomorrow. Where can they run to? There's always someone after the reward, if it isn't Mustafa the watchman, then it's Yusef the pump mechanic, or someone else of their breed. He had to be caught. He had to be returned.

What more? Should I tell you what he looked like when they brought him back, and what our neighbor Aryeh said and did? And how his mate, the lonely horse that had been left behind, neighed at the sight of him? Should I describe his appearance when he came back, and what that mane of his looked like, and everything else about him? And how I heard his cry—which nobody else did—when he came, a sort of cry which suffused the whole of me and has never left me since, a kind of don't-want-to, don't-want-to, don't-want-to which was too much to bear. And I couldn't look at his eyes, either. I just shut myself away in the house, shut myself up so that I shouldn't have to see the impossible change into the possible, into the here-and-now...

In our neighbor Aryeh's stable someone was laughing out loud as he hammered a heavy ringbolt into the concrete wall, and replaced the chain with one far heavier, and welded iron hoops onto the halter so that henceforth no one would take it into his head to bolt. He wouldn't be able to anymore; in fact, he would just have to stay on right here, where everything is predictable to the end, amid the clucking of the hens and the quacking of the ducks, where the fattened turkey puffs out his feathers by the water trough and the old raven, as always, roused everyone with his cawing.

Ah, that horse! Ah, that horse of mine! Ah, that horse!

Whoso Breaketh a Hedge a Snake Shall Bite Him

TRANSLATED BY YAEL LOTAN
FIRST PUBLISHED IN 1996

The start of the school day at Ben Shemen was signaled by two mighty ringing peals that spread out and reached the forest, passed lightly over it and mingled with the bells of Jerusalem and perhaps farther afield to fade away only over the haze of the Desert of Judea, or even the dreamy azure of Mount Nebo.

Instead of a bell they had taken an iron bar and suspended it between two cypresses and with the aid of two drumsticks entrusted to a pair of skilled hands eager to drum rapidly the chimes broke out in a vigorous volley such as only the youthful arms of a sixteen-year-old in the fullness of his powers could produce, fast and forcefully in a scintillating hail that could not be ignored with any pretext of I-didn't-hear, even if you stuffed a pillow over your head, longing for sleep or lying in late because you are young and no call to study can plumb your blissful depths that are exempt from everything.

Two series of chimes were rung, the first as a warning to gather your books and notebooks and sleepy bones along with the porridge you have gulped in haste and which is still slurping down unswallowed—and the second as the signal to enter the classrooms and start peering around for indications of what to expect today, the gap between the first chimes and the second being ten minutes or a quarter of an hour, depending on the ringer and his stamina this morning.

აₑ

Which is where our story begins about a young teacher who was similarly dozy and reluctant to hear any reveille in the world, be it even the messiah's ram's horn. The first chimes flung him out of bed though his head and mind were still unsettled and unawake, he dressed hastily and only half tucked his shirt into the trousers pulled on his meager limbs, shuffled in tired sandals toward the dining hall and mouthed the sickening insipid porridge with the sugar and cinnamon, and began to rally with the brackish remainder of the coffee-substitute, and when the second chimes subsided began to drag his infinitely weary legs toward the stairs of the "inner courtyard" building, past the hallway with the big, unmoving clock, may God help it.

And as in all good stories, this one too has a "one fine day," and one fine day as they say in the stories, while this sleepy-head teacher was climbing those stairs before God had given him any sense or increased his alertness, right there at the entrance to his classroom, in addition to all the barefoot sprinters converging from their beds and porridge bowls, the books dropping from their hands, handsome boys and girls, the latter still adjusting their clothes and their brushed hair while the former like their teacher disgracefully slovenly and shamefully disheveled—at the very door there was another, quite dissimilar gathering.

Such people we had not seen before. Citified gentlemen and ladies togged most respectably, some bespectacled and all armed with briefcases and files and exuding effort and diligence, and in the midst of this eminent company stood some elder eminences—elder being Ben Shemen for anyone who was not snot-nosed and hand-

266

wiped—and in loyalty to the truth and to the memory of very far-off days now that things are no longer so luminous, I may note that as well as being dressed like important gentlemen and as bald as important gentlemen and as gray-haired as important gentlemen who had evidently devoted their entire lives to learning and scholarship, there was no mistaking Professor Ernst Simon's humane smile, oval head and wise eyes, or Professor Eliezer Rieger's grave expression, scanty hair carefully combed back and general appearance of a big company executive, and Professor Dushkin (what was his first name) who looked like an American uncle, kindly and shortsighted in his thick gold-rimmed spectacles, and all were wreathed in highly educational smiles, seeking the teacher whose lesson and method they were there to hear that morning as a model lesson for students at the Jerusalem university, which they had announced in writing and confirmed many days ahead, everything being precise and filed and beyond question.

The surprise was complete. The teacher in his aforesaid appearance, porridge on his lips, his shirt half hanging out and half hastily tucked in, his head void and traces of his dream still evanescing, with nothing under his famously unkempt shock of hair but the murmur of their evaporation. And the learned guests and disciples who had taken the trouble to rise that morning in the small hours of the night in order to arrive on the dot and observe the marvels of rural education and the methods of open or experimental education, call it what you will, both groups were standing about disbelieving their eyes, alike the mob of pupils whom the blasting chimes had swept hither against their will, and the polite company of scholars who had journeyed the whole way from Jerusalem:

Someone had to take charge of the situation, which role inevitably fell to the teacher who was obliged by good manners to shake hands and murmur politenesses and with a raised hand politely to invite in while at the same time softly chiding his flock of pupils to go inside and sit down as well as seize and quickly make some order in the untidy room that had been untouched since the day before. At last the stage was set and the guests were introduced and

introduced themselves and the teacher raked five fingers through his
sleep-snarled hair, knowing that he was supposed to do something,
whatever was expected, for the sake of which these dignitaries had
bestirred themselves before the crack of dawn to reach Ben Shemen
via the tortuous roads between Jerusalem and Ramlah and Lydda
and the Youth Village.

God Almighty, what to do now? The shock of the visitors'
appearance had somewhat driven out the mists of sleep, but the
pupils' immobile faces had already turned to stone from awe and
shame, and from the eagerness for knowledge and progress on the
part of the humanists who were clustering to observe the "pedagogi-
cal poem" that had been promised them in writing. Everything was
present, all the actors and the entire set, only the curtain was yet to
rise and the leading actor had yet to come in and take a bow.

The Good Lord heard and sent a sign. We are now in the Book
of Ecclesiastes, the teacher, emerging momentarily from his daze, told
the visitors who immediately took out of their respectable briefcases
little immaculate Bibles, plus a few more pairs of spectacles, while the
pupils crouched to rummage in the bowels of their desks where they
might have forgotten the books, and someone was sent post-haste to
fetch some more. And two or three were crawling swiftly to gather
bits of papers and leftovers from the floor, and again comb their hair
with their fingers as best they could, and the moment came. There
was nothing for it. The books were present. Opened on Chapter Ten.
A few platitudes by way of introduction, to explain what fifteen-year-
olds have to do with Ecclesiastes and his vanity of vanities. Now what?
Nothing. Now comes the verse which is read aloud in unison:

*He that diggeth a pit shall fall into it, and whoso breaketh a hedge
a snake shall bite him.*

How wonderful it would be, in this very place, to ask kind, wise
and wise Professor Simon if he would please step over and say something, cede him the chair, move back against the wall and melt into it,
for there was a no more learned, thorough, multifariously scholarly
Jew than he, and he would have responded, great humanist that he
was, and we would have heard something memorable. Or Professor

Rieger, that wise renaissance man, or Professor Dushkin, an authority on education, who would have mined educational gems from that verse about the pit and the hedge. But no. Now it's you.

Right. We quickly disposed of the "pit"—meaning, a hole in the ground—and after, warning diggers to make sure and cover the pits before leaving, moved on to the stone boundary walls in the Arab fields in Haditha and Budrous and Daniel and Shilta and Bait Naballah, which we used to circle when drawing up reports for the Haganah, and could if we wished have told stories about snakes, especially adders, as well as scorpions and centipedes, and there was one Hanan who was an expert on creepy-crawlies and another Hanan (both had once been Hans), who did experiments with lizards and every quarter of an hour by his watch stuffed some crumbs of lizard food into this or that shirt pocket in order to measure something, I forget what exactly, and the paralysis in the class had somewhat thawed and here and there they woke from their shock, and could if we wished have talked a great deal more about "life in the country-side" and "stories of the rural life", and diggers of pits and builders of fieldstone hedges and what use such hedges were and since when do people break down a built boundary wall, and things would turn quite lively and bright.

It might also have been possible to stop and ask some light-footed lad to please pop over to the library and bring some commentaries and ancient texts about this chapter and verse, look them up and broaden the meaning, also about who this Ecclesiastes was anyway, and when and if he was, and all the other fine issues so familiar to those students from Jerusalem who knew that this was exactly what they would have done if they were giving a model lesson, and their tutors would have been pleased, and perhaps that was what they were busily scribbling on their elongated sheets, and the professors too, each with his respective notebook and creased brow, making notes for the concluding talk, and it was all going forward swimmingly, the porridge forgotten, sleep shaken off, the pupils laughing and everything being really delightful.

But no. Because just then something got into the teacher. It was not Ecclesiastes who had lived a thousand or two thousand or even more years ago, and may even have been a king in Jerusalem, and who is to say what had influenced him and why indeed he was not suppressed—no, it was not Ecclesiastes who stood up in that rural classroom but a new, young and fierce Ecclesiastes with a rampaging imagination. Whoso breaketh an hedge a snake shall bite him! he said, actually roared at them, certainly it might be possible not to break it and the snake would not bite, it might be possible to settle for the existing hedge, live within the accepted order, and no snakes would bite. Because the snake had not come to the hedge to get a suntan, it was sitting there in order to frighten off intruders. Oh that was some introduction. One teacher with unremarkable features but a storm in his innards turned into a prophet, utterly free of doubt, rose to his middling height and prophesied to his pupils, which was an easy matter, also to his wise visitors, and the people gathered outside who did not miss a word of his mighty voice, neither in the inner courtyard nor the outer one, nor the distant mountains and hills, and he grew and grew before their eyes, his stature became Ezekiel-like, his reproach Jeremiahish, his grand prose Isaiahish, and astonishingly they all sat stunned and open-mouthed around him, scarcely breathing at all.

There was a kind of hush in the room. There was total, minute attention. The pupils listened with their whole bodies and the visitors with all their might. They were in it. Nobody made notes because they were no longer in the business of note-making, only in that of the hedge and its demolition. But this was merely the start. The drama was just starting. The dramatist was warming up, he was the writer and the director and the scene-painter and the special-effects man, he was great in the middle of the room between the "unimportant" pupils and the surrounding yet absent visitors in their chairs, he was in the middle of doing the thing which was in his bones.

Examples? Ah, that good old publishing-house "Omanut": travelers and journeys, inventors and inventions, world discoverers and world expanders, Everest climbers and bold invaders of the heart of Africa, sailors crossing the seven seas in cockleshells—they would all have stayed home if they had not been bitten by the urge to break down hedges and overcome their fear of the snake, and where would we all be if the snake had intimidated them and overcome the urge to break through, take Columbus, hello Columbus, the teacher tugs at his shirt and stuffs it in, because right now he is Columbus, his sailors are mutinying, should he turn the ship, the Pinta or the Santa Maria, turn back, they cry, turn back, it's all so scary and hopeless and the ocean snake has already opened its maw like the gates of hell, but the captain faces them firmly, frightened men do not discover new countries, he reproaches them, or we shall not have America, he reproves them triumphantly, or take Vasco da Gama, hey Vasco, how're things, or Galileo Galilei, come come, don't be coy, welcome great man, here is Galileo in our classroom arguing before his Inquisitor-tormentors that the earth goes round and not the sun, thus breaking down the hedge of ignorance, and the snakes get ready to burn him at the stake, here is the stake and here the man and his speech to them, the speech of a man about to be burnt, and the world remains silent, and why only him, what about our own who went to the stake crying *Shema Israel!* refusing to succumb to the hedge-keepers, or Spinoza ostracized by the keepers of the hedge which he breaks down without giving a thought to snakes, and here is the marvelous Rosa Luxembourg addressing the birds from her prison cell, breaking down the exploiters' hedges on behalf of the exploited workers—for which the snakes kill her, and the examples come roaring out, reduced to small dramas by the smallness of the stage, yet actually exploding there in the center of the world, the justice of his argument being so overpowering that they come over and walk at his side, so repulsive and pathetic are the petty stupidity and cowardice of the hedge-keepers with their snakes that they turn away from them and come over to him, here too is the woman from *The Enchanted Soul,* rejecting all the conventions that confine woman's freedom and her rights over her body she proceeds to have her child without marriage but only with love, and now almost the whole spectrum of the deeds of the free man has been unfolded, of the man "who fears no snakes but despises danger and breaks down hedges, wait a minute, not all hedges and not all the time, or the world would lapse into savagery, savagery would rip through the world and everything would revert to chaos. Oh God Almighty.

What else? The rest is less clear. Only the great actor continued to pace on his stage in the middle, his hearers being overwhelmed, alike the little ones, the big ones and the very big ones. Instead of pouncing on him at the end of the lesson, was this a lesson was this teaching and where was the bibliography and what kind of improvised homiletic game was it instead of serious study and what about homework and the moral of the story, and all the rest, as they teach day after day and their students take down what they say, instead of shouting at him you scoundrel you waffler you fantasist, they did nothing of the sort but walked along with him, moved with him, mumbling what he had uttered with awe, oh how his arms flew between the ceiling and the floor, how his hands extended from wall to wall, how his voice dropped down to earth in moments of danger and rose and mounted to thundering roars when the danger was torn to shreds by contempt, and how the big and the small in the room clustered on the side of the just and together repelled the side of villainy, and how the taunts against the faint hearted who so feared the snake that they missed out on progress reached all the way to the woods, to the Herzl woods with its four extensions, and how all hearts concurred and there was universal agreement when the teacher reached the figure of the pioneer—oh the pioneer, oh the pioneer, oh the through-breaking pioneer, oh the pioneer—only then it turned out that the hour had passed and someone had already opened the door and said with an apologetic grin that it was over, not now but a while ago, and that already outside the windows and the door there was a considerable crowd which had heard the sounds and trembled at the moral without knowing if what they were hearing were cries for help or rallying cries, suddenly the lesson was finished and still no one stirred, literally did not move their feet, sitting with staring eyes waiting for something to happen that would bring the finish to an end, or bring the curtain down.

※

Some time ago, at an unexpected meeting, a man took hold of me, a man neither young nor familiar looking, who laid his hands on my shoulders, Don't you remember me? he demanded peremptorily, a not-unusual demand and a not-unknown disappointment, Where from? I asked, already knowing it had to be Ben Shemen, they were fifteen-year-olds fifty years ago, how was I to recognize this fat bald man whose unyouthful hands lay on my shoulders, What do you mean where from? the man wondered, From your lesson, The lesson? Yes, about the hedge and the snake and the hedge breaker, don't you remember? how's that possible? Ah yes, I stammered, it was so long ago, Long ago? like yesterday, the man shouted, Don't you remember? it goes like this: He that diggeth a pit shall fall into it, and whoso breaketh a hedge a snake shall bite him.

Suddenly I heard the volleys of those summoning chimes.

Harlamov

TRANSLATED BY HILLEL HALKIN
FIRST PUBLISHED IN 1996

Mr. Harlamov was a big man. He was a fearless man too and when he sat himself down at the harmonium (which was a kind of piano played with a foot bellows, or a kind of accordion with legs like a piano's, an exotic instrument that served as the standard medium of instruction in Music Pedagogy and Appreciation at the Bet Hakerem Hebrew Teachers College of Jerusalem)—when he sat himself down, as big and fearless, as a bear tickling a kitten, and picked out the keys with his big, fearless fingers whose palms covered the keyboard while pumping the bellows with his feet, the whole harmonium shook with its wheezing, creaking pedals as if about to give out in one last excruciating and unmusical gasp. Above the crash of its chords, Mr. Harlamov sang in his big, fearless voice. If he hadn't had to work the pedals he could have easily strode around the room with it instead of intermittently rearing in his seat to scan the class for anyone slacking or off-key, calling out parenthetically to the culprit without breaking the tempo of the song, You there, or That young lady in the back. Which was enough to make whoever it was cringe and join the mighty chorus.

If truth be told, the monumental sight of Mr. Harlamov thumping away at the wheezing harmonium while the class accompanied him at full volume was impressive. It was also comical, mixing giggles into the harmonies whose frequent parentheses were filled with a Hebrew that was far from untainted by Mr. Harlamov s big, fearless Russian errors. You please to sing, he would scold. No you laugh, you. And with a scowl he went on adjusting our mighty chorus to his big, fearless notes, hunching over his harmonium and fiercely rearing up to review his troops.

There was really nothing very fierce about him. There was even an inherent good nature that might have prevailed if only nothing had not been as it should have—neither the poor substitute for a piano, nor our voices that kept going flat, nor our young, grinning faces that showed scant respect for The Heavens Tell the Glory of the Lord. He was constantly correcting us. C! he would shout. C Major! The more roughshod we ran over the music, the more desperately he increased the volume of the harmonium to salvage what he could of its beauty, doing his best to drown us out while bent over his instrument, a very lonely, uncompromising man.

I never had much luck with Mr. Harmalov. I didn't even notice it when, while we were singing a choral number one day, he reared and signaled for silence so that he might spot the villain who was making a mockery of the music. For a moment nothing was heard but my unsuspecting voice, booming out the words of the Internationale. You, Mr. Harlamov whispered in a voice that made the ceiling recoil. You. Mr. Dinburg. Scram you from here! I tell dean he give you boot. I tell you without culture, murder music. I tell, for what I work? And maybe I tell too: if you know what is Russia and what is do to me there, you not sing that song. It wouldn't have helped if I had sworn on a stack of Bibles that it was only a harmless joke. It wouldn't even have cleared my own conscience. Why did I do it? Sometimes the only answer is because, and this because was a feeble one. Unless (but this wasn't something I could have said out loud, not even to myself) it was to make an impression on the flushed wearer of a brown sweater who was singing her heart out next to me.

Little wonder that I received a "D-" in music at the end of the term—and even that was an act of mercy to the young buffoon on the great man's part. Next to my "A"s in Bible, Literature, and History, it stood out like a sore thumb. (Not that my Arabic was any better; I flunked with an "F", courtesy of the esteemed and resplendent Jerusalem orientalist, Yosef Yoel Rivlin. And my English too, in the words of Mr. Morris, a short but stern pedagogue whose heels clicked when he walked, left "a great deal to be desired". To say nothing of math, all my efforts at which satisfied neither the sphinx-like Mr. Hevroni nor the laws of algebra.) I didn't do very well either when I tried pacifying Mr. Harlamov by remarking as I walked beside him, half-running to keep up with his big, fearless steps in the portico flanking the rocky lot that was slated to become an athletic field for our fabled gym teacher Mr. Yekutieli, that I, simple farm boy though I was, was so musically sophisticated that I had actually listened at my friend Habkin's house to records of Beethoven (mainly the Fifth), Mozart (the E-Minor), and Bach (the Third Brandenburg). At which point I committed the grievous faux pas of enthusiastically adding that I also liked the symphonies of Chopin. Breaking off his fearless stride, Mr. Harlamov threw me a downward, withering glance. Chopin write no symphonies! he said with disgusted finality, walking off to leave me more foolish than ever and unable to explain that I had meant Schumann, and especially the Spring Symphony, which had left me wet-eyed with *weltschmerz,* most of all for the wearer of a brown sweater whose shy beholder found her more adorable than approachable.

The fact was that all those European names, like Schumann and Chopin, could have confused anybody, especially if he was bad at languages, and most especially if he had an idealistic father who had insisted on speaking only Hebrew at home because that was what a proud Jew should speak. But go explain all that to Mr. Harlamov. The man was as big as the steppes of Russia, where he would have had a great future had not a cruel fate reduced him to a Palestinian music teacher who did not even have a proper piano.

Who could count the times I had been corrected with a tolerant smile by Habkin, who, with his gramophone, his record collection, and his violin, had such knowledge that, when he wasn't eking out a living as Professor Gruenfeld's secretary, he was copying scores in a calligraphic hand I never tired of watching, scrolling clefs and staffs and bars and notes, multi-angled and magical with the secret glyphs of music-making: It's not Ber Ahms. It's not Yiddish. It's Brahms, in a single syllable: Johannes Brahms.

Once, though, it was different. Once, as Mr. Harlamov was playing and singing while we sang along with him, grinning as we sometimes did, we suddenly found ourselves listening as if something were happening and we had to know what it was. All at once, without even a rear or a scowl, Mr. Harlamov was transformed at the faltering old harmonium, which gasped out great chords that seemed beyond its powers of endurance. Something was definitely happening. The chords and music were no longer the same. Although Mr. Harlamov was still singing and playing while hunched over the keys like a giant snail, or an eagle feeding its fledglings between its talons, the whole class had fallen silent with a great, concentrated attention. He was singing differently too, as though to himself, as though he were alone and had suddenly realized something and didn't care that no one else knew, or had discovered a new truth that was now coming into focus and of which he meanwhile only knew that it was on its way. It wasn't Tchaikovsky, in case you're wondering. It wasn't Borodin, or Scriabin, or one of your Rimski-Korsakoffs. It was different and special, not yet itself as he sang hunched like a snail in his big voice, which came through slightly muffled but clean the way something sounds when it's true and you know it's happening and isn't here yet and will be even more than you thought, beyond all your stupid jokes when you knew nothing about it.

It was happening to us too, so that, humbled and longing for what we now knew was there and had never known before, we listened with a catch in our throats. It would be easy to spout something about the vast steppes of Russia sobbing in that harmonium, or the Cossacks, or the Tartars, or the cold winds of Siberia, or something of the sort, but it wasn't that at all. It was only a man singing and you hearing and knowing that was it, a place beyond the class and the room and the Bet Hakerem Teachers College of Jerusalem, something coming from afar that was maybe a bit like the child Samuel when he heard the voice in the quiet of the night the voice that said Samuel Samuel and he answered here I am.

Then there was silence and it was over. Nobody knew what to do next, not even Mr. Harlamov, who finally rose all at once to become as tall as the ceiling and then let his shoulders slump and grew smaller again, his big hands dangling in air. His wiped his big, bald skull with a handkerchief and grew even smaller, and then he turned and walked without a word to the door and turned again when he reached it and waved a limp hand and was gone.

And still no one spoke. A few of us began getting to our feet. One by one, we stooped forlornly out of the classroom. I started down the stairs, not knowing what to say. Which way are you going? asked the girl in the brown sweater, who did not know what to say either. It was such an unanticipated question that the young man it was asked of forgot how long he had been waiting for it, and how many wonderful stories he had told himself about it, and how that now that it had happened he had never imagined that it would be like this. They descended the stairs. How about you? he asked with an awkward gesture. I'll walk you. He couldn't believe that it was so simple or that he had been so bold. I live quite near here, at the bottom of Hehalutz Street, she said. The Jerusalem cold brought a flush to her cheeks, and when, in her brown sweater, she noticed that he noticed, she blushed until she was as red as an autumn apple in a poem. She was so scandalously red that she would have liked to run away, but she raised her collar to blush level and the two of them headed for the steps of Hama'alot Street, skipping down them as if dancing not only because they were so skippety young, but because dance is a wordless art form. Of the sort we're most in need of at this moment, she added without words, the casuarina trees dripping wet pearls on a rain-washed street that was already Hehalutz. Three or four houses further on they turned to the right and there, on the ground floor, she lived.

They stood there, the rosy girl and the young man with the wild head of hair and too-slender back. He gives me piano lessons, she confessed. Mr. Harlamov. I didn't ask for them, but he asked me if I'd like them, and I asked if it wouldn't put him out, and he said no, he'd be glad to, I had a talent and he didn't even want to be paid. Believe me, that's the kind of man he is.

They stood there a while longer without thinking of anything to say, shifting their weight from leg to leg. Then they leaned their arms against a tree, an electric charge running between their fingers that were not yet ready to touch, the blush gone from her face that was now simply ruddy with cold. His heart was in his throat. He couldn't think of a word. It was great, what he played, she said. Tremendous, he said. Utterly fantastic. Extraordinary. Unbelievable. The drops falling from the needles of the casuarina trees were clean and pure enough to drink.

If he were to shake a branch it would shower down on her and make him laugh at her sudden shriek. Well, she said. Yes, he said. All right, then. She stood a while longer. I guess I'd better turn in. Good night. Good night. And still neither of them made a move to go. Well I'll see you, she said. She had chestnut hair above the warm brown of her sweater. Look how pearly the raindrops are, he said. Yes, she said. And he said, Yes, well, so long, and she came running back to him and planted a kiss on his cheek and spun around and fled down the stairs.

Incredulous, he stood there, his hand on his cheek. It was too much to take in but there it was. Like a drunk he staggered up the wet, empty street, breaking under his breath into The Heavens Tell the Glory of the Lord and then beginning to hum until he was roaring like an ox in the sleepy streets of Jerusalem whose good folk he was keeping awake. He wasn't thumbing a proletarian nose at them, he was simply letting them know the great truth newly revealed to him on Hehalutz Street that the heavens told the glory of the Lord. He went on singing even when it began to rain so wonderfully hard that he only wanted to let it be and turn cold and wet inside him. He only wanted to sing with the choir—*three, four!*—"His handiwork is written in the sky."

About the Author

S. Yizhar (Yizhar Smilansky, 1916-2006) was born in Rehovot, Israel, to a family of Russian immigrants who were members of the Zionist pioneer intelligentsia. He fought in the 1948 War of Independence, was a member of the political parties headed by David Ben Gurion and held a seat in the Knesset, the Israeli Parliament, for seventeen years. Yizhar was professor of education at the Hebrew University of Jerusalem and professor of Hebrew literature at Tel Aviv University. He started publishing in 1938, writing fiction for both adults and children. Yizhar was considered Israel's most illustrious writer. He was awarded the Israel Prize for his masterpiece, *Days of Ziklag* (1959). He also received the Brenner Prize, the Bialik Prize (1991) and the Emet Prize for Art, Science and Culture (2002). *Days of Ziklag* is included among *The 100 Greatest Works of Modern Jewish Literature* (2001).

The fonts used in this book are from the Garamond family

Other works by S. Yizhar available from *The* Toby Press

Preliminaries

The Toby Press publishes fine writing,
available at leading bookstores everywhere. For more
information, please visit www.tobypress.com